THE
CURIOUS CASE
OF
COMMANDER COLE

JACK WILLIAMS

NEWMAN SPRINGS PUBLISHING
320 Broad Street
Red Bank, NJ 07701

First originally published by Newman Springs Publishing 2023

ISBN 978-1-68498-783-2 (Paperback)
ISBN 978-1-68498-784-9 (Digital)

Printed in the United States of America

To my grampa Clarence, a man's man and a grandson's hero.

PREFACE

On writing *The Curious Case of Commander Cole.*

When growing up, every father and most of the grandfathers in the author's neighborhood were veterans of World War II. (The big one. Just ask them.) Every time families got together, the men would eventually get around to talking about their experiences while in the service. To say the author had a bad case of hero worship of these men is an understatement. Rather than spending all his time playing once the storytelling started, the author would sit quietly listening to the tales these men told.

Very little was related to the fighting these men experienced. The majority of the stories they told were about the odd ball things that occurred, the screw-ups, and the ways these citizen soldiers found to overcome needless red tape and beat the system in order to get the job done. It was the biggest adventure of their lives and other than a few horrific events, which they mostly kept to themselves, the stories were about funny things that occurred and how those things shaped them into the men they became.

The incidents described in this story are mostly true and are recited from the lips of the men who lived the events and told the tales. Granted there has been some literary license taken in order to fit the tales into the story, but undoubtedly no more literary license was taken in the writing than was taken in the telling.

Someone once said, to be a good writer you should write about things you know something about. *The Curious Case of Commander Cole* is a tale about mistaken identity and the lengths a person will go to, to succeed even when placed in a situation far outside their training and prior capabilities.

The inspiration for this story came from a situation the author found himself in while working on the construction of a nuclear power plant. The long and short of the situation was that while conducting the security background check there turned out to be another individual with the same name, same birthday, and same last four digits of his social security number as the authors. The individual had been a very naughty boy, and the author had to go to great pains to prove he was not the individual the background check thought him to be.

Eventually, the mistake was rectified and the author was able to obtain the proper security clearance. However, until it was resolved, a comedy of errors occurred that at best was something to be looked back on and laugh. At worst, it could have resulted in a CEE (Career Ending Event).

The Curious Case of Commander Cole is meant to poke fun at the pompous, the overzealous, and the individuals who take themselves too seriously. War is a matter of life and death and should be taken seriously, but life is meant to be enjoyed. Even in the midst of great stress and danger, it is human nature to try and find humor in any situation, if for no other reason than to keep from going crazy.

It is hoped that you enjoy this book and can see the humor in the tales it relates. Perhaps you will recognize yourself in some of the events depicted.

ACKNOWLEDGMENTS

*T*he *Curious Case of Commander Cole* is a work of fiction. Lest there be a misunderstanding readers should understand that the events described in this story did not happen aboard the real USS LST 121. Initially, all US Navy LSTs were assigned hull numbers instead of names. To bring this work to life a ship was needed around which the story could be developed. Since a fictitious name could not be applied a number was needed. Regardless of the number picked it would have represented the hull number of a ship ordered by the navy, commissioned, and sent to sea. LST 121 was selected because it fit the timeline and location of construction that was required to tell this tale.

Many of the events described in this work actually occurred at one time or another during WWII, but they did not all occur aboard a single ship and to the best of the author's knowledge none of them occurred aboard USS LST 121. USS LST 121 had an outstanding record and made a significant contribution to the United States' war effort during WW II. To honor the ship and her crew, the war record of USS LST 121 as written by the Naval History and Heritage Command appears below:

LST-121

LST-121 was laid down on 23 May 1943 at Jeffersonville, Ind., by the Jeffersonville Boat & Machine Co.; launched on 16 August 1943; sponsored by Mrs. H. A. Bayless; and commissioned on 29 September 1943, Lt. John P. Devaney, USNR, in command.

During World War II, *LST-121* was assigned to the Asiatic-Pacific theater and participated in the following operations:

Marshall Islands operation:

(a) Occupation of Kwajalein and Majuro Atolls-January and February 1944

Marianas operation:

(a) Capture and occupation of Saipan-June and July 1944

(b) Tinian capture and occupation-July 1944

Western Caroline Islands operation:

(a) Capture and occupation of southern Palau Islands-September and October 1944

Iwo Jima operation:

(a) Assault and occupation of Iwo Jima-February 1945

Following the war, *LST-121* was redesignated *LSTH-121* on 15 September 1945. She performed occupation duty in the Far East until mid-November 1945.

Upon her return to the United States, the ship was decommissioned on 21 March 1946. On 14 April 1946, she was sold to the Sun Shipbuilding & Drydock Co., of Chester, Pa., for scrapping. She was struck from the Navy list on 1 May 1946.

LSTH-121 earned five battle stars for World War II service as *LST-121*.

CHAPTER 1

O ctober 9, 1937, was a cool, crisp autumn Saturday in Washington DC. At the Main Navy and Munitions Building along Constitution Avenue Yeoman Third Cecil Elder and the rest of the clerical staff in his records unit were pulling extra duty and listening to the World Series on an old Philco radio one of the sailors had brought to the office for that purpose. The task wasn't hard, but it was boring. The records of all Naval personnel—current, reserve, or eligible for recall—were being updated to include the new Social Security numbers the government had begun issuing the previous November.

It was game four of the World Series. The Yankees were up three games to none, but Carl Hubbell was pitching a great game for the Giants. It was the Giants, 7, and the Yankees, 2, going into the ninth inning. Elder had a dollar riding on the game for a four-game sweep and a five-dollar bet on the Yankees to win the Series; however, the way Hubbell was throwing Elder could feel his wallet getting lighter. But the Yankees were the Yankees, and if there was a strike left in a game, they were still in it no matter how far behind they might be.

Elder was on pins and needles; a dollar was a lot of money in the depression economy and five bucks was a fortune. He didn't want to have to tell his wife about it if he lost six bucks. When Red Barber announced, "It's number four Lou Gehrig coming to the plate for the Yankees," Cecil entered a four in the Social Security number he was working on for Lieutenant Commander Jack Cole a distinguished officer who had an outstanding career in the Great War as captain of a destroyer. Lou launched one into the outfield seats, and in his excitement, Elder completely forgot to recheck his work.

Coincidentally, the resulting social security number Elder entered was that of another Jack Cole, a county superintendent of schools in Wellborn County, Nebraska, who not only shared the same name with Lieutenant Commander Cole but also happened to have the same birth date.

CHAPTER 2

Thursday morning, October 8, 1942, harvest was underway, geese were flying south, and one after another farmers were bringing wagon loads of picked corn to the Walnut Hill CO-OP elevator. Jack Cole was in his office going over the budget for the Walnut Hill Unified School District in Wellborn County Nebraska. This included the high school, and all the country schools throughout the county that would be sending their grade school students to Walnut Hill High School in the coming year. As county superintendent of schools, Jack had the responsibility of making sure each school was properly staffed and funded. By and large, it was a paper-pushing position, and he was very good at it. He was level-headed, active in the community, and well respected throughout the county. Unbeknownst to Jack, there were at least three single women in town that had their eye on him with matrimony in mind.

With harvest progressing, those not actually at work in the fields were in town shopping, visiting with friends, or getting prepared for the long winter that would soon be upon them. The businesses, cafés, and shops were doing a land office business that day so just about everyone saw the gray Navy staff car when it pulled up in front of the county court house where Jack's office was located.

After parking the car, two burly SPs and a Navy lieutenant got out and walked into the building asking where they might find Mr. Cole. Agnes Drake, who was the receptionist and also the county switchboard operator, stared open-mouthed at the three men from behind the Coke bottle lenses of her classes and simply pointed to her left. As the three Navy men marched down the hall, Agnes leaned over her counter and watched wide-eyed until they turned the corner out of her sight. She sat down for a moment, blinked her eyes a few times to make sure she wasn't seeing things, and dialed Mildred Schwartz, her best friend, to tell her all about it.

Agnes was just telling several of her other friends on a party line about what she'd seen when the lieutenant marched back past her desk, tipped his hat, and said, "Thank you for your help, ma'am."

Right behind the lieutenant came the two SPs. They had Jack by the arms dragging him along between them, toes up, and heels sliding along the marble courthouse floor. As the two sailors passed, Mrs. Drake placed her hand over the mouthpiece of the microphone hanging from around her neck, looked at Jack, and asked, "Will you be back after lunch Mr. Cole?"

The lieutenant held the door while the SPs dragged Jack down the courthouse steps, losing one of his shoes in the process and banging his head against the car door as they deposited him in the rear seat. The two SPs then got in front, the lieutenant got in back with Jack, and they drove away while everyone downtown came out of their shops and stores to watch. Among them were Jeannie Evans, Angie Jenkins, and Helen Brant who had rushed into the street from their jobs in the Woolworth's, Peterson's Hardware, and Schultz's Jewelry waving their hankies at the staff car as it drove away. Then noticing each other and seeing the rest of the town staring at them each one quickly put away their hankies and went back to their jobs; all three with tears in their eyes. Agnes Drake went back to her switchboard and called Mildred Schwartz. Agnes was relentless when it came to gossip, and with the news of Jeannie, Angie, and Helen crying when Jack Cole left town, there might even be a little scandal in the making. This was just too good to keep to herself.

CHAPTER 3

When Jack had been taken from his office and thrown in the back of the Navy staff car, he was irate. He demanded to know why he had been forcibly removed from his office, where they were taking him, and what was going on.

The Navy lieutenant in charge abruptly told Jack he was lucky the Navy didn't have him arrested, tried for treason, and shot. Apparently, the Navy had been sending Jack letters and telegrams since the war started telling him to report to the recruiting office in Lincoln, Nebraska, for reinduction, and Uncle Sam didn't take kindly to being ignored.

Jack told the lieutenant he'd received the letters and telegrams, but he'd never been in the Navy so he wrote the Navy, told them they had the wrong man, and after that, ignored the rest of the letters and telegrams.

The lieutenant informed Jack the Navy was not in the habit of making mistakes and referred to Jack's protests as a bunch of b———l s———t excuses. Then he told Jack that if he had a war record like his from the Great War he'd be chomping at the bit to get back in and do his part. Jack started to reply, but the lieutenant told Jack he didn't want to hear any more about it and to sit there and keep his f———g mouth shut until they got to Offutt Airfield where he would be put on a Navy transport and flown to Washington DC.

CHAPTER 4

After an all-night flight, the transport landed at Anacostia Naval Air Station in Washington DC where another Navy staff car was waiting for him on the tarmac. This time, in addition to two SPs, there was an ensign and a lieutenant JG who got in on either side of Jack. Neither man said a word as they were driven to the Main Navy and Munitions Building. Once there the SPs, one on either side of Jack, followed by the ensign and the lieutenant JG escorted Jack into the building where he was placed under the care of another pair of SPs and a Navy commander.

The commander looked Jack up and down taking in the rumpled suit jacket, wrinkled trousers, unshaven face, bloodshot eyes, and missing shoe. He shook his head and took Jack to the office of Rear Admiral Randall Bryton, assistant chief of naval personnel. The admiral looked up from his desk into the bleary-eyed face of Jack Cole and bellowed, "What the h——l do you think you're doing, Cole?"

Not having what he thought was a real good response to the question, Jack just stood there and collected his thoughts. It had been a long time since he'd had any sleep. He was tired, hungry, and he could smell his own body odor. For a man who prided himself in appearance and grooming that was bad enough. But he'd worn a hole in the sock on his shoeless foot, and walking around in one shoe with his big toe sticking out of his sock was not only embarrassing, but it didn't help to improve his mood. He'd tried to find out what was going on, but every time, he tried to explain that the Navy had made a mistake he'd been told to knock it off and keep quiet. He'd been up for thirty-two hours straight and had no idea why he was here or what was wanted of him. Now this big shot admiral wanted to know what he thought he was doing. Jack decided to tell him.

"H——l if I know, why don't you tell me why YOU think I'm here?" Jack said. "Because I haven't the foggiest idea and nobody else seems to know either."

Jack's comment did not sit well with Admiral Bryton who, in a volcanic tirade, informed Jack there would be a cell waiting for him in Rhode Island at the Portsmouth Naval Prison if he heard another crack like that. From the red face, bulging eyes, and spittle that was flying as the enraged admiral yelled, Jack guessed the admiral was serious so he fought the urge to make any type of reply and kept his mouth shut.

Then Admiral Bryton stepped from behind his desk holding a sheaf of papers in his hand and shook them in Jack's face. "This is a copy of your service record. It's outstanding, and that's the only thing that's keeping me from throwing you in the brig right now, so watch your mouth."

"I can't have a record. I was never in the Navy," Jack yelled.

"Knock off the b——l s——t," the admiral roared and shoved the fistful of papers within an inch of Jack's nose. Pointing to the first page, he yelled, "Is that your name?"

Jack tucked his chin and leaned back so he could read the paper and said, "Yes."

"The proper answer, Mr. Cole, is *yes sir*," the admiral barked.

"Yes, sir," Jack mumbled through gritted teeth.

The admiral then pulled the top sheet aside and pointed at the second page. "Is that your date of birth?" he yelled.

"Yes...sir!" Jack replied almost forgetting to add "sir" at the end of his reply.

The admiral then pointed to the third page and growled, "Is that your Social Security number, Mr. Cole?"

Jack looked at the number and said, "Yes, sir!"

"Congratulations, Cole, you just passed your first recall exam for active duty. I expect you to do equally well on the rest of your recall training. Just so we are clear. If I hear about you not giving your duties everything you've got, you're going to land your a——s in Portsmouth where you will spend the duration of this war and as many years afterward as I can arrange, in prison. Oh and by the way, if you do not perform at the exemplary level that you did during the Great War the same will apply, so I'd better not hear of you making any mistakes." Then he shoved the sheaf of papers into Jack's hand, turned toward the office door, and yelled, "Johnson!"

The door immediately opened and the commander who had escorted Jack to the admiral's office entered. "Yes, sir?" he said.

"Commander Johnson, I want you to see that Lieutenant Commander Cole is escorted to the Navy Exchange and properly outfitted. Charge his uniforms against his pay and make sure he has all the appropriate medals and ribbons due him for his rank and prior service. Is that clear?"

"Yes, sir!" the commander barked and escorted Jack from the office.

Johnson turned Jack over to an ensign who saw that Jack purchased the proper uniforms and accessories and then escorted him to the transient officer's quarters. Jack had no idea what went where on a uniform, so he shanghaied the ensign into attaching all the proper medals and insignia to the uniform of the day with straight pins.

When he was done, the ensign gave Jack the business card of a seamstress who could do all of the sewing and have it completed by the end of the next day. The ensign said he would be happy to take the uniforms to her and pick them up when she was done. Jack handed the ensign everything that needed to be sewn and the money to cover it along with a nice tip.

"Uh, sir," the ensign said, "this is the United States Navy. We don't tip." Then he turned and left.

After the ensign was gone, Jack carefully put on the uniform of the day and with the pins still in place walked over to the officers club and got his first meal in forty-eight hours. While Jack was eating, he noticed he wasn't the only officer to be eating there that had his insignia attached with silver straight pins. Apparently Admiral Bryton was doing a land office business recalling officers to active duty. After eating, Jack returned to the transient officers' quarters read through the papers the admiral had given him, which included the real Lieutenant Commander Cole's service record, undressed, laid down, and promptly fell asleep.

The next day, Jack started a three-day program to reorient officers recalled to active duty. The classes addressed changes in Navy courtesies, communications, and electronics; nothing in the way of ship handling or managing a crew was covered. It was a given that those who were reinducted already had those skills and were only being given an overview on the new customs and technology the Navy had adopted since 1918.

By the time the course was finished, Jack felt like he knew who to salute, who should salute him, what to wear, and when to wear it. Beyond that the only things he learned were the name and function of radar, sonar, long-range radio, and short-range talk between ship (TBS) radio.

CHAPTER 5

The morning after he finished the class, Jack and the rest of the officers, who completed the course with him, were driven to Union Station at 50 Massachusetts Avenue NE and placed aboard various trains bound for their duty assignments. As they all shook hands and headed their separate ways, Jack noticed that the others in his class were taking trains to places like, Norfolk, Bremerton, Pensacola, and San Francisco. Jack's ticket read Evansville, Indiana. When he saw that everyone else was heading to the coasts and he was headed inland, he felt a wave of relief wash over him. Maybe, just maybe, he was going to be given some sort of desk job where he would be pushing papers. If so, he felt pretty sure he could bluff his way through whatever was required of him until the Navy figured out their SNAFU and got the real Lieutenant Commander Cole back in uniform. For the first time, he began to think he might get through this without being locked up, shot, or singlehandedly losing the war for Uncle Sam.

When Jack got off the train in Evansville, the station was a mad house. Hundreds of people were pushing and jostling, each trying to get somewhere other than where they were at that moment. Jack's orders were to report to the Missouri Valley Bridge and Iron Co. shipyard with his assignment to be determined. Jack caught a cab at the stand in front of the station which took him to the main gate of the MVBI shipyard where he checked in. The SPs made a phone call and shortly a Navy Jeep arrived to pick up Jack and his baggage.

As the driver navigated his way through the warehouses and work shacks, piles of steel, and other materials neatly stacked about, Jack noticed they were headed toward some taller buildings which seemed to be the center of the complex. As they drew nearer, Jack was actually starting to feel better about the whole situation until the Jeep driver roared past the administrative buildings and straight toward the slipways along the river bank.

The driver slid to a stop alongside a huge slab-sided Navy gray monstrosity of a ship that was so ugly only a mother could love it. Jack shot a questioning look at the driver who jumped out of the jeep, grabbed Jack's luggage, and proudly barked, "Welcome to your new command, Commander, USS *LST 121*, newest ship in the United States Navy and the first of her kind to be completed here at Evansville." Then beaming, he took Jack's luggage and deposited it at the foot of the ship's gangway where another sailor grabbed it and disappeared up the gangway aboard the ship.

Jack stood there a moment gazing at the ship trying to gather his thoughts. Then with his hands clasped behind his back, he walked along the pier toward the bow where he looked long and hard at what appeared to be a pair of doors, which opened out exposing the interior of the ship. He spent a moment taking in the enormous interior of the ship then turned and walked along the pier toward the stern where he stood gazing at the upper works which was the only thing that stuck up above deck level that he could see.

All the time as he paced the pier, he was asking himself, *How the h———l did I get into this mess? If I screw up, I'm going to prison. If I try to tell someone, I'm not the guy they think I am I'm going to prison. If I take this ship to sea, I could get everybody killed. I wonder what sin I committed in a prior life to deserve this? H———l what sins did the men aboard this ship commit to deserve me?* Finally, resigned to the fact that he would shortly be arrested and spend the rest of his life on an all-expense paid vacation in Portsmouth Rhode Island, he thought, *Well, I'd better get this over with.* Then he turned, walked toward the gangway, and boarded his ship.

While Jack was on the pier wrestling with his thoughts, his crew, which had been mustered to show the proper courtesies when their commanding officer came aboard, was nervously awaiting his arrival at the top of the gangway. The boatswain had the crew assembled per Naval ritual and was waiting with his boatswain's pipe primed and ready. When the skipper didn't show, he carefully looked over the side and saw Jack walk from bow to stern on the pier below. The executive officer, a lieutenant JG asked, "Boats, what is he doing?"

The boatswain took one more look and said, "He's walking the length of the ship inspecting her."

"Why is he doing that?" the lieutenant asked.

"It's what the really good skippers used to do before they took command. They'd be rowed around the ship to see how she's sitting in the water, and then they'd adjust the cargo so the ship sits even at the waterline. This guy really knows his stuff."

"Hear that, everybody?" the lieutenant said to the crew. "Be on your toes the skipper is a real pro."

The men began exchanging worried looks. Then they started adjusting their dixie cups, making sure their gig lines were straight, retucking and reblousing their shirts, and adjusting their trousers. A few of them after glancing down at themselves were standing on one leg or the other rubbing the tops of their shoes on the backs of their trouser legs trying to coax a shine out of a dull finish.

When Jack finished his pacing, he walked to the bottom of the gangway, gathered himself, and strode up the gangway to his ship. The thought of prison was running through his mind, and it showed on his face in the form of a scowl that would curdle milk. When he topped the gangway, he saw a hundred wide-eyed men and two hundred eyeballs staring at him as if he was the devil incarnate.

The crew snapped to attention, the boatswain piped Jack aboard, Jack made the proper salutes, then stood there wondering what to do next. The crew and officers wilted under his glare until the boatswain looked at the executive officer and gave him a "get on with it" jerk of the head.

The executive officer snapped out of his stupor and said, "Excuse me, sir, seaman Parker will show you to your quarters. I'll await your orders, sir."

Then as Jack was led to his quarters the executive officer looked at the boatswain and shrugged his shoulders palms up in a what-just-happened manner.

The boatswain said, "He was waiting for you to follow procedure. This guy is old Navy. We're going to have to be on our toes."

The executive officer said, "Thanks, Boats."

Meanwhile, in his quarters, Jack was contemplating things. He'd made it aboard without embarrassing himself or falling off the gangway. That was a good start. Now what would a real captain do? Luckily, Jack didn't have to make that decision. There was a knock at his door, and a sailor entered to hand Jack a manila envelope. As soon as the sailor left Jack opened the envelope to find his sailing orders. He was to get underway as soon as the ship was ready and take her to New Orleans for final outfitting and await further orders.

Since the trip would take them down the Ohio River to the Mississippi River and then south to New Orleans, a river pilot would be assigned, and Jack could get underway as soon as the pilot reported aboard and Jack felt the ship was ready. Approximately ten minutes after Jack had received his orders, the river pilot showed up at the gangway and was escorted to Jack's quarters. When the pilot knocked and entered, Jack was sitting at his desk rereading his sailing orders.

"Are you aware of our orders?" Jack asked.

"Yes, sir," the pilot replied.

"Then let's get going," Jack said.

The pilot left Jack's quarters, and then it dawned on Jack he hadn't asked the man his name.

I've got to be sharper than that from now on, Jack thought. This put Jack on edge, and then it struck him he didn't even know where the bridge was. *Oh, Lord,* Jack thought. *This is going to be a disaster.*

Then after putting his orders in his safe, he looked through the manuals, and other technical papers stored in his quarters until he found a diagram of the ship to see if he could figure out where to find the bridge.

CHAPTER 6

When the pilot entered the bridge, he found it fully manned and ready. The officer of the deck was the executive officer who asked the pilot if he'd met the skipper, and if so, what did he think of him. The pilot whose name was Masters said, "Yeah, I just came from his quarters. Man, he's sharp. I reported to him, and all he asked me was if I was aware of the orders. When I told him I was, he just said, 'Then let's get going.' He doesn't waste any time at all. I thought he'd spend a few days or a week going over the ship's systems and exercising the crew. He must be planning to work up the crew on our way to New Orleans. It looks to me like he wants to get into the war as soon as possible. I'd say you guys have got a real sea dog."

With that, the executive officer glanced at the bridge crew, and they all smiled and stood a little taller.

Following the captain's orders, Masters began the process of getting underway. By the time Jack found his way through the maze of passageways and ship's ladders to the bridge, the engines were rumbling, the gangway was hauled aboard, the crew was at their stations, and the lines were shortened up.

When Jack stepped onto the bridge, the first man to see him yelled, "The captain is on the bridge." Jack froze where he stood and looked at the men as they stared at him with great anticipation. The first thought that went through his head was he was in the wrong place, or he wasn't dressed properly. Somewhat defensively, Jack said, "Well?"

The bridge crew immediately snapped too, and the bridge came alive with activity. Within an hour of his taking command, USS *LST 121* cast off all lines, backed into the stream, and began her maiden voyage from Evansville to New Orleans. As she pulled away, the yard commander grabbed his binoculars and watched as the ship headed downriver. Then he turned to one of his aids and said, "Send word that USS *LST 121* is underway in record time."

Within the hour, Commander Johnson knocked and entered Admiral Bryton's office in the Main Navy and Munitions Building and announced, "Sir, just received word that *LST 121* has departed the shipyard in Evansville and is underway, Lieutenant Commander Cole commanding, sir."

Admiral Bryton glanced at the calendar on his wall and said, "Underway already? He must have just gotten there."

"Sir, the yard commander reports that Commander Cole slipped his mooring lines and was underway within an hour of arriving, sir," Johnson commented.

Admiral Bryton slapped his hand down on his desk and said, "Now that's more like it. Record time, hey, good…That's very good. Keep me posted on anything that comes in about Commander Cole and put a note in his file about getting his ship underway in record time. I want to keep an eye on our reluctant warrior. So far, I'd say he's off to a good start."

Jack spent the rest of the day on the bridge watching and listening as Masters conned the ship on the way south. Operating on Mark Twain's principle, "It is better to be silent and thought the fool than open one's mouth and remove all doubt," Jack stood at the rear of the bridge out of the way and watched as the men went about their duties. The only time he took his eyes off the activities was when he jotted something down or was presented with some piece of paperwork that required his signature. The rest of the time, he was silent as a stone with a clipboard in his hand taking notes as they made their way downriver.

Of course, this made everyone nervous, particularly the river pilot. He was used to carrying on a casual conversation and enjoying his time on the water as he worked his way up and down the rivers. The silent intensity of the captain, his manic notetaking, and his ever-watchful eyes were just about more than the riverboat captain could stand. The skipper's silence dominated the atmosphere, and no one spoke a word beyond what was necessary to do their duties.

When officers changed watch and enlisted men relieved each other at their stations, Jack made notes of what was said and how each change was made. Not knowing what the Skipper was writing, the men naturally assumed he was evaluating them. As a result, they made sure every move they made and every word they said was straight out of the *Blue Jacket's Manual* and executed with perfection. P. T. Barnum couldn't have put on a better show.

At the end of the day, they tied up along the shore. Jack remained on the bridge taking notes until every hawser, running light, and sentry was in place. Then he tried to find his way back to his quarters. This resulted in an impromptu tour of the ship. He wandered from compartment to compartment looking for something he recognized to give him a clue where he was and hopefully an idea of where he needed to go to get back to his cabin. He'd stick his head in a compartment take a look around to see if anything looked familiar and if not he'd move on. Jack finally stumbled across his cabin around midnight and slept like a rock until the ship's steward Franklyn Ingolls woke him up with a cup of coffee and asked him if he wanted ham or bacon with his eggs.

Jack stared at Ingolls, a medium-sized black man, out of one eye and asked him what time it was.

"Oh, five hundred," the steward replied.

"What?" Jack roared and jumped out of his bunk with the intention of strangling Ingolls but restrained himself. Ingolls took a step back, set the cup of coffee on the desk next to Jack's bunk, and ran out the cabin door.

Realizing he'd probably scared the man half to death, Jack figured he was awake so he might as well get dressed and start his day. He washed his face and underarms, grabbed a quick shave, and stepped into the officer's ward room where he found Ingolls wide-eyed backed up against the pantry door.

"Sorry about snapping at you like that," Jack said. "I'm not used to getting up at this hour."

"Yes, sir, sorry, sir. I'll see that it doesn't happen again," Ingolls stammered.

"That's okay," Jack said. "I'll just have to get used to it."

CHAPTER 7

J ack took a bite of toast with marmalade followed by a sip of coffee. With a grimace like he had just eaten a persimmon before the first frost, Jack said, "Did you make this coffee?"

Ingolls said, "No, sir. It was sent up from the galley. Cookie or one of his men made it."

"Good lord," Jack said, trying to get the taste out of his mouth by wiping his tongue on a napkin. "This is terrible. He isn't serving this to the crew, is he?"

"Well, sir, if you don't mind, let me see if I can do somethin' 'bout that." Ingolls stepped into the pantry while Jack scooped up a fork full of scrambled eggs. His reaction to the eggs was very similar to his reaction to the coffee, but he finished the eggs. A few minutes later, Ingolls came back and handed Jack a fresh cup of coffee.

"Try this, sir."

Jack took a tentative sip and his eyebrows shot up. "Now that's a cup of coffee. What did you do to it, Franklyn?"

"Well, sir, I puts a little chickaree in it and just a dash of baking soda. The chickaree kills bitter taste, and the baking soda gets rida the acid."

"This is the best cup of coffee I've ever tasted. Where did you learn to make coffee like this?" Jack asked.

"That's the way my momma makes it. Ever'body says she makes the best coffee in the parish."

"Well, you thank your momma for me, Franklyn. She's a marvel." Jack finished his toast and coffee and left the wardroom.

Franklyn just beamed.

The other officers wandered into the ward room just before 0600, and Franklyn served them their breakfast. Finally, the executive officer Lieutenant JG Dale Purvis asked, "Franklyn, is the captain up yet?"

Franklyn replied, "Sir, he's been here and done gone."

"Oh s——t," the executive officer said. "When did he leave?"

Ingolls glanced at the clock on the bulkhead wall and said, "It's been about twenty minutes now. He was up at oh five hunerd, and boy was he sore I woke him up so late. I don't know what time he normally gets up, but it shore ain't oh five hunerd. I thought he was gonna wring my neck, but he let it go and said he'd get used to it."

Purvis looked at the rest of the officers gathered and said, "Men, we've got a real tiger by the tail. We'd better be here at oh five fifteen from now on. The skipper is a go getter."

With that, they finished their breakfast and dashed out. As he was passing, Purvis said to Ingolls, "Say that's about the best coffee I've ever tasted. Pass that along, will you?"

"Shore 'nough," Ingolls said, throwing out his chest with pride. "I'll be shore ta do that."

As soon as Franklyn had a few minutes to spare, he wrote his mother and told her what the captain had said about her coffee and that he'd said she was a marvel. He could just see his mother back in Waterproof, Louisiana, beaming with pride when she read that in his letter. He spent the rest of the day humming as he worked and thinking, *That Captain Cole is shore nuff good people.*

CHAPTER 8

As soon as he left the ward room, Jack got lost again and wandered around for ten minutes before he finally found himself on the main deck. Since it was still dark and they wouldn't be getting underway until first light, he walked the length of the main deck looking at one thing and another wondering what each piece of equipment was called and what it did. He almost stumbled into a sentry who had been standing behind what looked like the entrance to a prairie tornado shelter.

The sentry stepped from behind the structure, popped to attention, and asked, "May I help you, sir?"

At the sentry's first move and the sound of his voice, Jack about jumped out of his skin. He was about to yell, *Yes, you can. Don't ever do that again.* But he caught himself, and instead, it came out, "Yes, you can…What's your name, what's your job, and what are you doing now?"

It was dark, but Jack could see that the sailor was very young and very nervous. He was probably away from home for the first time, was home sick, and was afraid he'd screwed up in front of the captain.

The young sailor told Jack his name was Wilford Burwell, SC2, at the moment his job was to guard the "booby hatch" and make sure no one came or went without proper authorization.

So that's what this thing is called, Jack thought.

Then Jack pointed at one piece of machinery after another and asked, "What's that, and what does it do?"

Young Burwell answered each of Jack's questions, not only telling him what each piece of machinery was called and what it was used for, but how it was operated as well. By the time he was finished asking questions, Jack had learned quite a bit.

Jack said, "Thank you, Wilford. Can I call you Will?

"Yes, sir!" Burwell said.

"Well, Will, you really know your stuff. Where are you from?"

The young sailor said with pride, "I'm from Hamburg, Iowa, sir."

"No kidding," Jack said. "I'm from Walnut Hill, Nebraska, myself. We're practically neighbors. I don't suppose you've ever been to the Sydney Rodeo, have you?"

The young sailor's face lit up. "I sure have. Matter of fact, I won the junior division bull riding competition last year."

"Are you kidding me?" Jack said. "You must be tough as wang leather. I'll rest easy knowing I've got a man like you aboard. It was good talking to you, Will. Thanks for all the information."

Jack shook his hand and then dropped down the booby hatch to go below. SC2 Burwell stood there bursting with pride. He'd been grilled by the captain and passed with flying colors; the captain even said he knew his stuff, and then he told him he would rest easy with a man like him aboard. Suddenly, Burwell didn't feel so lonely or homesick.

CHAPTER 9

J ack was waiting on the bridge when Masters arrived to take the ship on downriver. Jack was in deep thought about the process of getting underway. They would be pulling away from the bank with the current running. At Evansville, they started from the shipyard in slack water; today should be a completely new experience. He was making notes on what to watch for when Masters stepped onto the bridge and greeted Jack with a friendly, "Good morning, Commander." Jack was still in deep thought as he scribbled notes and completely missed Master's comment.

When Jack finished making his last entry on his clipboard and glanced up, he found Masters staring at him. Taken by surprise, Jack stared at Masters for a moment lost for words. The only thing Jack could think of to say was, "Carry on, Mr. Masters." Jack had heard some of the officers at the reorientation class use that phrase, and it seemed to be one of those all-purpose throwaway lines officers used when they didn't have anything else to say. Then after he'd said it, he hoped it would fit the situation because he had no idea what Masters had just said to him.

Masters, on the other hand, was thinking he had appeared to Commander Cole as hesitant and unsure so Cole had in effect told him to get going and do his job. An order Commander Cole should not have had to give. Masters had screwed up and he knew it. However, Commander Cole had not reprimanded him as he could have and instead allowed him to keep his dignity in front of the bridge crew.

Masters was thinking, *He reminded me to do my job without reprimanding me. He is a really good leader. I'd be glad to serve under a man like this.*

Jack watched and made notes as Masters gave the necessary commands to cast off and pull away from shore. After watching things on the bridge for an hour, Jack realized they were settling into the same routine he had witnessed the day before. Not needing to spend all day watching the bridge crew repeat what he'd already learned, Jack decided to go below and tour the ship.

After Jack left, the ensign on deck turned to the boatswain and asked, "Wasn't the captain supposed to announce he was leaving the bridge and turn command over to me?"

"Mr. Price," the boatswain said, glancing sideways at him, "the skipper never took command. Mr. Masters is in command. Our captain is one heck of a sailor and knows procedure like you know the back of your hand. We're d——n lucky to have a man like that taking us out."

Without taking his eyes off the channel ahead of him, Masters uttered, "You can say that again, Boats."

CHAPTER 10

Jack proceeded from the bridge forward to the 40 mm. gun tubs, looked over the rail at the bow wave, and then thought about what to do next. He thought about returning to his cabin to review the ship's diagrams and performance specifications, but he'd learned so much from seaman Burwell he thought it might be a better use of his time to find his way around the ship, meet some of the crew, and see what else they could teach him.

He entered the booby hatch Burwell had been guarding earlier and went down a set of stairs. Because they were so steep, he wondered if they were called stairs or if they had some other name for them in the Navy. He was wondering what else they could be called when he reached the bottom and a sailor came pounding out of a side companion way and almost ran into Jack. The sailor jumped to attention and said, "Sorry, sir, I didn't see you coming down the ladder. Excuse me, sir.

So that's what those things are called, Jack thought.

Not knowing what else to say and not wanting to look like he didn't know what he was doing, Jack said, "That's not a problem. I like to see a man hustle when he's working."

"Um, I'm not exactly working, sir. I was on my way to the head, sir."

"Oh..." Jack paused for moment, lost for words, then said, "Well, you've got a critical mission to perform so get on with it," and stepped out of the sailor's way.

The sailor barked, "Aye, aye, sir" and ran down the companionway.

CHAPTER 11

One of Jack's immediate goals, along with trying to learn how to be a captain, was to meet each of his crew members. He didn't know how long it was going to be until the Navy figured out they had the wrong man in command, but in the meantime, he figured they were all in this together and the more he knew about his people the better off everyone would be. After all, if the Navy had its way, he might end up taking them to sea, and if that happened, he'd need to know how good each man was at his job and who he could depend on. Together, they'd need all the help they could get.

The evening before, he had begun to memorize the crew's names. Now he wanted to put faces with the names. He also wanted to learn how to get from one place to another without getting lost. The Navy was bound and determined to put him in command of a ship, but he didn't think it would show very good leadership if the captain had to keep asking the crew where he was or how to find his way back to his cabin.

Learning the names of his crew members wasn't hard. Jack had learned the names of all the students, parents, teachers, and staff in his school district as well as most of the people in Wellborn County, Nebraska. Remembering names came easy once Jack had met a person and gotten to know something about him. So as Jack toured the ship, he'd ask each man who he was, what department he was in, what his job was, and how he did his job. Then he'd shake the man's hand and move on.

Jack worked his way down the port side from the bow toward the stern, shaking each man's hand and learning as much as he could as he went. Time was of the essence. He needed to learn as much as possible as quickly as possible and asking the men who did the work was the best way he knew how to get the job done.

To Jack, shaking a man's hand was a common courtesy. However, the crew, most of whom were drafted and had become used to being treated as nameless faces in the crowd, felt like the captain was taking a personal interest in them. They were especially impressed by how interested he was in knowing how they did their jobs.

Scuttlebutt raced throughout the ship as Jack worked his way toward the stern. *The Skipper is testing each man to see how well he knows his job.* This put the men on edge, but it also made them sharp and the personal interview with the captain made each man feel like he was the most important man on the crew.

CHAPTER 12

By the time Jack reached the engine room, it was close to midday, so he left the engine room for later and found his way to the ship's galley. One of the things Jack had learned about people was if they were well fed, it just naturally improved their outlook on life and made them more amenable to things that might otherwise get under their skin.

Bud Stamwell who ran Stamwell's Livestock Auction House in Walnut Hill had confided this to Jack one evening following an Elks Club meeting when Bud had a little too much spiked punch from the punch bowl. Bud's livestock auction house served the best breakfast and lunch in the county, but his restaurant was only open on auction days. As Bud had put it, "I don't feed people well because I like to see 'em eat. I feed them well so they'll bid high, sell low, and enjoy doing it."

Jack thought Bud's philosophy could be put to good use in his current situation. He may not know anything about being a sailor, but at least he could make sure his men got the best food he could provide. So far no one knew he was a fraud, but he wanted his crew to be happy in their ignorance.

Figuring people are people no matter where you go, Jack had already determined he would need to keep his men active and in good spirits if he stood any chance of keeping himself out of Portsmouth. He had some ideas about how to bring this about, but he would need some items he was sure were not Navy issue to get the job done. He'd made a list of what he needed, but he'd start with the food and work on his other ideas when the opportunity presented itself.

After meeting the galley crew, Jack watched them work until sailors began to arrive for their meals. At this point, Jack asked Bill

Spence, the ship's cook, about how they moved sailors through the chow line. After listening to Spence describe the process, Jack asked him if there were any problems and if so what Bill would recommend to smooth things out. Spence thought about it for a moment and said, "Well, sir, we're okay right now, but when we get a bunch of troops aboard, I think we might run into some problems getting everyone fed on time.

"Why's that?" Jack asked.

"Well, sir, we feed our people three times a day and the Army only feeds their people twice a day. If we feed the troops in between the meals, we feed the crew we'll be feeding pretty much nonstop all day long. That ain't no problem, but I'm concerned about getting all our trays and silverware cleaned between meals. We need to wash them with soap and water and then hit them with steam to get them sanitary, and I don't know if we've got the capacity to do that with the dishwashing machinery we've got."

"Okay, Bill," Jack said. "If it comes to that, here's what we'll do. We'll weld up some racks, have the troops scrub their trays and silverware in soapy water, put the trays on the racks as they leave the mess, and then we can hit them with live steam from a steam hose to sanitize them. That ought to speed up the process."

Jack didn't want to tell the cook, but he'd seen this done on a five-thousand-man WPA construction site in the Black Hills before the war. Bill, on the other hand, thought, *Man, this guy is sharp. He just came up with that off the top of his head.*

"And don't worry about trying to get everything done with your own people. If it comes down to it, we'll shanghai some troops to pitch in and do whatever you think will get the job done. Got it?"

"Yes, sir!" Spence replied, beaming.

"Oh, one more thing, Bill," Jack said. "How many coffee pots do we have?"

"Coffee pots, sir?" Spence asked.

"Yeah, coffee pots, you know like the ones everybody has in their kitchen at home? I haven't seen one in any of the departments. I don't want the men to have to leave their duty stations to grab a cup of coffee and I don't want them to go without. It cuts down on our efficiency and ruins morale. While I'm thinking about it, who do you have making the coffee?"

"Reynolds, sir," Cookie said, nodding at the man.

"Have you tasted his coffee?" Jack asked.

"No, sir. I don't drink coffee myself, never acquired a taste for it. Why? Is there a problem?"

"Not unless we want to win the war. There isn't," Jack said with a sour look on his face.

"Okay, sir, I'll jump his a———s and get him on the ball," Cookie said, looking at the back of Reynolds's head with a scowl that could have penetrated a bulkhead.

"Don't do anything yet," Jack said. "His coffee is the worst I've ever tasted, but it's probably not that much worse than most Navy coffee. I'm going to have Franklyn Ingolls bring down a pot of coffee from the ward room. I want Franklyn to show Reynolds how he makes it. It's Franklyn's momma's recipe. It's the best I've ever tasted."

"While we're at it, let's make something for the guys to chew on during their watch. I'm not talking about sandwiches or anything like that and I don't want it to put a bunch of extra work on you and your men, I just want them to have something to go with a cup of coffee. It'll keep them happy, and they'll think you walk on water. Whatever you do though, don't tell them I had anything to do with it. Got me?"

"Yes, sir," Spence said. "How about donuts?"

"Yeah, that sounds good to me," Jack replied, "as long as it doesn't put an extra burden on you and your men."

"No, sir. We can mix up a bunch of batter in our slack time, roll it into hollow tubes, and freeze it. Then all we'll have to do is cut pieces off the roll and toss them in the friar. Shouldn't be a problem at all."

"Now, what about those coffee pots; how many do we have?"

Cookie rolled his eyes to the overhead in deep thought. "There's only two I can think of, sir. There's one in the officers mess and one in the officers pantry. The rest of the coffee is brewed here in those big urns," he said, jerking his thumb over his shoulder at the huge kitchen coffee urns.

28

"Okay," Jack said. "I'll have to see what we can do about the coffee pots. In the meantime have you got anything you can put coffee in that will keep it hot?"

"Well, sir. I've got plenty of metal pitchers with lids. I could wrap them in towels. That would keep the coffee hot for a couple of hours I imagine."

"Good. That'll work. Wait until Franklyn shows Reynolds how to make coffee first, then start sending coffee to all the departments every two hours, and keep that schedule going until we get enough coffee pots for every department."

From the galley and mess deck, Jack moved on to the engine room. After speaking with the crew in the engine room, Jack headed for the quartermaster's office. When Jack stuck his head into the quartermaster's department, he found Chief Quincy Barton sitting behind his desk with his back to the door pouring over a sheaf of papers. When the chief didn't react to him entering, Jack cleared his throat and said, "Chief, you got a minute?"

The chief swung around so quickly Jack almost jumped. The chief had a narrow-eyed squint on his face and looked like he was ready to fight until he saw who it was that had interrupted him. Then he jumped up and bellowed, "Excuse me, sir, I didn't hear you come in. Sorry, sir!"

"No problem, Chief. What are you working on?" Jack said, reaching over and picking up the sheaf of papers the chief had dropped on the desk when he jumped up.

The chief reached for the papers and said, "Oh, nothing you'd be interested in, sir. Just some inventory reports is all."

But it was too late, Jack had already started to read down the list which read like a sale bill, listing an item and its equivalent in other items. Jack knew what it was immediately. I see you have a shopping list, Chief. Is this for the ship or for uh…shall we say personal use?"

Knowing he was caught, Chief Barton fell back on that old tried and true adage, "If you don't know what else to say, tell the truth."

"Well, sir, you see it's like this. The navy only issues a certain amount of equipment to each ship, and they don't always get it right. Sometimes, there isn't enough to get the job done, and sometimes there's too much, and it just sits around getting in the way. So us chiefs in quartermaster sort of even things out and get the equipment distributed the way the Navy uh…intended it to be in the first place…sir."

"I see," Jack said. "That's very interesting and all, but it doesn't answer my original question, does it?"

"Uh wha…uh, what's that, sir?" Barton stammered.

"Is this for the ship or for personal use?"

"Well, sir…It's for the ship, but there's no such thing as a straight swap. The quartermaster chiefs are right guys, but they know if they've got sumpin', you need they got ya by the short hairs so's to speak an they'll stick it to ya if they can. I just sees that as handlin' charges and the cost of doin' bidness, so if I make out on a deal, I puts the extra into uh…escrow so to speak for the future…you know in case I gotta have sumpin an gotta pay through the nose to get it, sir."

"I see, and where do you keep your…escrow account, chief?"

"Oh, I've got it squirreled away here and there so's it don't get in nobody's way."

"Well, Chief, I may have a job for a man with your, let's say, talents. Let's you and me take a little stroll and see what you have in inventory."

The chief was as nervous as a lightning rod salesman in a thunder storm. This telling the truth was new to him, and he didn't know quite what to think of it. But the captain had him dead to rights, and there was only one thing he could do at this point. He'd never been very religious, but he began to silently recite John 3:16. After all, God takes care of drunks and fools. He didn't qualify on the one hand, but he figured he had the other covered in spades.

When Jack was working on equipping the Walnut Hill High School's band and football team, he had resorted to a little horse trading and dickering himself to get what he needed for his kids. When he took over as county superintendent of schools, every township had a one room school house. Over time, as the one room schools were consolidated into multigrade elementary buildings, Jack found himself with an overabundance of equipment which was of no value to the school district but was of considerable sentimental value to the district patrons and neighboring county schools. To outfit the band and the football team, he traded the school bells, desks, and chalkboards to other school districts for instruments and football equipment. He then turned around and auctioned off memorabilia such as class pictures, trophies, and other sentimental items, and sold the doors, windows, and potbellied stoves. Once a building had been stripped of all useful items, Jack sold the lumber for salvage and rented the land for agriculture.

When Jack discovered Chief Barton was heavily involved in the redistribution of wealth, he knew he had found a diamond in the rough. After digging into the dark recesses of the ship and seeing the plethora of equipment Barton had in escrow, Jack gave Barton a list of items he wanted for the ship.

Barton looked at the "shopping list" as he called it. When he was finished, he said, "Sir, I don't know what you want or need this stuff for, but I don't see any problem getting all of it except this here item at the bottom of the list. An ice cream maker might be a bit of a stretch, even for me."

Jack laid a hand on Barton's shoulder, looked him in the eye, and said, "Quincy, a man can never rise to his full potential if he limits himself to what he has already accomplished. Think of this as an opportunity to excel at a level no other quartermaster has yet achieved."

Chief Barton stood there, looking at the list, and then his face suddenly lit up. "Yeah, this'll be somethin' ain't nobody never been able to do. I'll get right on this, sir."

"Oh and, Chief, let's keep this strictly between you and me, got it?"

"D——n straight…Uh, I mean, *yes*, sir."

Jack went back to his quarters where he found that Franklyn had a hot meal waiting for him.

"Have the other officers eaten yet, Franklyn?" Jack asked.

"Yes, sir," Franklyn replied.

"What about Mr. Masters, our pilot? Has he eaten yet?"

"Yes, sir. I took him his meal. He ate on the bridge so we could stay underway, just like we did yesterday, sir."

"Okay," Jack said, all the time thinking, *I dodged that bullet.*

CHAPTER 13

The biggest concern Jack had was meeting his officers. He figured since his officers had completed officer training, they would know what they were doing and immediately spot him for the fraud he was. Jack avoided meeting them his first night aboard by making the rounds familiarizing himself with the ship. But he knew he couldn't do that again, and he didn't know how he was going to deal with that problem.

Jack planned to spend the rest of the day working his way through the remainder of the ship and be on the bridge to witness the ship being tied up to the bank for the second time.

During the afternoon, while Jack was making his rounds and meeting the crew, the executive officer and first lieutenant were conferring at the back of the bridge. In hushed tones, they were speculating on why the captain had not invited all his officers to the officers' mess his first night aboard. Their general consensus was that after watching how things were being run, the new skipper was not happy with their performance and was probably planning a way to get rid of them and find some more qualified officers. All in all, it was not an optimistic conversation.

As they went over what could have dissatisfied the captain, they developed quite a list of possible transgressions. However, as each man threw out a suggestion, they knew the crew's performance had been outstanding and that neither them nor any of the officers had performed poorly. That is what was really bothering them; they didn't know why the captain was dissatisfied with them.

Standing beside the helmsman, Chief Boatswain's Mate Art Gardener couldn't help but overhear bits and pieces of the conversation. Finally, taking a step back, Gardener said, "Excuse me, sirs. I couldn't help but overhear your conversation. May I?"

The two officers looked at each other, and then the executive officer Lieutenant JG Dale Purvis said, "Sure, Boats. What's on your mind?"

"Well, sirs, it's tradition for the senior officer to hold a gathering for all the officers as soon as he takes command. However, the commanding officer is the senior officer so by default the captain performs this duty."

"And?" both officers asked with puzzled looks on their faces.

"Well, technically, until he is relieved, Mr. Masters is in command when the ship is underway and knowing naval tradition like he does, Commander Cole may feel it is inappropriate for him to initiate such a gathering until he has full and complete command of the ship."

Purvis looked at the first lieutenant, Lieutenant JG Wayne Young. "What do you think, Wayne?"

"Boats is probably right." And then both officers looked at Masters, the river pilot.

Sensing their stare, Masters turned to face the three men and said. "What?"

"You understand better than we do, Boats. You tell him," Purvis said.

After Gardener explained what he thought might be happening, Masters said, "Okay, let's say Boats is right. What do you want me to do about it?"

All three sets of eyes turned to Boatswain Gardener.

"It's not my place to say, but if you ask me?" Gardener said and stopped, looking at the three men.

Purvis gave the boatswain a "come on, spit it out" motion with his hands. "Come on, Boats. If you've got it figured out, let's hear it."

"Okay," Boats said. "Here's the way I see it. Mr. Masters and the captain are in a joint command, so to speak, and the skipper sees it as a log jam. He's not going to go to a civilian. No offense," Gardener said, looking at Masters who rolled his eyes and shook his head in a none-taken manner. "To ask permission, so to speak, to hold a dinner for his officers on his own ship. Maybe if Mr. Masters went to the skipper and suggested they hold a dinner for the officers jointly, it might break the ice. Mr. Masters would be asking permission, and in so doing, he would in effect be recognizing the captain as senior officer and under his authority."

"What do you think, Mr. Masters?" Purvis said.

"Sounds good to me. As far as I'm concerned, there's no question he's in full command. But if you think it's causing a problem, hey, I'm ready to do whatever it takes to get the job done."

"Okay," Purvis said. "How about you ask him as soon as we tie up this evening?"

"H———l, we've got a stretch of smooth water with no shoals or bars coming up. As soon as we get into that, I'll go talk to him."

CHAPTER 14

Commander Cole was on the tank deck aft in the steering compartment listening to SF1c Bill Davis and SF2c Angelo Marguchi explain the operation of the steering gear when Masters popped into the compartment and asked permission to speak with the captain.

Cole shook hands with both men and said, "Thanks, Bill. Thanks, Angie. I'll be back as soon as I'm finished with Mr. Masters. I want to know more about the secondary backup system and those hydraulic transfer pumps."

Davis handed Jack a shop rag to wipe the grease off his hands from the handshake, saying, "Sorry about that, sir."

"Don't worry about it," Jack said, wiping his hands on the rag and tossing it back to Davis. "It's a badge of honor. Shaking men's hands who know what they're doing and how to make things work."

Jack stepped into the companionway and said, "What can I do for you, Mr. Masters? It must be important for you to leave the bridge and come down here. What do you need?"

Jack was annoyed that Masters had found him below deck. The last thing he needed was Masters telling the officers the skipper is below asking the crew how everything works. He felt like Masters had caught him with his hand in the cookie jar.

Jack's brisk manner set Masters back on his heels. Obviously, the captain expected him to be doing his job and took exception to him not being on the bridge conning the ship. Thinking fast, Masters said, "I thought I'd let you know we are in a long straight stretch of water with no bars, shoals, or other obstructions in case you had any maneuvers or exercises you wanted to run, sir."

"Oh...Thank you, Mr. Masters. I don't believe that will be necessary at this time. Carry on." There was that throwaway line again. *It sure comes in handy when you don't know what you're doing*, Jack thought.

When Masters entered the bridge, Purvis and Young looked at him with expectant eyes. Masters just shook his head and said, "He about skinned me alive for leaving the bridge and not doing my job. You guys are on your own."

Below in the steering compartment, Jack listened to the ship fitters explain the secondary steering system and the backup hydraulic pumps one more time and told them he thought he understood, but he'd probably be back for a refresher. Then he left the tank deck and began working his way back toward the bridge figuring he'd better do something somewhere where his officers could see him before they figured out he was avoiding them.

Jack still wasn't that familiar with the ship and managed to get lost again trying to find the bridge. He stopped several times to get his bearings as he wandered from one corridor to the next and finally found himself in the passageway behind the bridge. Feeling pretty pleased with himself, Jack glanced at his wristwatch to see how long it had taken him to find the bridge this time. When he looked down at his watch, he noticed a large glob of grease on one shoe which he must have picked up in the steering compartment. As he reached down to wipe it off, he threw up his hand to balance himself against the bulkhead and accidentally leaned on the battlestation's alarm.

This set off a mad house response throughout the ship. Sailors were running every which way, throwing on life jackets, grabbing their steel pots, racing up or down ships ladders, and dashing first one way then the other trying to remember where their battle station was.

Jack froze. The bridge crew had not been immune to the general panic that swept through the ship, and after running into each other and slamming into various pieces of equipment in their frenzy to get into their life jackets and steel pots, they were in place with their battlestations, manned, wide-eyed, and ready for action.

In the few seconds it took to get to their battlestations, no one noticed Jack standing in the passageway at the back of the bridge. The departments were reporting manned and ready when Lieutenant Young noticed Jack. The first lieutenant jumped to attention and was just beginning to speak when Jack said, "Shut that thing off, would you, Mr. Young?"

Before Young could move, one of the bridge talkers reached over and shut off the battle stations claxon. Jack stood there for a moment, embarrassment turning his face a deep shade of red. With all eyes staring at him, Jack said, "Carry on." Turned and stepped onto the starboard bridge wing without saying another word.

Not knowing what else to do and fighting his growing embarrassment, Jack glanced down at his watch, looked at the ship from bow to stern, turned, and left the bridge wing to go below to his cabin.

Purvis relieved everyone from their battle stations, and the crew went back to their normal duties.

CHAPTER 15

Ⅰn his cabin, Jack was sitting at his desk contemplating his future
in Portsmouth, Rhode Island, while thumbing through one of
the ship's technical manuals when Ingolls knocked, entered, and
handed Jack a steaming cup of coffee. Jack was too embarrassed to
look at Ingolls, so all he said was, "Thank you, Franklyn. A cup of
your momma's coffee is just what I need right now."

Franklyn had just returned to his pantry when Lieutenant
Purvis stuck his head through the pantry door and asked in a whisper, "Franklyn, what's he doing?"

Franklyn slowly turned and glanced into the captain's cabin, then
turned back to Purvis. "He's jist sittin' there like nothin' happened."

"Is he mad?" Purvis asked.

"He don't look it, but I cain't tell. He neva looked at me. He jist
took the cupa coffee I give him and's sitting there quiet as can be with
a tekical manual," Franklyn replied.

Purvis was thinking, *Oh s——t that battle stations drill was a
complete cluster f——k. He was so mad his face turned beet red. He
checked his watch to see how long it took us to get to battle stations and
then left the bridge. He probably wants to have us all shot, but he's too
level-headed to lose his cool. He never gets ruffled, puts us through our
paces, and acts like nothing happened.*

"I 'spect he figures we'd better know our bidness and hop to
when he say jump," Franklyn said.

"I think you're right, Franklyn. Do you think he'd let us eat with
him this evening?" Purvis asked.

"H——l if I know," Franklyn said. "Whyn't you ast him?"

"Would you do it for us, Franklyn? Just tell him the officer's request permission to dine with him this evening, if it meets his approval, at whatever time he chooses." Purvis was almost pleading.

Franklyn looked from Purvis into the captain's cabin again and back to Purvis. "Okay, but if he throws me ovaboard I'm comin' back and haunt you."

"You got a deal," Purvis said. "I'll wait in the ward room while you talk to him."

Purvis ducked into the ward room before Franklyn could change his mind and closed the ward room door behind him. Franklyn stood there for a moment gathering his courage and finally knocked on Jack's doorframe and went in. "The officers ast parmission to dine wit' you dis evenin', sir."

Jack had been thinking about life behind bars when Franklyn stuck his head in the door and asked his question. Jack slowly turned his head toward Franklyn and said, "Why?"

"I cain't answer that, sir. They knowd you was busy so they ast me to ast you if they could eat wit you at whadever time you say."

Jack thought, *Well, this is it. They've figured me out. D——n, I thought I'd last longer than two days.*

"Sure, Franklyn. You pick the time. Whatever works best for you is fine with me," Jack said with a sigh.

"How 'bout eight bells, sir? We should be tied up along shore by then wit everthin' secure and guards posted."

"Sure...Fine," Jack said thinking, *What the h——l time is eight bells?*

Franklyn left the captain's cabin and met Purvis in the ward room. "Captain say eight bells."

"Thanks, Franklyn. Any problems? How'd he act? Is this going to work or are we gonna get keel hauled?"

"No idea. He act like it was jist anotha thang he had ta do but warn't really cited about doin' it."

"Okay. Thanks, Franklyn," Purvis said and left.

CHAPTER 16

Purvis spread the word to the other officers that they would be dining with the captain at eight bells in the ward room. When asked what to expect he just told the other officers. "I don't know what's going to happen. Just be prepared for anything."

At eight bells, the officers and Mr. Masters were waiting in the ward room for the captain to arrive. They didn't dare sit down for fear the captain would enter and find them seated before he had given them permission. After Purvis glanced at the bulkhead clock for the third time, Franklyn took the hint and went to the captain's cabin to remind him of his dinner with the officers. Not finding the captain in his cabin, Franklyn began to search for the captain whom he ultimately found talking to seaman Burwell at the port side booby hatch.

Burwell was in the middle of a tale about the bull riding circuit when Franklyn walked up and cleared his throat to catch their attention. They turned, and Franklyn said, "You have the officers dinin' wit you at eight bells, sir."

Just then, the bell started to toll, and Jack said, "Is it that time already? Will, don't forget where you left off. I want to hear the rest of your story about the Grand Forks rodeo." Then he said, "Okay, Franklyn, let's go."

As he was walking away, Burwell thought to himself, *He sounds more like he's going to a funeral than going to a dinner party.*

It was 2008 hours when Jack walked into the ward room. All the officers were standing behind their chairs at parade rest. At a silent signal from Purvis, they all said, "Good evening, sir."

Jack stood there for a second, not knowing what to do, then walked to the head of the table and sat down. The officers all remained standing while Jack stared at them wondering, *What the h——l are they doing now?*

Finally, Purvis asked, "Permission to be seated, sir?"

Jack, who had been dreading the moment of being exposed, looked at each officer in turn and said, "Yes, of course. Be seated, gentlemen."

After they were all seated, Franklyn, Tyree Higby, and Luscious Tanner, the other two ships' stewards, began serving the meal. Not a word was spoken as the stewards served each course. Finally, as the officers were each enjoying a scoop of lime sherbet for desert, Jack laid down his spoon and asked, "Franklyn, is this the same meal the men are being served this evening?"

"No, sir!" Franklyn said.

"Who selected this menu?" Jack asked.

"Um, I did, sir."

"Well, you tell Bill I said the meal was delicious, but from now on, let's have the officers eat the same meal as the crew regardless of the occasion. How's that sound to you, Franklyn?"

"Sorry, sir, I…uh…I…" Franklyn began to stammer.

"No need, Franklyn. You selected an excellent menu, and the cooks prepared it magnificently. I just don't want us"—here he looked around the ward room at his officers—"eating better than the crew. It's just common courtesy. Wouldn't you say so, gentlemen?"

A chorus of "yes sirs" came from the officers.

"Now how about some of that outstanding coffee of yours?" Jack asked.

After the coffee was served, Franklyn, Tyree, and Luscious withdrew to the pantry. Jack took a sip of his coffee, set the cup in the saucer, leaned forward, put both elbows on the table, and said, "Okay, this is your meeting. Let's get it over with."

All eyes turned to Lieutenant Purvis. He glanced sideways at the officers beside him and across the table then cleared his throat and said, "Well, sir, we know you are old Navy, and we know we haven't measured up to your standards. We were hoping we could find out what our shortcomings have been, and you could tell us how to improve so we can meet your expectations, sir."

This took Jack by surprise, and he tried to keep the surprised look off his face by tenting his fingers in front of his face and leaning forward on his thumbs. He'd expected something more along the lines of a mutiny rather than his officers apologizing for poor performance and asking how they could improve.

The first thing that went through Jack's mind was, *These aren't trained Naval officers. They're boys.* Then it struck him. *You poor kids, you're so green you haven't got a clue, how to lead men, or how the world works....I don't need to worry about being found to be a fraud by them. They have no idea what they're doing. I'm going to have my work cut out for me trying to learn how to be a ship's captain and train them how to be officers at the same time. Oh, Lord!*

Trying to buy some time so he could think how to handle the situation, Jack leaned back in his chair and folded his arms across his chest. "Why don't you tell me why you think I'm disappointed in your performance, where you think you need improvement, and tell me what needs to be done to correct the situation. We'll start with you, Mr. Davis I believe you are the junior officer aboard."

Jack regularly attended school board meetings at one of his country schools where the board president always asked for the youngest school board member's input first. The board president was a longtime rancher and a very prosperous one to boot. He said he always wanted the youngest man's opinion first. That way, the young fella would be encouraged to speak his mind rather than follow the lead of the "gray beards" as he called himself and the rest of the older board members. When asked why that was important, the old gentleman said, "If we don't get some new ideas, we'll never get any better than we are today. That's d——n good you understand, but we can always get better."

Jack decided he'd use the same approach here.

Ensign John Davis was the junior officer and got off to a stuttering and stammering start, but when he saw he wasn't going to be interrupted by the captain or the other officers, he started to relax and laid out a number of things he felt could be done better in his engineering department.

Next was Ensign Adam Jensen the gunnery officer; followed by Ensign William Wesley, the communications officer; Ensign Aaron Price, the assistant first lieutenant; Lieutenant JG Wayne Young, the first lieutenant; and Lieutenant JG Dale Purvis, the executive officer. When they were finished, Jack turned to Mr. Masters and said, "Owen, you're not an officer of this ship, but I'd like your input as well."

The list of transgressions included things like hair being too long, shirt tails untucked, grease on machinery or tools, delays in hauling in mooring lines, rust spots showing on deck or hull fittings, failure to have gig lines straight, pleats in trousers not sharp enough, slow to battle stations, etc.

After hearing everything his officers and Mr. Masters had to say, Jack asked, "Do you gentlemen really think the things you've mentioned are cause for me to be dissatisfied with your performance or the performance of the crew?"

They all looked at each other, and no one answered. Finally, Jack said, "Gentlemen, to the best of my knowledge, no one knows anything about an LST because the Navy has never had LSTs before. They are new to the Navy, and the Navy doesn't have any history to draw upon to train crews on these vessels. We will be among the first to take one to sea. If I thought you weren't doing your job, I would have told you. In the meantime, I'm trying to find out as much about an LST as I can. And the only people who know anything about this ship are the people who built her and the crew they trained to operate her. We can't function as a well-oiled machine unless we know how all the parts work.

"Don't for a minute believe the things you've each identified are actions or lack thereof that would disappoint me. But I'll tell you this. If you honestly believe any of the things you've identified are shortcomings by you or your men, then why the h———l haven't you done anything about it? If I ever hear of one of my officers finding a problem and not solving it, I'll kick you out of my scho—er, ship so fast, it will make your head swim. Now I've got a few comments of my own to make so listen up."

Jack sat there for a moment trying to think of how he wanted to get his message across. The whole situation reminded him of the first day with teachers and staff at the beginning of a new school year. So he launched into a modified version of his beginning-of-the-year speech.

"First of all, I haven't seen any training or drills on operation of the systems on this ship. By that, I mean how to operate the elevators, bow doors, bow ramp, stern winch, ballast tanks, anti-aircraft guns, radar, communications, or any of the million other things we need to know how to operate once we get to sea. He thought: *It's a good thing I've been reading those technical manuals. I don't know how any of that stuff works, but at least, I know they have something to do with the ship.* And if I have an officer aboard this ship who thinks he has to wait for me to tell him to do this, then you are sadly mistaken. While I'm at it, Mr. Masters, how many of my officers have you trained to maneuver this ship? How many helmsmen have you been training to steer this vessel? Now I won't fault you for not taking the initiative for doing that. I accept that responsibility. So hear me loud and clear. Although you are not an officer of this ship, I suggest you make training an active part of your daily routine from here on out on this voyage and every other voyage you take when delivering a ship to the Navy."

Looking at his officers, Jack said, "Starting tomorrow, Owen will man the bridge as an adviser, and officers will conn the ship. Owen, your job will be to see that they learn what they are supposed to do and insure that they do it correctly. He thought: *H———l I need that as much or more than they do.* You point out the course, and it will be the officer in command who will give the orders to steer the ship through whatever maneuvers are required. Again: *I need to be on the bridge as much as possible so I can learn all that stuff too.* I want helmsmen changed every two hours, and I want officers to stand standard watches. And mix it up. I don't want the same officers and same helmsmen standing watch together all the time. I want everybody on the bridge to know how to work together regardless who they are paired with.

"In the meantime, the rest of the ship's crew will be conducting drills on every function, real or imaginary, that you can think of which we might be required to perform. When you've run out of things to do get with your senior crew members and ask them for ideas. I'm not real big on rank, but I am a believer in experience. Just because you've got a man that hasn't been in the Navy very long doesn't mean he didn't bring a lot of knowledge with him when he joined. *And in my case, the opposite is true.* Get to know your men. Pick their brains. *Lord knows that's what I'm doing.* Figure out how to do things faster, safer, and better every time you run a drill.

"Mr. Purvis, whose job do you think it is to set up the training schedule and make sure we are not at cross purposes? And by cross purposes, I mean seeing that we don't conduct drills that work against each other or put the men and the ship in any sort of danger?"

Lieutenant Purvis swallowed hard, jumped to his feet, and said, "Mine, sir."

"That is correct. Please sit down. This is a discussion. You're not on trial."

Everyone laughed at that, and Purvis sat down with a smile on his face.

"That's better," Jack said. "Now whose job do you think it is to coordinate all this for you so you can manage the training program?"

Purvis got a panicked look on his face for a split second and then confidently said, "The first lieutenant, sir."

"Correct again, Dale. Wayne, whose responsibility is it to determine what the drills are for each department?

"Uh, the…the department heads, sir?" Lieutenant JG Wayne Young stammered.

"That's right. Now whose responsibility is it to make sure each department is conducting the drills they need to be conducting and doing them correct?"

"I think that would be me, sir?"

"Correct, Wayne. That would be you. So to make sure you do your job correctly, what are you going to need to do?"

"Uh…I'm going to have to know everything about every department aboard ship, sir?" Lieutenant Young asked.

"That's correct, Wayne. Dale, how are you going to know whether Mr. Young is doing his job?"

Purvis looked startled but said, "I'll have to learn everything there is to know about this ship, sir." This time, Purvis answered with confidence, and Jack thought, *I might just be getting through to this young man.*

"And how will I know if you are doing your job correctly, Dale?" Jack asked.

"You'll have to learn everything there is to know about this ship, sir," Purvis snapped.

"Now we're thinking like a team. Dale, you will also be the ship's navigator, and, Wayne, you are assistant navigator. Dale, it will be your responsibility to see that each of us stays sharp on navigation. That includes me. Everyone will shoot the sun at noon each day, and Mr. Purvis will check our work. We will all compare our findings. It's a big ocean out there, and I want to know where we are at all times. No one can know too much about navigation so Dale start us all from the beginning as if none of us knows anything about navigating."

In the back of his mind, Jack was thinking, *One of us doesn't know anything about navigating. If the river didn't run between two banks, I'd probably end up in Albuquerque. I hope Dale is as good a navigator as his fitness report says he is.*

"Ensign Wesley, what drills and training will you need to be conducting as communications officer?"

"I…I'm not sure, sir," Wesley replied.

"Good. You said the right thing. I can't speak for any other officer in the Navy, but with me, when you don't know the answer to a question or you don't know what to do, ask. I'll never hold you accountable for something unless I've told you it's your responsibility. That goes for everyone. If you have a problem, your department has a problem, and if your department has a problem, the ship has a problem, and if the ship has a problem, we all have a problem. Got it?"

Jack looked from man to man, not looking from one to the next until he got a nod or a positive response from each one.

"Now, Bill…Can I call you Bill?" Jack asked.

"Yes, sir!" Wesley replied.

"Now, Bill, find out how many men you have that can operate and repair our radios and radar. Once you know that, find out who on this ship has any experience with radios, telegraph, or any other form of communication and get them trained so we have at least six people aboard who can operate and repair our radios and radar. And I want at least two men in each department who can send and receive Morse code by dit dah and wig wag. If we haven't got that many, train them. You'll get the names of your trainees from the department heads. Got that?"

"Yes, sir!" Wesley snapped.

"And while we're talking about code, how many among us can comfortably send and receive by dit dah and wig wag?" Jack asked.

No hands went up. "Okay, Bill. Include us in the classes as well, and by us, I mean me too. I don't want any officer on this ship that isn't completely comfortable sending and receiving code."

"Adam, we've got two twin 40 mm., four single 40 mm, and twelve 20 mm. I don't just want our gunners trained on those weapons. I want them trained on our small arms as well, and I want enough men trained that we can go three deep on every weapon we've got. That's three deep on each twin 40, three deep on each single 40, and three deep on each 20. When you train them, make sure everyone in a gun crew knows every job on that gun and can take over any position required. As soon as we can, we will begin live fire exercises. That may not be until we reach the gulf, but if there's a place we can use while we are on the river we'll use it, so make sure everyone is ready. Also, I want training on rifles for every man aboard ship, officers included. I don't care what a sailor scored in boot camp or what his job is aboard ship. Everyone will learn to shoot, strip, clean, and repair an M1. While you're at it, let's make sure everyone learns to do the same with a Colt .45 pistol. We might have a need for that as well.

"Make sure you include safety at all times, Mr. Jensen. Not only in operating the weapons, but in handling ammunition, safe guarding the ship's magazine, firefighting in and around the guns, and the

48

ready-use ammunition at each gun. By the way, you will also be my cargo officer. You will determine what goes where in the tank deck and on the main deck. Remember to load in reverse order of what will be needed. Do you know what I mean by that?"

"Yes, sir. What is needed first goes in last," Jensen said.

"Correct," Jack replied. "Now, Mr. Davis, you're my engineering officer and that doesn't just mean the ship's engines. That means everything from the bow doors and bow ramp to the Danforth anchor and the stern winch, and everything in between. If it's got power to it, it creates power, it turns, it goes up and down, in and out, or side to side you own it. You have some outstanding men in your department. Don't be afraid to ask them how something works, how to fix it, or how to keep it working. I've been asking them and they've been great at showing me things and explaining how they operate. Make sure everyone knows how to operate everything. When we run drills, make sure you rotate your men so everyone not only knows about the machinery but gets to operate it as well. Got that?"

"Yes, sir!" Ensign Davis replied. "Sir, what about damage control?"

"That is an excellent question, John. I'm glad you brought it up. Except for your own equipment, damage control will not be your responsibility. Damage control will fall to you, Mr. Price, and you will be in charge of every department not currently assigned. Can you tell me what that will include, Mr. Price?"

Jack expected Ensign Aaron Price to be overwhelmed. To Jack's surprise, Ensign Price did not bat an eye and said, "Yes, sir, damage control, commissary, ship's stores, quartermaster, pharmacy, ship's boats, yeomen, ship's music, and moral. Unless assigned to engineering, I will also have ship fitters and water tenders."

Jack sat there stumped for something to say for a moment, then replied, "Very good, Mr. Price. I will have Mr. Davis keep ship fitters and water tenders along with maintenance and repair of ship's boats. You will be in charge of managing ship's boats activities as well as the other departments you mentioned."

"Aye, aye, sir!" Price bellowed.

The speech he had given was basically the same speech he gave every year to his teachers and staff at the beginning of the school year. He just substituted departments for classes, training drills for teaching exercises, etc. Jack felt good about how things had just gone. His officers were young and green, but they were eager. They were like first year teachers. They wanted to do a good job. They wanted to be the best they could be. It was obvious from the list of things they thought they were doing poorly that they needed confidence. All they need is someone to provide the leadership so they can gain that confidence while learning their jobs. Then Jack thought, *h———l that's the same thing I need.*

At his beginning-of-the-year speech, Jack always made it a point to end with something light so the teachers and staff began the year on a positive note, and he followed suit with his officers.

"Now, gentlemen, there is one final thing I want you all to remember, and this is very important so don't forget it." At this point, Jack paused for effect, and with the straightest face he could muster, he said, "Port is left, and starboard is right."

His officers sat there for a second with shocked looks on their faces and Jack thought, *Oh no, I've ruined everything.* Then Ensign Davis burst out laughing, Lieutenant Purvis spit out a mouth full of coffee he had just sipped, and the rest of the officers broke up. Tears started running down Masters's cheeks, Wesley got a pain from laughing so hard and had to hold his sides, Young laughed so hard he began to choke, and Jensen tried to give him a glass of water but instead spilled it down the front of Young's shirt into his lap. And that made everybody laugh even harder. Price grabbed a towel, stood up to help Jensen and Young, tripped on a table leg, and landed flat on the floor. That just added to the hilarity.

Jack let the laughter play out on its own. His joke wasn't that funny. What was causing the laughter was the release of tension. At the beginning of the meeting, his officers thought they had displeased the captain only to find out the captain was trying to learn enough about the ship to give them direction and now that they knew what was expected they were relieved.

When they finally got settled down, Jack told them he was glad to have them aboard and what a fine group of officers they appeared to be. Each man smiled broadly and stood a little taller. After dismissing them and watching them leave the ward room, Jack thought, *Between the bunch of them, they've got more pimples than they do whiskers.*

He wasn't disappointed, but he was nervous. He had hoped to have at least one seasoned officer aboard that knew what he was doing. Then it dawned on him, the Navy had put him in command with the same thought in mind.

Oh Lord!

CHAPTER 17

It is 190 miles from Evansville to Cairo where the Ohio empties into the Mississippi. At a cruising speed of nine knots, which is roughly ten miles per hour, and a current of about one mile per hour, Jack figured they would travel about eighty-eight miles per day. That should get them into Cairo by midmorning of the third day. However, there are four locks on the Ohio between Evansville and Cairo. With the amount of river traffic due to the war effort, the wait time to get through a lock could be anywhere from an hour to fifteen hours. Owen Masters had calculated about a two hour average wait for each lock which would add another day to the sailing time and put them into Cairo by midmorning of the fourth day. However, the cumulative wait time ended up adding another day and a half to the sailing time and put them into Cairo about midafternoon on the sixth day.

The four days following Jack's meeting with his officers resulted in a beehive of activity aboard the ship. All departments were running drills on everything the officers and department heads could think of. They took advantage of the wait time at the locks to practice beach landings by running the ship up on sand bars and mud banks. The gunners practiced training their guns and tracking passing aircraft. The ship's two LCVPs were lowered and retrieved, cargo nets were slung and retrieved, surprise fire drills were held, collision mats were deployed internally and externally to simulate damage to the hull, and men were designated with specific wounds and taken to the dispensary during battle drill.

Each time they tied up for the evening near some small town, Chief Barton went ashore, "with captain's permission." He would disappear for a few hours and return to the ship. Sometimes when he left the ship, he would take a man or two with him carrying things in boxes or secured in empty ammunition cans. Generally, when Barton returned, he and his men were carrying something other than what they left with wrapped in paper, in boxes, or in large wooden crates. When they pulled in at Paducah, Chief Barton took four men with him and didn't return until the early hours of the next morning just in time to cast off.

When asked about this by Lieutenant Purvis who was in charge of assigning shore leave, Jack looked him in the eye and said, "He's just filling some requisitions for me."

For a split second, Purvis looked like he wanted to ask a question but thought better of it and said, "Yes, sir!"

When they reached Cairo, Jack immediately authorized shore leave for the entire crew. Mr. Purvis assigned shore leave by division and watch so the men who worked together could get a chance to socialize together. Jack was a big believer in the old adage that if you worked hard and played hard, you'd have people who stuck together when the going got tough.

Nebraska wasn't the Wild West, but it was common for cattlemen and farm hands to come to town on a Friday or Saturday night and paint the town red. Jack understood this so he was prepared to field some complaints from the Cairo police, mayor, or city council. What he wasn't prepared for was one of his men being dumped at the foot of the gangway beaten to a bloody pulp. A car had driven onto the wharf, S1c Eddie Hartnet was rolled out of the back seat onto the concrete, and the car sped away without stopping.

Ensign Aaron Price was officer of the deck. He saw the car coming and expecting some sort of excitement was waiting at the foot of the gangway when the car slowed to toss Hartnet out. Price got the license number and called the local hospital which sent an ambulance and delivered Hartnet to the emergency room. While Price was waiting for the ambulance, the ship's pharmacist mate Andy Richards and Captain Cole were called.

Andy took care of Eddie until the ambulance arrived and then rode to the emergency room with him. Jack managed to get Eddie to give an account of what happened and immediately called the local police.

According to Eddie, he and a half dozen of his buddies took a taxi to the GEM Theatre on Eighth Street between Poplar Street and Commercial Avenue. Eddie had already seen the movie that was playing so he decided to walk back to the ship which was moored along the wharf just off Ohio Street between Fourth Street and Second Street. He was walking down Commercial when he came to the Riverman bar. He decided to stop in, get a drink, and then come on back to the ship which was only about two blocks away. Eddie said he walked into the bar saw it was full of zoot suiters and turned to leave. Someone grabbed him from behind and started yelling, "The Navy was buyin' drinks for the house!"

Eddie said he tried to laugh it off, but when he tried to pull free from the man holding his arms behind his back, things started getting ugly. Eddie told them he wasn't buying drinks for the house, and then someone punched him in the face. What started out as one punch turned into a beating when the zoot suiters started taking turns hitting and kicking Eddie until he finally blacked out. The last thing he remembered was lying on the floor being kicked and someone grabbing his wallet.

Walnut Hill, Nebraska, isn't what people normally think of when they talk about the Wild West. But the Oregon Trail passed through Wellborn County and Rock Creek Station where Wild Bill Hickok had a shootout with David McCanles in 1861 was only a few miles down the road. The spirit of the Old West was alive and well in Wellborn County, and folks lived and grew up there were brought up to "ride for the brand."

When Jack called the police station, he was told that they would send someone around in the morning to take a statement. Jack was furious and demanded immediate action. He was told that wasn't going to happen. Since the zoot suit riots that summer, it was probably all started by his men, and if he kept it up, no one would be investigating anything. Jack asked to speak with the chief of police but was told the chief was gone for the day and wasn't to be disturbed. The man on the phone said he was in command of the night shift, and if

Jack didn't like the way he was handling things, he could, f——k off, take his d——n row boat, and get the h——l out of town.

Mustering all the restraint he could, Jack set the phone back in its cradle and called Ensign Price to the bridge. The cowboy in Jack wasn't about to let this pass.

There were thirty-five men and two officers ashore on liberty; they were due back no later than 2400 hours. It was currently 2230 hours. Jack told Price to gather all but a skeleton crew from the men still aboard, arm them with nightsticks and billy clubs, and have them form up on the main deck forward of the elevator hatch no later than 2330 hours. As men returned to the ship from shore leave, those who were sober were to be armed and join the men forming up on the main deck. Anyone drunk or inebriated to the point their coordination or judgment was impaired were to be released from duty and told to turn in.

At 2357 hours, all crew members had reported aboard. When Ensign Price reported this to Jack, he calmly left his sea cabin behind the bridge and marched down to the main deck where he climbed onto the elevator hatch and addressed his men.

"Gentlemen, there has been an incident this evening which I will not permit to be ignored. The complete details will be released to you at a later time. Suffice it to say, one of our own, Seaman Hartnet, was accosted at the Riverman bar this evening and is currently in the hospital."

A menacing rumble emanated from the men formed up on the main deck.

"It is not acceptable for this type of behavior to occur much less to occur to one of my...er, our men. In order to remedy the situation and see that it does not occur again, shore leave will be extended until 0200 and will be restricted to the Riverman bar a half block north of Fourth Street on Commercial Avenue.

"Seaman Hartnet's wallet was stolen. He was beaten to a bloody pulp and thrown from a moving car onto the pier in front of the ship. The police are unwilling to address this issue until morning. I do not care to wait that long. At no time will any one of you initiate any trouble. However, I expect every man to do his duty, and I will be greatly disappointed if I hear any of you are disrespected in any fashion without proper corrective action being taken. I want Seaman Hartnet's wallet returned with all the money he was carrying. As he was unable to tell me what that amount was, I will leave that to you gentlemen to determine. If it is somewhat unclear to the individuals who stole Seaman Hartnet's wallet as to how much money he was carrying, please inform all the patrons of the bar that on Seaman Hartnet's behalf, donations will gladly be accepted.

"Mr. Jensen, as gunnery officer, you will pick eight men, arm them with rifles and side arms, issue SP armbands and helmets, and have them accompany our men to the Riverman and back to make sure everyone conducts themselves in an orderly manner. You and your men will remain outside during the duration of this leave. Before anyone enters the bar, I want the telephone cable leading into and out of the Riverman checked to make sure it is in good working order. Mr. Wesley, as communications officer, this will be your responsibility. I am sure the lines will need to be taken down immediately upon arrival in order to inspect them properly. See that that is done and make sure they are left in good working order after our men are through with their business. Mr. Purvis, Mr. Young, Mr. Davis, and Mr. Price, I want you available for consultation in the event questions arise as to the conduct of the patrons of the bar. I have every confidence that our men will conduct themselves in a manner befitting the reputation of the United States Navy. However, in the event someone should disagree, you gentlemen will be there to witness all actions that occur. As nonpartisan observers, you will be the final arbiters of any misunderstandings or disagreements as to who did what. Do I make myself clear, gentlemen?"

A roar of "Yes, sir!" thundered from the crew.

Jack bellowed, "Attention!"

The men snapped to attention in a fashion that would have warmed the cockles of any drill instructor's heart. In a voice he reserved only for calling rowdy children to order on the far side of the playground, Jack shouted, "Enjoy your shore leave, gentlemen. Dismissed."

There was a general stampede toward the gangway but no pushing or shoving. Once off the ship, the men moved along in an orderly fashion silently disappearing into the murky glow of the street lights. Jack climbed to the starboard bridge wing and settled into his captain's chair for the long wait to hear the results of his ship's first combat.

CHAPTER 18

At 0147 hours, singing could be heard coming from shore. As the singing grew louder, the crew of USS *LST 121* came in sight through the dim light of the street lamps. They were marching along singing "The Monkeys Have No Tails In Zamboanga" carrying various pieces of clothing, slouch hats, five- and six-foot-long watch chains, and other paraphernalia which had obviously originated from many different zoot suits. As the men neared the wharf, Chief Gardener called them to order and marched them the last block, this time singing "The Battle Hymn of the Republic." As the men paraded onto the wharf, Chief Gardener brought them to attention alongside the ship, ordered a left face, so the men were facing Jack who was standing at the head of the gangway, and bellowed, "Sir, the men of USS *LST 121* reporting from leave, sir."

"Yes, Chief, I see that they look to be in fine fettle. Do you have anything to report?"

The chief bellowed, "Yes, sir. A good time was had by all. The patrons of the Riverman bar were very hospitable. They apologized profusely for the injury to Seaman Hartnet, and when asked, they not only returned his wallet but took up a collection of $137.42 to reimburse him for the money which had mysteriously disappeared from his wallet while in their keeping. To show how sorry they were for the trouble, they caused they also donated a large amount of clothing to be given to the War Production Board for the war effort."

"I see," Jack said. At this time, the officers came walking up behind the men. They had been following the group as they returned.

"Mr. Purvis, do you or any of the other officers have anything to add, corrections to make, or comments that might clarify Boat's report?"

"No, sir. Our men conducted themselves like gentlemen at all times. No disrespect was shown to our men, and the patrons of the bar went out of their way to comply with the requests our men made for the return of Seaman Hartnet's wallet as well as our suggestion they might want to donate excess clothing to the war effort."

"Well, gentlemen, it sounds to me like your actions this evening reflect great credit on the United States Navy. I am indeed proud of each and every one of you. I am designating tomorrow as a ship's holiday. No drills will be conducted. Instead we will hold rifle and pistol competitions, wrestling and boxing matches, and will send crew members in groups of ten to visit Seaman Hartnet in the hospital. The first group of visitors will leave the ship at 0530. We will rotate visitors every two hours. To show our support for Seaman Hartnet, we will not leave him without visitors until he is released from the hospital. Mr. Purvis will set up the rotation and see that arrangements are made for transportation. Please come aboard."

As the crew filed past, they dropped off the clothing they had gathered at the Riverman. As the pile grew, Jack noticed socks, underwear, and T-shirts among the items that had been donated. It was early October; it wasn't freezing, but the air had a distinct chill to it. He imagined that some of the Riverman patrons had a difficult time getting home with no money and no clothes.

A line of taxi cabs left the dock at 05:30. At 07:30, a new line of taxis appeared at the foot of the gangway. These taxis returned the first group of visitors to the hospital, loaded the waiting sailors, and returned to the hospital with the new visitors. At 08:00, rifle and pistol competition commenced, using a high steep mud bank on the far side of the river as a safety backstop. At 08:30, six patrol cars pulled up along the wharf and emptied two dozen of Cairo's finest at the foot of the gangplank.

Jack had anticipated this and was waiting at the head of the gangway when the squad cars pulled up. As the chief of police started up the gangway, Jack said, "It is customary to ask permission before attempting to board a United States Navy vessel. Without doing so, it might be interpreted as a hostile act, and I would be forced to repel boarders."

With a nod of his head, Chief Boatswain's Mate Gardener signaled the ten men waiting in line to shoot to step forward and man the rail.

When the chief of police saw the armed men along the rail, he stopped, backed down the gangway, and stood on the wharf.

"May I help you, Chief?" Jack asked.

"Yeah. Just what in the h———l do you think you're doing?"

Without giving him a chance to continue, Jack replied, "We're having a ship's holiday, Chief. We're having rifle and pistol competitions, boxing and wrestling between divisions, and a little later, we will be having an open-air picnic on the main deck. Would you and your men like to join us?"

"You're d———n right we'll join you." And the chief started up the gangway again.

Chief Boatswain's Mate Gardener barked an order, and all ten armed men along the rail charged their weapons. The sound of ten rifles cycling a live round into the chamber brought the chief to a halt.

Jack said in a calm voice, "I warned you once, Chief. This is like *Simon Says*. You have to ask permission to board, and I haven't heard that request yet."

"I don't need your f———g permission to come and arrest you and your men," the chief roared.

"Oh, but you do, Chief!" Jack said. "Chief, Mr. Jensen, if you please?"

At once ten more armed men appeared at the rail and both twin 40 mm., the two starboard single 40mm., and all the starboard 20 mm. swung out and trained in the direction of the police standing on the wharf.

"Now if you ask real nice, I might let you and your men come aboard. However, if you cannot summon the common courtesy to ask first, then you can stand on the wharf until you rot for all I care."

The chief of police thought over his options for a moment, then said, "Permission to come aboard, Captain?"

"Why certainly, Chief. Since you asked so nicely, I'd be happy to have you come aboard. That invitation is also extended to your men."

The chief of police and his men began to walk up the gangway. Just as the police chief reached the top of the gangway, Jack said, "Chief Boatswain's Mate Gardener will relieve you and your men of your weapons before you set foot on the deck. You understand, of course, that the United States Navy does not allow armed persons aboard ship unless they are members of the crew or on temporary duty assigned to this ship."

The police chief's face turned a dark shade of red. He began to spit and sputter under his breath, but with his men backed up on the gangway behind him, he couldn't turn around and walk back down without looking like a fool, so he reached for his pistol, pulled it from his holster, and said, "Of course." Then he handed it to Chief Boatswain's Mate Gardener who passed it to Tyree Higby who dropped it into a sea bag he'd brought along just for that purpose.

"Your handcuffs and nightstick too," Chief Boatswain's Mate Gardener said.

The police chief turned his head and looked angrily at Jack.

"You heard the man, Chief," Jack said. "Your handcuffs and nightstick too."

The police chief gave Chief Boatswain's Mate Gardener his handcuffs and nightstick and stepped aboard, followed by the rest of his men who turned over their weapons and handcuffs as well.

Jack stepped forward shook the police chief's hand and said, "Welcome aboard, Chief. I thought you might be dropping by this morning so I've arranged a little tour of the ship for you and your men."

Then turning to Chief Gardener, Jack said, "Carry, on Boats."

Chief Boatswain's Mate Gardener quickly divided the police officers into twelve groups of two and assigned each pair to a group of four seamen who had been preparing for the boxing and wrestling matches along with a chief or department head. As the patrolmen were led away, Jack called his officers together and they escorted the police chief to the officers ward room. Franklyn Ingolls and Luscious

Tanner had coffee and pastries prepared and waiting when the ship's officers escorted the police chief into the ward room.

After being seated, Jack took a sip of coffee smacked his lips and said, "Once again, Franklyn, you have outdone yourself with this coffee. Try a sip, Chief."

"I don't want any of your f——g coffee. Especially if some n——r made it," the chief said caustically.

"I see," Jack said. "Well, let me put it this way, Chief. Take a sip of the coffee!" There was no mistaking the threat in Jack's voice, the chief picked up his cup and took a sip. "Isn't that the best cup of coffee you've ever tasted, Chief?"

"Tastes like s——t to me," the chief growled.

"You know, Chief, that is the second offensive statement you've made since accepting our hospitality in the ward room. That is unacceptable. Mr. Davis, there is a yellow jacket on the back of the chief's head. Please swat that thing before it stings the chief."

Ensign Davis, who was sitting next to the police chief, craned his neck around to the back of the chief's head and slapped the chief in the back of the head hard enough to cause him to spill his coffee.

"Did you get him, Mr. Davis?" Jack asked.

"I'm not sure, sir. I'll keep an eye out for him in case I missed, and he returns."

"Good. You do that, Mr. Davis." Then Jack turned to Ingolls. "Franklyn, would you top off the chief's coffee? His cup is nearly empty, and he'll have another."

After Franklyn topped off the chief's coffee, he left the pot on the table and retired to the pantry with Tyree Higby and Luscious Tanner.

"Now that we have the pleasantries out of the way, Chief, to what do I owe the pleasure of this visit?"

"You know d——n well why I'm here," the chief said.

Jack looked at Mr. Davis. "Keep an eye out for that yellow jacket, Mr. Davis. I don't want him to try and sting the chief again."

The chief, expecting another slap, tucked his head in between his shoulder blades like a turtle ducking into his shell. When the slap did not come, he relaxed and sat up straight. That's when Mr. Davis cuffed him in the back of the head again and said, "I think I got him that time, sir!"

"Good. Good work, Mr. Davis. Don't worry, Chief. We'll keep those pesky insects away from you. I think it's foul language and bigotry that brings them out like that. Now you were saying?"

"Your men took over the Riverman bar last night, robbed the patrons of all their money, and then stole their clothes after forcing them to disrobe."

"That's quite a fanciful story, Chief. Mr. Purvis, I believe you were on shore leave last night. Did you by any chance happen by the...What did you call it, Chief? The Riverman bar? Yes, I believe that's what you called it. Mr. Purvis, did you happen by the Riverman bar last night?

"Why yes, sir, I did. Mr. Wesley, Mr. Jensen, Mr. Young, Mr. Davis, and Mr. Price also happened by at about the same time."

"When was this, Mr. Purvis?"

"I'd say it was somewhere around 0015 hours, sir."

"Did any of you see anything like the chief described take place?"

Mr. Price piped up, "No, sir. Chief Boatswain's Mate Gardener asked the patrons of the bar if they were aware Seaman Hartnet had been brutally beaten earlier in the evening. They said they were aware of it and apologized for the actions of, as they put it, a few bad apples, when asked if they would help find Seaman Hartnet's wallet they were more than helpful. His wallet was located, and when it was pointed out to them that the wallet was empty, they took up a collection to reimburse Seaman Hartnet for the money which had disappeared from his wallet. It was strictly voluntary on their part, sir."

"I see," Jack said.

"Did any of you other officers see anything that might help clarify the situation for the chief?"

"Yes, sir," Lieutenant Young said. "Chief Grubowski commented that it sure took a lot of cloth to make a zoot suit and one of the zoot suiter's agreed. Chief Grubowski asked the man if he didn't feel a little guilty using up all that material when it was needed for the war effort. The man took off his jacket and handed it to the chief.

He told the chief he'd like to donate it to the war effort. That must have struck a patriotic chord with the rest of the bar patrons because they all started donating clothing. Some were so eager to help Uncle Sam they gave their all."

At that comment, Jack bit his lip and turned away from the police chief, trying not to laugh. "Well, that was very patriotic indeed. Were there any female patrons in the bar who made donations?"

"No, sir!" Ensign Davis said.

"Are you sure?" Jack asked.

"Yes, sir! The men would have noticed if there had been," Davis replied.

"Yes, I'm sure they would have," Jack said, trying his hardest not to laugh out loud. As it was, laughter was heard coming from the pantry, and Jack used this as an excuse to turn away from the police chief and ask, "Is everything all right in there, men?"

"Yes, sir!" came the joint reply from Ingolls, Higby, and Tanner.

"Okay, does anyone have anything else to add?"

Ensign Wesley said, "Yes, sir. When I arrived, someone said the telephone wasn't working in the bar, so I hunted around outside until I found the telephone wire. I inspected it and repaired it and reattached it. The problem was some worn insulation that caused a short in the system. I took it down, cut away the faulty section of wire, and reconnected it. It should be in perfect working order now and should remain that way as long as the proprietor exercises some preventive maintenance from time to time."

"I see. Did you charge the owner of the bar for your repair work, Mr. Jensen?"

"Uh, no, sir. I thought it was the right thing to do and would help foster goodwill between the Navy and the citizens of Cairo, sir."

"And quite right you were, Ensign. That was a nice gesture on your part."

Then turning to the police chief, Jack said, "Well, there you go, Chief. It appears some of the patrons had remorse over their generosity last evening, perhaps feeling they had donated excessively. That is understandable, but they should be proud of themselves for taking the initiative to right a wrong. I took the liberty of writing a report on last night's incident and forwarding copies to the Navy Department in Washington DC as well as the War Production Board, the mayor of Cairo, and the governor of Illinois. I am sure there will be communications waiting for you when you return to your office as well as invitations from the mayor and the governor to explain why your night duty officer refused to respond to the incident when it was first reported last evening.

"By the way, in my report to the Navy, I suggested that since there will be a large number of Navy vessels passing through Cairo on the way to the war, if anything like this happens again, it might be in the best interest of the War Department to declare Cairo off-limits to military personnel or place the city under martial law. I pointed out the economic impact either of those actions could have on Cairo in my letters to the mayor and the governor. I'm sure you will be hearing from both gentlemen shortly.

"Chief, I can't tell you how much I've enjoyed our chance to visit. Mr. Purvis will escort you to the gangway. I hope you take this in the spirit it is intended when I tell you I hope we never meet again."

Shortly after the meeting with the Cairo chief of police, Chief Barton was called to the captain's sea cabin. Jack added two more items to the list he had given the chief earlier. Chief Barton left Jack's sea cabin staring at the list, scratching his head, and mumbling to himself.

CHAPTER 19

Two days later, Seaman Hartnet had recovered enough to be released from the hospital and return to the ship. The hospital staff had raised cane with Jack over his crewmen staying beyond visiting hours, but as Jack told them, it was as much for their protection as it was for Hartnet's. After the beating he'd taken, if anything happened to Seaman Hartnet, Jack didn't want to be responsible for trying to keep his men from being, as he put it, "overprotective."

Mr. Purvis was in command when USS *LST 121* was preparing to leave Cairo. Things were going smoothly with Mr. Masters casually offering a hint here and there to aid the process. Jack particularly liked the way Masters handled this. He would lean forward and whisper something in Purvis's ear when needed. Since all eyes were focused forward, no one noticed when Owen stepped in to help.

Jack was thinking, *Masters would make an outstanding teacher* when he noticed several women standing on the wharf waving. Jack glanced down at the main deck and saw several of his men standing at the rail waving their dixie cups. Jack had heard the old adage about a girl in every port, but until now, he never thought there was any truth to it. As they were preparing to cast off all lines and pull into the current a taxi pulled up beside the ship, three nurses jumped out and ran to the edge of the wharf waving, blowing kisses, and tossing small remembrances up to a sailor on deck. As the mooring lines were cast off and the ship began to pull away, Jack could see the sailor the nurses were interested in was Eddie Hartnet. From the look on Hartnet's face, Jack couldn't help but think Eddie was going to have more to remember about Cairo than the beating he took in the Riverman Bar.

CHAPTER 20

Two days later, Admiral Bryton was notified that the governor of Illinois, both of its senators, several of its House members, and the mayor of Cairo had contacted the Navy expressing their admiration for the service and everything the Navy stood for. They also pledged that they would do everything in their power to see that all Navy personnel were treated with the utmost respect at all times. The messages contained various forms of apology for the conduct of a few miscreant locals and heaped praise on the crew and commanding officer of *LST 121* for the patience and restraint they showed during the recent incident. Almost all the messages ended with some form of assurance that the welcome mat was always out for the Navy and the hope that the Navy would see its way clear to give Cairo and the State of Illinois one more chance to be good hosts.

Admiral Bryton called Commander Johnson into his office and asked, "Isn't Lieutenant Commander Cole in command of *LST 121*?"

"Yes, sir."

Admiral Bryton said, "Good! d——n good. Make a note of that, attach it to this memo, and drop it in Cole's file will you?"

"Yes, sir. Anything else, sir?"

"No, that will be all, Johnson." Then the admiral glanced up at a painting of the Navy's battle with the Barbary Pirates in Tripoli that was hanging on his office wall. He paused for a moment thinking and then went back to the tasks at hand.

CHAPTER 21

The current on the Mississippi is a little stronger than the current on the Ohio. Jack anticipated they would cover a little over one hundred miles a day. With a distance of 859 miles between Cairo and New Orleans, they would arrive around noon of the ninth day of sailing if he took the ship straight through. But Jack planned to give the men some shore leave along the way and work on beaching as much as he could. With what he had planned, he thought ten to twelve days should put them in the Big Easy.

The days were filled with drill after drill. Jack began each morning with battlestations before sunrise and finished the day with battle stations before they put into shore and tied up.

There were a few small towns with good mooring facilities along the way, and Jack gave the men some shore time as soon as the ship was secured for the night. The incident at the Riverman was always in the back of his mind when he let men go ashore, and after watching Eddie Hartnet's harem bid him goodbye when they left Cairo, the thought of an angry father with a shotgun was another item to worry about.

Periodically, Jack would call Chief Barton to his cabin for an update and strategy session. The chief had been picking up items here and there as they worked their way downriver and managed to find enough coffee pots to provide one for each department as well as a few spares. In addition to the coffee pots, he'd been able to fill some of the items on the shopping list; however, most of the bartering he'd done so far was to collect items he knew he could use to "trade up" as he put it when he got to a port with a navy base.

Reports from the fighting in North Africa and the Solomons had convinced Jack that the war was going to be about supply.

Whichever side was able to keep their troops better supplied was ultimately going to win. The Japs and the Krauts had much shorter supply lines. The United States would have to move men and supplies halfway around the world to keep her fighting forces adequately equipped.

As Jack saw it, an LST would be a prime target for German or Japanese aircraft. The ship's defenses against air attack were substantial, but he felt like the ship was woefully undergunned based on the reports he'd read about the intensity of the air strikes thrown against shipping in the Mediterranean and the Solomons. He needed more defensive firepower, and he was determined to get it in order to prevent *LST 121* from becoming a sitting duck. Jack realized his "shopping list" was far from complete; he would have to try and figure out a way to increase his ship's firepower which most likely meant he would have to look beyond the Navy quartermaster network.

Jack told Chief Barton not to feel obligated to work his magic only in the confines of the navy and pointed out that when they pulled into Memphis, he shouldn't overlook the Army's Memphis Supply Depot as a possible "garden spot."

If the officer of the deck knew what to listen for, he would have noticed that when Chief Barton returned from shore leave many of the boxes, crates, and containers he carried aboard made a sloshing sound. These items were particularly dangerous to handle and store because of the Navy's rules against alcohol aboard ship, human nature being what it is, and the crew being normal red-blooded American males. The danger with handling large amounts of alcohol-based trading stock, in addition to the navy regs against it, was what could happen if sailors knew about it and tried to get into it. Chief Barton could not store his trading stock in the nooks and crannies he normally used for his escrow materials because they were secret, but not secure. The only two sites aboard the ship that could be secured were the brig and the magazine. Based on the assumption that men would be men, Jack wanted to avoid the brig. There was always the chance that he might have to use it for its original intention, and alcohol and sailors don't mix so he chose the magazine.

Prohibition ended in 1933, but the thirteen-year dry spell between 1920 and 1933 had seen the proliferation of the moonshine business. The Ohio and Mississippi Rivers ran right through the heart of moonshine country, and Chief Barton took full advantage of the opportunity to build his escrow account. Crates of moonshine were labeled EXPLOSIVES and stacked in the magazine until there was no more room. To accommodate all his trading stock, Chief Barton opened the troops' berthing quarters and locked the remainder of the crates in the armory provided for soldiers and marines to store their personal weapons while they were in transit to the fighting. By the time they reached Memphis, it would not have been unfair to say the ship was more tanker than anything else.

When they tied up at Memphis, Jack gave the men liberty and turned Chief Barton loose. They hadn't been tied up more than four hours before Chief Barton returned to the ship with a small convoy of army vehicles. Mr. Wesley was officer of the deck. He heard the convoy coming long before he saw it. When it finally came into sight, it consisted of an MP Jeep with siren blaring, an olive drab staff car, followed by a six-by-six deuce and a half truck, and another MP Jeep also with its siren blaring. The convoy pulled to a stop on the quay alongside the ship and Chief Barton got out of the lead MP Jeep. Ensign Wesley immediately sent word for the captain.

As Jack was coming forward to the head of the gangway, he saw Chief Barton have a quick word with Chief Grubowski who wandered down the gangway to speak with the Army drivers and MPs. He then began introducing Colonel Archer Agnew, his aide de camp, and two of his staff officers to Mr. Wesley. When Jack arrived, the colonel and the colonel's entourage were introduced, and Colonel Agnew said, "Just how can we help you, Commander?"

This took Jack completely by surprise, but Chief Barton jumped in and said, "Sir, I was explaining to Colonel Agnew the problem we were having working out our vehicle loading diagram, and he offered to allow us to practice some of the various configurations we discussed."

Jack's eyebrows slowly began to creep up his forehead as he listened to Chief Barton. Then Colonel Agnew entered the discussion saying, "Yes, your chief here was telling one of my master sergeants all about these wonderful new ships you Navy boys have come up with to land men and equipment right on the beach and how you've been trying to figure out the best parking arrangements to get the most vehicles on board at one time.

"Well, I'm here to tell you that the Army is all for that and the Army Quartermaster Supply Depot would be happy to help in any way we can. The chief here said you would be in Memphis for several days, and I got to thinking we've got a big war bond drive coming up so why not bring the mechanized equipment you need down here and let you try the various plans you've come up with and see what works best? We could invite people to come and watch and use the event to promote bond sales."

Jack turned to Chief Barton and said, "You managed to arrange all this in four hours?"

Chief Barton said, beaming, "Well, sir, these Army guys are really sharp. They're not like the Navy and Marine quartermasters. The Army is trying to win the war. Sometimes I think our quartermasters are working for the Krauts and the Japs. I was just griping about the problems we were faced with and the sergeant, that would be Master Sergeant Bell, sir, Linden Bell. Anyway right away, he sees the predicament we're in, and he goes up the chain of command and when Colonel Agnew heard about our problem, well, Sergeant Bell, he says to me, he says, the colonel, told him by gum the Army'll just have to come down here and get the Navy on the ball. Yes, sir, that's what Sergeant Bell told me, sir."

Colonel Agnew cleared his throat, threw his shoulders back, placed both hands on his chest, and said, "Well, now, Chief, that may be a little bit of an exaggeration, not much of one, but a little bit of an exaggeration, we here at the Army Quartermaster Supply Depot feel we're doing just as much to win the war as the boys over there doing the fighting are. I'm not taking anything away from the fighting men you understand. They do their part too, but by gum, the work we do here would overwhelm lesser men. I can tell you that, yes, sir. It would overwhelm lesser men by gum. At any rate, I know you're on a tight schedule to get to New Orleans and on out to the war so I figure we've got to act fast. You give me a list of everything you'll need, and I'll see to it that it is here tomorrow morning as early as you want it. Now as I understand it, this ship of yours has doors in the front? Is that correct? Doors in the front. What will they think of next. Doors in the front that you drive vehicles in, and then when you get to the beach, you open the doors and the vehicles just drive right out. Is that correct?"

"Yes, Colonel, that is exactly how it works," Jack said.

Then Chief Barton pulled out a sheet of paper and handed it to Jack, saying, "Uh, sir, this is a list of the equipment we were discussing the other day at our planning session. I just happened to have it with me. I thought you might want to take a look at it and see if this is everything you were wanting. It's a copy of the last list we developed. It's the most up-to-date list we have prepared, sir."

Jack took the list Chief Barton handed him. Knowing Chief Barton was up to something and never having seen the list before, Jack needed a little time to think, so he ran his finger down the sheet. He slowed as he got near the end of the sheet and a gleam shone in his eyes, "Yes, Chief, this looks good. However, there is one thing we did not discuss that I just thought of. We don't know whether we'll have enough clearance in the overhead to bring any of those halftracks with the quad .50 caliber machinegun mounts in the rear aboard without hanging up in the overhead crane on the tank deck."

Chief Barton's eyebrows shot up, and he looked at Jack with a newfound admiration. Turning to Colonel Agnew, Jack said, "You wouldn't, by any chance, have any of those types of halftracks we could use for this experiment would you, sir?"

"Why yes, we do, Commander, They're called MCMGs that stands for motor carriage multi gun. I'll see to it that we send you some of those as well. Now if you don't mind, I'll take that list with me and make all the necessary arrangements for tomorrow. I'm sure the mayor, city council, fire chief, police chief, and other civic minded individuals will want to participate as well. We'll use this as a means of generating goodwill and promoting the war bond rally within the Memphis area. Once they see what the Quartermaster Depot is doing to help win the war, I'm sure this will make all the papers. A little press never hurts, does it, Commander." At this point, Colonel Agnew gave Jack a wink and a light nudge in the ribs with his elbow.

"No, sir," Jack replied. "It will be an excellent opportunity. You might think about making a parade out of it on the way back through town. Everybody loves a parade."

"Say, that's a great idea. It would be a good excuse to get the Depot band out and make a big to do about the whole thing. With a few phone calls to the right people, I bet we can turn this into a major event without too much trouble. Too bad we won't be able to get you and your men involved, but I know you have a tight schedule and will probably be leaving right after we're done, won't you." The "won't you" wasn't a question. In officer speak, it was an order—one that Jack would be glad to obey.

As they escorted Colonel Agnew and his entourage to the gang-way, Jack gave Chief Barton a questioning look. "Ice cream machine," Barton mouthed silently. Jack nodded his head and smiled.

When Colonel Agnew was preparing to leave, the driver of the six-by-six deuce and a half truck couldn't get it to start so it was left behind on the quay. Jack promised he'd have his engineering department take a look at it, and if they could get it started, he'd send it back to the Depot as soon as possible. Colonel Agnew thanked him and told Jack he'd leave word at the gate to let the truck through and give the driver a ride back to the ship. Once Agnew and his men were gone, Jack called his officers and chiefs together in the ward room for a council of war.

CHAPTER 22

Three hours later, Jack said. "Okay, does everyone understand their part in this operation?" Jack looked around the table, and everyone nodded. Okay, we'll kick off Operation Pilfer as soon as we get the truck running and load it up."

Jack looked at Chief Grubowski and said, "You think you can get that truck running, Chief?"

Grubowski stood up and tossed a coil wire on the ward room table. "Yeah I'm pretty d———n sure we can. This here oughta help."

Everybody laughed. Then Jack looked first at Barton and then at Grubowski. "Does anyone other than Master Sergeant Bell know anything about this?"

Before Chief Barton could respond, Chief Grubowski said, "Ain't none a them Army boys knows nothin' about that coil wire, sir, includin' Bell. Barton ast me to keep that truck from getting' back to the Army Depot, so while I was chattin' up the driver and MPs darned if the coil wire on that there truck didn't just fall out. We was jist lucky one a my boys was takin' a little break at the time, and it fell right inta his lap so to speak. Heck, if he hadn't been there, that coil wire woulda prolly got lost. Jist lucky he happen ta be there when he was."

"Is it a common practice for your men to take a break while under a truck, Chief?" Jack asked.

Without a pause, Chief Grubowski replied, "Well, sir, as hard as I work my boys, when they sees a oppatunity to grab a break, they do, sir."

Jack shook his head laughing, Barton grinned like a Cheshire cat, and everyone in the ward room broke up.

CHAPTER 23

C hief Barton and Boatswain Gardener were sitting in the front of the six-by-six deuce and a half truck when it pulled up to the main gate at the Memphis Army Quartermaster Supply Depot. In the rear of the truck sat four of Boat's most able-bodied seamen, meaning the biggest and strongest of his deck hands. They were hidden behind a small mountain of Chief Barton's finest 90-proof trading stock. The canvas top was pulled tight knotted and crosstied just as it had been when it was left behind at the dock.

The MPs at the gate stopped the truck and asked Chief Barton what his business was. The chief, who was driving, nodded his head at Boatswain Gardener sitting on the other side of the cab. Boats said, "We're here to return this truck. It broke down when Colonel Agnew was down to the dock visitin' with our skipper. He asked us to return it if we could get the d——n thing started. Well, here we are. He said he'd leave word that we was comin'.'"

The MP ran his finger down his clipboard, stopped about halfway down, and said, "Yeah, here you are. Take it on in. Do you know where you're going?"

"Yep, Master Sergeant Bell told us to come see him, and he'd tell us where he wanted it."

"Okay, you're good to go." Then while one MP raised the crossbar on the gate, the other waved Boat's truck on through.

Barton headed into the depot and immediately made a right turn at the first side street to get out of the sentry's eye sight. "Okay, let's find Bell and get this show on the road," Gardener said.

When they pulled up in front of Master Sergeant Bell's Quonset, he was out front sitting in a jeep. He had four good-sized men in the jeep with him. "Hey, Barton, any trouble gettin' in?"

"Naw, went smooth as silk. You ready for us?"

"Yeah."

"Where ya want it?"

"Folla me."

Bell roared off in the Jeep with Barton right behind.

They unloaded the moonshine into an empty ammunition bunker and went back to Bell's quonset to load the ice cream machine into the back of the six-by-six. Bell's men jumped in the back of the truck with Gardener's deck hands, the three noncoms pulled the canvas tight, knotted it, and crosstied it like it was when they arrived, then hopped in and headed for the river.

While Jack was planning Operation Pilfer, Lieutenant Purvis and Mr. Masters pulled the ship away from the pier and beached her in the slack current behind a channel break water. When Barton, Gardener, and Bell got to the river, the bow doors were already open, and the ramp was down. Barton drove straight into the ship and pulled up alongside one of the troop berthing compartments. Between Bell's men and Gardener's deckhands, the ice cream machine was unloaded in no time. Bell hopped into the driver's seat, his men hopped in back, and Gardener's men retied the canvas cover just like it had been.

Barton asked Bell, "Okay, is everything ready to go? You added those MCMGs the skipper wanted, right?"

"Yep."

"The manifest is in pencil so's you can change it when we're done?"

"Yep."

"Okay, it's good workin' with ya. See ya tomorra."

"Gotcha." And Bell drove back to the Memphis Supply Depot.

At 0600, a stream of Army mechanized equipment began rolling through town on its way to the river front. Once there, the vehicles were backed into USS *LST 121* one after another in various configurations on the main deck and tank deck until Jack, his officers, and Chiefs were satisfied they had figured out the best parking plan for the ship to carry the maximum number of vehicles possible. Trucks, tanks, halftracks, jeeps, trailers, towed artillery, and every other type of mechanized vehicle the Army used in combat were run in and out through the day from 0600 to 1700 hours. Colonel Agnew, his staff officers, the mayor, fire chief, police chief, city council, and just about everyone in Memphis who didn't have to work or could slip away was there to watch.

When vehicles weren't actually moving in or out of the ship, soldiers were giving tours of the equipment. Children were climbing in and out of tanks, halftracks, trucks, and jeeps. Parents were chasing their kids, trying to make sure none of them got under the wheels or treads, and MPs were everywhere trying to make sure some enterprising individual or souvenir hunter didn't take off with some piece of equipment they thought they needed more than the Army did. In short, the operation was organized chaos, which was just what Jack was hoping for.

Altogether there were over one hundred vehicles involved in the loading trials. Not all of them were in use all the time, so some were always sitting unattended either on the main deck, on the tank deck, or outside. Master Sergeant Bell was keeping close watch on the inventory of everything the depot provided. Colonel Agnew and his staff were hob knobbing with the local dignitaries, and the depot band was standing off to one side playing to entertain the locals who had come to watch.

In all the commotion, no one noticed when a MCMG was backed in behind a wrecker and parked there until it was needed elsewhere. In addition, no one noticed that when the MCMG drove off, the quad .50 caliber machine gun turret remained behind swinging from the hook on the wrecker's winch and cable. Nor did anyone notice when Chief Grubowski and his men lowered the machine gun turret onto a floor dolly and wheeled it off to parts unknown. This happened on four separate occasions during the day, and each time a MCMG was marked as a depot inventory item when it drove aboard ship, it was redesignated as a halftrack when it drove off the ship.

When the loading trials were complete, Colonel Agnew and his staff scrambled into the backs of open halftracks along with city dignitaries of equivalent relative importance, the depot band climbed aboard the deck of an empty tank transporter, and the convoy of

Army mechanized equipment began a slow parade back through town just in time to catch those who had finished work as they were leaving their offices and shops and beginning to head home for the day. In the midst of the roaring engines of the Army vehicles, the honking horns of impatient workers trying to get through the parade of equipment, the band playing every march in the military song book, the roar of the cheering citizens, and the sirens blaring on the MP jeeps, no one noticed as USS *LST 121* retracted her ramp, closed her enormous clam shell bow doors, backed off the beach, and swung into the stream to continue her voyage downriver. No one—that is, except Master Sergeant Bell who stood on shore with his vehicle inventory erasing one six-by-six deuce and a half truck and a jeep from the list of vehicles used in the loading trials.

Coincidentally, the vehicles with the corresponding serial numbers to those just erased from Sergeant Bell's inventory were chained to the tank deck floor next to the paint shop in the ship as she sailed south. In his hand, Master Sergeant Bell held signed requisition forms for one six-by-six deuce and a half truck and one four-by-four quarter-ton truck (jeep) assigned to account number 212020–122021, the numerical equivalent of *USS LST* and signed by C. Barton of the 121st Amphibious Tank Transporter unit.

When USS *LST 121* was clear of the beach and had completed her turn to head downstream, Master Sergeant Bell snapped off a razor-sharp military salute, which was acknowledged by a blast of "shave and a haircut two bits" from the ship's horn. Jack called Lieutenant Purvis to one side and said quietly, "You'll find a six-by-six and a jeep chained to the deck just outside the paint shop. I want those painted Navy gray and stenciled with Navy serial numbers. From now on, any time we give the men shore leave, you will set up a ship's taxi service. I do not want a repeat of the Cairo incident. Got it, Mr. Purvis?"

"Yes, sir," Purvis answered with a big smile. "I'll see to it, sir."

CHAPTER 24

When USS *LST 121* backed into the stream and pulled away from Memphis, Jack only took her downriver a few miles before the sun started to set. Once they were out of sight of Memphis, he had Mr. Davis take her to the Arkansas side and tie up there. Not knowing if they had been successful with Operation Pilfer or not, Jack felt it was better to be safe than sorry.

The next morning, Jack got underway at day light wanting to clear the *scene,* as he thought of it, as soon as possible. As they passed small river towns, people could be seen on shore waving as they went by. This wasn't too unusual, they had seen people waving from shore ever since they left Evansville. However, those were mostly children who had been playing along the riverbank when the ship went by. The people they were seeing now were adults. In addition to waving, a lot of them were carrying flags, and everyone seemed to be cheering. The farther south they went, the more people they saw. When they started seeing police cars and fire trucks, Jack got a little uneasy, but the police and firefighters were waving with big smiles on their faces, their sirens wailing and their lights flashing. In some cases, the firemen had run hoses down to the river and were shooting streams of water in the air.

As they worked their way downriver, the crew was unaware of their popularity in the national press. The Memphis radio stations had broadcast live coverage of the loading trials describing everything in great detail as well as the war bond rally that followed. The Memphis newspapers carried stories and pictures approved by the Army censors the following morning. The national news organizations picked up the story, and for the next several days, the loading trials and the war bond rally in Memphis were big news around the nation. Colonel Agnew's face was on the front page of every paper in the country as was Walter Chandler's the mayor of Memphis.

When they came to the Ben Humphreys Bridge, the whole span was lined with people, squad cars, fire trucks, and ambulances. As they neared the span, flowers began to cascade down from above. When they passed under the bridge, Ensign Jensen who had the bridge sounded the ship's horn and had his gun crews spin the 40 mm. anti-aircraft guns in circles. This brought a thunderous cheer from the crowd that could be heard over the sound of the ship's engines. It also brought a pair of braziers floating down from two young ladies who were obviously in the Mardi Gras spirit. This show of patriotism inspired the crew to start chanting, "Show us your t——s." Several rather buxom young ladies complied with the request and another brazier came floating down. This caused a mad scramble on deck that looked like it would turn ugly until Jack announced over the ship's PA that all contraband received aboard ship would be considered war trophies and displayed for all to see. When Boatswain Gardener collected the garments and brought them to the bridge, Jack had them hoisted on the signal staff, which brought a huge cheer from the crew.

Three days later in the Main Navy and Munitions building, Washington DC. Commander Johnson walked into Admiral Bryton's office with a box of newspaper clippings and set it on the admiral's desk.

"What the h——l is this, Johnson?"

"Sir, we've been receiving these from the War Finance Committee, War Production Board, Navy PR section, Memphis newspapers and radio stations, the governor of Tennessee, and even the Army. They are coming in from everywhere, sir."

"What are they about?"

"Well, sir, it seems the War Bond sales for Tennessee set a national record following a War Bond rally there three days ago in Memphis."

"That's very nice to hear, Johnson, but what has that got to do with us here in BuNavPer and why are you showing me this?" The admiral was starting to get perturbed with Johnson for wasting his time.

"Sir, it seems the key to the success of the drive was a demonstration of the loading abilities of an LST conducted between the Army's Memphis Supply Depot and *LST 121*."

"D——n, Johnson, I...Wait a minute did you say *121*?

"Yes, sir."

"Cole again?"

"Yes, sir."

"D——n, that man is a tiger. Drop all that in his file and keep an eye on him. He's going places."

Meanwhile back on the Mississippi River, still concerned about the possibility the Memphis Supply Depot might discover their inventory was out of kilter, Jack beached the ship on mud flats in mid channel and got underway early each morning. Once they were south of the Arkansas border, Jack figured they were far enough out of the Tennessee authorities jurisdiction that he could afford to take a chance and pull into shore for the evening. They pulled into slack water and beached the ship, opened the bow doors, and dropped the ramp a mile upriver from Mayersville, Mississippi. Lieutenant Purvis and Boatswain Gardener took the jeep and headed into town to nose around and find out if anyone was looking for them. When Purvis and Boats came back to the ship, half the town of Mayersville came with them. Purvis and the chief had discovered that USS *LST 121* and her crew were national celebrities and the folks in Mayersville were anxious to see the famous ship.

Earlier that day, Chief Grubowski and his ship fitters finished installing the ice cream machine and got it up and running. Cookie served ice cream that evening and instantly became the most popular man aboard the ship. To Bill's credit, he let it be known that Boatswain Gardener, Chief Barton, and several others were the ones who managed to obtain the ice cream machine. He was just the man that operated it.

When Purvis and Gardener returned to the ship, they drove up the ramp onto the tank deck, and the crowd followed them. Jack was alarmed at having all these people aboard. He didn't like the idea of civilians aboard ship *running free* as he thought of it. While he had everyone corralled, so to speak, on the tank deck, he climbed on the elevator, had it raised six feet off the tank deck floor so everyone could see and hear him, and gave an impromptu speech about the ship and its capabilities. At the end of the speech, he identified his officers and chiefs and had Mr. Purvis divide the crowd into groups gathered around an officer or chief. Once this was accomplished, Jack instructed each officer and chief to show their group around the tank deck and main deck, answered all the questions they could without violating security, and led them through the mess deck before exiting the ship down the ramp through the bow doors. Jack pulled Bill Spence aside and told him to give everyone a scoop of ice cream as they were leaving the mess deck. Cookie had his men fold writing paper into cones and handed an ice cream cone to every member of the crowd as they finished their tour and left the ship.

The remainder of the trip to New Orleans proceeded much the same way everywhere the ship stopped. Word spread downriver and the crowds that greeted the ship grew each time they tied up for the night. When they tied up at Vicksburg, Mississippi, Jack sent the six-by-six to Jackson, Mississippi, to pick up additional ingredients so Cookie wouldn't run out of ice cream before they reached New Orleans.

When the ship reached New Orleans, they were inundated with requests for tours. Not all the requests came from civilians. Andrew Higgins came aboard with representatives from the New Orleans Port of Embarkation for a tour and Navy, Marine, and Army officers showed up almost daily to see what an LST was like and what it could do.

They spent three days in New Orleans for their final fitting out and were ready for sea two days earlier than it was expected to take to get the ship from Evansville to New Orleans and ready to join the fleet. This was duly noted and forwarded to Washington where Admiral Bryton read the report, smiled, and handed it to Commander Johnson for insertion into Jack's file.

Commander Johnson noted, "Commander Cole is really getting things done, sir."

To which Admiral Bryton replied, "Yes, it's amazing what the threat of life in prison will do to inspire a man. Now I'm beginning to understand why the Royal Navy was so fond of the cat-o'-nine tails."

Commander Johnson stared at Admiral Bryton for a split second cleared his throat and said, "Yes, sir," turned and left the admiral's office.

The final fitting out was supposed to have taken six days but helped along by the liberal distribution of liquid trading stock and ice cream, both of which seemed to be in short supply and high demand throughout the city, USS *LST 121* was ready in record time. Jack gave serious consideration to writing a commendation for Chief Barton for his assistance in getting the work done so quickly. However, after several attempts, he found he was unable to convey that Chief Barton's outstanding efforts consisted of beating the system, providing unauthorized incentives to the shipyard workers, and absconding with anything that wasn't nailed down to barter for placing the ship first in line for work to be completed. At least not without making it sound like it was a bad thing.

CHAPTER 25

L *ST 121* was the first of her kind to finish fitting out. As a result, when she headed south toward the Gulf of Mexico, Jack's orders were to moor at Pilottown and provide demonstration cruises daily for Army, Navy, and Marine personnel until further orders were received. Owen Masters stayed aboard to act as pilot when the ship passed from Pilottown into the Gulf and returned at the end of each day to her mooring.

Pilottown was located eighty-five miles south of New Orleans and ten miles north of Head of Passes. This gave Jack the option of reaching the gulf through Southwest Pass, Pass A Loutre, or South Pass. Depending on the day's assignment, any one of the three passes could be used.

There was absolutely nothing to do at Pilottown so visiting military personnel rarely stayed aboard ship. They would generally arrive early in the morning and leave late in the evening. Each day, Mr. Masters would monitor one of the officers as he took the ship downriver. Jack would conduct the drills and demonstrations requested, and Mr. Masters would monitor another officer as he took the ship back up river to their mooring.

It didn't take long for monotony to set in. Being on the move daily had presented no problem for the crew coming downriver. There was always something new to see, and while underway, there were plenty of drills to keep everyone occupied. With guests aboard, this was not possible. Many of the visitors were high-ranking officers. After one major general complained that there was so much activity aboard ship, he was unable to concentrate on evaluating the trials being conducted, it was suggested to Jack by the rear admiral commanding the New Orleans Port of Embarkation that at the request of the United States Army Transportation Corps he "consider the demonstrations he conducted as his training exercises for the day and ease up on the other activities so the 'observers' could concentrate on their evaluations." This galled Jack no end, but he had learned as a county superintendent that when the school board "asked" it was not a request.

After several days of watching his crew's morale begin to slip, Jack had had enough. New military personnel arrived almost daily delivered by PT boat. The PT boats were fast and handy. Their skippers were young and cocky and made quite a show of bringing personnel downriver. The PT boat skippers would bring the little fighting ships downstream at forty-five knots cut the power and glide smoothly alongside the LST. While the passengers climbed the accommodation ladder, the PT boats would wait alongside, engines idling, but as soon as they were given the okay to cast off the PT boat, skippers would haul their boats around and advance their throttles to maximum power. The boats would then rocket away, engines roaring, and spray flying until they disappeared out of sight upriver.

When new personnel came aboard, they often asked for drills and demonstrations that had already been conducted. Most of the drills asked for were beaching techniques and demonstrations of how equipment could be loaded and unloaded directly onto the beach. These were conducted in the channel, relieving Jack of the need to take his ship out into the open waters of the gulf of Mexico.

When they were asked to demonstrate the ship's ability to ballast down for deepwater sailing, two subchasers were assigned as escorts. It was not widely known, but German U-boats were running wild in the gulf. Until the convoy system was implemented, tankers were being sunk almost as fast as they could be loaded. Except for the lack of a midship's superstructure, an LST looked similar to a tanker at a distance when ballasted down, and the Navy was unwilling to lose their first LST to German submarines before it even got out of sight of land.

Unlike the PT boat skippers and their crews, the subchasers were manned by older men, men who had experience handling small ships on the open ocean. Other than a few youngsters fresh aboard from radar or sonar school the skippers and crewmen of the sub-chasers were native to the coast and had made their living prior to the war handling shrimp boats, tuna boats, coasters, and other types of small craft, which plied the coastal waters of the gulf eking out a living from the sea.

The subchasers tied up at Pilottown along with the LST they were guarding. It didn't take long before the crews started to mingle. This led to some impromptu basketball games played inside the LST on the tank deck, a few cookouts, and various other activities which were "officially" unknown to the ship's officers. Drinking, gambling, sports, and hunting and fishing in the swamps helped the men burn off some excess energy, but what they really wanted was women.

There were several pilots who lived at Pilottown with their wives and families. Men being men and women being women, Jack and the subchaser skippers soon found themselves dealing with real and imaginary problems between the locals and the ship's crews. Pilottown is in the middle of Cajun country, and two things became very apparent. Creole men have hot tempers, and they possess a great deal of pride when it comes to their wives and families. They took offense to anything that in their mind was seen as an inappropriate gesture toward their wives and daughters. A look interpreted as lewd was met with a dangerous glare, cat calls, and whistles were met with curses and obscene gestures, and any physical contact, even shaking hands led to an instant fight.

By and large, Jack felt that his men and the men of the sub-chasers did not mean to be disrespectful. However, he could see, that with all the attention the men were paying to the few women in Pilottown, why the local men would react the way they did. Not only was there the potential for danger, but if things got nasty, Jack could find himself in a cell. Something had to be done.

Jack invited Rene Buochard, the unelected mayor of Pilottown to dine with him and the skippers of the subchasers, Lieutenant Henry Burk, and Lieutenant Raymond Hart. Jack asked Rene to bring along a couple of the more influential members of the Pilottown community. After introductions and a few platitudes, the men got down to the business at hand. It soon became apparent that the Pilottown men were just as concerned about settling things as Jack, Henry, and Ray. As Rene Bouchard said in his Creole accent, "These war she ees a terrouble ting, but it ees bring wealth to Pilottown lak nevair before. The lass ting we want is to kill these goose she lay de golden egg."

Everyone agreed with Rene and once it was understood that all parties wanted to resolve the issue without outside authorities becoming involved a plan began to take shape. At this point, Chief Boatswain's Mate Gardener and Chief Barton were called to the ward room. Details of the plan began to fall in place, and by 2200 hours, the men all shook hands, and the guests were seen to the railing. Two more days of meetings, one of which involved the PT boat skippers, were needed to tie up all the loose ends, and Operation Charleston was born.

Operation Charleston was an example of logistics coordination and mutual cooperation between the Navy, local civilians, USO, and the jazz community of New Orleans. As with any military operation, Charleston depended on highly detailed planning, precise timing, and secrecy from the enemy. In this case, the enemy was determined to be the US Navy, US Army, and possibly the Coast Guard.

November 24 was the date selected for Operation Charleston. This allowed two weeks preparation to pull everything together. The operation was a complex affair with many facets. Information was released on a "need to know" basis only. Aboard ship, no one except Jack, Boatswain Gardener, and Chief Barton knew the full scope of the plan. Aboard the subchasers Henry Burk and Ray Hart knew the complete details of the operation and ashore only Rene Bouchard and two of the local men had the complete story. Other than those few individuals, no one had any idea what the complete picture looked like. Jack was depending on this. As with any "secret" aboard ship, word spread like wildfire each time crewmembers were asked to perform some job outside their normal duties. When the men asked why they were doing something, all they were told was they would find out on the twenty-fourth. This generated rumors which only increased the crews' expectation that something big was about to happen and everyone needed to be on their toes.

The daily drills and exercises continued for the visiting military personnel, but instead of morale plummeting, the crew became sharper, each man working to the best of his ability in order to be prepared for whatever was about to happen. There was a spirit and drive aboard ship that could be felt. New personnel coming aboard to observe the drills and exercises noticed this and comments were made to the rear admiral in charge of the New Orleans Port of Embarkation who in turn forwarded them to Washington where they found their way to Admiral Bryton's desk. After reading them, the admiral had Commander Johnson add them to Jack's service file. As Johnson was leaving the office, he noticed the admiral smiling like a pirate counting his gold doubloons. This sent a slight shudder down the commander's back.

The rumor mill was working overtime and speculation was running wild. When Jack sent one of the ship's LCVPs into the swamps with six of his best riflemen, Rene Bouchard, and a local hunter, word had it that German commandoes hand infiltrated the swamps and the ship had been assigned to ferret them out. Instead, the men returned with four wild pigs that were butchered and placed in the ship's freezer. When both LCVPs were sent out with ten men and two Cajun fishermen in each boat the word was they were testing out a new method of finding German U-boats. Instead they returned with clams, oysters, and mussels, which were packed in seaweed and stored in one of the ship's voids, which was partially filled with sea water.

Everyone had an answer for whatever was going on. Two shrimp boats pulled alongside, and thirty men were sent out with the Creole captains and their crews. For sure, this was to pick up spies who were returning from missions in South America. The boats returned with their holds full of shrimp, which were loaded into boxes on the bow ramp and transferred to the ship's coolers where they were packed in ice.

There was one thing that puzzled everyone and produced no rumors to explained it, that was when Boat's, Chief Barton, Franklyn Ingolls, Tyree Higby, Lucious Tanner, and six of Gardener's deck apes drove the ship's jeep into an LCVP loaded several crates in along with it and disappeared up river only to return midmorning of the next day. The crates Chief Barton had stowed aboard were missing, but a piano and drum set were tied down in their place. That evening, when the ship returned to Pilottown, the military personnel who had been aboard as observers were loaded aboard the waiting PT boats, and as soon as the visitors were out of sight, Boats drove the jeep onto the tank deck, the piano and drum set were loaded into the back of the six-by-six, the canvas top was pulled tight, cross tied, and secured, and everyone went back to business as usual. That had everyone stumped.

CHAPTER 26

On the twenty-third, the drills and exercises ceased at 1200 hours. They were cut short at the request of a brigadier general who wanted to get back to New Orleans to, as he put it, "get prepared for Thanksgiving," whatever that meant.

As soon as the ship was secured along the pier, the subchasers pulled in and rafted on the upstream side. After securing bumpers and gangways between the ships an accommodation ladder was installed from the inboard subchaser to the LST. Work details were mustered to place cargo nets along the edges of the pier that were secured at the bottom and held aloft by booms slung out from the ship's side. This created a net wall around the entire perimeter of the pier. When one of the crew asked Boats what the nets were for, he said, "Them there walls is so nobody feeds the gattors tanight."

Once the gattor walls were completed, Chief Barton broke out crates from various hidey holes around the ship and men began to string Christmas lights, Japanese lanterns, and streamers between the booms, across the cargo nets, and along the ship's rail. Inside on the tank deck, the piano and drum set were set up along the starboard side on top of a pile of pallets Boats had erected for that purpose, covered with plywood, and draped with canvas. Colored lights were strung from the overhead, Chief Barton pulled out a mirrored globe from some deep dark corner no one knew about, and Chief Grubowski hung it in the center of the tank deck overhead.

The six-by-six had been left ashore when the ship pulled out that morning. After the piano and drum set were unloaded, the six-by-six disappeared and returned an hour later with a load of sand that was dumped on the center of the pier in the middle of a ring of wharf timbers about six feet wide and twenty feet long. The six-by-six disappeared again and came back with a load of firewood and rocks, which were stacked alongside.

Just before 1700 hours, Jack, Lieutenant Burk, and Lieutenant Hart gathered on the port bridge wing where they could be seen by everyone on the pier and aboard ship. Ensign Jensen, the ship's communications officer, announced over the ship's PA, "Now hear this. Now hear this, Captain Cole, Captain, Burk, and Captain Hart will address the men of USS *LST 121*, USS *SC-584*, and USS *SC-499*."

Ensign Jensen then handed the microphone to Jack who announced, "Gentlemen, at 1700 hours, you will be dismissed from all duties for the remainder of the day." A cheer went up from the crews of all three ships.

"At that time, you will retire to your quarters where you will shower, shave, and don your dress blues." A moan swept through the men.

"You will prepare yourselves in every way deemed appropriate to receive visitors who will be arriving via PT boat beginning at approximately 1900 hours." Another moan went through the men. Obviously, they thought more military personnel would be arriving for some sort of grandstand showing of the ship to impress the brass.

"These visitors will be our guests and are to be extended every courtesy. I expect each of you to act as the gentlemen you are and conduct yourselves accordingly." There was complete silence. "There are one or two items I must mention in order to make sure there are no misunderstandings during the course of the evening. Number one, the rule against drinking alcohol aboard United States Naval Vessels will remain in place aboard this ship. However, that does not apply to the pier alongside. Captain Burk and Captain Hart may have something to say regarding that rule aboard their vessels. That is not in my purview to address."

There was a stirring among the men at this, and smiles began to appear on what a few moments before had been rather somber faces.

"Number 2. Except for the tank deck, main deck, and the port booby hatch stairwell, all parts of the ship will be off-limits to civilians." This produced a few questioning comments and puzzled looks.

"And finally, gentlemen, number 3. No means no. Do you all understand that?"

This one completely dumbfounded the men, but it produced a resounding "Yes, sir."

Jack then turned to Burk and Hart and asked, "Gentlemen, do you have anything further to add?"

Lieutenant Burk took the mic and said, "Gentlemen, there will be no civilians and no drinking alcohol aboard USS *SC-584* this evening. Is that understood?"

A chorus of "yes, sir" rose from the crew of SC-584.

"That goes for everyone. Is that understood?" Burk repeated somewhat forcefully. This time, everyone replied, "Yes, sir."

"That is all I have." Burk then turned to Lieutenant Hart. "Do you have anything to add, Captain Hart?"

"Yes, thank you, Captain Burk. Gentlemen, the same holds for drinking and civilians aboard *SC-499*. There will be no drinking and no civilians aboard ship this evening or tomorrow. I have one other thing to add to what Captain Cole and Captain Burk have already mentioned. Even though as captain I am authorized to conduct marriages aboard my ship, I will not do so under any circumstance this evening, tomorrow, or most likely ever. Do I make myself clear?"

At this, the men just stood dumbfounded and looked at each other.

"I said, do I make myself clear?" Hart bellowed.

"Yes, sir," came a thunderous reply from the men.

Lieutenant Hart handed the mic back to Jack who handed it to Ensign Jensen who announced, "That is all."

During the day, a few pirogues and bateaus had drifted in from the swamps, poled or paddled by Cajun families from back in the bayous. By 1700 hours, when the ship's crews headed to their quarters to shower, shave, and put on their dress blues, a sizable crowd of locals had gathered on shore. When the pier cleared of sailors, the men and women of Pilottown carried baskets of food and spices onto the pier. The men built fires on the sand covering the middle of the pier, and the women placed large cooking pots over the fires filled with water and seasonings. More Creole families began to arrive by small craft of all types including a few by shrimpers and oyster boats. Rene Bouchard and the men went below where Bill Spence was waiting in the galley for them. The Pilottown men carried the shrimp, oysters, clams, mussels, and pork onto the pier where everyone pitched in and helped shuck oysters, peel shrimp, husk corn, and wash potatoes. Then tossing all the ingredients into the pots and fryers, the women began to prepare low country boil, gumbo, fried clams, boiled shrimp, and barbeque.

It didn't take long for the aroma to draw the sailors to the deck. Men were crowding the rail to see what was going on when a man hailed the deck from the forward twin 40 mm. gun tub. "They's PT boats a comin' this way and you ain't gonna believe what they're carryin'."

Counting the ship's crews and the locals, there were almost two hundred people in, on, or around the pier when the first PT boat pulled up to the LST. The bow doors had been opened, and the ramp lowered to deck height of a PT boat. When the first PT boat bounced against the bumpers laid across the end of the ramp to fend off damage to its plywood hull the crews of the LST and subchasers went absolutely wild. Twenty young women from the New Orleans USO stepped daintily from the bobbing PTs onto the ramp and were immediately swarmed by the waiting sailors. The next boat carried more girls as did the two following that one. When the fifth PT boat arrived half a dozen girls and a dozen black musicians off loaded. The band members made their way to the piano and drum set in the middle of the tank deck and in a few minutes the tank deck began to jump to the sound of hot Dixieland jazz.

The accommodation ladder was lowered from the LST to the pier and men and women began to come and go up and down the ladder in and out of the tank deck on to the pier and back and forth. The PT boats were rafted up river of the subchasers and the boats crews ran across the gangways up the starboard accommodation ladder and joined the fun. Operation Charleston was in full swing.

The food was laid out in the middle of the pier next to the cooking pots from which it was served. Right in the middle of the food was the refreshment table serving Chief Barton's trading stock cut with Cookie's powdered lemonade and gallons of ice cream which was kept frozen by periodic shots of CO_2 from the ship's fire extinguishers.

With the bow doors open and the ventilators running, the music poured out over the pier and across the bayous. It soon became apparent why Jack had the gattor walls erected. Dancing couples, sober or otherwise, caroming across the pier or the tank deck jitter bugging to the music and lost in the spirit of the moment were bouncing off other couples and into the nets. This produced squeals of laughter from the USO girls and loud guffaws from the men as they tried to disentangle themselves from the nets and get back to dancing. Things were ramping up, and Jack noticed that the sailors and Cajuns were talking, drinking, and eating together. Operation Charleston was accomplishing its objective.

As the evening wore on, couples began to pair off, and the gattor walls served a second purpose by keeping everyone corralled on the tank deck, pier, or main deck. Jack was sure there was more going on than a few kisses and passionate embraces, but that was life. Young men and women would do what young men and women had been doing since Adam and Eve. It was a fact of life and nothing would change that.

At his age, Jack thought he had developed a certain resistance to Mother Nature's urge to see couples pair off for the good of the species. He'd been married in his early twenties but soon found that in order to make a successful marriage, a couple had to want the same things out of life and be willing to work together to reach their mutual goals. Unfortunately, that hadn't turned out to be the case for Jack and his bride. He and his wife had barely gotten beyond the honeymoon when it became apparent they were both in love with the idea of being married but didn't share the same vision of where they wanted to take their lives and how they planned to get there. Just shy of two months after the wedding, they sought an annulment and went their separate ways.

Jack was leaning on the rail of the port bridge wing watching the party and thinking about his life when a movement on deck below caught his attention. He looked down and saw Rene Bouchard strolling along at the head of a small group of men and women laughing and talking using big animated gestures so important to Creole communication. As the party drew closer, Rene looked up and shouted in a somewhat slurred voice, "Capeetan Cole, you no having fun, yes? These party she be tres bon everyone good frens now. Come drink with us, eat with us, perhaps maybe so, if you are good fun, my beautiful seister, she let you dance with her. What you say, mon amee?"

Then turning to a lovely dark-eyed beauty, Rene said, "Annette, the capeetan he not so ugly. You would not dance weith heim, yes?"

Annette turned, and with a sideways glance, she looked up at Jack. Jack could see her silhouette against the light of the lanterns and cooking fires. "I don't know, Rene, he is so far away. I cannot tell if he is an ugly duck or a proud peacock. Besides, he cannot dance from way up there if I am way down here."

Rene and the rest of his party roared with laughter. "Capeetan Cole, is not every man he get to dance weith my beautiful seister. What you say? You come dance, no?"

Jack couldn't help but laugh, and showing off to the best of his ability, he spun around put one foot on each hand rail of the bridge ladder and slid down landing at Annette's feet. He gave her a very deep bow and then scooped her into his arms, twirled her around, set her down at arm's length, and said, "Well, what do you think, too ugly to dance with?"

Annette threw her head back and laughed, then extended both arms and said, "I've danced with worse."

Jack spent the rest of the evening dancing, eating, and drinking with Rene and his wife, Rene's sister Annette, and Rene's friends. As the clock wound into the early hours of the twenty-fourth, and the party neared its end Jack thought for the first time in as long as he could remember he didn't want the night to end.

At 0200 hours, the boarding call for the PT boats was announced, and a careful headcount was made of the USO girls. This took some time. It appeared many of the young women weren't that eager to call it a night. Quite a few had to be coaxed out of the dark corners and deep shadows of the main deck, tank deck, and booby hatch stairwell with their lovers in tow. As the girls gathered on the tank deck near the bow ramp, Jack noticed some of them seemed to be somewhat disheveled, and many of the men escorting them had lipstick smears on their faces and collars. Mother Nature hadn't lost her touch. Jack was glad Lieutenant Hart had nixed the idea of shipboard marriages.

When everyone was rounded up, the PT boats began to take on passengers for the return trip to New Orleans. The loading was slowed by couples locked in embraces saying their goodbyes and doing their best to make a good night kiss last as long as possible. It was obvious no one wanted the night to end. The boats pulled away amidst a flurry of waving hankies, blown kisses, and tears. The band continued playing even after they boarded a waiting PT. Taking the sobriety of the partiers into consideration, instead of rocketing off like they normally did, the PT boat skippers cruised along at a comfortable speed making sure no one fell overboard. At about 0300 hours, the last faint strains of music could be heard carrying over the water as the boats pulled into the night.

CHAPTER 27

T he next day being Thanksgiving, no visitors arrived to observe the ship's capabilities so the day was devoted to cleaning up after the party. Ensign Jensen managed to pick up the Detroit Lions football game over the short wave and piped it throughout the ship. The work progressed smoothly but quietly through the day. There was the occasional man who made a trip to the side to be sick over the railing from the effects of the previous night, but no one was incapacitated to the point that they couldn't put in a full days duty.

Pilottown was quiet that day as well. A few locals came and went on their daily business, and the pilot boat carried three pilots in and out, but other than that, everything was peaceful and silent. Once the residue of the party was collected and disposed of and Chief Barton had tucked his lanterns, lights, and other decorations away for safe keeping, the sun set on an idyllic fall day in the Mississippi River delta. Operation Charleston was over. It was deemed a complete success, and a pleasant calm cast its spell over the little hamlet.

After seeing that the guards were posted, the ship secured, and everything was in order, Jack took a tour along the pier to make sure nothing had been overlooked in the cleanup effort. He had completed his inspection from the accommodation ladder to the river end of the pier and was walking back along the pier toward shore when he saw movement in the shadows by the ship's stern. He stepped to the middle of the pier, which gave him more time to react in case someone had something in mind other than fond memories of a wonderful party the night before and continued to walk toward the end of the pier. Suddenly and unexpectedly Annette stepped from the shadows and stood waiting for him. When Jack came near, Annette threw her arms open and rushed to him. He held her close, her perfume was intoxicating, her hair smelled like blossoms, and her skin was so smooth and soft she felt like silk in his arms.

Jack said nothing; he held her close enraptured by her presence. Slowly, she lifted her face to him, and he saw she was crying. He bend to kiss the tears from her cheeks, and suddenly, they were locked in an embrace like none he'd ever felt before. Her kisses were passionate, insistent, yet soft and warm. Jack's head began to swirl, and before he knew it, he was running his hands up and down her spine. She leaned into him pressing hard against his chest until with a shudder, she leaned back and looked into his eyes.

"I will never forget you, Jack Cole. If not for this war we would never have met, but I fear the war will soon take you from me. Please come back to me, will you, if only to hold me one more time? I know it is foolish, but I think I am in love with you. Please, please, please do not think me a foolish girl. I am a woman and my feelings for you are those of a woman. I will never forget you."

With that, Annette kissed him one more time, then slipped from his embrace, and hurried a short way down the pier where she stopped, turned, ran back, kissed him once more, and then fled into the night. Jack stood there staring into the darkness listening to the sound of her footsteps. He hadn't said a word. He couldn't think of a thing to say. Finally, when he could hear her footsteps no longer he began to turn and walk back toward the accommodation ladder, but a voice stopped him, "She is a beuteeful woman, my seister. She knows her heart and cannot help herself. You are a good man, Capeetan Cole. You don't make promises you do not plan to keep. You do not lie to her. You make her happy. I weesh you well in these war. Until these fight she is over, tink of her often as I am sure she will tink of you. Remember these place and these people. There is a place for you here if you desire but feel no obligation to return. Annette, she understand this. She know two sheeps they pass, but maybe they should meet again no?"

Rene turned and walked away slowly waving his hand above his head not looking back.

As with all good things they must come to an end. The next day, Jack received sailing orders. They were going to war.

CHAPTER 28

Jack was ordered to be prepared to get underway within twenty-four hours of notification. This is an order which means the captain should have his ship in such a state that he can sail within twenty-four hours of receiving orders to go to sea. Having never been in the Navy Jack did not understand this and thought he was to be ready to go to sea within the next twenty-four hours. Since he had been taking the ship out daily, Jack was ready to go; all he needed to do was top off the tanks and replenish the food and other sundries that had been expended when demonstrating the capabilities of his LST to Army and Navy personnel.

Jack immediately cast off and traveled up river to New Orleans where he replenished, refueled, and took on a full load of ammunition plus an additional five hundred thousand rounds of .50 caliber ammunition for the MCMG turrets he had absconded with in Memphis. Following completion of his preparations he reported USS *LST 121* ready for sea. Jack received his orders to get prepared at 0600 hours and reported ready for sea at 1400 hours. This was passed up the chain of command and a copy landed on Admiral Bryton's desk late that afternoon. After reading the notification, Admiral Bryton handed it to Commander Johnson for inclusion in Commander Cole's file and said, "You know, Johnson, I can't figure this man out. We had to drag him in here kicking and screaming that we had the wrong man and he'd never been in the Navy, yet everything he's done since returning to duty has been outstanding. He's the most gung ho returning officer we've got. I wish I had a hundred more just like him. Maybe I should threaten every officer the way I did him."

Commander Johnson started to smile at Admiral Bryton's joke until he saw the look on the admiral's face and realized he wasn't joking.

The Navy hadn't planned on sending *LST 121* to sea until a larger group of LSTs could be assembled and made part of a convoy; however, the notification that the ship was ready to sail caused the Navy brass to rethink this idea. Subchasers were needed in the Mediterranean. Seven newly completed subchasers were ready to go in Rockport, Texas, but without a tanker to travel with them, they were just sitting there tied up at the pier. The subchasers were capable of deepwater sailing, but they didn't have the range to make the crossing from the United States to the Mediterranean without being refueled in route. An alternative would be to lift a subchaser aboard a tanker or cargo ship and transfer it as deck cargo, but the deck space was needed for the vital war supplies to fight Rommel and his Africa Corp.

A naval officer who had come aboard Jack's ship to observe the capabilities of an LST noted that when sailing in the open ocean an LST was required to ballast down in order to remain sea worthy. He had mentioned this in his report along with a note that an LST could ballast down with fuel oil or diesel fuel and serve as an interim tanker should the need arise. This item in the report had not fallen on deaf ears. Instead, it captured the imagination of Navy brass who were looking for ways to keep the fuel flowing to England and North Africa. With seven armed subchasers as escorts an LST would be more that adequately protected on an Atlantic crossing and could possibly help offset the heavy losses of tankers to German U-boats.

When Jack reported ready for sea, a few key Navy brass put their heads together and decided to use this opportunity as an experiment to see if an LST could serve in the role of tanker while carrying vital equipment and supplies overseas. Two days after reporting ready for sea, Jack received orders to proceed to the chandler's pier in New Orleans. Here refueling equipment was loaded aboard and made fast as deck cargo. Jack was then ordered to the Shell Central Facilities Seaplane base in Southwest Pass to take on diesel fuel as ballast in lieu of saltwater.

Jack remained at the Shell refueling pier for twenty-four hours wondering why he had been required to fill his ballast tanks with diesel fuel until finally a pilot boat dropped off his orders as it headed to sea to deliver a pilot to an incoming ship. Jack retired to his cabin, tore open his orders, and began to read them. Things looked fairly straight forward. He was ordered to rendezvous with a small flotilla of seven subchasers at the mouth of Southwest Pass. From Southwest Pass he was to proceed to Gulf Port, Mississippi, via Chandeleur Sound. At Gulf Port, Jack was to pick up a Seabee battalion, load their equipment and materials, and proceed to Casablanca, Morocco, via Key West Naval Station, Trinidad, and Cape Verde. During the Atlantic crossing, he would refuel the subchasers as needed from the diesel fuel he carried for ballast. This operation, codenamed Fountain, was designed to evaluate the feasibility of using an LST in lieu of a tanker when required. He was to keep detailed notes on all aspects of the refueling process until he completed the Atlantic crossing. When he arrived in Casablanca, he would file his report and receive new orders.

Bringing his ship down the Mississippi was one thing, especially when he had a river pilot, but an open ocean voyage from North America to Africa; that was something else. However, as he was reading his orders he began to think that perhaps he could deal with the situation. Certainly, Boatswain Gardener would be able to handle the mechanics of rigging the lines and hoses necessary for the refueling. His officers and men were very capable and would do their utmost to make the operation a success. The more he thought about it, the better he felt. He'd be in a convoy with seven other ships. He would have to study hard to make sure he was on top of all the convoy maneuvers, signals, and protocols as well as the refueling procedures, but if worse came to worse, all he would really need to do was follow the ship ahead of him and let his men do their jobs. It would be just like running a school district. He didn't teach every class or clean every building. He managed the process and made sure everything that needed to be done was done correctly and on time. As long as he followed procedure and the convoy commander's orders, he'd be all right. Then just as he was beginning to feel that he would be able to get the job done he read the final line of his orders. "As ranking officer, you will be convoy commander of TG 4.7 and in command of Operation Fountain."

Jack froze where he sat. A bolt of fear went through him like an electric shock. He had no idea what to do. How would he find Casablanca? It was clear across the Atlantic. He had no more idea how to find his way from Pilottown to Africa than he could fly. He didn't even know where to begin. This was insane. He'd been forced into this and was only here to keep from being thrown in prison. Somehow he'd managed to blunder from Evansville down the Mississippi to New Orleans without getting anyone hurt or damaging the ship. But this? This could cost the lives of hundreds of men and the loss of millions of dollars' worth of ships, supplies, and equipment. He'd already tried to tell the Navy they had the wrong man, but they wouldn't listen. If he refused the orders, he could be shot, and that wasn't a threat. It was a fact. This was a time of war and refusal of an order would be his death sentence. Jack had never felt as close to panic as he was now, and he had no idea how he was going to deal with the situation.

There was no one he could turn to. He certainly couldn't confide in his officers or men that he shouldn't be there and had absolutely no idea what he was doing. It was up to him to figure things out. The only thing he could think of was to follow his standard procedure when preparing for a district board meeting. He sat down and made a list of the items that needed to be addressed. Then he prioritized them. He put some items under the heading of old business, some items under the heading of new business, and the rest he grouped under standing business. Standing business would include food, fuel, personnel, paint, repairs, spare parts, etc. In other words, the standard items required for daily operation of the ship. Old business included crew training, communications training, radar training, Morse code training, navigation, and gunnery. In short, the additional training he had added since taking command. New business included convoy organization and operating procedures, refueling procedures, communication between ships, convoy formation, emergency procedures, convoy defense air, convoy defense submarine, convoy defense surface attack, storms, fog, and the final item…unknown.

When Jack was preparing for a school board meeting, it was his standard practice to call his building principals, administrators, and department heads together and go over everything that needed to be covered. In this case, Jack called all his officers, division heads, and department lead men together to go over every aspect they could think of which was related to the convoy. This included Boatswain Gardener, Chief Barton, Bob Parks Radioman first class, Bill Davis Ship Fitter first class, Chief Grubowski Motor Machinist, Jimmy Tinker Fire Controlman second class, Andy Jennings Radarman second class, Herman Winkle Electricians Mate first class, Roger Kinkaid Water Tender second class, Alonzo Peters Fireman first class, Andy Richards Pharmacist's Mate first class, and Bill Spence Ship's Cook.

Jack went over the orders, then went around the table making assignments, checking on training progress, asking questions, and making suggestions where needed. He was particularly interested in the development of additional radio and radar operators and the progress his officers were making in navigation training. Following those reports, Jack gave each man an hour to get with his division personnel and return with any questions, comments, or observations that hadn't been covered during their first meeting. This would be the unknowns.

When the meeting resumed, Bill Davis reported he didn't have enough steel to build gun tubs for the MCMG turrets. Jack said, "Draw up your plans and see Chief Barton."

Then turning to Barton, Jack said, "Chief, see what you can do when we get to Gulf Port. If anybody can get us some steel, it ought to be the Seabees. In the meantime, if you can find it anyplace else, don't be bashful about getting it. Just make sure it isn't missed."

Everyone laughed at that. Barton just placed his palms together and rolled his eyes toward the overhead smiling like a beatific little angel.

Boats piped up, "Sir, I'll need to drill my deck apes on shooting lines, rigging those refueling hoses, and transferring fuel. Is there any way we can work on that while underway? I'd like to get in a few practice runs at doing it before we rendezvous with those subchasers. I don't want to learn as we go and dump diesel fuel all over the Atlantic."

"Sure, Boats." Then turning and pointing at Lieutenant Purvis with the eraser end of his pencil, he said, "Dale, get on the horn and find out what Burk and Hart are doing. See if they can spare the time to work with us."

"Yes, sir," Purvis replied, then added, "You want one or both of them, sir?"

"I hadn't thought about it. What are you thinking?"

"Well, sir. If we can run our drills in one of the passes, we'll only need one subchaser, but if we go out, I'd feel better if we had both. One could ping for subs while we run our drills with the other."

"Good idea, Dale. See what you can do to get both of them. Let me know as soon as you can."

Then looking at the group, Jack asked, "Anyone else?"

There were no replies, only shaking of heads.

Jack was ready to end the meeting. "Okay, let's hop to. Chief Grubowski, can you stay for a moment? I've got some questions?"

The room quickly emptied, and Jack asked, "Chief, is there any way we can squeeze another knot or two out of this ship?"

Chief Grubowski sat down at the ward room table and looked up at the overhead thinking. "Well, sir, there's only so much we can do. We can't change the hull design so we've got to get more power out of the engines. With the engines the way they are, we're getting all we can now. Without making some changes, we're pretty much as fast as we're ever going to be."

Jack leaned forward on his elbows, his forearms crossed, thinking. "You mentioned changes. What kind of changes are we talking about?"

Grubowski took a big breath and let it out like it was a great effort to do so then pushed his CPO cap back on his head, "Well, sir, if we cool the intake air, that would help. We could probably work out something using the freezer units or maybe we could get some freezer units just for cooling the air. We could clean up and expand the exhaust manifolds by filing all the slag and burs out of the casting, but we'd have to shut down the engines and let them cool to do that."

"Can you shut them down one at a time for that?" Jack asked.

"Yeah, that would work. We could keep underway on one engine while I pull the manifold off the other then switch engines and do the other one. Yeah we could do that," Grubowski replied tentatively.

"Okay, what else?"

"Well, we could do a lot with high-performance injectors, but we don't have any of those."

"Is that something Chief Barton could…ah…assist you with?"

"Well, I don't know if the Navy carries any or not, but Chief Barton should be able to find out, I guess. Maybe he could check and see if there were any freezer units sitting around too."

Chief Grubowski was starting to get enthusiastic about the possibilities. "You know, if we built a fuel reservoir a little higher than the engine, we could pump the fuel into that and feed the engines from there under static pressure. That would reduce the work load on the fuel pumps and allow the injectors to work more efficiently which would give us a boost, but if we really wanted to improve the horsepower on those engines, what we need are blowers."

Chief Grubowski was grinning now, with a faraway look on his face, like he was in another place. "Yeah, if we could do all those things and add blowers, I'll bet we could get maybe another two knots out of her, sir."

"Okay," Jack said. "Does the Navy have any of these…ah… What did you call them, blowers?"

"No, sir," Grubowski replied. "But if we could get our hands on the right stuff, we could make our own."

Grubowski was still in that faraway place only now he was visibly excited. Jack let him wander there for a few moments then said, "Okay, Chief, I don't get it, but you know what you're doing. Work it out and come show me what you need to do. Just make sure the engines are as dependable when you're done as they are now. I want more speed, but I want dependability to go along with it."

Grubowski popped up out of his chair said, "Yes, sir," and dashed out of the ward room.

Jack was in his cabin when Lieutenant Purvis knocked and stuck his head in the door. "Sir, Captain Burk and Captain Hart both say they are tied up at Pilottown waiting for orders. They want to work with us, but don't think it's a good idea to go out with only one escort pinging for subs. They said they'd feel better if they were both on the lookout while we were working on refueling."

Jack spun around in his chair. "Okay, got any ideas?"

Lieutenant Purvis looked surprised when asked for his thoughts. "Well…yes, sir. We could see about using a PT boat, but they burn avgas so we wouldn't be able to transfer fuel. Even though it's smaller, we could lower one of our LCVP's and practice on that. An LCVP can turn twelve knots. Heck, they're just as fast as we are. They burn diesel so we could drop one over the side with its tanks almost empty and pump fuel directly into them. I'd say if we can refuel something that small bobbing all over the ocean we should be able to refuel anything."

Jack stood up and slapped Purvis on the shoulder. "Great idea. Get a hold of those subchasers and make it happen. While you're at it, tell Boats to get his men ready to rig the refueling gear. There's nothing in the orders about showing us how it's done so we'll teach ourselves. I want to be ready to go as soon as those subchasers get here."

CHAPTER 29

Shortly before 1100 hours, *SC 584* and *SC 499* pulled up alongside USS *LST 121* and Captains Burk and Hart came aboard via the accommodation ladder. Jack went over what he planned to do, and both men went back to their ships. When the subchasers were clear of the side, Jack had one of the LCVPs lowered with a dozen men and the tackle necessary to secure a line from the LST. Boats had drilled his deck crew on the process of shooting a line, pulling a cable, and hauling a hose from one ship to the other. They knew what they were supposed to do and were eager to get at it.

They spent the remainder of the day practicing shooting lines, pulling cable, hauling hose, and pumping diesel fuel. Jack practiced into the wind, with the wind, across the wind and with quartering winds off the bow and stern. The LCVP bobbed like a cork, rolled, and pitched in the swells and danced on the bow wave the LST kicked up, but it didn't take long and Ensign Price, and his boat crew handled the LCVP like it was an America's cup yacht. Boats's deck crew had trouble early on, primarily with the Lyle gun and properly flaking the line. Jack noticed that Boats handled his men well. He was at least twenty years older than his deck hands, but instead of berating them for their errors, he was patient and used every opportunity to teach them how to do things properly. Once he got the idea across that they had to lead their target when firing the Lyle gun and to make sure that when they laid out their line it wasn't twisted, everything started coming together. It took a while, but after the first three or four tries, the men started handling their duties like they'd been refueling from ship to ship all their lives.

It had been a long day, but a good day. When they pulled in and tied up at the Shell refueling pier, there was a small delegation waiting for them. A lieutenant, one lieutenant JG, two ensigns, and a dozen seamen requested permission to come aboard. Jack met them at the head of the accommodation ladder still dressed in his dungarees which he had ordered as uniform of the day for refueling training. He left the sailors in the care of Boatswain Gardener and invited the officers to the ward room. Jack was just about to make introductions between his officers and the visitors when the lieutenant cleared his throat and announced, "Gentlemen, my name is Lieutenant Jason Turner United States Naval Academy class of 1940. I am in command of the training detachment sent here to teach you how to handle refueling while underway. Until further notice, you will be under my command and take your orders directly from me. Is that understood?"

Then turning to Jack, he said, "Captain, I'd like to know why you were not at the refueling pier when I arrived. I've been waiting here since 1200 hours, cooling my heels on this d——n pier, and I don't like it one bit. I checked before leaving New Orleans, and you did not have sailing orders. You were supposed to be tied up here at the refueling pier, but instead, you were out gallivanting around in the gulf with a United States Navy vessel without orders. Whether you realize it or not, Mr. Cole, this ship is not your personal property, and you do not just go to sea willy-nilly whenever you feel like it. This is the United States Navy, and you will follow orders. I'm not about to put up with something like that. I am going to report you for dereliction of duty and unauthorized use of a naval vessel. I am considering having you thrown in the brig so your excuse for whatever you have been doing had better be d——n good, or I'll see to it that you are court marshaled. Do you understand me, Mister..."

Franklyn Ingolls had just stepped into the ward room when Lieutenant Turner started his harangue. He was prepared to serve coffee but froze in the pantry doorway and tried to look invisible. Jack's officers listened in shock as the lieutenant worked up to an indignant rant. Even the officers that accompanied Turner aboard ship seemed embarrassed by the tongue lashing Jack was receiving.

Jack sat in his chair at the head of the ward room table. His face was growing redder by the moment and his hands were turning white from the force of his grip on the arms of his chair. His eyes rested on Lieutenant Turner in a deadly squint, and the muscles in his neck stood out like cords of rope.

Fighting to keep himself under control, Jack stood slowly and said to the other officers. "Gentlemen, please make yourselves comfortable. I believe you will find that Mr. Ingolls makes the best coffee in the Navy. Franklyn, perhaps you could inquire of our visitors if they have eaten. Gentlemen, we dined at sea as we returned to the pier. If you haven't eaten, Mr. Ingolls will see to it that you are fed and taken care of. Enjoy your coffee."

Then turning to Turner, Jack motioned to his cabin door and said, "Lieutenant, if you'll join me, I'd like to speak to you in my cabin."

Jack opened his cabin door and held it for Lieutenant Turner to enter. Once inside, Jack closed the door. In the ward room, silence prevailed. Everyone was listening to hear what was going to happen. They didn't have to wait long.

Ships cabins are not meant to be sound-proof. Except for the hatches that lead onto the open deck very few passages have water tight doors above the main deck. The ward room and officers' quarters on an LST are no exception. Though they couldn't clearly determine what was being said due to the ambient noise level aboard ship the officers in the ward room could tell the difference between Turner's voice and Jack's voice when they were speaking. The discussion went back and forth for a few moments rising in volume until Turner suddenly went silent; after that, only Jack's muffled voice could be heard. A few moments later, the cabin door opened.

Lieutenant Turner stepped through the door, turned and said, "Yes, sir, Commander." He then turned and walked through the ward room. As he passed the officers present, he glared at them and mumbled, "How was I to know he was a lieutenant commander? He was wearing dungarees for crying out loud." Lieutenant Turner did not say another word as he left the ward room.

A few moments later, Jack entered the ward room and said, "Mr. Purvis, find quarters for our guests for the evening and see to it that they are properly taken care of. Also contact Captain Burk and

Captain Hart and inform them that we will be conducting refueling exercises again tomorrow."

Then addressing everyone in the ward room, Jack said, "Gentlemen, I'm sorry I can't spend any more time with you this evening, but I have a report to write. We will be getting underway tomorrow at 0600 hours. I suggest you turn in and get some rest. Good night."

CHAPTER 30

Forty-eight hours later, Jack rendezvoused with the subchaser flotilla five miles off the mouth of Southwest Pass. Jack was extremely anxious about leading the convoy to Gulf Port. However, when he picked up the Inter Coastal waterway, the buoys and markers were clearly marked, and he stayed in the channel all the way to Gulf Port. This would allow him to stay in the shallow waters in shore to minimize the possibility of submarine attack. Jack formed the convoy around his LST with three subchasers in an arrowhead formation ahead and two subchasers on each side port and starboard. With the help of the intercoastal buoys and markers, Jack found it wasn't difficult to navigate through the reefs and shoals of Chandeleur Sound to Gulf Port. The fact that he was never out of sight of land was a great comfort, but he was still amazed when he managed to bring his convoy into Gulf Port without losing anyone or running aground. Cruising at a steady nine knots the convoy raised Gulf Port in fifteen hours. After passing through the submarine nets, they dropped anchor in the road stead, and Jack reported to the commanding officer of the Gulf Port naval station.

In the commanding officer's office, Jack was introduced to the Seabee battalion commanding officer, Commander Peter Meriwether, who had been an electrical contractor in Indianapolis, Indiana, prior to the war. The two men hit it off immediately, and Jack invited him and his executive officer to dine aboard ship that evening along with the commanding officers of the subchasers.

The following morning, they wasted no time in getting the loading process underway. After receiving his guests, Jack conned the ship alongside a loading pier and drove her up on the beach. By doing so, Jack could load deck cargo off the pier and drive tank deck cargo aboard at the same time. Thirty-six hours had been allotted to load the battalion. They were finished in eighteen hours. This was almost entirely due to the ability to drive the majority of the equipment and supplies aboard rather than having to lift, sway, and stow everything in a cargo hold by crane. The other contributing factors were application of the parking plan they had worked out in Memphis and the talent and skills of the Seabees in handling their equipment and their knowledge of how best to arrange lumber, pipe, cement, and other supplies to pack the most material into the smallest space.

Jack reported loading completed and ready for sea twenty-four hours ahead of schedule and left Gulf Port with the evening tide. The next morning in the Main Navy and Munitions Building, Commander Johnson laid a copy of a message on Admiral Bryton's desk informing CinCLant that the convoy was underway.

Bryton looked at the message, read it, and asked, "Cole again?"

Commander Johnson nodded his head and handed the admiral a file folder. The admiral opened it and found it contained two reports. One was from Owen Masters, the river pilot, and the other was from the admiral in charge of the New Orleans Port of Embarkation. Mr. Masters's report was a glowing assessment of Lieutenant Commander Cole's abilities, leadership, and determination to get the job done regardless of the difficulties encountered. The second was a notification that Lieutenant Commander Cole had apparently straightened out an underperforming Lieutenant named Turner who since spending two days with Lieutenant Commander Cole had done a complete reversal on his prior performance and appeared to be on his way to becoming a satisfactory officer. Admiral Bryton raised his eyes from the reports, slapped the palm of his hand on his desk top, and with a smile, said, "Drop these in Cole's file."

Johnson picked up the message and reports and left Bryton's office.

CHAPTER 31

A ship sails exactly the same at night as it does in the daylight. But try telling that to a skipper who has never commanded a ship before, sailed at night, or has little or no faith in his ability to navigate by the stars. Jack was up the entire night. He knew his men knew what they were doing and the only man aboard that he was worried about was the captain. He knew that man had no idea what was going on, and that wasn't a real confidence builder.

Through the night, Jack moved from the bridge to the radar room, to the bridge wing where he shot the stars, and then to his sea cabin to work out his location after which he checked his findings against the shore line that showed on the radar screen. After confirming with the coast outline that his navigation plot was correct, he would return to the bridge for an hour or so and repeat the process all over again. Each time he issued a course change to zigzag across the convoy's heading, he was as nervous as a new bride on her wedding night. Finally, dawn broke, and Jack was thrilled to see that all ships were still with him and on station. He left the bridge and retired to his sea cabin where he caught a few hours' sleep until called to the bridge for an aircraft sighting.

Radar had identified it as a friend via the IFF (Identification Friend or Foe) signal it broadcast, but Jack called the ship to battle stations and did not have the crew stand down until he had visual confirmation. The Navy PBY circled the convoy twice and then went on about its patrol duties. At noon, all the officers gathered on the bridge wings to shoot the sun, they worked out their plots, and Jack was pleased to find that everyone had fixed their plot accurately, including him.

Approximately midafternoon, the subchaser on the starboard wing of the arrowhead formation reported a contact and the entire convoy went to battle stations. Jack released the lead subchaser on his starboard side to assist on the contact and the trailing ship on the port side swung across the LST's wake to take up station and close the gap on the starboard side that was left open as the two subchasers went after the contact. After ten minutes of intense searching, both ships made contact, Jack cleared them to attack, and radioed the PBY they had seen earlier that they had a positive contact.

The subchasers bored in on the echo in a crisscross pattern and made several depth charge attacks without producing any wreckage, oil, or flotsam. The contact was finally lost, but by then, the PBY had arrived and patrolled around the convoy until returning to Pensacola to refuel.

As the first PBY disappeared to the north, another PBY lumbered in and continued to patrol around the convoy until dark when a Navy K class blimp arrived from NAS Richmond and escorted the convoy into Key West.

As at Gulf Port, all ships were refueled and resupplied before upping anchor and setting course for Trinidad. The convoy track took them from Key West southeast along the North Atlantic side of Cuba where the subchasers refueled at sea under air cover provided by Cuban Air Force PBYs out of newly completed air bases near San Antonio de los Baños and Pinar del Rio. Once out of Cuban waters, the task group again received air cover and was escorted past Haiti and the Dominican Republic by US Coast Guard planes out of Haiti and US Army Air Corp aircraft out of Puerto Rico.

After rounding the southeastern tip of the Dominican Republic at Punta Cana the convoy set course to the south southeast and entered the Caribbean, passing between Isla de Mona and Rojo Cabo on the west coast of Puerto Rico. Again Jack refueled the subchasers, this time while under air cover of patrolling US Army Air Corps B-18 Bolos. From there, Jack charted a course directly to Trinidad across the great expanse of the eastern Caribbean Sea.

The subchasers made another contact at the intersect of lines running south to north from Caracas, Venezuela, and east to west of

St. Lucia, but the contact quickly disappeared and a pod of whales was spotted in the vicinity of the contact shortly afterward. The remainder of the voyage to Trinidad was uneventful to everyone except Jack who barely slept during the two-thousand-mile, nineteen-day trip.

CHAPTER 32

T hough the trip was uneventful, it was not without action and excitement. When Jack pulled into Gulf Port, Chief Barton had taken the ship's six-by-six two-and-a-half-ton truck, Bill Davis, Angello Marguchi, an oxyacetylene cutting torch, and disappeared. He returned late that evening, picked up a few items from his escrow account, and disappeared again. Dawn found the ship's six-by-six parked on the loading pier with Chief Barton asleep in the cab, and Davis and Marguchi bedded down in the truck bed with a load of pipe, plate steel, and a half-dozen large wooden crates carefully concealed under a heavy tarp.

After reporting aboard, Barton left Davis and Marguchi to oversee delivery of the steel and sundry items to the machine shop while he reported to Jack. After finishing his report, Jack had the starboard LCVP lowered, and Chief Barton disappeared into the morning mist with a coxswain, six of Boatswain Gardener's deck hands, the oxyacetylene torch, and a portable chain hoist.

Chief Barton returned shortly after noon with a massive amount of rusted steel plate which was lifted aboard from the LCVP and transferred below deck to the machine shop. The LCVP was lifted back aboard, and the men returned to their regular duties.

After leaving Gulf Port, Bill Davis and Angello Marguchi began working on gun tubs for the MCMG turrets. The Seabees were interested in any construction or fabrication project so naturally they were drawn to the machine shop. When they found out what Davis and Marguchi were doing, they practically begged to get involved and jumped at the chance to pitch in and help. In no time, patterns were drawn in chalk on the machine shop floor and four gun tubs along with support legs and mounting brackets were fabricated and ready for installation. When the convoy pulled into Key West, all the welding on the exterior of the hull to attach mounting brackets was completed, primed, and finished in Navy gray before the convoy weighed anchor and left port. Once at sea, the gun tubs were swung in place, and the MCMG turrets were mounted.

The excitement of the voyage wasn't limited to the machine shop. Between Gulf Port and Key West, Jack held anti-aircraft target practice using Army Air Force and Navy tow planes out of Tampa, Sarasota, Bonita Springs, and Key West. The planes made passes over the convoy pulling target sleeves for each of the subchasers. Then for his own ship, he had the target tugs pull sleeves for the 40 mm. guns and another set of sleeves for the 20 mm. guns. Jack sent two gallons of ice cream to the subchaser with the best score each time target practice was held. He put the name of his ship's top scoring 40 mm. gun and top scoring 20 mm. gun on display in the mess hall for all to see. When the MCMG turrets became operational, the Cuban Air Force pulled target sleeves for Jack's gunners, and he added the top scoring .50 caliber gun turret on each practice session to the wall as well. The crew began referring to the growing number of plagues adorning the bulk head as Murderer's Row and the competition to get a gun crew's name on the wall became quite intense.

The Seabees had been trained in small arms and light machine guns and wanted to get in on the competition. Commander Meriwether approached Jack about this, and Jack approved target practice for the Seabees based on whatever Pete thought would be best for his men. The Seabees put their heads together and came up with a rifle competition firing at targets they mounted on towed sea sleds. The sleds were lowered over the side and allowed to fall behind the ship to whatever distance Meriwether selected for the days shooting. Pete split his men into teams, and the Seabees shot for scores which were tabulated each time a sled was retrieved. Individual high scorers and highest scoring teams were posted on the bulkhead outside the battalion's berthing quarters. The morale of the ship's crew and the Seabee battalion soared.

Not to be out done the subchaser skippers requested permission to practice on surface targets with their three-inch .23 caliber deck guns. Jack had Meriwether build more target sleds. He towed them far enough behind the LST that if a three-inch shell hit the sled instead of passing through the target sheet splinters and debris would not rain down on Jack's ship or men. Another two gallons of ice cream was sent over to the high scoring ship after every round of surface target practice. By the time the task group reached Trinidad, the ship's gun crews didn't feel they had to take a back seat to anyone when it came to defending their convoy.

The excitement of the cruise did not end with building the gun tubs and target practice. In Gulf Port, when Chief Barton originally contacted the Seabees about steel and high-performance injectors, they didn't have access to anything they could give him, but they had been instrumental in locating pipe and plate steel that wouldn't be missed and helped Chief Barton and his men cut up a partially sunken derelict tuna boat that had been abandoned in the back waters of Gulf Port. They also promised him that he needn't worry about the injectors. Once they got aboard, they would make them in the machine shop and help Chief Grubowski tune them for maximum performance.

At sea, Grubowski explained what the captain wanted done. He then explained his ideas on how to make it happen. This was right up the Seabees alley, and they fell to with a will; they worked on Grubowski's engines like they were their babies. In ten days, new injectors had been fabricated and tested, an overhead fuel reservoir had been constructed and installed, modified, and enlarged exhaust stacks were waiting for an engine shut down so they could be mounted, and after modifying an Ingersoll Rand air compressor, the Seabees had built an air intake cooling box that could drop the outside air temperature as much as twenty degrees even on the hottest days.

Pride of accomplishment and increased performance were gratifying, but what really caused a stir was when Grubowski unpacked the crates Barton had brought aboard and unveiled six Federal Signal Thunderbolt air raid sirens. That in itself was odd enough, but when asked what he planned on doing with them, Grubowski said he was going to make superchargers out of them for the engines.

All a siren is, is a high-speed fan that blows large amounts of air into a tube with holes in the side. Inside that tube is another smaller tube with holes in it as well and fan blades on the ends. The air blowing through the tube causes the inside tube to spin and when the holes in both tubes match up the escaping air makes a loud wailing sound. Grubowski wasn't interested in the tubes that make the sound what he wanted were the high-speed fans. The fans on the federal sirens were special. They were known as Roots blowers. They were small in diameter and lightweight but were able to move an enormous amount of air. By using a rheostat, Grubowski knew he could adjust the speed of the fan and that would allow him to control the air pressure or PSI entering the engine. In essence, he could control the fuel and air mixture with the high-performance injectors and the rheostat and produce as much power as he wanted until the engine blew up. That was the thing Grubowski had to be careful of.

Companies that build engines with superchargers, which are also known as blowers, run countless tests to know what pressures the engines can stand. They print these limits on the engine so the operators don't exceed them. Grubowski didn't have that information, so he had to be careful and not produce too much horse power. No matter what the reason, blowing up an engine wasn't on Lieutenant Commander Cole's list of things to do.

Sailors and construction men are by nature adventurous and risk takers, but they are also practical and well-grounded in science and applied physics so when Grubowski said he could make a supercharger for the ship's engines out of air raid sirens the betting started, and Chief Barton was right in the middle of it.

Grubowski knew about the betting, and he knew almost everyone was betting against him. However, when someone would ask him a question about his blower project he would explain what he was going to do and why it would work. Generally, the person would listen to what Grubowski had to say, nod his head, and walk off just as confused as he was before he asked the question. Everything Grubowski planned to do and his reasons for doing it were out in the open, but it had no effect one way or the other on the betting.

The majority of the crew, and over half the Seabees still thought Grubowski was full of hot air and they bet heavily against him.

Even Barton, who was betting on Grubowski, was beginning to sweat the outcome of the project. Barton had all of his money, remaining "liquid" assets, and most of his escrow account tied up as collateral. But all the bets he took from the sailors, and Seabees were placed in cash and to make sure nothing "funny" happened to the cash Barton had Bill Davis build him a steel box. When Barton refused to take any more bets, he put all the cash in the box and had Bill weld it shut and bolt it to the floor in the mess hall.

Grubowski cordoned off a corner of the machine shop, hung tarps around it, and got to work. Periodically, the ear-splitting blast of an air raid siren would emanate from behind the tarps, but other than that, whatever Chief Grubowski was doing was known only to him and his helpers.

By the time the task group dropped anchor at Trinidad, Grubowski and his buddies had been finished with their project for several days. They couldn't wait for the engines to be shut down and cool, so they could get everything in place. When the engines finally cooled, Grubowski pulled the exhaust manifolds, honed all the burs out of the castings, and polished the insides like a mirror. Then the manifolds were replaced, and the oversized exhaust system was connected. When all the preliminary work was completed, Grubowski ordered everyone out of the engine room. He and his cohorts hauled in their blower equipment and worked nonstop for twelve hours straight. When they were done, they opened the water tight doors to the engine room and invited the captain and Commander Meriwether to inspect their work.

As he developed his plans for the engine modifications, Grubowski had kept Jack informed every step of the way, but even so, when Jack stepped into the engine room, he was flabbergasted. There was a huge tank in the overhead between the engines, a giant box was welded in place against the back wall of the engine room with a compressor sitting on top of it, the main induction pipes for engine air ran into the box from above and two large ducts ran, one from each side of the box to the engines where they split into three separate air ducts, each duct had what looked like a large can attached to it with electric wires running in and out, "Them there is the blowers, sir." Grubowski said when he saw Jack staring at the cans. "They's made outa the sireens we got back in Gulf Port."

An air duct ran from each can to an intake plenum on top of the engines, three ducts to each engine. The stack from each exhaust manifold was half again bigger that it had been. The engine room looked like it had been converted into some sort of Rube Goldberg contraption. But Jack had to give Grubowski credit. It was spotless, and the workmanship looked first rate. If he didn't know better, he would have sworn the new equipment looked like it had been installed during construction.

Jack stood there, looking around the engine room from the overhead to the deck and from port to starboard. When Grubowski said, "Well, sir, what do you think?" Jack realized he had been staring at the maze before him with his mouth open. He quickly snapped his jaw shut and looked to see if anyone had noticed before saying, "Bill, I've never seen anything like it!"

Grubowski just beamed. His chest swelled, and he turned to his band of helpers and said, "Ya see, guys, I told ya he'd love it!"

Jack turned to Meriwether and said, "What about you, Pete? Have you ever seen anything like this before?"

Pete stood there for a second, collecting his thoughts, stuck his hands in his pockets, looked jack in the eye, and said, "Jack, I can honestly say I've never in my life seen anything like this."

Grubowski's Seabees cheered and started slapping each other on the back. As soon as everyone calmed down, Jack said, "Bill, why don't you let everybody who has an interest see what you've done, and then let's start these engines and see what they'll do. I want to make sure you have everything tested and dialed in before we head to Africa."

Even though sailors don't salute aboard ship, Grubowski jumped to attention, snapped off a razor-sharp salute that would have made a Marine drill instructor envious, and said, "Yes, sir!"

CHAPTER 33

It took an hour for everyone to parade through the engine room and see what Grubowski and his helpers had done. When the tours were over, Bill called the bridge and told them he was ready to start the engines as soon as the captain gave the go ahead. Jack had been in his sea cabin behind the bridge and gave an immediate approval. Within a few moments, the engines rumbled to life, and Grubowski called the bridge to tell Jack he wanted a few minutes to double-check everything and let the engines warm up. Once that was taken care of, Jack gave the order to up anchor and get underway.

The Gulf of Paria is a large shallow body of water bordered by Venezuela to the west and the tiny nation of Trinidad and Tobago to the east. At its deepest, it is barely over one hundred feet deep. As a result, it is very dangerous for submarines to operate in and they avoid entering the gulf except at night and then only on the surface. Even though the chances of encountering a German U-boat were very slim, Jack still took two subchasers with him when he proceeded into the gulf to test the new engine upgrades.

The results were amazing. At flank speed, the results far exceeded Chief Grubowski's estimates. Jack found they could make just over thirteen knots without the blowers, and once the blowers were engaged, they could turn just under fifteen and a half knots. The increased performance didn't just effect their flank speed. It also allowed Jack to up their cruise speed from nine knots to ten and a half. Grubowski said in an emergency they could get more speed if he engaged all six blowers, but he was still working on adjusting the injector settings with the blower pressures, and he didn't want to risk running on all six blowers until he had a chance to work out accurate settings.

That evening, back at anchor the subchaser captains were enthusiastic about the increase in cruise speed. They said the higher cruise speed would make their ships ride more comfortably in the South Atlantic rollers. All that was left to do now was complete refueling, resupply, and rearming, and they were ready to go to Africa.

CHAPTER 34

When the convoy left Trinidad, the Navy put on quite a show to send it on its way. Knowing German U-boats dare not enter the Gulf of Paria, it was suspected that they would lie in wait where the deepwater began not far beyond Columbus Channel and the Bocas del Dragón, which were the only entrances and exits from the gulf. Jack hadn't considered the Navy would do anything different than they had when he left Gulf Port or Key West. At those locations, he had notified the harbormaster when he planned to leave, upped anchor, and away they went. As they approached the submarine nets, the net tenders pulled the nets back far enough for the ships to pass through and then closed them behind them when the convoy was clear of the nets.

At Trinidad, it was a completely different story. Because of the U-boat threat outside the nets as the eight ships of the task group neared the submarine nets, four destroyer escorts rushed past them at flank speed passing through the nets just as they were pulled open. Immediately they fanned out and started dropping depth charges over their sterns and launching them to each side via K guns. Jack had gone to battle stations once they upped anchor and ordered the convoy to flank speed. The task group passed through the submarine nets following the DEs at fifteen knots. The subchasers were already at battle stations and began to actively ping for contacts quartering ahead and alongside the LST like bird dogs searching for quail. Five miles outside the submarine nets, the DEs quit dropping depth charges. But they stayed with Jack and his ships until the convoy was on its planned course for Cape Verde 2,700 miles away.

When the escorting DEs left the convoy and swung back toward Trinidad, the flotilla leader flashed "God Speed." Jack signaled back "John 3:16," and they were on their way.

CHAPTER 35

The South Atlantic is nothing like the cold storm filled north Atlantic. Due to the close proximity to the equator, it is hot. The sun can beat down with a vengeance when there is no breeze, but fortunately, with the trade winds and the ship's speed there was always air moving across the decks and through the ship's ventilators. Unlike the rough choppy ice-cold waters of the North Atlantic, the South Atlantic is warm with long rollers, which produced a comfortable ride rather than the crashing and battering ride of the North Atlantic.

Jack had calculated a voyage of twelve days between Trinidad and Cape Verde, but that had been with a cruise speed of nine knots. With the increased engine performance, Jack had set the cruise speed at ten knots, and after running for two days at that speed, Grubowski reported he had better data on the manifold pressures and suggested Jack could increase the cruise speed to twelve knots.

In this type weather and pleasant sailing conditions, Jack knew it would be easy for the men to be lulled into a false sense of security. This put him on edge, and he constantly racked his brain to come up with ways of keeping his crew and his escorts on their toes. Target practice helped, but without tow planes, only the Seabees and sub-chasers got much excitement out of that. Drills and maintenance chores were getting old hat, and Jack was seeing a diminishing of effort so he modified the training schedule and increased the work on maintenance projects, but even with the variety, this provided he could see his men becoming more and more lackadaisical as the days went by.

All this changed however, on the seventh day of the voyage when radar reported a contact seventy-five miles out at an altitude of ten thousand feet and closing fast. All eyes were searching the sky to the north northeast on the bearing indicated by the radar plot. Finally, a large four-engine aircraft was seen outlined against a background of white cumulus clouds. At first, cheers went up from the crew thinking that because it had four engines, the plane must be an Army Air Force B-17 or B-24. But as soon as the plane came within range of the lookouts and their binoculars, swastikas could be seen on the wings and tail. It was a Focke-Wulf Fw-200, and no one cheered about that.

Lufthansa, the German national airline, ran regular currier and passenger flights to South America using the long-range Focke-Wulf Fw-200 Condor. That could be bad news because anything spotted by Lufthansa would be reported to the Kriegsmarine and would probably result in routing U-boats or surface raiders to intercept the convoy. The other danger was the Luftwaffe also used the Focke-Wulf Condor for long-range reconnaissance and as an attack aircraft. The Luftwaffe version of the Condor was fast, heavily armed, and carried a bomb load big enough to sink anything up to the size of a cruiser.

As the plane approached, it began to climb and changed course so as not to pass directly over the convoy. To Jack, this meant the aircraft was a Lufthansa plane and would not be attacking. It appeared to avoid the convoy in order to stay out of range of the ship's anti-aircraft guns. The Condor then circled the task group twice before returning to its original heading and disappearing over the horizon. From here on, Jack had no problem keeping his men on their toes.

Over the next several days, reports of submarine periscope sightings were rampant and not just aboard the LST. The subchasers had the jitters too, and anytime someone aboard a subchaser thought they saw a periscope, the little ship went to battle stations, began active pinging, and charged off in the direction of the sighting. A few spouting whales got beat up by depth charges, but no actual contacts were made on enemy submarines.

In addition to false periscope sightings, every odd coloration of cloud on the horizon was reported as funnel gas and the entire convoy went to battle stations in anticipation of an attack by a surface raider. The thought of meeting a German raider was constantly on

Jack's mind. The reality was if they ran into a surface raider, they had no chance at all. The German pocket battleships carried eleven-inch guns and were so much faster than the ships of the convoy they could run circles around them. It would be a slaughter. The commerce raiders the Germans sent to sea had six-inch guns, and even though they were only slightly faster than the convoy, they could still stand off at any range they chose and pick off the ships one at a time. The only defense Jack could think of was a smokescreen to disappear in or if he got lucky a rain squall he might be able to duck into, but the weather had been fair since leaving Trinidad, and he felt there was little chance of a squall coming up just when he needed one. As a result, Jack reviewed his plans for deploying a smoke screen and made sure each vessel thoroughly checked their smoke generators to guarantee they would work when and if needed.

Jack was losing sleep, he was losing weight, and his nerves were constantly on edge. He felt like he was falling apart. However, to the crew, he looked calm, almost detached as he went about the business of managing the convoy operations. Watching Jack as he carried out his duties inspired the younger officers who tried to emulate his relaxed, but confident demeanor. To them, it was not unlike whistling when you walked past a graveyard. They appeared calm on the outside but were quaking on the inside. To Jack, it was like living in a pressure cooker.

Finally on day 9 of the voyage, a PBY out of Cape Verde was spotted. PBYs stayed with the task group in relays until they made port on day 10 of their voyage. When the convoy passed through the submarine nets and anchored safely in the harbor at Mindelo, Jack reported in and returned to his cabin where he slept like he had died.

Forty-eight hours later, Admiral Bryton learned Jack had arrived in Cape Verde two days earlier than anticipated. He handed the message to Commander Johnson and said, "Look into this. Someone must have their dates screwed up. There is no way Cole could be in Mindelo two days early. Find out what's going on."

CHAPTER 36

After refueling, Jack pulled out of Mindelo the same evening he arrived and set sail for Tenerife in the Canaries Islands—a nine-hundred-mile trip that should have taken a little over four days at nine knots but took just over three days cruising at twelve knots. The trip north along the west coast of Africa was completed without incident primarily due to the air patrols conducted by the Army Air Force out of the Canaries and occupied Morocco but also because of the heavy antisubmarine surface patrols guarding the shipping lanes from South Africa to England.

The convoy arrived in Casablanca a little over a month after Operation Torch, the invasion of North Africa. As Jack pulled into the anchorage signs of the damage were still evident. Most of the warehouses and buildings along the waterfront bore the scares of battle; many were without roofs, others were nothing more than collapsed piles of rubble, and still more showed signs of fire damage and pock marks from shell fragments and bullets.

The harbor was littered with damaged or destroyed French warships. At a quick glance, Jack saw one battleship sunk at its moorings, a beached cruiser reduced to nothing more than a burned-out hulk, and the superstructures of several destroyers and submarines protruding from the water at various places in and around the harbor. It was a somber sight for the men of the LST as they dropped anchor. The war wasn't just a newspaper article or a newsreel at the theater anymore; it was real, and it looked and smelled nothing like it did in the movies.

After reporting in and filing his report on Operation Fountain, Jack was about to return to the ship when he was handed a message from the civilian harbormaster to pull alongside the cargo pier and begin landing the Seabee battalion. When Jack arrived back aboard, he found that an admiral and a Seabee Captain had arrived while he was gone and were waiting on the bridge for him. Both men wanted to observe the unloading and find out firsthand what an LST was all about. Jack conned the ship alongside the cargo pier and beached her just as he had done at Gulf Port. The bow doors were opened, the ramp was lowered, and the first vehicles were just driving ashore when Jack received a radio call from the harbormaster. Since he was occupied, Jack had the radio call transferred to the bridge speaker so he could talk while he continued to work.

Not being familiar with an LST, the harbormaster had determined Jack had run his ship aground as he was trying to dock. As soon as the bridge talker acknowledged that the captain was listening, a Frenchman speaking heavily accented English began a scathing tirade about Jack running his ship aground while trying to dock and how his poor seamanship was going to cost the harbormaster days of delays in unloading while they tried to pull his ship free of the beach. Before the man could finish, Jack reached for the handset on the bulkhead, but the admiral grabbed it first, turned to Jack, and said, "May I?" He then proceeded to give the harbormaster a chewing out like Jack hadn't heard since a truck backed into the holding pen at Stamwell's Livestock Auction House and let one hundred head of wild winter range cattle loose in Walnut Hill.

When the admiral was finished, he calmly hung the handset back in its holder and said, "Thank you, Commander. That f——g French a——s h——e has been nothing but a pain in my a——s since we got here, and I appreciate the opportunity to be on the righteous side of an argument with that little s——t for once. I hope you didn't mind me butting in."

"No, sir, not at all," Jack said. "If you don't mind my saying so, I believe that is the finest a——s chewing I've heard in a long time… Maybe ever."

"Well…ahem…Thank you, Commander," the admiral said. "I came up through the ranks. It's been awhile, but I'm glad to see I haven't lost my touch."

CHAPTER 37

Jack spent the next several months operating out of Casablanca running supplies up and down the Moroccan coast, into the Mediterranean, and to ports in North Africa supplying Patton's seventh army as it fought its way east against Rommel. This allowed stateside mail to finally catch up with the ship. For the first time since leaving Evansville, the crew received letters and packages from home. For most, it was like Christmas. For some, it was just another day, and for a few unlucky sailors who received a "Dear John" letter, mail call was a black day indeed.

Not having any close family members to correspond with Jack was surprised to find he had received a sizable stack of letters. He placed them in calendar order and sorted them into piles he mentally categorized as Navy, business, and personal. The superintendent in him would not allow him to read the personal letters until he had finished all his business so he set to, plowed through the Navy correspondence, wrote the necessary replies, and waded into the business mail. He was disappointed to find most of these were from the Nebraska State Board of Education and the local school board pertaining to his abrupt departure from the Walnut Hill Unified School District. He had written to both organizations shortly after taking command of his ship explaining what had taken place so after reading the first few he set the remainder aside without opening them. This left the personal pile. When he was sorting his mail, he noticed several letters were addressed to him in decidedly feminine hand writing. He set those aside and worked his way through the remainder of his personal mail. These letters were from his church, the various service organizations he belonged to, clubs, etc. All wishing him well, thanking him for coming to the defense of the country, notifying him of upcoming meetings and the like. When he was done with these, he picked up the small pile of letters remaining with great anticipation wondering who could be writing him.

The letters were from Jeannie Evans, Angie Jenkins, Helen Brant, and Annette Bouchard.

Jack opened each letter in chronological order. To say he was surprised by the content of the letters would be a major understatement. Jack had no idea Jeannie, Angie, or Helen had the feelings for him they expressed in their letters. Jack had asked the women to local events like the Lady's club ice cream social, church hay rides, Elks Club, Kiwanis, and Eagles dances. He'd invited each one to the movies on occasion and taken them out to dinner, but beyond a peck on the cheek, none of them had shown "that" kind of interest in his attentions, and he had come to view them more like "good" friends. But the content of their letters revealed how badly he had misread them. Each letter was slightly more intimate than the last until Jack could feel his face flush from what was implied.

Jack had always thought of Jeannie as lots of fun but rather prim and proper. Angie seemed to him to be something of a tomboy in crinoline, very outgoing, but perhaps a little shy. He had suspected that Helen could be very passionate but was reserved and under control at all times as if it wasn't polite to show emotion.

Obviously, Jack had no insight into the female mind. Jeannie's comment that she looked forward to his return with great anticipation and her suggestion that "it would be nice to have a picnic at Turner Lake with a dip in the lake to follow" set his imagination to envisioning her wearing something other than a dress or slacks—a not altogether unpleasant sight.

Angie was a little more foreword in her letters. She said she was looking forward to his return. She always enjoyed the hay rides he invited her on but thought she would enjoy them even more if there weren't so many people around so they could do a little "snuggling under the hay."

Helen's letters were more detailed regarding what she thought would be fun to do once Jack returned home. He had guessed right when he thought she could be passionate but missed the mark entirely when he thought she would be too reserved and polite to show any emotion. Among other things, she suggested that they would have a lot of fun if they went to Des Moines, Iowa, and attended the Iowa State Fair where as she put it, "No one would recognize us and we could share a room to cut down on expenses." Helen had several other ideas, all of which required traveling far enough from Walnut Hill that no one would know them, and they could "let their hair down."

While those letters were full of promise of one sort or another the letters that he valued the most were from Annette. Her letters were more intimate; she opened herself up and shared her feelings about her family and friends, what was going on in the little community of Pilottown and what was happening around the gulf and up the river to New Orleans and beyond. Her letters were full of warmth and humor that wasn't apparent in the letters from Jeannie, Angie, and Helen. Annette made him feel like he was there in Pilottown as a member of the community participating in everything that occurred. In short, he felt like he was a part of Pilottown in ways he had never been a part of Walnut Hill.

Somewhere he had heard the term "dofer," which was a name given to a person who liked to do things for people—a dofer. In Walnut Hill, Jack was a dofer. He did things for people, all sorts of things for all sorts of people. He enjoyed doing these things, but after reading the letters from Annette, he realized that was all he was in Walnut Hill, a person who did things for people. Thinking about it, he never got invited anywhere just to attend an activity. He was there because he was asked to help organize the event or run it. People always came up and talked to him and were very pleasant and fun to be with, but the conversations always started because of some issue regarding the planning or organization of the activity. In other words, "Is everything going to be ready to go when we start?" never how are you doing. Even Jeannie, Angie, and Helen's letters were about what he could do for them. They were things that would be fun, but the way the women discussed them seemed shallow and self-serving, almost like a business arrangement was being proposed. They didn't even ask him how he was doing and if he was okay.

Annette's letters were about life, about her feelings, about what was happening in Pilottown, and how events affected her life and the lives of those in her family and the community. She wanted to know all about what he was doing, what he thought about this and that, and she reveled in being able to tell him about things which were indirectly caused by something he or one of his men had said or done. Even though they were on the other side of the world, Jack and the men of *LST 121* were thought of as part of the community and in Jack's case a part of the Bouchard family. Not once in any of her letters did Annette ask anything of him, she shared things with him without demanding anything in return and always passed along the thoughts and good wishes of her family and the friends he had made in Pilottown. Each letter ended with the admonition "Take care and don't let anything happen to you. You are cared for very deeply."

The ship had no sailing orders for the next two days, so Jack declared the following afternoon would be a ship's holiday with a dinner and entertainment on the main deck. Almost as an after-thought, he added, "Guests may be invited."

Based on their experience with past ship's holidays and Operation Charleston, the crew fell to with a will. The only question Jack received was from Lieutenant Purvis who asked if the same pro-tocols would apply to the dinner and entertainment as those applied at Pilottown. After thinking about it for a moment, Jack replied, "Yes, with the exception that all activities will be restricted to the dock and main deck. No one will be allowed access to any part of the ship other than the main deck."

Purvis replied, "Yes, sir! What about…ahem…ladies facilities, sir?"

For a split second, Jack thought, *What are you talking about?* But then, it dawned on him the ship had been in and out of Casablanca enough times for the men to have made contact with the locals, and since he had allowed guests to be invited, there was the possibility some women may be coming aboard.

He'd announced guests were welcome. It was too late to change that so he dodged the question by asking, "What do you have in mind, Mr. Purvis?"

"Well, sir, I thought we might designate the officer's head as a ladies…ah…powder room, sir. We could erect a barricade across the companion way beyond the door to the officer's head and lock all cabin doors between the main deck entry and the barricade."

"Good thinking, Mr. Purvis. Make it so," Jack replied. He'd read that "make it so" line in a C. S. Forrester novel he was reading and liked the sound of it. Apparently, Lieutenant Purvis did too. He replied, "Aye, aye, sir!" turned and left with a spring in his step.

Looking back on it, Jack admitted to himself he should have gotten more involved in the details of organizing the dinner and entertainment, but he had a good crew, and he trusted his officers and men to get things done based on their past performance. Jack was right to trust his officers and men to get things done. They were hard workers, forthright, and enterprising, representing the best of what being an American was all about. The only thing Jack failed to take into consideration was just how enterprising they could be and how well they could get things done.

The following morning, the main deck was crammed with men touching up the paint work, hanging lights, stringing Chinese lanterns, erecting tables, setting up chairs, cordoning off a dance floor, and building a band stand. There were even men over the side in bosun's chairs painting over the rust stains beneath the ship's drains and along the waterline. The band stand should have tipped Jack off that things were accelerating quickly and fast growing into an event far beyond what he had originally intended. But the enthusiasm of the men and the obvious pride they were taking in their ship and what they were doing was contagious, and Jack fell into the festive mood that permeated the ship.

The first hint Jack got that things might be getting out of hand came when Yoeman Vickers began relaying messages of acceptance to him. They came from Admiral Hunt, the port admiral, the skipper of the USS *Tuscaloosa*, the chief of staff of II Corps, the head of medical services at the Casablanca army hospital, the proprietor of the Anfa Hotel, the commanding officer and chief surgeon of the Navy hospital ship USS Relief, and many more. Somehow every major military unit, American and allied, and the head of every department in the city government had been invited to the ship's holiday and were eager to attend. In Jack's mind, there was only one possible explanation.

A few moments later, an announcement over the ship's PA interrupted the work on the main deck. "Now hear this, now hear this. Chief Barton is to report to the captain's cabin immediately. I repeat, Chief Barton is to report to the captain's cabin immediately. That is all."

Following a brief discussion with the chief in Jack's cabin an all call went out for Boatswain Gardener, Lieutenant Purvis, Chief Grubowski, Ensign Price, and ship's cook, Bill Spence, to report to the ward room.

After the men arrived and the door to the ward room was closed, a person in the companion way outside the door would have heard many voices participating in a general discussion. However, there was one voice that was conspicuous by its absence from the conversation, and that was Jack's. After his opening comment, "Okay, you guys fill me in." The only contribution he made was an occasional "Uh-huh" or "Why?"

As it turned out, whatever it was that made Barton tick was rubbing off on the rest of the crew. Lieutenant Purvis coordinated the effort, but each man had pretty much used their own initiative and made arrangements, cut deals, and finagled the system so that that evening beginning at 1700 hours, baring an air raid, the biggest ship's holiday in the history of ship's holidays was about to occur aboard USS *LST 121*.

Adhering strictly to regulations barring alcohol aboard United States Navy vessels, cocktails would be served on the dock alongside. Chief Barton had gone to great lengths to acquire a plethora of empty whiskey bottles of all types which would be refilled and used to serve the finest he had to offer from his reserves in the escrow account. He had even gone to the trouble of acquiring food coloring, which would be added to the moonshine in an effort to differentiate bourbon from rye, brandy from scotch, and blended whiskey from malt whiskey.

As he said, "H——l after the first drink, nobody will be able to tell the difference by taste, but they'll sure as h——l remember what color it was."

Which, when Jack thought about it, was probably true. He just hoped Barton wouldn't run out of food coloring.

Promptly at 1800 hours, the attendees would be called to dinner aboard ship where they would dine under the stars served by the maître d' and his service staff from the Anfa Hotel in exchange for a ten-gallon Navy coffee urn and one hundred pounds of sugar. Bill Spence said the coffee urn was one he got in a three-way swap between a tank destroyer unit, a signal battalion, and a fighter squadron. He had to take it in order to get the sugar, so as he said, "We didn't lose nothin' in the deal."

The floor show would begin at 1930 hours and would include belly dancing and an exhibition of sword swallowing provided by the mayor of Casablanca in an attempt to curry favor from the Allied forces occupying his town. Lieutenant Purvis said he let him off easy; he only charged him five get-out-of-jail free passes so if anybody had a man get tossed in the hoosegow, they should let him know. Short of murder, he could get him off scot free.

Following the floor show, the USS *Tuscaloosa* band would perform dance music from the libraries of Glenn Miller, Tommy Dorsey, Benny Goodman, Charlie Barnett, and many other swing bands. According to Ensign Price, the skipper of the *Tuscaloosa* thought that was the least he could do for the generous gift of twenty gallons of ice cream his ship received.

The dance floor would be a teak parquet unit laid over the steel of the main deck and polished to a high gloss. The chief of staff of II Corps heard about the dance from the commanding officer of the Army's Sixth General Hospital who had been invited and planned to attend taking as many of his nurses with him as he could. The II Corps chief of staff had his eye on one of the Sixth General Hospital nurses and decided he wanted to attend. When Grubowski heard about it through the II Corps motor pool he let it be known they were in need of something better than a steel deck to dance on. After working its way up and down the sergeant's network the dance floor was removed from the ball room in the hotel II Corps occupied as their headquarters, trucked to the ship, and the chief of staff got his invitation.

The 202nd MP Company provided traffic control, security, and valet parking in return for the donation of two gallons of Tennessee sippin' whiskey and six gallons of ice cream. Boat's said, "Those MPs are right, guys, but they're d———n poor poker players. With a few more hands I could a got 'em for nothin', but I had ta get back to the ship."

Fresh beef, potatoes and vegetables were provided by the officers of the 304th Army commissary Battalion for the privilege of attending. Spence said, "H———l they called me and practically begged. What else was I supposed to do?"

And last, but far from least every allied Army, Navy, and Red Cross unit commander was invited as long as he or she agreed to bring at least ten nurses with them.

Following the summary of events Jack leaned back in his chair, crossed his arms over his chest, and stared at the smiling faces of the men before him. They were proud of what they had accomplished in such a short time and each one of them was positive their actions were well within the parameters of their individual authority and in full compliance with the expectations Jack had of them.

Jack just sat there and smiled at his men while shaking his head and said, "Very well, it seems like you gentlemen have thought of everything and have everything under control. Carry on."

The ward room emptied in a flash, and Jack sat there contemplating whether he had built the finest crew a skipper could ask for or created a monster.

CHAPTER 38

The evening got off to a grand start. The men of the 202nd were dressed in their finest. When a vehicle pulled up at the head of the pier, the guests were greeted by big strapping MPs, each well over six feet tall, dressed in their class A uniform, with white MP helmets, white gloves, white leggings, and yellow foulards. They were an imposing presence. Wearing their .45s holstered and attached to lanyards, billy clubs at the ready they gave those attending the impression that *LST 121*'s ship's holiday was as an extremely important event warranting security as tight as or tighter than it had been for Churchill and Roosevelt at the Casablanca Conference held a few months earlier. In a manner of speaking, this event *was* more important, at least to Jack's men. The Casablanca Conference only involved Roosevelt and Churchill. Tonight's ship's holiday would involve women. In the men's minds, the scale of importance definitely leaned toward the women.

Attendees didn't just come by land. The first ship's boat to arrive was that of the USS *Tuscaloosa*. In addition to her skipper, officers, and the ship's band, they had stopped along the way and picked up what would be the first of several boat loads of Navy nurses from the USS *Relief*. The nurses were allowed to board first. Each one was met at the head of the accommodation ladder by one of Jack's men who offered their arm and escorted the nurses across the deck and down the starboard ladder to the dock where cocktails were being served. The *Tuscaloosa*'s officers and the band were summarily ignored and left to their own devices to get aboard.

The admiral and his staff arrived at the same time as a six-by-six filled with nurses from the Sixth General Hospital. Even though he was in full uniform, ribbons and gold braid included, the admiral was just another swabby to the MPs as they helped the nurses from the truck and escorted them to the head of the pier. The general from II Corps and his staff were greeted in the same manner as the admiral so at least the MPs weren't showing any partiality to one branch of the service over the other.

The MPs were really on their game. They arrived early and cordoned off a huge section of the wharf to use for parking. This made it easier for them to park and retrieve vehicles and to keep an eye out for any light fingered locals. When asked by the mayor of Casablanca why all the extra precautions were being taken about the parking an MP looked him square in the eye and said, "If we don't watch out them d———n Arabs (he pronounced Arab like Ahab from *Moby Dick*) will steal anything that ain't set in concrete. The mayor tried to look indignant, but finally shrugged, nodded his head in agreement, and handed the sergeant five dollars in script and asked him to keep a special eye on his Citron.

Chief Barton was doing a land office business. He set up at the end of the dock and had his men rig a cargo boom from the ship out over the bar. He hung a sign on the boom that from a distance appeared to read LST. However, when the party goers got closer they saw it actually read Lost Souls Tavern below which was a smaller sign that read, DRINKS $.10 PER SHOT LADIES DRINK FREE. What he didn't advertise was that all the ladies drinks were doubles. With drinks going for $.25 a shot ashore, Barton's prices were ridiculously low, and the party goers drank like fish. With his overhead practically zero, Barton was making a killing.

Jack watched from the starboard bridge wing as the crowd grew and mingled on the dock below. He noted that Lieutenant Purvis had rigged cargo netting around the pier to prevent any of the party goers from taking an unintentional swim and also noticed that as people started to climb the accommodation ladder to the main deck Lieutenant Davis and Ensign Wesley had positioned themselves at the top of the ladder to politely remind the guests that liquor was not allowed aboard United States Naval Vessels.

When Jack saw Admiral Hunt ascending the ladder with a glass in his hand, he sensed a problem was about to occur and stepped toward the bridge ladder to dash to the main deck. Before he could begin his decent, Ensign Wesley stepped forward and took charge of the situation.

"Good evening, Admiral. We are extremely pleased that you have joined us this evening. If you don't mind, I'll take that drink for you. No liquor is allowed aboard Unite States Naval vessels, and our ship's holiday is no exception."

As Wesley reached for the admiral's glass, the admiral pulled it up and away out of Wesley's immediate reach and said in a very slurred voice, "Ensign, I'll have you know I am in command of this port. I not only outrank you, but I've been in this man's Navy since 1923."

Wesley never batted an eye. He reached for the admiral's glass, took it from his hand, threw the contents overboard, and handed the empty glass back to the astonished admiral, saying, "Excellent, sir. Then I don't need to tell you the importance of setting a good example for the enlisted men. I'm sure they will be encouraged by your demonstration of leadership."

The admiral leaned back threw out his chest and said, "Ahem... That is correct, Ensign. We must set a good example for the men. I congratulate you on your attention to duty! Ah...Carry on." Then the admiral turned to the nurse accompanying him and said, "This way, Jennifer. This young man has a job to do."

As the admiral walked by with the lovely Jennifer on his arm, she gave Wesley a look that was the most blatant invitation Jack had ever seen a woman give a man. When she turned away, Wesley glanced up at the bridge, and Jack gave him a thumbs-up.

The guests were piped to dinner promptly at 1800 hours by the ringing of the ship's bell and an all call over the ship's PA announcing, "Dinner is served. Please make your way to seats on the main deck."

Immediately following the PA announcement, someone began to blow mess call on a trumpet from someplace near the forward 40 mm. twin mount. The second time through the call everyone joined in and sang, "Piggy, piggy, piggy, come and eat your slop. Piggy, piggy, piggy, come and eat your slop," along with the trumpeter. Jack happened to glance in the direction of the skipper of the *Tuscaloosa* at the time and watched him turn nine shades of red before grabbing one of his officers and sending him forward to find the prankster in the band.

Jack silently shook his head and thought, *Ah the joys of command.*

Once everyone was done milling around and had seated themselves Jack left the bridge, stepped up onto the band stand, introduced himself, and began to speak. "Admiral, General, *mesdames et messieurs,* ladies and gentlemen welcome aboard USS *LST 121,* one of the first of her kind to join the fleet. She is a good ship with a fine crew. This evenings ship's holiday is a celebration of that crew, and the work they have done here in North Africa a long, long, way from their homes in the United States. For security reasons, no one will be allowed below deck. However, feel free to tour the main deck at your leisure, you will find the door ways and hatches are all locked with the exception of the hatchway in the superstructure which leads to the ladies...ah...powder room."

At this point, Admiral Hunt jumped up and holding his water glass high said, "Let's hope they don't blow up the ship."

That got a big laugh, and after acknowledging the applause and laughter with several bows of his head, he sat back down.

Jack went on, "Yes, Admiral, I'm sure we all share those sentiments. As I was saying, you will find the hatches and doorways locked. Please honor our security measures. As you know during war time espionage is punishable by firing squad, and we have some very good shots aboard this ship."

That got a little chuckle; however, Jack did not smile before, during, or after he said it.

Jack continued, "In closing, I'd like to say once again, please enjoy yourselves. This is a ship's holiday. It was earned by the men of my crew. You are their guests, not mine. Please acknowledge that as you mix and mingle. Now, before we enjoy this evening's fine meal, let me say one final thing. As captain of this ship, I am authorized to perform marriages at sea. However, we are in port so my authority in that regard ended at the submarine nets. Please do not ask me to make any exceptions. Thank you."

The last comment brought a huge roar from the partygoers and a grand round of applause.

The meal was a huge success. Bill Spence and his staff out did themselves and were brought up on the band stand for recognition. From forward, a trumpet blew charge, and the crowd cheered. Bill and his men accepted the accolades with bows and left the stage. The captain of the *Tuscaloosa* shot a withering look at his executive officer who immediately jumped up grabbed another officer and both men went forward one on each side of the forward 40 mm. gun tub.

As ice cream was being served, the floor show began. The mayor of Casablanca introduced the dancers and sword swallower in very good English and gave a running dialogue of what the various belly dancing movements meant. As part of the show, he encouraged any-one who wanted to try it to come up on the stage so the dancers could instruct them on the various techniques. Obviously, he had hoped to entice one or more of the nurses to participate, but instead a dozen of Boat's deck apes charged the stage peeling off their dress blue jackets and tossing them aside as they clambered up on the band stand.

The resulting antics on the stage brought peals of laughter from everyone especially the participants. Finally, when the sailors began to get to aggressive in response to the dancers running their hands over the men's stomachs, the mayor ended that part of the show and brought on the sword swallower. While the sword swallower was entertaining the crowd, the *Tuscaloosa*'s band began to set up behind him. With the lights trained on the man with the swords it was hard to see the band members in the background. But Jack noticed the two officers from the *Tuscaloosa* that had gone forward earlier stand-ing to one side of the stage on either side of a man holding a trumpet. The officers looked rather perturbed, but the trumpet player had a look on his face like he didn't have a care in the world. Obviously he was a reservist, probably drafted from one of the big bands just wait-ing for the war to get over so he could get back on the road.

When the sword swallower was done and the applause died away, the band began to play and they were good. The trumpet player wasn't the only one Jack suspected of being drafted from a really good dance band. They had a trombone player that was as good as any Jack had ever heard, live or on the radio, and the piano player was no one to be sneezed at.

Soon, the dance floor was filled with people swaying to the music. Jack noticed that there was a steady stream of couples going to and returning from the dock. The Lost Souls Tavern was still drawing a crowd.

The longer the band played the larger the crowd on the dance floor grew until it was filled to overflowing with people dancing everything from the Fox Trot to the Jitter Bug. It was one giant swaying, throbbing mass of people crammed together writhing to the music. That's when the air raid sirens began to howl and the lights of Casablanca died turning the African port into a black ink spot on the Atlantic coast.

The moment the air raid sirens went off, all the ship's lights were killed, and the klaxon for battle stations blared throughout the ship. The crew was quick to spring to their battlestations, in some cases embarrassingly quick. Gunner's Mate 2c Herman York jumped over the gun tub splinter shield to dive into his pointer director's seat on the forward twin 40 mm. guns, only to find it was already occupied. He spun the seat around, saying, "Hit the road this seat is taken," and found a wide-eyed young couple staring back at him. The man was without his tunic, wearing only his undershirt and skivvies, his face was smeared with lipstick, and the young nurse sitting across his lap was naked from the waist up wearing only a very skimpy pair of panties.

When York landed out of nowhere from the inky blackness and spun the seat around, the young lady began screaming and jumped off the man's lap trying to cover herself as best she could with her hands while searching frantically for her skirt and tunic all the while staring in wide-eyed terror at Herman. Not able to think of anything more appropriate to say or do York pulled off his helmet and thrust it into her hands so she could cover her naked breasts saying, "Here, ma'am, I think you need this more than I do right now."

As crew members jumped from the deck to the port side 20 mm. gun platform a pair of naked bottoms, which appeared startlingly white in the moonlight, were seen to run up the forward gun platform access ladder and disappear behind the port booby hatch. On the stern the starboard 40 mm. single mount traverse gears were temporarily jammed by what turned out later to be a pair of silk stockings and a size 7 woman's pump with very stylish metal buckles. Initially when the gun crews on both port side quad .50 cal. machinegun turrets could not see through their ring sights they thought they had been sabotaged. Luckily, it only took them a second to determine nothing was wrong with the sights; they were just obscured by loose clothing which had been draped across the guns and abandoned for reasons known only to the former owners of the garments in question.

The air raid turned out to be a single German snooper which had flown in under the radar and popped up to make a pass over the harbor.

Jack's ship was tied to the pier in the southeast corner of the harbor next to the dry dock. When the alert was sounded, the snooper came roaring in from the northeast on a course that would take it directly over Jack's LST. It made its way unscathed past the ships at anchor in the harbor and those tied up to the piers and wharfs. That made Jack's ship the last ship the plane would fly over before making its escape. Where the Naval warships had been taken by surprise and did not have time to man their anti-aircraft defenses Jack's men were ready and waiting as the Dornier Do 17 came speeding toward them. The Luftwaffe pilot and his crew never had a chance. Honed to a sharp edge by all the anti-aircraft practice they had done; every portside gun opened fire as soon as the plane was in range. The Dornier was caught in the center of a spider web of converging tracer fire and immediately burst into flames. As it passed over the ship, the starboard guns engaged. What had been a burning aircraft was turned into a blazing inferno and exploded showering the Bourgogne district of Casablanca with scorched wreckage.

The lights in Casablanca quickly came back on, and the sirens stopped their wailing. Things happened so fast that when the ship's lights came back on, the dance floor was still filled with couples, and the band was still playing "A Hot Time in the Old Town Tonight," which everyone later agreed was a very appropriate tune for the events which had just transpired.

Those who realized what had taken place began to head for the accommodation ladders, others soon followed, and the party broke up. The following morning, during clean up, many interesting things were discovered from the night before. For instance, a major general's tunic was discovered with red lipstick stains on the collar. It was returned to II Corps rolled up in a chart tube and marked II CORPS CHIEF OF STAFF—GENERAL'S EYES ONLY. A large box of Navy nurses apparel was gathered up and sent to the USS *Relief* care of the head of nursing. All clothing with laundry tags identifying the owner and/or unit was returned to where it belonged. The remaining odds and ends such as garments without tags, items which were gender neutral, and paraphernalia of indeterminate service origin were gathered up and tossed into the ship's slop chest. As one of the men put it, "It's a good idea to hang on to all this stuff. You just never know when you might need a size 9 left shoe or a khaki field scarf to turn the tide of battle."

The only item not returned to its owner or tossed into the slop chest was a pair of pink ladies panties, which were found in the shower in the officer's head/ladies powder room. Jack made the command decision to add those to the ship's collection of war prizes along with the brassieres that had fluttered down on them from the Ben Humphreys Bridge.

Once the cleanup was finished and all lost items returned, the ship was ready for business as usual. Jack filed his after-action report and pulled out of Casablanca that evening with a load of lumber, pipe, construction vehicles, and oil well control valves. They were routed to Tunis and ordered to wait for further orders once they arrived.

CHAPTER 39

The trip up the coast through the night was quiet and uneventful. Jack had made this trip many times and choose to stay close in-shore as he moved along the coast. He didn't like the fact that the ship's silhouette was backlit by the lights ashore at night, but he only drew a little over eight feet forward and fourteen feet aft. His shallow draft even when fully loaded allowed him to stay in waters too shallow for submarines to operate submerged and in shore far enough to be well out of torpedo range.

An hour after dawn of the following day found them just north of Asilah and the Caves of Hercules nearing the approaches to the Straits of Gibraltar. When a small aircraft was sighted heading toward them, Jack immediately went to battle stations. As the plane approached, he could see it was a high winged olive drab monoplane sporting US Army Air Corps roundels. Back home in Walnut Hill, the plane would have been yellow with a black lightning bolt running down each side. It was a Piper J-3, better known as a Cub, and in the Army, it was referred to as an L-4.

The Piper Cub was one of the most useful small aircraft currently flying. The Cub could land just about anywhere and take off again. It couldn't carry a lot of weight, but it could haul two adults and as much equipment as could be piled in with the passenger and it could be flown from either the front seat or the rear seat. Ranchers used them in lieu of horses to keep an eye on their herds, mend fence, and run errands on the range. They even used them to keep the coyote population down by hunting the coyotes from the air, firing out of the side door of the little planes.

The plane circled the ship and made a pass just over the LST's superstructure. It dropped a capsule tied to a streamer, which landed on top of a load of pipe on the main deck. The capsule was retrieved immediately and brought to the bridge. It contained a message that read,

U-boat sighted five miles ahead bearing 325
degrees your position. Aircraft on way.

Jack read the message then asked radar if they had spotted anything. The report came back negative so Jack knew the sub was running submerged. The Army L-4 must have spotted the sub's periscope or seen its outline under water.

The ship was still at battlestations, all lookouts were aware of the sub warning, and Mr. Jensen had his gunners primed and ready. Jack was too far in shore to be worried about a torpedo attack from a submerged submarine but not out of range of a U-boat's deck guns. Jack thought it very unlikely that a U-boat commander would risk his ship by attacking on the surface in daylight; even this early in the morning. But when the lookouts reported a disturbance on the surface at eight thousand yards on the port side Jack had second thoughts.

A submarine is an extremely dangerous vessel; however, there are two moments when a submarine is completely blind and helpless. Those times are when it is committed to surfacing or committed to diving. In both cases, until a sub can open its hatches and man its deck guns or completely submerge and get underway it can't see, hear, or fight. As soon as the top of the conning tower broke water, Mr. Jensen opened fire. Jack ordered full speed, and Grubowski gave the engines everything he thought they could stand. The hail of flak from the 40 mm. and 20 mm. anti-aircraft guns and the .50 caliber rounds bouncing off the conning tower and pressure hull drove the sub back down while Jack and his ship departed the area at fifteen knots.

The U-boat captain must have been counting on surprise. If Jack had not been warned by the L-4, his men would not have been at battle stations. This would have given the U-boat plenty of time to surface and man its guns while Jack was calling his crew to battle stations. If that had occurred, the U-boat would have been able to put several shells into its target, submerge, and be gone in fifteen minutes or less with plenty of time to exit the area before ships or aircraft could respond. However, with the unexpected surprise, the U-boat commander received when trying to surface there was no way his men could man the deck guns. The U-boat commander was lucky to get away.

Approximately fifteen minutes after the engagement, a pair of Army Air Corps P-38s came screaming overhead and disappeared toward the last known location of the sub. Thirty minutes later, a B-24 flew past at about four thousand feet heading in the same direction as the P-38s.

Being in combat two days in a row had the crew wound tighter than a watch spring. Shooting down a German bomber and firing on a U-boat was more action than anyone aboard ship ever expected to see, and the men were walking on air. The men in the paint shop made a sign and hung it on the bulkhead in the mess hall next to Murderer's Row. It was titled "Victims," and a German bomber wearing a swastika was painted below the sign. Right next to it, the men painted a submarine with a big question mark painted in the middle of it. Just to make sure the rest of the Navy knew about their combat success, the same images were painted on the port and starboard sides of the bridge like the kills recorded by fighter pilots and painted below their cockpits. It was good to see his men were proud of their accomplishments; they should be, but Jack wondered what kind of trouble their swagger was going to cause in the bars and night spots when his men got to bragging about their combat record with other ship's crews and Army units sitting within ear shot. After thinking about it for a little while, he thought, *To h——l with it, whatever happens, happens.* His crew should be proud, and they deserve to be a little cocky. He looked at it like the years when the Walnut Hill football team or basketball team won the conference championship. Everything went smoother for the rest of the school year, whereas nothing seemed to go quite right for the rest of the year when the school had a losing season. Jack figured he'd just have to make sure

Mr. Purvis ran his taxi service with a few extra men along as muscle, just in case.

The remainder of the voyage to Tunis was completed without incident. In his after-action report, Jack credited the Army L-4 with preventing damage to or destruction of his ship by sighting the submarine and alerting them to its presence. Jack also made a mental note to find out what unit the L-4 was attached to and send them a couple of gallons of "Thank You Juice" out of the escrow account.

CHAPTER 40

Two days after the engagement with the U-boat, Commander Johnson laid an after-action report on Admiral Bryton's desk. The admiral glanced at it and said, "What the h——l do I want with an after-action report from North Africa, Johnson?"

"You still want everything that comes in about Commander Cole, don't you, sir?" Johnson asked.

"You're d——n right I do. What's this got to do with Cole?" Bryton snarled.

"He and his men shot down a German bomber at Casablanca." Then Johnson set another after-action report on top of the first one. "They also fought a surface engagement with a U-boat outside the Straits of Gibraltar, sir. It appears they contributed substantially to its sinking. Cole and his men knocked a hole in one of its fuel tanks, the Air Corps followed the oil slick, and a B-24 sank it with depth charges. That after-action report is from the Air Corps. Cole is still on his way to Tunis and doesn't know the U-boats been sunk yet."

Admiral Bryton leaned back in his office chair with a smile on his face. "That d——n Cole what's he going to do next?"

Then the smile turned to a frown, and Bryton asked, "Did you find out about those sailing dates?"

"Yes, sir. They are all accurate. I don't know how he did it, but he cut the transit time by two days."

"Hmm...He must be flogging those engines of his awfully hard. I want that checked into. If he hasn't blown his engines already he will soon. I admire his initiative, but I don't want him destroying his ship.

"Yes, sir," Johnson replied and left Admiral Bryton's office.

CHAPTER 41

When they dropped the hook in Tunis harbor, Jack reported ashore and found he had a letter and a package waiting for him. To his surprise, Admiral Hunt in Casablanca had forwarded a congratulatory message to him on, as he put it, "Bagging one of Goering's boys." And the II Corps chief of staff had shipped him a chunk of aluminum with a swastika on it recovered from the downed bomber. His package also contained a note which read, "Outstanding work. I thought you and your men might like to have this as a souvenir. PS. Thanks for the eyes only message."

Later that day at the general mail call for the ship, Jack received a letter from Helen Brant explaining that she was so sorry, but she had met an Air Force officer at a USO dance who was training to become a P-47 pilot. One thing led to another, and she probably wouldn't be writing any more. He mustn't feel disappointed. It was just one of those things, and she hoped they could still be friends. Jack couldn't help but smile to himself. He had a pretty good idea that the Air Force officer would probably be receiving a similar letter shortly after he went overseas.

CHAPTER 42

When Jack returned to the ship, he put Mr. Wesley in charge of finding the unit the L-4 belonged to and notified Mr. Purvis about the changes he wanted in the ship's taxi service. He had just finished these tasks when he was requested to come ashore again. When Jack pulled alongside the pier, there stood Pete Meriwether, a general's aid de camp and a small crowd of other officers—both Army and Navy. After salutes and introductions were exchanged the aid de camp got right to the point. "Sir, I'm sorry I missed you earlier and had to have you make another trip in. You got here quicker than expected. We were led to believe these LSTs were slow and cruised at about nine knots. You must have cruised a lot faster than that to get here this soon.

"Yes…Ahem…Well, we have one h——l of a chief motor machinist who with a little help from Mr. Meriwether's Seabees happens to be able to get quite a bit more out of our ship than most," Jack replied, shooting Meriwether a quick glance out of the corner of his eye.

"I see," the aid de camp replied, looking from Jack to Pete and back to Jack. He knew there was some hidden meaning to Jack's comment but decided to let it drop. "Well, General Patton has some very specific needs for an upcoming operation, and it was suggested that you, and Mr. Meriwether are the men to solve these needs. If you will accompany me, gentlemen"—at this, he looked around, taking in all the officers present—"the general has set up a secure conference sight here and would like you to get started on the problem right away."

The first thing that went through Jack's mind was *Oh s——t, there is no way I can bluff my way through this. Hello Portsmouth, Rhode Island, here I come.* But with no other recourse, he sent his gig back to the ship with instructions that he would call for it when he was ready to return all the time, thinking, *If I return.*

There were a number of Army staff cars waiting at the end of the pier, which took the entire entourage to the Tunisia Palace Hotel just a few blocks from the shore of Lake Tunis where the officers were ushered into a large ornate conference room full of maps, charts, tide tables, and other documents hanging from the walls and spread across a giant conference table. In attendance were a mix of American and Allied personnel up to and including both a British and an American admiral.

A US Army full bird colonel opened the meeting with a brief explanation of the need. The challenge was to come up with a way to land tanks, artillery, and heavy equipment on beaches considered impossible to be used for a major amphibious landing. He reviewed the reasons the beaches were considered impossible to be used and then went on with his presentation. Not only did the horrible conditions of the beaches need to be overcome, but the equipment had to be unloaded quickly while under fire from the shore, air attack, and possibly engaged by surface craft. He then turned to Jack and said, "Commander Cole, it is our understanding that these new LSTs of yours can off load tanks, trucks, artillery, and any other form of vehicle simply by running your ship up on the beach, opening a door in the front, and driving them off. Is that correct?"

Scared witless and afraid to say something that would give him away, Jack stood up and replied, "Yes, sir." Then he sat back down.

The colonel was somewhat taken aback by the short answer and, looking at Jack, said, "Would you like to elaborate or add anything to that?"

Again Jack stood up and said, "No, sir, you described what we can do very accurately." Then he sat back down again.

"Yes...Well, Commander, do you think your LSTs can handle the challenge we are putting before you?" the colonel asked.

At this, Commander Meriwether tugged on Jack's sleeve and motioned Jack to bend down so he could whisper in his ear. Jack listened intently and then stood up, looked the colonel in the eye, and said, "Yes, sir." Then he sat back down again.

A frown crossed the colonel's face, and he said somewhat testily, "Would you care to explain?"

Jack jumped back to his feet and said, "Yes, sir. With Commander Meriwether's assistance, I would be glad to explain, sir."

Before Jack could sit back down, the colonel motioned him to the front of the room. Jack and Commander Meriwether both walked to the head of the table, all the while Jack feeling like a condemned man walking to the gallows. Pete moved a flip chart on an easel in place. Jack cleared his throat and began, "The condition of the beaches you have described can be overcome if the unloading can be accomplished from a distance away from the beach. However, the vehicles cannot be driven through surf that deep so the solution is to bridge the distance between our LSTs and the shoreline. Commander Meriwether has the latest information on a, for lack of a better term, secret weapon the Seabees have developed which will solve the problem."

Then, turning to Pete Jack said, "Commander, would you care to explain how the Seabee's new secret weapon can be utilized in this particular case?"

Jack was never so glad to turn a presentation over to another individual in his life.

"Thank you, Commander. Yes, I would be happy to do so," Pete replied. Then picking up a marking pen, he opened the flip chart to a blank page and drew a three dimensional representation of a rectangular box. "This, gentlemen, is what we Seabees call a pontoon. It is a 5 ×7 × 5 watertight steel box that can be attached to as many other pontoons as needed to form a causeway. Our solution is to prefabricate causeways, hang them from the sides of an LST, drop them in the water when the ship arrives at the invasion site, bolt them together so they overlap, then use the LST to push them up on the beach. Once the causeway is beached, we anchor it in place then lower the ramp on the LST and drive all the mechanized equipment ashore. Since it will be anchored in place ships of all types, not just LSTs can use it to unload their men and supplies."

While he was speaking Pete drew an overhead view of a causeway overlapped and bolted together. He then stepped back and asked, "Are there any questions?"

The colonel stood up and somewhat pompously asked, "How long have the Seabees had these…these…secret weapons, and why hasn't the Army been informed?"

Commander Meriwether looked at the colonel and said, "Sir, the only reason I know about the pontoon is because I was involved in development of the attachment hardware. The Navy Bureau of Docks and Yards under Admiral Moreell was running the acceptance trials on the pontoon when I brought my battalion from Davisville, Rhode Island, to Gulf Port, Mississippi. Since arriving in North Africa, I have been informed that the acceptance trials are complete, and I will be receiving a large shipment of unassembled pontoons within the month. Why you are not aware of the pontoon is a question I cannot answer."

The colonel glared at Commander Meriwether for what seemed to be a long time, then picked up a telephone which was sitting on the conference table and said, "Get me the chief of staff's office." Then he glared at Pete until he was patched through. "Yeah, Harold, this is Bill. Can you ask the old man if he knows anything about something called a pontoon? Yeah, it's some sort of a whizz bang gizmo the Seabees have come up with. I want to know what kinds of games are being played and why we don't know anything about it. Yeah, I'll wait."

After a pause of several minutes, someone came back on the line, and the colonel said, "Yeah, it's still me.

Jack could only hear one side of the discussion, but it went as follows, "Go ahead…Yeah…Okay…When?…Well, why weren't we told?…Uh-huh…Yeah…Okay, so they weren't informed ahead of time?…Well that would have been nice to know…Yeah, yeah, yeah…Okay…Right. You too."

The colonel hung up the phone and turned to Jack and Pete. "Okay…Apparently, we did know about the pontoon, but nobody had ever heard of one or what it could do so somebody decided not to pass that information along. Apparently, what this meeting was supposed to be about wasn't to figure out how to land the equipment. You two are the most knowledgeable men in the Middle East about LSTs and pontoons, and this meeting was supposed to be held for our benefit so you two could tell us how the pontoon was going to be used to solve our problem. If I understand correctly, neither of you men were informed about this meeting prior to us bringing you here today. Is that correct?"

"Yes, sir," Jack and Pete responded in unison.

At this point, both admirals stood and left the conference room. The colonel watched them leave, then said, "d———n sometimes I wonder if we aren't our own worst enemy. Okay, unless you have anything else to add, I guess we're done here. I'll see to it that we get you back to your ship, Commander Cole and Commander Meriwether, I'll see to it you are dropped off at your battalion headquarters."

With that, both men saluted, the colonel returned the salute, and the conference room immediately emptied.

CHAPTER 43

J ack and Pete both jumped in the same staff car. "Take us to the harbor to drop the commander off. Then you can run me out to my outfit," Pete told the driver.

As they were making the short drive to the harbor, Pete asked, "Have you got a little time today? I've got a problem, and I think you and your pirates are the ones to solve it."

Jack, who was just getting his pulse back to normal and thanking his lucky stars things went the way they did, had been taking in the sights and smells of Tunis looking out the side window. After Pete's comment, he slowly turned his head and looked at Commander Meriwether. "Pirates?…Me…and my pirates? Is that any way to speak to the most knowledgeable LST man in the Mediterranean? Why I'd be offended if it wasn't true."

"Yeah, right," Pete said. "Listen, we've got a problem, and I can't seem to find a way through the red tape to get it solved. By the time you and your crew were finished in Gulf Port, I'm surprised the mayor didn't give you a certificate of appreciation for removing all that unsightly scrap iron that was lying around all over town. H——l you and your men about picked the place clean."

"What can I say? We're civic minded," Jack replied.

Both men started laughing, and then Pete got straight to the point.

"Okay, it's this way. That load of equipment you have on board is for me. The Army's over run the oil fields in Libya, and I'm supposed to send part of my battalion there to repair what the Krauts blew up and get the wells pumping again. That's not a problem I've got the men to do it, and you're carrying just about everything they're going to need to get the job done. The problem is 'just about every-

159

thing we need' ain't gonna cut it. This is a joint project between the Army and the Navy and those two don't see eye to eye on what needs to be done. The Navy knows the oil fields will need to be rebuilt after the Krauts blew 'em up, but the Army says it's just a repair job."

"So what's the problem?" Jack asked.

"The problem is the Army controls the TO&E [Table of Organization and Equipment], and since they call it a repair job, they don't think we need a crane. They also shorted us on well casing, drill pipe, control heads, and head tees. H———l I can't pull and replace broken casings, without a crane, and I can't set control heads, and install valves that I don't have."

"Okay, so where do I come in?" Jack asked.

"Well," Pete said, scratching the back of his neck. "I can requisition the extra well casing, drill pipe, control heads, and head tees, but I can't get my hands on a crane. I figure from the way you handled things at Gulf Port, Key West, and Trinidad, you and your men might be able to come up with some way of helpin' us get a crane."

"Okay." Jack leaned forward and tapped the driver on the shoulder. "You can drop us both off at the harbor. I'll see to it that Commander Meriwether gets back to his unit."

CHAPTER 44

B y the time the ship's gig pulled alongside the pier, Jack had a pretty good idea of how to handle the situation, but to make sure he had every last detail covered, he called a council of war in the ward room to go over everything and make sure nothing had been overlooked.

Jack started the meeting by making a list of the things that needed to be done, and then, he prioritized them. A few touches were added here and there, but the basic plan Jack had come up with passed muster and the men got to work. Jack had the starboard LCVP lowered and pulled around to the bow where the ship's jeep was backed into it, and Commander Meriwether was taken to the beach. When the bow ramp of the LCVP was lowered, the jeep rolled out with Boats driving, Meriwether riding shotgun, and Barton and Grubowski in the back.

As they drove along the harbor road, all four men had their eyes peeled looking for what they needed, to get Operation Hernia completed successfully. After approximately thirty minutes of driving up and down and in and out of the labyrinth of back alleys and side streets that made up the warehouse district along the dock side Meriwether nudged Boats with his elbow and motioned him to slow down. Meriwether grabbed the windshield of the jeep and stood up for a better look. When he sat back down, he told Boats, "Stop the jeep. This is the place."

Meriwether hopped out of the jeep and jogged up to the fence surrounding a large military compound with a sign reading 142nd Battle Damage Assessment and Repair. He spent a little time looking through a knot hole and finally came back to the jeep. "Okay, they've got what I need. You can see the *A* frame for the boom hoist tackle sticking up just beyond that tank retriever. Can you see it?"

All three men craned their necks to see over the fence. Boats stood up on his driver's seat, Grubowski jumped up on the jeep's rear seat, and Barton hopped down, ran around to the front of the jeep, and climbed up on the hood. Boats and Grubowski saw it immediately. Barton couldn't see it at all. Finally, Grubowski said, "Barton, you blind son of a b———h, you see those metal legs stickin' up with a pipe on top? It looks like a big swing set with lines running down from the pipe?"

"Yeah?"

"Well, that's what we're lookin' for."

"Well, h———l, why didn't ya say so in the first place?"

The other three men all gave Barton a caustic look.

"What?" Barton said, lifting his hands palms up and shrugging his shoulders.

"H———l, I ain't no construction whiz. I'm in procurement and distribution," he said with a holier-than-thou look on his face and his nose in the air.

"Just cause I don't know what a crane looks like in a repair depot in the middle of the night don't mean I can't help ya snatch it."

The other three men broke into laughter.

Everybody jumped back in their seats, and the jeep sped off.

CHAPTER 45

The afternoon of the following day, the harbormaster signaled Jack to position his ship alongside the jetty opposite the port gantries. Jack conned the ship in place and ran her up on the beach, opened the bow doors, and lowered the ramp. Shortly, a convoy of Army transporters drove up at the foot of the jetty with loads of well casings, drill pipe, well heads, valves, and well head tees. An Army captain stepped down from the lead transporter and asked permission to come aboard. Jack met him at the head of the gangway. The Army captain saluted, handed Jack a cargo manifest, and smiling said, "Captain Bill Larson 383rd transport unit, sir. It took some doing, but we got everything the Seabee's needed. Is there anything else we can do for you?"

Jack looked at the manifest, looked at the line of trucks along the jetty, and looked back at the Army captain. "This looks good captain, but where is the crane?"

"Crane, sir?" the captain asked.

"Yes, Captain, the crane. Where's the crane?"

"What crane is that, sir?" the captain replied with a puzzled look on his face.

"The one to unload your trucks and load all that equipment aboard ship," Jack said.

"I…Uh…I don't know, sir. Nobody said anything to me about a crane. My orders were to gather up all this equipment and material ASAP and get it to the jetty. Apparently, the Seabees need all this stuff to fix the oil wells in Libya, and they need it there like yesterday. That's all I know, sir. I've been running from one supply depot to the next all morning trying to find the stuff on that list and scrounge up enough trucks to get it here. No one said anything to me about a crane, sir," the captain stammered.

"Hmm…well, h——l, Captain, that's not your fault. You've done your job. But that material isn't going to load itself and you and I sure as h——l aren't going to carry it aboard by hand, are we?" Jack threw in a little chuckle and the captain smiled somewhat hesitantly at Jack's joke.

"How'd you get all that stuff loaded onto your trucks in the first place?" Jack asked.

"Well, I just pulled into one depot yard after another, handed them the Seabee manifest and if they had what was needed they loaded it with one of the cranes they had sitting there."

"Well, there's our answer. We just need to get a crane down here. Can you move one with your trucks?" Jack asked.

"S——t yeah…er…Excuse me, sir." The captain looked embarrassed for his language in front of a superior officer.

"Yes, I can move anything up to and including a Sherman tank, sir." the captain was beaming with pride.

"Okay, well, I have a land line hooked up here aboard ship. Why don't you get on the horn and find a crane we can use to get this stuff loaded?"

As soon as Captain Larson started making calls, Jack stepped out on the starboard bridge wing where he spotted Gardener on the main deck below. When Gardener looked up, Jack gave him a nod. Gardener gave Jack a thumbs-up, picked up a handset, and called Grubowski. When Grubowski answered, Boats said, "It's on." and hung up. His next call was to Chief Barton with the same message. Boats then turned toward the bridge and gave Jack the universal signal for okay by making a circle with his thumb and forefinger. Jack nodded, then returned to his sea cabin and asked Captain Larson if he'd had any luck.

Captain Larson turned around in Jack's chair, stood up, and said, "No, sir, every depot is using their cranes. The soonest I can get a crane will be tomorrow afternoon. Can we move the ship to one of the gantry piers and load it there?"

"No, Captain, I asked already. The harbormaster has those gantry piers set aside for unloading cargo from the holds of freighters. They've got every gantry in use and four freighters waiting to unload. They're going full bore over there and can't squeeze us in. Have you tried everybody?"

Just then, there was a knock on Jack's door casing and Chief Grubowski stood there wiping his oily hands on a grease rag.

"What is it, Chief?" Jack asked.

"I don't mean to interrupt, sir. I was just wondering if you've heard back from that Army repair depot on the repairs they were making to the winch for our Danforth anchor, sir?"

Jack shot a quick glance sideways at Captain Larson and said, "No, sorry, Chief. No word yet."

When Larson just stood there Jack made a slight nod of his head toward the captain that only Grubowski could see.

Grubowski saw the signal and said, "Well, sir, they told me they'd get right to it after they finished work on a crane they had in for repairs. They said they'd be done working on the crane yesterday afternoon and get to our winch first thing this morning. They should be done by now."

Larson still stood there staring into space, seemingly oblivious to the conversation Jack and Chief Grubowski were having.

Jack said, "Well, Chief, they might not be able to get to our winch if they have a crane sitting there in the way." At this, Jack turned his head slightly so he could see Larson. Larson was off wool gathering someplace and just stood there.

Grubowski picked up the conversation. "That's proly zactly what's happenin'. Too bad there ain't nobody round that could move a crane so's they could get the thing outa the way and get working on our winch."

Still nothing from Larson. Finally in frustration Jack turned to Larson. "Say, didn't you say you could move a crane captain?"

"Uh…Yes, sir, I did. We can move anything up to—"

"Yes, you mentioned that. Anything up to and including a Sherman tank, right?"

"Yes, sir." Larson beamed.

"And you said all the depots are using their cranes and one won't be free until sometime tomorrow; is that right?" Jack asked, practically begging Larson to see the light.

"Yes, sir, that's correct. None of the depots have one sitting around that isn't being used right now."

Grubowski rolled his eyes and said, "You don't suppose there might be a crane sittin' around somewhere other than in a depot yard, do you? One that's maybe just sitting there doing nothing, maybe just sitting there getting in the way?"

Captain Larson stood there thinking, crossed his arms over his chest, and rested his chin in the palm of his hand, then stared up at the overhead. All the time Jack and Grubowski were silently pleading for him to connect the dots. Finally, after what seemed like forever, Larson's eyes lit up. He snapped his fingers and said, "Say, why don't I check with the repair depot? They might just have a crane in for repairs that hasn't been sent back to its unit yet. What do you think about that commander?"

Jack suddenly realized he'd been standing there holding his breath ever since Larson crossed his arms and put his chin in the palm of his hand. "Why that's a brilliant idea, Captain." Then looking a Grubowski, he said, "Why didn't we think of that, Chief?"

"I don't know, sir. I guess it just took an Army man to figure out a Navy problem. Nice job, Captain." Grubowski stuck out his greasy paw and shook Captain Larson's hand.

Captain Larson was smiling from ear to ear and said, "Sir, if you don't mind. I'll just get on the horn here and see if the repair depot might have a crane." Then looking at his greasy hand, he wiped it on a piece of scrap paper and picked up the land line.

When he turned toward the desk, Captain Larson never saw Chief Grubowski make a strangling motion with his hands at the back of Larson's neck or Jack close his eyes, drop his head to his chest, shake it back and forth, and then look to the heavens in a why me motion.

It didn't take long, and Larson sent one of his transporters to the repair depot to pick up the crane and deliver it to the jetty. As the transporter was pulling out of the Battle Damage Assessment and

Repair Depot Barton was driving in with a pair of large boxes in the rear of his jeep. One box contained two gallons of liquid escrow and four gallons of ice cream. In exchange for which Barton watched as Master Sergeant Alvin Tiddle filed an assessment on the crane which had just left his depot yard writing it off as a complete loss due to battle damage. Barton's next stop was the harbormaster's office where he left the second box, which contained two gallons of ice cream and a slightly used West Bend electric percolator coffee pot in gratitude for assistance rendered in getting the LST assigned to load at the jetty.

When the casing, drill pipe, control heads, and head tees were all loaded, the Seabee crane operator lowered the boom, reeled in the hook, drove the crane to the end of the jetty, onto shore, turned, and drove down the bank straight into the LST. As soon as the crane was secured, Jack raised the ramp, closed the bow doors, and conned his ship back to its original position in the road stead where he anchored and waited for his sailing orders.

The next afternoon, Jack was underway for Libya with Commander Meriwether's oil field unit, their materials, supplies, and one crane which did not appear on the cargo manifest.

CHAPTER 46

When Jack returned from Libya, the official announcement of the sinking of a German U-boat with the assistance of *LST 121* and the 422nd Heavy Artillery Observation Squadron was made. Both commanding officers were called to Allied headquarters where a presentation of medals was made. When Jack found out he would be meeting the commanding officer of the 422nd, he had Barton fill a new unused jerry can full of "Thank You Juice," paint it blue, and stencil it "Diesel Fuel." Jack's rational was fighters and bombers all burned high octane gasoline and tanks, trucks, and jeeps burned low octane gasoline so the present he had for the 422nd should be safe from light fingered opportunists until he was able to get it into the hands of the 422nd commanding officer.

The presentation ceremony was held at Allied headquarters. It was quite a lengthy ceremony and Jack was as nervous as a w——e in church afraid he'd be called out by someone who knew the real Lieutenant Commander Cole. British, Australian, Canadian, American, New Zealand, and Indian service men were there to be decorated. The court yard at Allied headquarters was filled with representatives from each nation. General Eisenhower as Allied commander witnessed the ceremony along with Air Chief Marshall Tedder, commander of Allied air forces, and Admiral Cunningham as commander of Allied naval forces in the Mediterranean.

General Jimmy Doolittle made the presentation of the Air Medal to Major Hal Dunwitty of the 422nd Heavy Artillery Observation Squadron and Admiral Hunt pinned the Navy and Marine Corps Medal on Jack's chest. When the ceremony was completed, Jack made a beeline for the exit where he ran into Major Dunwitty. Jack introduced himself and after chatting for a few moments Jack said, "If you don't mind, let's get out of here. I've got a little something for you to go along with that Air Medal."

Dunwitty followed Jack outside to the staff car that brought him to Allied headquarters, opened the trunk, pulled out the blue jerry can, and handed it to the major. "This is for you and your unit. If it hadn't been for you guys we'd probably been sunk by that sub. That stencil may be somewhat misleading. This particular fuel is for internal consumption. I hope you and your men enjoy it."

Major Dunwitty unscrewed the top, put his lips to the spout, and took a sip. He immediately started coughing, and his eyes started to water. Screwing the top back on tight, he managed to say between coughs and gasps, "Say…that's some mighty smooth sippin' whiskey. I sure do appreciate this. Where'd you get this here cactus cola?"

Major Dunwitty had a decidedly Texas accent.

"Well, Hal," Jack replied, "that is a closely guarded military secret, and I'd have to kill you if I told you so let's just say it's American made and leave it at that."

Dunwitty's face slowly broke into the biggest sloppiest grin Jack had ever seen on a human being. It kind of reminded him of a one-hundred-pound blue catfish he'd seen at the fish market in Omaha. The grin seemed to start somewhere back around his right ear, work its way across his face, disappear around the side of his jaw and ended up some place back by his left ear.

Dunwitty slapped Jack on the back in a friendly fashion that almost knocked Jack off his feet and said, "I like you. Whata ya say we lock this up fer safe keepin', and we go try to find the bottom of a bottle in one a these here joints they try to pass off as a saloon?"

Jack's relief at making it through the medal ceremony without coming to grief was just wearing off, the staff car had a driver, the ship was loaded for its next run, but he wasn't scheduled to sail for twenty-four hours so Jack thought, *Why not?*

There are all types of drinkers. Some get silent and morose when they drink, some get mean when they drink, and others get wobbly and can't walk straight. Jack was more of a tea teetotaler. He liked a drink now and again, and he certainly didn't hold it against a man if he occasionally had too much to drink. But Jack had never seen a man drink the way Hal Dunwitty drank.

Hal would pour a drink while he was telling a story, start to lift the glass to his lips, stop while he was telling his story, and then put the glass down while he was laughing at his own joke. Hal did this over and over all afternoon. He'd finish one story, stop someone walking by, introduce himself, pour the man a drink, and then launch into another story all the time holding his glass, but never managing to quite take the time to get it to his lips. They had been to four different places, and Hal hadn't tasted a drink yet nor had he told the same story twice. The man never stopped talking.

They were sitting in a small French bistro when two Royal Canadian Nursing Sisters walked in. Jack was facing the entrance while Hal was regaling a pair of British Naval officers about the merits of Longhorn cattle over Herefords. There was something about one of the nurses that caused Jack to walk up and ask, "Would you like to join us? It would be my pleasure to buy supper for you if you wouldn't mind."

As soon as the words left his mouth, the thought struck him, *I've never been this forward with a woman in my life.* The nurse Jack was speaking to looked at him then cocked her head slightly to one side as if thinking and said, "Why…I'd be delighted."

Turning to the nurse with her, she said, "What do you say, June?"

June looked somewhat annoyed with the boldness of the brash American and Jack thought she might nix his invitation, but when she saw the pleading look in her friends eyes, she relented and said, "Okay, sure…Why not. My name is June and this is Shelley. Do you have a table?"

Jack was just about to answer when the two British Naval officers sitting with Hal got up and walked off, laughing and shaking their heads. Hal turned toward the seat Jack had been in, saw he wasn't there, and looking around yelled, "Jack, where'd you go, son?" Then he stood up, spotted Jack, and hollered, "Well, there you are cowboy. Looks like you found yerself a coupla strays."

Jack offered Shelley his arm and with a flourish and a bow he waved his hand toward the table, saying, "This way, ladies. I'll introduce you to Major Hal Dunwitty, the latest recipient of the much coveted US Army Air Corps Air Medal. You'll have to excuse him. He's from Texas. He isn't house broken yet, but he *is* on our side. Hal, I'd like you to meet June and Shelley. If I read their tunics correctly they are Canadian Nursing Sisters and should be treated with the utmost dignity and respect. Please try to overcome your shyness and say hello."

Jack could feel Shelley's grip on his arm tighten, but June broke into a big smile and said, "Well, howdy partner. Where's yer chaps and six gun?"

It turned out June was from Saskatchewan and lived on a cattle ranch between Keoma and Nightingale not far from Calgary. As opposed to his first impression of her, Jack found out June was anything but standoffish. She was even more of a wild hare than Hal. The two of them hit it off and between yehaws, and by gollies, it was a lot like being in a Gene Autry movie.

Once she realized Hal was a male iteration of June, Shelley relaxed, and she and Jack had a lovely evening. The meal was excellent French cuisine with good wine. Later on, Jack couldn't recall what they had ordered or anything about the meal other than it was good and Shelley's eyes seemed to be as big as two blue moons floating over lips that were the color of poppies on Armistice Day. Other than those two remembrances, the rest of the evening was a pleasant blur. They talked all evening. He remembered holding her when they danced and the smell of her shampoo and perfume and how she felt in his arms, but it was all so intoxicating that later on he couldn't remember what they talked about or having ever asked her to dance. They just seemed to melt into one another and float around the dance floor.

On the way back to the ship, Jack heard the staff car driver tell Hal that he and June had really cut a rug jitter bugging. Hal asked, "What about the swabby?" nodding his head toward Jack.

The driver said, "Him? He and his girl just stood in the middle of the room swaying to the music while you and that babe you were with tore up the dance floor all around them. That was news to Jack. He never knew anyone else was on the dance floor. It was a magical evening, and then it was final call and the evening was over. Jack walked Shelley to the street and put her and June into a taxi to take them back to their quarters, and the evening was over. Jack stood there on the curb watching the cab pull away, Shelley's face in the rear window waving, and then she was gone. Not until that moment did Jack realize he didn't even know Shelley's last name.

Hal slapped Jack on the back and said, "Buddy boy, you can shore pick 'em. That June would make a guy want to give up his citizenship and punch cows in Canada. What'd you think of that gal o yorn? What was her name?"

"Shelley," Jack almost whispered. "Her name is Shelley."

Jack didn't remember the drive back to the ship, but after walking up the gangway, saluting the colors, and signing in, he was handed a message telling him the ship's sailing orders were moved up. By dawn, Jack was underway and standing out to sea with the morning tide.

CHAPTER 47

During the next month, Jack was constantly on the move transferring men, equipment, and supplies from the west coast African ports into the Mediterranean. More and more LSTs began to arrive as well as smaller ocean going beach landing craft such as LCTs and LCIs. More destroyers, mine sweepers, cruisers, and other types of warships began to appear in the sea lanes along with thousands of aircraft which seemed to form a continuous umbrella overhead. Something big was coming, and the rumor mill went into overdrive.

There were those who thought the allies were preparing to invade southern France. Others thought the allies were going back to Cyprus and Greece. Still more thought Italy was the target. Regardless of the final destination supplies and equipment were being stockpiled along the North African coast by the millions of tons.

In the midst of the constant runs into the Mediterranean, up and down the Atlantic coast, and across North Africa, it was difficult for mail to catch up with the ship, but when it did, mail call was like Christmas. Jack had been corresponding with Jeannie, Angie, and Annette on a regular basis, writing and mailing letters almost every time he made port. Their letters in return arrived in bunches because the ship was always on the move.

The letters made him ache inside for home and the people he knew, but they also made him wonder about his future, if there was a future, and would any of these women be a part of that future. Jack had been alone a long time, and he had grown used to his own company. He wondered whether he had what it would take to build a life with someone else in it. All these things ran through his mind as he read about the comings and goings in Pilottown, the plans Jeannie and Angie had for the future and how he could fit into those plans. But as he read the letters, thoughts of the Canadian nurse Shelley would creep into his mind and hover in the back of his consciousness like a soft breeze on a warm night.

He remembered how lost he'd felt when he was suddenly thrust into command. The feeling of events being totally beyond his control and the fear he had about what would happen if he failed or was found to be a fraud by the crew. He likened his feelings when he read the letters from Jeannie, Angie, and Annette to the feelings he had at that time. And then there was the issue of Shelley. He didn't even know her last name or how to contact her, but she also played into his feelings in a way he didn't understand. It was frustrating and being on the other side of the world out of direct contact didn't make it any easier for Jack to sort things out.

When Jack received a letter from Jeannie telling him that she had left her job at the Woolworths in Walnut Hill and moved to Omaha where she was working in a bomber assembly plant, he initially thought, *That's great,* and he was excited for her and proud that she was contributing to the war effort. But as he read on he realized there was more to the move than met the eye. Jeannie indicated she would not be moving back to Walnut Hill and didn't know what she was going to do after the war. She ended her letter by telling Jack that she was thinking of him and wished him well, ending her letter with "Perhaps we'll meet again sometime, somewhere in the future."

At first, Jack didn't know what to make of the letter, but he felt for sure that he wouldn't be hearing from Jeannie ever again. However, several weeks later, he received a letter from Jeannie in which was enclosed a clipping from the *Omaha World Herald* announcing the coming nuptials of Ms. Jeannie Evans and Mr. Everett Dortmund. There was nothing else in the letter, but across the back of the clipping was scrawled, "I'm sorry. I didn't know how to tell you. Please don't hate me."

In response, Jack composed a letter telling Jeannie how happy he was for her and Everett and enclosed a $25 war bond made out in her name. He really didn't know how he felt about Jeannie or how this impacted his life. He knew he didn't love her; he liked her, but he had no deep feelings for her. Obviously, she felt something for him which was much greater than what he felt for her.

For a few minutes, he felt disappointed, but not angry. He was confused and wondered how his life would end up. Was he destined to go back to Walnut Hill and pick up where he left off or was there something else he was yet to discover that would lead to a new path in life? He wondered if he would remain alone or if there was someone who was willing to share their life with him? Was he incapable of feeling love? Was he cold inside only able to deal with issues where there was a clear right or wrong answer?

As he thought about it, he realized he was much better off with these doubts and fears than without them. He was fretting over his options and if he would make the right choices. Once he realized that, he came to the conclusion that he was looking forward, not backward. That hadn't been the case for a long, long time. Before, his life had been one of order and predictability, no risk, but nothing exciting, he was always in control. The thoughts he was having now were about taking a chance on life, the feeling of having both feet planted firmly in midair, and the challenge of the unknown. It was something he hadn't felt in years and now that he was beginning to understand what he was feeling, it felt good, real good.

Jack wasn't the only one. He noticed the lovely Jennifer was waiting on the dock for Ensign Wesley whenever they returned to Casablanca. Lieutenants Purvis and Young appeared to have a special flair for the ladies. Regardless of the port, neither of them was ever seen ashore without the company of a WAC or a nurse. Ensigns Davis, Price, and Jensen also seemed to be making time with the Allied nurses and some of the young local French beauties or *jeunes beautés françaises* as they were known. Jack couldn't help but think, *My boys are growing up.*

The enlisted men were no different. Right down the ship's roster from Dennis Anderson to Allan Zimmer, the men were doing their best to spread their version of goodwill throughout North Africa. Jack thought, *I hope that's all they're spreading* and made a mental note to make sure Andy Richards and Joe Martinsdale, the ship's Pharmacist Mates, were holding regular "short arm" inspections.

The ports along the North African coast were beautiful exotic places, but they could also be deadly. Robbery and murder were a cottage industry in the back alleys and dives. The ship's taxi service kept the men from having to walk the streets from bar to bar and the taxi crew was constantly on the lookout for crewmates who were drunk, seeing to it that they got back to the ship unharmed. As a result, none of Jack's crew fell prey to anything more serious than a severe hangover or getting gyped on the purchase of fake artifacts. No one said anything about it, but the men knew Jack was looking out for them and knew he had their back.

Jack's policy of letting his men have as much leave as possible, even if it was only an hour or two ashore, paid big dividends in moral. His ship moved more cargo than any other LST largely due to shorter loading and unloading times which was due directly to the enthusiasm of the crew. Of course it didn't hurt that Jack routinely cruised at twelve knots as opposed to the nine knots the rest of the LSTs could make. The men worked hard, and they were proud of the work they were doing. When they won a blue *E* award for logistics management efficiency, the men were as proud as if they had won a battle star. The blue *E* was added to each bridge wing along with the swastika for the airplane they shot down, and the image of the U-boat they helped sink. In the mess hall, the chunk of aluminum from the bomber was proudly displayed on a bulkhead as a war trophy and a big blue *E* was painted at the head of the chow line so everyone walked past it to get their meals. *LST 121* was a good ship, with a good crew, and if asked, the men would say they had an excellent skipper.

CHAPTER 48

T he massive build up in North Africa worked just like any large scale operation; nobody seemed to have enough of something they needed while everyone had too much of something they didn't. This is where the redistribution system the quartermasters conducted came to be so important.

Because of his experience with the crawler crane Commander Meriwether let it be known that Jack Cole was a no nonsense commanding officer who ran a tight ship but placed a high priority on getting the job done first and then figuring out how to make it fit within the rules and regulations afterward.

As a result, when a unit was in a pinch and couldn't get their hands on something they needed, the unit's QM would contact Barton and Barton would take the request to Jack. Jack would sit down with the unit commander, make a list of the things that would need to be done to acquire the needed tools or equipment, prioritize the items on the list, and launch an operation to secure whatever it was that the unit commander needed. As long as it was available somewhere in a unit that didn't need it, Jack saw it as part of his duty to help sort out the problem. Consequently, Jack was owed favors all up and down the Moroccan coast and across North Africa. With Chief Barton involved in the redistribution process it was likely there were a lot more favors owed than Jack was aware of. Mulling it over one day, he thought, *I wouldn't be surprised if Rommel owes us a favor or two.*

Jack hadn't needed to call in any favors, but he was assured that if he ever needed anything the Army, Navy, Air Corps, and Seabees would put him at the head of the line. As one Air Corps quartermaster sergeant said after Jack was able to finagle a motorized engine hoist for him, "Commander, we was about ta kill ourselves tryin' ta change engines without that hoist, if you ever need a favor, you know like an airplane ride or somebody killed you just let us know."

Jack thought that was a pretty funny line and almost started to laugh until he saw the look on the QM sergeant's face and realized he wasn't kidding.

Jack also made a habit of sending ice cream back with a unit when they came to pick up their supplies. He would even have his men recharge the CO_2 bottles the troops brought along with them to keep the ice cream frozen until they got it back to their unit. So when *LST 121* pulled into port it was like Santa Claus had arrived or Black Beard the Pirate depending on how you looked at it.

CHAPTER 49

Jack was a stickler for anti-aircraft practice and after the run in with the U-boat he had his men work on surface targets as well. Generally a PT boat or a subchaser would pull a target sled for them, but once a British destroyer pulled alongside and offered to tow a sled because they heard that they could get some ice cream if they did. That started a good relationship between Jack and the Royal Navy. Periodically, Royal Navy ships would pull alongside and offer to pull a target sled or make a fast run to deliver 121's mail to port because they knew they could get some ice cream.

On shore, Wilmer Burwell ran into a bunch of British sailors on shore leave. When they found out, Wilmer was from *LST 121* one man, in a heavy cockney accent, said, "You blokes on *LST 121* are all right. If it wasn't for the fact you can't speak English, we'd swear you was British."

The Air Corps was too heavily engaged in the desert air war to spend time towing target sleeves for an LST, but the search and rescue units and patrol squadrons were happy to do so. If they weren't available, Jack could count on one of the heavy artillery observation squadrons to make a few passes. That is what got Jack back in touch with Major Dunwitty.

They had just completed a round of antiaircraft target practice when Jack got called to the radio shack. When he walked in Ensign Wesley, the communications officer, and Bob Parks the radio operator on duty were ashen faced and looking like they wanted to be any place except where they were.

"What's up?" Jack asked.

Parks pulled off his cans and handed them to Jack, "You'd better take this in private, sir. It's the squadron commander from the unit

179

that just towed the target for us, and he ain't happy. He says we hit his plane!" Parks was really concerned.

"Naw, put it on speaker," Jack said and handed the cans back to Parks.

Parks took the cans and glanced warily at Ensign Wesley. Wesley nodded, and Parks said, "Yes, sir," as he threw the switch from head phones to speaker.

"This is Commander Cole. Go ahead."

"Just what in the h——l do you sailor boys think yer a doin? Ya'll just put a buncha holes in one a my aereeoplanes. Cain't ya'll tell the difference tween a US f——g Army L-4 an a target sleeve?" It was the thick Texas accent of Hal Dunwitty.

"What makes you think I should believe we hit your airplane?"

"Cause I wasa flyin' it by d——n."

"Well, I wish we had known it was you flying it Hal. I'd have told my men to shoot to kill."

"How ya doin', ol' buddy?" Hal bellowed in response.

Jack turned, looked at Wesley and Park, and winked. "Just fine, Hal. It's good to hear your voice. Thanks for towing for us."

"Hey, no prolem. Next time you make port, gimme a call on the field phone. We're settled in for a while, and they should be able to find us. I need to discuss sompin', and this hear radio ain't the place ta do er. Over."

"Will do. Out."

Jack looked at Wesley and Parks who had questioning looks on their faces, "Friend of mine," he said and left the radio shack for the bridge.

As Jack left, Wesley and Parks both looked at each other. Wesley shrugged, and Parks shook his head. The more senior an officer got, the weirder they got.

**

In the Main Navy and Munitions Building in Washington DC. Commander Johnson walked into Admiral Bryton's office. Bryton looked up and said, "Yes?"

"There's a fellow out here that says his name is Jack Cole. He's demanding to know why he hasn't been recalled to active duty. I looked into it and we've got a problem, sir," Johnson replied.

***

Jack made port two days later and contacted the 422nd heavy artillery observation squadron as Hal had requested.

"There's a meetin' in Tunis you need to attend. If I send a plane to pick you up can you make it tomorrow?" was Hal's question as soon as Jack got him on the line. No hello, no friendly banter, no joking around. Just straight to the point.

"Well, we're loading now, and I'm scheduled to leave with the tide tonight. What's up?" Jack replied.

"Okay, here it is. I can't go into any detail on a field phone, but if you push your sailing date back, can you make it?"

"I can't push the sailing date back. We've got to get a cargo load to Sfax ASAP. What's going on?"

"H——l, what about your exec? Can he handle the ship? If he makes the run, can you come to Tunis?"

"Well, of course he can handle the ship and make the run. I don't know about the Air Corps, but here in the Navy, they kind of frown on skippers just taking off and leaving the ship to the second in command without at least asking, "Pretty please."

"Yeah, yeah, yeah. You'll probably be getting orders within the hour so be prepared." Then the line went dead. Hal was finished.

Jack thought, *I bet that's the shortest conversation Hal's ever had in his life.*

Forty-five minutes later, Jack's orders arrived.

The flight to Tunis was uneventful. When Jack arrived, a jeep was waiting for him and he was driven to the Tunisia Palace Hotel. The meeting was held in the same ornate conference room where they discussed the Seabee pontoons. This time, however, there were far fewer people in attendance. In addition to Jack and Hal, there was a British delegation, which included Admiral Springset who had attended the pontoon meeting, one captain, two commanders, and a lieutenant commander. The Americans present included Admiral Beyard who was at the pontoon meeting, an Air Corps colonel, a lieutenant colonel wearing artillery insignia, Pete Meriwether, and another Seabee officer wearing commanders braid on his cuffs that Jack didn't recognize.

Admiral Springset opened the meeting. Speaking to Jack and Hal, he said, "I suppose you know why you are here?"

Hal answered, "Yes, sir."

Jack, who was always on edge when he was away from the ship, especially in a place where someone might know the real Lieutenant Commander Cole, glanced at Hal who was sitting beside him, stood, and nervously replied, "No, sir." Then he sat back down.

In a very casual voice, Admiral Beyard said, "Tony he was at sea and could not be briefed over the radio. We'll have to fill him in. He just arrived by plane and came straight here."

The British admiral looked somewhat surprised but nodded his head and said, "Certainly...Well, secrecy must be our first priority. Yes...So let's fill you in commander, shall we? The purpose of this meeting is to discuss an extension of the problem you and Commander Meriwether resolved for us the last time we met in this room."

This caused a stir among all those present. No one other than the admirals had attended the prior meeting and it caught everyone off guard. It also gave the rest of the officers present a new respect for the two lowest-ranking officers in attendance. At this point, Admiral Springset paused and looked around the room. "Gentlemen, the next allied move against our friends Mr. Hilter and Mr. Mussolini is in its final planning stages. I don't need to tell you that what is said here is top secret and does not go beyond this room. Understood, gentlemen?" This last statement was specifically directed at Jack.

Everyone nodded their head except Jack who responded, "Yes, sir!"

Admiral Springset looked around. "Very good. Now here is the situation. For reasons I won't go into, no aircraft carriers will be available to provide air support for our upcoming operation. Air cover will be provided by aircraft flying from our bases in North Africa and Malta. On paper, this looks feasible. Aircraft providing cover against air attack should be able to maintain a constant combat air patrol over the landing areas during daylight hours. However, aircraft attacking ground targets will be hampered by the need to fly to and from their distant bases to rearm. The aircraft will have the fuel to loiter over their targets, but once they expend their munitions, they will be required to return to base to rearm. As you can imagine, we are very concerned about this. When aircraft are not available for close air support it will be the Navy's responsibility to provide fire support for the landing forces. We are very capable of doing this. However, there are issues we must address.

"Commander Cole, you and Commander Meriwether have been instrumental in developing the solution to our problem of landing across these beaches so I believe that you are the best men to go to for ideas on solving our present dilemma.

"There are two areas of concern. First, the shallow waters and shifting sand bars off the landing beaches will not allow our larger war ships to come in close enough for their observers to mark each ship's fall of shot, especially once they push inland. We would like to use observers on shore to call in direct fire support, but that leads us to our second concern. Normally, we use field telephones to adjust artillery fire. That way, each observer can communicate directly with his supporting guns. However, in this case, because the artillery will be at sea, the observers would have to use radios and as you can imagine the airwaves will be crowded with requests. Our fear is that in the heat of battle, radio discipline will break down, and it will become very difficult to properly control the gun fire from the sea. What we need to do is place spotter aircraft over the beaches that can communicate with the observers on the ground and coordinate the gunfire as needed. This will reduce the radio chatter and allow for more accurate fire control. The Navy can use their float planes, but putting up a plane from each ship would result in more radio clutter and frankly it would be better to have Army observers speaking to Army spotter planes to cut down on confusion. That is where Major Dunwitty and his observation aircraft come into play.

"The major assures us that his unit is more than capable of handling the job with one exception. His aircraft do not have the range to fly to and from Tunis or Malta and still have adequate fuel reserves to loiter over the target area. What we need to come up with is a way to place his observation aircraft over the beachhead and maintain them there as long as they are needed."

Then turning to Admiral Beyard, he asked, "Admiral, do you have anything to add?"

"Just one thing, Tony, Commander Cole it is my understanding that you were convoy commander of Task Group 4.7 and in command of Operation Fountain. You have demonstrated your ability to handle a task group and your crew has extensive experience handling fuel at sea. Both of these attributes may prove to be very valuable in finding a solution to this problem."

Then turning to the British admiral, he said, "I think that covers everything."

"Quite...Very well then, now that you are aware of the challenge before you we will leave you to your deliberations. Please keep in mind that this is a vital task and time is of the essence."

Both admirals then left the room accompanied by their staff officers.

Jack turned to Commander Meriwether. "Pete, you got any ideas?"

"H——l I was about to ask you the same thing," Pete said.

"What about you, Hal? Any ideas?" Major Dunwitty turned his hands palms up and shrugged his shoulders.

Jack walked to the front of the room and turned the flip chart to a blank page. "Okay, why don't we start by making a list..."

***

After an hour of brainstorming and discussion, it was agreed that the L-4s could be carried to the invasion site and flown off an LST if a flight deck was erected over the main deck. Pete indicated his Seabees could build the flight deck without any problem and

Hal said when his planes were being transported they could easily be stored under the flight deck out of the way.

To get them airborne, the planes could be raised from the main deck to the flight deck by erecting a second level on top of the aft elevator. When the elevator was raised to the main deck level, the second level of the elevator would become a part of the flight deck, when the elevator was lowered to the tank deck the second level of the elevator would rest flush with the main deck allowing the L-4s to be moved from the main deck to the flight deck for takeoff.

The highly volatile aviation fuel could be stored in one of the ship's voids and pumped top side using pressurized CO_2 as a propellant when needed for refueling. This would significantly reduce the problem of gasoline fumes accumulating and becoming a fire hazard.

What was stumping the group was what to do after the L-4s were launched and had completed their mission. The planes could be launched from the improvised flight deck, but there was no way to land them back aboard. The aft superstructure was in the way. They couldn't just launch them and forget them. They needed to be refueled and maintained in order to keep aircraft over the beaches. The question was how could Hal's maintenance crews service the aircraft and keep them flying? No one knew how long the spotter planes would be needed at the invasion site before airfields could be established. They needed to come up with a way to keep the aircraft operating fully supported for an unspecified length of time.

Finally after staring at the sketch, they had developed of an LST with a flight deck built over the main deck Jack said, "Do we have to land the planes back aboard ship?"

"Well, what the h——l else do you expect us to do—park 'em on a cloud and shimmy down a rope?" Hal barked.

"No, no, no," Jack said. "Why can't you land on the beach?" We can run a causeway up on the beach, secure it, and run the maintenance crew and supplies ashore as needed."

Hal sat there with his jaw resting on the palm of his hand, his elbow planted on the conference table, and said, "Hmm."

Jack turned to Pete with a questioning look. "That just might work."

Pete said, "Hal, if you bend one of your birds, we can haul it back to the ship across the causeway where we've got the whole machine shop to do any repairs you need. If they can't hold the beachhead, we pull the plug, burn the planes, and get the h———l out of Dodge. What do you think?"

Hal looked at Pete then looked at Jack and said, "d———n that'll work."

***

When the three men exited the conference room, they passed the hotel lounge and saw Admiral Springset and Admiral Beyard with their staffs sitting at the bar having a drink. Pete walked up to Admiral Beyard and said, "Sir, we're done, if you would care to take a look."

This surprised everyone in the bar. Admiral Springset frowned and leaning back in his chair sputtered, "When I said time was of the essence, I didn't mean to throw something together half baked. I want a feasible solution not some…what do you Yanks call it… hare-brained idea."

This caused Admiral Beyard's brows to nit and his eyes narrow to a squint. He turned to Admiral Springset and in an icy tone said, "Tony, you asked for our best men for this project. That is what I've given you. I don't know about the Royal Navy, but in the United States Navy, when we give our best men an assignment, we expect results, and we expect them fast."

With that, Beyard stood and said, "Gentlemen, why don't you show us what you have."

As he walked past Pete, he said in a voice no one else could hear, "This better be good." Then he walked toward the conference room with the rest of his entourage in tow. Admiral Springset sat where he was for a moment white in the face, then abruptly stood, straightened his tunic, turned to his staff, and said, "Gentlemen!" then followed the Americans into the conference room.

Thirty minutes later, everyone exited the conference room with smiles and handshakes all around. Admiral Springset turned to his counterpart and said, "Bill, I have to say that I was skeptical that a satisfactory solution could be developed in a little over an hour, but your men came through, and I have every confidence this will give us exactly what we need."

Turning to Jack, Pete, and Hal, he shook each man's hand and said, "Well done...Well done indeed." Then he turned and left with his staff officers following. Admiral Beyard looked at the three, winked, and left.

As Jack, Pete, and Hal were walking out, Jack stopped Hal and asked, "Have you seen or heard anything from those Canadian nurses we met here last time we were in Tunis?"

Hal looked at Jack and said, "As a matter of fact..."

CHAPTER 50

Later that same day on the other side of the world in the Main Navy and Munitions Building in Washington DC. Admiral Bryton was fuming mad. He looked at a small pile of papers before him, slammed his fist down on his desk, and said, "s——t." Which given the circumstance, seemed to sum up the situation succinctly.

"D——n how in h——l could this have happened?" It was meant as a rhetorical question, but Commander Johnson answered anyway. "It appears there was a typo when the records were being updated to include the new social security numbers. As impossible as it sounds, the typo turned out to be the social security number of another Jack Cole and we've got the wrong man in command of an LST in the Mediterranean."

"I know that d——n it," the admiral barked. "That's not what I'm concerned about. How can we put a man who has never been in the Navy in command of a ship and have him succeed at the level he has with no prior military experience or training of any kind. H——l it makes us look bad. If word of this gets to the press our whole training program from the lowest boot to an Annapolis graduate will be deemed a waste of money, we might as well be British and let our officers purchase their commissions. Now we've got to do something about this and do it fast. Get me the JAG's office and make it snappy."

Commander Johnson turned and left the admiral's office, thinking, *I'm glad I'm not that poor SOB out there in the Mediterranean. By*

*the time the Navy gets through with him, he'll be lucky if they don't try
him as a war criminal and shoot him.*

***

As it turned out, June's nursing unit had moved to a bivouac
area near Tunis and Hal had run into her in the officer's bar at Allied
headquarters. They picked up where they had left off, and Hal was
seeing her every chance he got. When Jack asked about Shelly, Hal
told him she had been with June and asked about him. At the time,
Hal didn't know where to tell her Jack was or how to contact him,
but he was seeing June that evening, and Jack was welcome to come
along if he was free.

The thought of seeing Shelly again made Jack's heart pound
and his pulse quicken. It surprised him how much he wanted to see
her. But he was in the middle of modifications to his ship that were
taking place around the clock and wouldn't be able to get away until
they were finished. Hal told Jack he would pass the word to Shelly
that he was in port if he saw her. He also got the berthing number for
the ship just in case. Then Hal hopped into his Jeep when his driver
pulled up alongside the curb and headed back to his unit.

With visions of Shelly in mind, Jack stepped off the curb and
crossed the street to his Jeep which was waiting for him on the other
side of the boulevard. A taxi swerved to miss him, another just barely
stopped in time to keep from running him down, and the driver of
a New Zealand Bren gun carrier hit the brakes and spun his vehicle
just in the nick of time narrowly missing Jack and sliding past him
sideways with sparks flying from the tracks as they slid on the paving
stones in the street. Amid blaring horns, squealing brakes, and some
very colorful language from the Kiwi, Jack casually got into his Jeep
and the driver asked, "Sir, are you all right?"

Jack, snapped out of his reverie, looked at him in surprise and
said, "Yeah, why do you ask?"

The driver just shook his head, said, "Oh nothing, sir," and
drove back to the ship.

CHAPTER 51

In Tunis harbor, Commander Meriwether and his Seabees were swarming over Jack's ship like ants. In the last three days, they had built a steel structure to support the flight deck, and now they were attaching stringers and decking it over. Jack climbed to the bridge and was watching the progress, hoping Hal would see Shelly and he would be able to see her. While he was daydreaming about seeing Shelly, he happened to notice Chief Barton and Boatswain Gardener standing on the main deck watching the construction, talking, and shaking their heads. Jack called down to them, and they came up to the port bridge wing.

"How's it going, Boats? You satisfied with what they're doing to your ship?" Jack asked.

"Oh, yeah, they're doin' a great job, good buncha guys, work hard, and they're smart. When they get done, we're gonna look like a hunch backed escort carrier."

"You and Barton don't look all that happy. Something wrong?"

Boats turned and looked at Barton, "Go ahead an' tell 'em what ya tole me. The skipper'll un'erstan'."

When Barton hesitated, Jack looked at him and made a come on out with it motion with his hand.

Barton looked uncomfortable but finally screwed up his courage and said, "Well, sir, it's like this. Whenever we've had sumpin' needed ta be done, we didn't go aroun' askin' permission. We just went ahead and did it. Most a the time, we had ta do it on the QT so's ta speak, but everthin' always turned out fine. Now we got the system on are side, and well…it just don't feel right. Makes me kinda queasy thinkin' 'bout it, kinda like sumpin' bad's gonna happen cause ever thin's goin' are way fer once."

Jack looked at Barton for a few seconds and started to grin. "Chief, would it make you feel better if I sent you out to abscond with something, so things feel like normal?"

Barton looked puzzled, glanced at Boats, then back at Jack. "I don' know, sir. It might…if I knew what abscond meant." Jack and Boats broke up laughing.

What Jack didn't realize was that after a lifetime of wheeling and dealing Chief Barton's ability to sense trouble was second to none, and trouble was indeed on the way.

***

Just before noon the next day, Jack was in the machine shop listening as Chief Grubowski explained the installation of the fuel line from the void to the main deck for the aviation fuel when he got a call on the machine shop squawk box.

"Sir, there's an officer to see you." It was the assistant first lieutenant, Ensign Price.

"Who is it and what does he want?" Jack asked.

"The officer didn't say, sir," Price relied.

"I'm with Chief Grubowski going over the installation of the fuel line for the airplanes. Can it wait?"

"I don't know, sir. I'll ask."

The squawk box was silent for a moment, and then Price came back. "Sir, the officer says it's regarding Inter Allied Communications, sir."

"Okay, send him down."

"Ah, sir, the officer would rather speak to you on the pier if possible."

"Well, what the h——l is that all about?"

"I don't know, sir. I'm just relaying the request."

"Well, tell him to go away. I'll contact him as soon as I can."

"Ah, sir, I don't think you want to do that."

"What? Why not!"

There was an edge to Jack's voice that was sharper than he had intended. He'd been working extraordinarily hard to get on top of things. When he wasn't on deck or on the bridge, he was reading ship's manuals, memorizing procedures, learning Morse code and navigation, and how every piece of equipment aboard ship worked and was operated. When he wasn't working on those things he was administering the ship's operation and looking out for the welfare of the 111 lives that had been placed in his care. He was mentally tired, and it was starting to show. Other than the meetings, he had to attend and the two ship's holidays he hadn't taken any shore leave or left the ship since they left Pilottown. By his own admission, he was getting tired.

He thought, *I'll have to watch that. I don't want to be biting a man's head off for doing his job.*

"Well, sir, I think you'll see when you get up here. The officer will be waiting for you on the pier."

"D——n. Okay, I'll be right up, but whoever this a——s h——e is, he'd better have a pretty d——n good reason why I have to meet him now, and he can't come aboard."

"Oh, I'm sure there's a good reason, sir. Price out."

Shortly Jack popped out of the port booby hatch and stalked across the deck toward Price who was manning the rail at the gangway in the midst of a group of sailors Jack assumed were either signing out for or returning from liberty. Price handed Jack his clipboard and said, "I'm sure you will need to sign out for a trip ashore to handle this, sir."

All the men started smiling and jabbing each other in the ribs with their elbows like a bunch of school boys on the playground. Jack snatched the clipboard out of Price's hand and saw Price had already entered the reason for going ashore as an "Inter Allied Communications meeting."

"What the h——l is this?" Jack flared. That caused the men to start laughing among themselves.

Ensign Price handed Jack his pencil and hooked his thumb over his shoulder toward the pier at the base of the gangway. Jack grabbed the pencil and signed while glancing at the men who were starting to crowd in around him. Then he looked over the side. There stood Shelly.

CHAPTER 52

While Jack's ship was undergoing modifications, Major Dunwitty had been running his pilots through short landing and takeoff drills. Boats worked with Hal's maintenance chief, Master Sergeant Clarence Palmer, to develop a routine for handling aircraft on the flight deck, and use of the elevator to move planes up and down between the flight deck and the main deck. By the time they were finished, they had gone from a sketch and a bunch of notes on a piece of paper to an operational unit ready for combat in seven days.

Invasion preparations were moving forward at a frantic pace, but even with all the work that had to be done, Jack managed to find time to see Shelly. He grabbed a half hour with her here a couple of hours with her there sandwiching time with Shelly in between all the hundreds of demands thrust upon him and his sailing orders to various ports moving men and equipment as needed. He only managed a few hours' sleep each night, but he had never been happier in his life. He felt alive like he had never felt before, and no matter how tired he was, every time he saw Shelly, the weariness melted away.

At the same time, Jack was preparing the ship for action JAG Captain Dean Cassidy stepped off a Navy transport at the airport in Casablanca with orders to apprehend Jack Cole.

Lucky for Jack, Cassidy reported to Admiral Hunt, explained the reason for his presence, and asked for the admiral's assistance in finding Cole. During his audience with the admiral, Cassidy made the mistake of ending the explanation of his orders by saying, "I'm here to find this clown and run him out of the Navy."

Following his meeting with Captain Cassidy, Admiral Hunt had his aid de camp look into Cassidy's service record. Cassidy was on a fast track having made captain twelve years after graduating from the naval academy. He had been in the Navy for fifteen years and had never been to sea. There was nothing Admiral Hunt despised more than a senior-ranking Navy officer who had never been to sea.

Hunt knew a good officer when he saw one and in Jack Cole he saw a good officer. In Cassidy, he saw an over officious paper pusher on a mission the admiral found distasteful. It was painfully obvious that Jack was not guilty of anything worse than being cashiered into the Navy against his will and doing an outstanding job in a position for which he was totally unqualified and unprepared. All of which made Admiral Hunt admire Jack even more.

Admiral Hunt instantly made up his mind that he wasn't going to let Cole get hung out to dry for a mistake the Navy made and fired off a memo to Admiral Bryton in Washington DC. In the memo, he extolled the virtues of Lieutenant Commander Cole and stated in no uncertain terms that regardless of the circumstances surrounding Cole's entry into the Navy he was an extremely competent officer and currently involved in a mission so important to an upcoming operation that he could not be relieved from his duties for any cause.

Unfortunately, due to the secrecy surrounding Operation Husky, Admiral Hunt could not mention the upcoming invasion or go into any detail regarding Jack's role in the operation. Admiral Bryton received the memo, and because there was nothing explaining why Cole's mission was so important, he summarily dismissed it. In return, he notified Admiral Hunt that there was nothing so important that a man could not be replaced, especially one who was "masquerading" as a naval officer.

The term "masquerading" was the deciding factor in Admiral Hunt's ensuing actions. Hunt was a shirttail relative of Admiral Frank Jack Fletcher and Admiral Frank Friday Fletcher both Congressional Medal of Honor winners; Frank Jack Fletcher having won it twice. Hunt didn't have the fame his relatives enjoyed, but he had inherited the same fighting spirit. The admiral quickly formed a plan to throw Cassidy off the scent and delay him as much as possible in finding Commander Cole. The admiral sent word to Cassidy that his staff would check into Commander Cole's sailing orders, and the captain was to report to Admiral Hunt's office each day for an update and to handle assignments as needed by Admiral Hunt. Of course, the admiral had no intention of providing Cassidy with Cole's scheduled ports of call and planned to send him on every wild goose chase he could think of. In between times, he planned to keep him buried in paperwork until Operation Husky was completed; longer if possible.

Unfortunately, Captain Cassidy wasn't as gullible as Admiral Hunt had hoped. After several days of reporting to Admiral Hunt's office only to receive a mountain of various personnel issues, which needed to be resolved and no news of Jack's next port of call, he realized the admiral was not going to be of any assistance in finding Cole. Cassidy took it upon himself to dig into the matter and was finally able to determine where Jack's next port of call would be. He shanghaied a junior officer into dealing with the paperwork and left immediately by air to beat Jack to the next stop on his itinerary where he planned to apprehend Commander Cole and throw him out of the Navy.

Captain Cassidy was not on the fast track without cause. He was a very capable individual with drive and determination. He was the type of officer that when given an order would walk through the fires of Hades to get the job done. Unfortunately for Cassidy, Commander Cole was well liked in North Africa, and when Admiral Hunt found out Cassidy was on his way to confront Commander Cole, he played the ace card in his deck. He passed word to the senior enlisted men through his ranking yeoman that Cassidy was on a mission to apprehend Cole and cashier him out of the service. Hunt didn't tell his yeoman why Cassidy was after Cole. As far as Hunt was concerned, the fewer people who knew, the better. Just knowing that a good officer who took care of his men and anyone else that needed help was about to get the axe was enough.

Word spread fast, and when Cassidy landed in Bizerte, he found his ground transportation had not been notified of his arrival, and he ended up spending a miserable night at an Army Air Corps aux-iliary airfield sleeping on the floor in a maintenance hut, which was the only building he could find that wasn't locked. He was unable to secure ground transport until the next afternoon, and by the time he made it to the harbor in Bizerte, Jack had sailed.

Going back to his sources for Jack's next port of call, Cassidy was unable to secure air transport so he spent two days traveling in an Army hospital column as it wound its way along the North African coast to Algiers where Cassidy found he'd missed Cole again. After two more missed attempts at catching up with Cole, Cassidy realized he was being thwarted purposefully and redoubled his efforts. The chase was on, and the only one who was unaware of it seemed to be Jack who continued his duties ignorant of the fact that there was a sword hanging over his head, one thread away from falling on his neck.

CHAPTER 53

As the date for the invasion of Sicily fast approached, activities all along the North African coast picked up. Massive amounts of men and equipment were moved from the Atlantic coast of North Africa to bases along the Tunisian coast where the invasion was being staged.

Because of his experience working with Commander Meriwether on the Seabee pontoons, Jack was put in charge of training the LST officers and men in assembling and deploying pontoons as a cause way. This kept Jack in port at Tunis for approximately a week supervising the instruction program and running his "students" through the curriculum he designed. While this was good for the LST crews, good for the invasion, and allowed Jack to see Shelly more often, it made Jack a sitting duck, and Captain Cassidy finally homed in on his target.

Boats and Barton had been keeping tabs on the whereabouts of Cassidy through the chief's network. When word reached them that Captain Cassidy was on his way to Tunis, Barton created what became known as Operation Magic. Operation Magic was on such a large scale that even the redoubtable Barton required some assistance in putting it together and pulling it off. As it turned out, it was a lucky thing Jack had developed the relationships he had with the allies in North Africa because Operation Magic required interservice cooperation and allied support.

The day before Cassidy was due to arrive in Tunis, Boats began work on repainting the ship. Due to the scratches and gouges caused by raising and lowering pontoons alongside for the training classes, Boats had no trouble convincing Jack that painting was required. His plan was to start at the bow and stern where the work was most difficult and paint the slab-sided amidships when the pontoon training was finished. The first thing that needed to be done was paint over the ship's hull numbers port, starboard, bow, and stern.

When Cassidy arrived in Tunis, he found the harbor jammed with Allied shipping. He immediately went to the harbormaster and asked where he could find *LST 121*. The harbormaster offered Cassidy a seat in his office, and his secretary gave him a fresh cup of coffee. Captain Cassidy sat quietly sipping his coffee while the harbormaster thumbed his way through page after page on a clipboard he pulled from the nail it was hanging on next to his desk. In the meantime, the harbormaster's secretary was on the telephone in the outer office where she placed a call to *LST 121* via ship to shore telephone and asked for Boatswain Gardener.

After consulting several other clipboards and a map of the harbor anchor buoys, the harbormaster asked in heavily accented English, "What sheep do you say you are lookeeng for?"

This caused Cassidy to set his jaw and reply, "*LST 121.*"

The harbormaster rocked back in his office chair, took a sheaf of papers from the credenza behind his desk, and slowly worked his way through page by page, studying each one in great detail. He continued to study the pages until his secretary caught his eye through the office window behind Captain Cassidy and gave him a nod. She then walked into the harbormaster's office and refilled Cassidy's cup from a used West Bend percolator. At that point, the harbormaster leaned forward in his chair and said, "Monsieur, are you sure you are lookeeng for *LST 152?*"

Cassidy sat upright in his chair and put the coffee cup down on the harbormaster's desk much harder than he intended to and after plastering the most sincere fake smile he was able to fabricate on his face said, "No, I'm looking for *LST 121.*"

"Well, why do you not say so, Capeetan? You have waste my time searcheeng for a sheep who she does not exist. You British are all alike. You theenk you own the seas and all that is on the water. You should know your beesiness before asking for someteeng you do not want. Now leave my office at once. Pft"—he made a spitting noise—"on your King."

"I am not British. I am an American," Cassidy replied icily.

"Well," shouted the Frenchman, "why do you not say theese before to me, we French, we love America. Do you know Joe DiMaggio?"

Thirty minutes later, after assuring the harbormaster that he thought the Yankees would be every bit as good after the war was over as they were before and that Ted Williams was the only player that had a chance to beat Babe Ruth's home run record, Cassidy left the office to find a launch that would take him out to the ship. He scoured the docks for a Navy launch that could run him out, but every coxswain he approached was committed to other duties that required him to stay moored to the pier until his officer returned. Cassidy finally found a liberty boat that could take him out, but he would have to wait until all the sailors were delivered to their ships before he could be taken to the LST as the liberty boat returned to shore for its next load.

On the way out, the liberty boat passed several LSTs as the coxswain ran from one vessel to the next delivering sailors to their ships. Each time they neared an LST Cassidy asked the coxswain to pull alongside so he could ask where *LST 121* was anchored. But each time, the coxswain's response was, "Sorry, sir, I have my orders." Try as he might, Cassidy was unable to spot an LST with the hull number 121. It just didn't appear to be in the anchorage; although he did notice one that was being painted and thought he might give that one a try as soon as the coxswain was finished delivering the sailors to their ships.

Finally after an hour of zigzagging through the maze of ships through choppy water and a heavy spray, Cassidy was the last man aboard. The coxswain turned toward shore and glanced at his watch. Cassidy noticed this and said, "Run me out to that LST that's being painted. That might be the ship I'm looking for."

The coxswain looked at his watch again and said, "Sir, I'm afraid I won't have time. If we knew that was the ship you're looking for, I might be able to run you out to it, but I'm already running late, and I have to get back to the pier to pick up the next load, or I won't be able to get the men to their ships before their liberty expires. You're welcome to ride with me again, and maybe we can swing by that ship at the end of the next run."

Cassidy didn't respond but stepped ashore when the liberty boat landed and stalked off into the night wet, tired, and hungry. As he vanished into the darkness, the coxswain picked up his Aldis lamp and signaled *LST 121, Enemy in retreat.*

Boatswain Gardener read the message and replied, "*Well done*" with a flashlight he took from his pocket. Immediately, the anchorage lit up like a field full of fireflies as messages were flashed informing everyone Operation Magic had begun.

CHAPTER 54

The next day, the MPs from the 202nd Military Police Company stopped Cassidy when he tried to pass through security at the harbor. They found that he wasn't listed as a member of the local Naval detachment and was not listed as an officer or crew member of any US Navy ship in the harbor. When the 202nd MPs checked with allied military headquarters, they were informed by Admiral Hunt's chief yeoman that there was no Captain Dean Canidy in the North African theater of operations. Cassidy was hand cuffed and held in custody until the mix up over the pronunciation of his name was straightened out, and it could be proven that he wasn't an Axis spy. As a result, he lost an entire day in his hunt for Lieutenant Commander Cole.

The next day, all the coxswain's of the US Navy launches along the pier were again committed to their current duties, but Cassidy noticed a British launch that was preparing to leave the quay and asked the coxswain if he could drop him off at *LST 121* when he returned to his ship. The coxswain signaled his ship and after receiving a reply said he would be more than happy to do so. However, as the launch was motoring out into the harbor three loud whoop, whoop, whoops were heard from the British destroyer's siren and the coxswain made a dash for his ship. The launch was hoisted aboard as the ship was getting underway, and Cassidy spent two days aboard the tribal class destroyer HMS Ashanti as the ship charged out to sea and escorted a small coastal supply convoy into Tunis. The Ashanti's captain and officers welcomed Cassidy into their midst and regaled him with stories of the Mediterranean fighting over dinner that evening which was topped off by a large serving of ice cream the captain said he had received as a gift from an American ship for towing a target sled for them. Unfortunately, Cassidy lost the dinner and the ice cream over the rail later that night due to the fact that this was his first time aboard ship in the open ocean and he came down with a bad case of *mal de mar*.

Following his return to Tunis Cassidy spent the next day in his quarters recovering from the after effects of his adventures with the Royal Navy. After recuperating sufficiently to return to his mission, Cassidy arrived at the harbor in time to watch *LST 121* sail out of the harbor with spanking new hull numbers painted over a brand new coat of Navy gray.

A little further down the quay, a Canadian nurse stood next to a bollard holding a handkerchief to dab away her tears and waving to the ship as it departed. She watched the ship until it disappeared from sight and then walked away crying into her tear soaked hankie.

When Cassidy tried to check out through the harbor security, he found there was an arrest order out on him for being AWOL and traveling without proper authorization. Once again, he was hand-cuffed and taken to the regional military police station, processed, finger-printed, and tossed into a cell.

CHAPTER 55

Two months earlier, on May 13, the Africa Corps and the Africa Settentrionale forty-two divisions of the Italian Royal Army, had surrendered. The battle for North Africa was over, and Operation Husky, the invasion of Sicily, was on. Preinvasion plans were completed in June and Army units were assigned to transports and landing craft. These were organized into squadrons for command and control purposes. Each squadron was assigned specific Army units. They were also assigned their landing sites and the order they would hit the beach. Because he had been convoy commander of Task Group 4.7 Jack was assigned command of a squadron of LSTs. In addition to the L-4s Jack was carrying, he had a company of tank destroyers and an Army film and photographic unit aboard. The other LSTs in his squadron were carrying anti-aircraft guns, combat engineers, construction equipment, and replacement Sherman tanks.

Counting his own ship, Jack was in command of a total of six LSTs. Because of the cargo and troops they were carrying their units would not be landed until the beach heads were secured, and then Jack's squadron would land their troops and equipment when and where needed. Following the discharge of their cargoes, Jack would remain on site supporting Hal's L-4s and the remaining five LSTs would return to Tunis harbor to pick up additional troops and equipment.

While the initial landings were taking place, Jack's squadron was to loiter at sea ready to bring their units to shore as soon as the beaches were secured. He had been assigned a holding area ten miles out to sea that would make it a short run to get to the beaches. Hal would launch his planes as needed and land them on a predesignated beach where they would wait until Jack brought his ship in to support them.

Jack managed one last meeting with Shelley at a small French bistro just outside the harbor security area in Tunis. When they pulled up in front of the café, Jack jumped out of the Jeep and dashed in through the bistro's bat wing doors.

Shelly was waiting for him when Jack rushed in. He went to her and sat looking into her eyes. They had only taken a sip of their wine when Jack reached across the table and took Shelly's hand in his. Shelly looked down at his hand, then gripped it firmly with both of hers and looked up. Tears had begun to form. As she blinked them away, Jack stood and took Shelly in his arms. She melted into him laying her head against his chest. Jack could feel the tears soaking through his uniform, wet against his chest. Shelly looked up at him and said, "I don't think I can live without you, Jack. Please come back to me."

Then she buried her head in his chest, and he could feel her heart pounding against his. At that moment, he knew he would move heaven and earth to spend the rest of his life with her. He hugged her tight, and when she looked up again, he kissed her like he had never kissed a woman before. In that one brief kiss, he felt every emotion he'd ever known flow through him like an electric charge. He became lightheaded and never wanted the kiss to end, but it had to. And when they parted, Jack walked to the bistro's swinging doors, Shelly watching him. When he reached the doors, he stopped, turned, and before going through, he said, "I love you."

Shelly replied, "I know."

And Jack was gone.

In the Jeep, the driver looked at his skipper, waiting for his orders. When they didn't come, he asked, "Back to the ship, sir?"

All Jack said was, "Yeah."

The driver revved the engine, popped the clutch, and headed back toward the harbor. What neither he nor Jack saw was Shelly standing in the doorway looking over the bat wing doors crying her heart out as the Jeep disappeared down the street.

CHAPTER 56

That evening, July 8, the invasion armada began to form up for the trip across the Mediterranean to Sicily. Late in the afternoon of July 9, the wind started picking up, and by the time paratroopers and gliders were over their drop zones, the winds were howling with gusts up to forty-five miles per hour. At sea, the conditions were no better and the invasion fleet battled, the wind and waves through the night to be in place for the landings the morning of July 10.

Ashore, the airborne troops were widely scattered causing delays in their attacks on bridges and other strategic targets as they tried to consolidate their forces during the night. When the seaborne troops hit the beach the morning of the tenth, resistance was light, and the troops were able to come ashore without a great deal of difficulty. However, because many of the bridges leading to the landing beaches were not able to be captured or destroyed the evening before, reinforcements were able to be rushed in making it difficult to move very far inland.

The high winds also hampered the fighters and bombers from Tunisia and Malta. Though the allies put up a large number of aircraft over the landing beaches, the Regia Aeronautica and the Luftwaffe took full advantage of the weather affecting allied ability to maintain constant air superiority and drove home their attacks on the ships at sea and the troops on shore.

Jack's squadron stood off shore the day of the invasion waiting to be called to the beach. The Luftwaffe and Regia Aeronautica attacked throughout the day after fighting their way through the defending fighter force or when the weather caused scheduling problems in the fighter relays and left gaps in the air coverage.

Mr. Jensen's gunners brought down one Ju 87 dive bomber and an Italian SM.79 torpedo plane. They hit several more that limped away damaged trailing smoke. All of which was caught on film by the Army film unit camera men who seemed to be everywhere and had to be cautioned not to get in the way.

During the afternoon of the tenth, the 422nd was called upon for spotter work. In the midst of the fighting, Jack managed to get four L-4s flown off while fighting off attacking enemy aircraft, without any damage to the planes or the ship. After the L-4s were launched, Jack lowered both LCVPs and sent the 422nd ground crewmen, fuel, oil, spare parts, food, tents, and ammunition ashore to support the L-4s. Hal and the crews of the remaining aircraft stayed aboard to launch additional aircraft when called upon. A pair of Army camera men also accompanied Hal's ground crew and support personnel.

Both LCVPs were strafed by a lone Italian CR.42 on the fifteen-mile trip east to the beach. But the combat air patrol spotted the intruder and a pair of P-40s brought it down. Two of Hal's men were slightly wounded, by flying splinters and one camera man fell overboard in an attempt to get a shot of the P-40s attacking the Italian fighter. The coxswain of the LCVP circled, picked him up, and the landing craft made it to the beach without any further incidents.

The attacks on the LSTs did not let up. During the night, the squadron was attacked by Italian motor torpedo boats, but they were detected on radar, and Jack maneuvered his ship in between the torpedo boats and his squadron of LSTs. Again, Mr. Jensen's gunners proved the effectiveness of the ship's firepower and drove them off, sinking one and damaging two others in the process. At dawn, one of the damaged torpedo boats was discovered abandoned and in a sinking condition.

Later the morning of the eleventh, a request for two more spotter planes was received. Hal and another pilot flew off shortly before the LST squadron was called to unload. After completing the unloading, Jack transferred command of the LSTs and proceeded east to the site of the beach airfield where he pushed his assembled cause way up on shore and used the ship's six-by-six and jeep to quickly unload the remainder of the 422nd's supplies and equipment.

The beach allied command selected for Hal's operation was located in the twenty-five-mile gap between the US Army landing sites along the south central coast of Sicily and the British landing sites on the south east coast. The invasion plan called for the allies to consolidate the area between the two invasion sites within hours of the initial landings. This would place the 422nd out of harm's way, safely located in a position to provide artillery spotting for both the American and British sectors. However, due to the winds that disrupted the paratroop landings, the area had not been secured, and the 422nd's airfield had in effect been set up in axis territory.

CHAPTER 57

When allied troops failed to meet them at the beach, Jack contacted allied command who assured him there was nothing to worry about. Paratroops had landed farther inland and secured the area. Jack was ordered to remain where he was and "carry on." There was that throw-away phrase again, knowing how it was used a shudder went down Jack's back.

The beach the 422nd occupied lay at the base of rocky cliffs which fell away inland to become a narrow valley. The far side of the valley floor rose in a series of rugged ledges and rocky outcroppings, which eventually formed the low mountains of the Sicilian high lands.

There were no allied troops to be seen, and Jack wasn't about to bet his life and the lives of the men he commanded on what allied command thought was going on. If there were paratroops farther inland protecting the airfield, Jack couldn't see them, so he applied the best military advice he'd ever been taught, which was *Be prepared*. Even though he'd learned it as a Boy Scout, it was good advice for any situation. He just regretted the Scouts had never offered a merit badge in hand to hand combat.

Jack was no military man, but everybody in Nebraska knew you never left your fences untended if you wanted to keep your cattle in and the predators out, so he established a series of outposts on the cliffs above the beach. Radio silence was still in effect so he equipped each post with a battery powered Aldis lamp and a set of signal flags. He manned his outposts with six man teams—two to handle signals and four riflemen for protection. He had them dig in and armed them to the teeth. Absent any real military know-how, it was the best he could think of. An Army camera man went along with them and dug in as well.

It was a tough climb to get from the beach to the top of the cliffs so once he had men on top Jack had Boats rig bosun's chairs to run men, supplies, and hot meals to and from the beach to each of the lookout posts on the cliffs.

The beach was wide, flat, and deep. It provided Hal's pilots a perfect base of operations and plenty of room to take off and land without obstruction, except to the north where the cliffs rose to a considerable height. The squadron operated out of the beach airfield for the remainder of the day and through the morning of the twelfth without incident until signals were received from the top of the cliff that a cloud of dust was seen and appeared to be heading in the direction of the beach. Jack had Hal send one of his planes to reconnoiter. The pilot and observer returned and reported a large column of Italian mechanized vehicles making its way to the coast along a narrow twisting road, which consisted of a series of switchbacks carved into the mountainous terrain.

As they were returning to the beach, the observer noticed a group of paratroopers moving inland several miles in front of the enemy column on the same road. To make sure the paratroopers were aware of the Italian armor, he scribbled a note and dropped it as the pilot overflew the troops.

The paratroops acknowledged the message and began scrambling up the sides of the narrow roadway to get out of the path of the oncoming Italian armor. The observer dropped another message advising them of the location of the 422nd and the outposts. The paratroops hurried over the broken terrain and made contact with the observation posts on the cliff approximately thirty minutes later.

When Jack was informed of the Italian armor, he contacted allied command and began to get ready to pull out if necessary. Hal was calling for gunfire support on the Italian column but was informed there was nothing close enough to fire on those specific targets. The 422nd was in axis occupied territory in the gap between the two landing sites where no naval fire support had been allocated. Ships would have to be repositioned in order to be in range of the coordinates specified. The fighting was getting heavier at the beach heads as the Italians and Germans began throwing reinforcements into the battle. Fleet gun fire was critical at the moment and could not be spared. Jack was told he would have to hang on as long as he could and keep the observation planes operating at all costs.

Jack's anti-aircraft guns weren't designed to lob shells over obstacles like a howitzer could; they would be of no use against the Italian armor if the column chose to come his direction and attack the airfield. Pulling out was not an option his orders wouldn't allow it; it could mean the death of thousands of men on the beaches. But if he was caught on the beach and the aircraft were destroyed, the same end result would occur. He had to come up with a plan.

So as not to be taken by surprise, Jack asked Hal if he could spare one of his aircraft to keep an eye on the Italian column. Hal sent one of his L-4s to loiter in the general area but told the pilot not to get too close or draw any fire. The pilot was about to take off when one of the Army camera men asked Hal if he could go along. Since the plane would not be directing any artillery fire, the observer wasn't needed, and Hal gave the camera man the okay to go.

Hal and his pilots were in and out of the beach continuously. He had eight L-4s in the air spotting artillery fire plus the one he had watching the Italians. He kept the other three either ready to cover new target areas or held in reserve in case of a break down or loss of an aircraft. By rotating his planes and aircrews Hal was able to keep his men and planes as fresh as possible. The spotting effort was working as planned and allied command ordered Jack to keep it operating regardless of the situation he faced.

Aboard a ship, there is no such thing as a secret. When word got around that an Italian armored column was approaching, but the skipper had been ordered to hold on at all costs a feeling of fear, apprehension, and near panic went through the crew. They didn't know what was going to happen, but if the Italians were sending an armored column, they would be sitting ducks. Firing down on them from the cliffs above would be like shooting fish in a barrel.

Jack had never faced an "at all costs" situation before. Realizing what the implications were, the thought, *This could end up being a bad day* flashed through his mind. It was such an outlandish thought that he began to laugh at himself. When the bridge crew saw this, word raced through the ship that the skipper was laughing at the danger and spoiling for a fight. The men figured the skipper must have something up his sleeve and the talk aboard ship quickly changed from "What is that armored column going to do to us?" to "What are we going to do to that armored column?"

When the paratroops joined Jack's men atop the cliff, they were deployed in fighting positions between the observation posts by their commanding officer Second Lieutenant Abner (Abe) Schromber and dug in. The lieutenant rode a bosun's chair down to the beach and reported to Jack aboard ship. It turned out that Second Lieutenant Abe Schromber wasn't the commanding officer of a unit; he was the ranking officer among a rag tag group of paratroops that had been widely dispersed by the wind. Schromber had gathered them up in ones and twos as he moved through the country side trying to find his unit.

Not being able to find his own people, Schromber took command of the paratroops he'd collected and headed inland to destroy the three bridges his unit was assigned. When Hal's pilot dropped the message about the Italian armor, Schromber realized the Italians had already crossed his target bridges and was glad to join up with other American forces.

Lieutenant Young was in command of the outposts on top of the cliff. Jack put Abe under Young's command with the understanding that Young would call the shots, but Schromber would set up the defenses and direct the fighting if it came to that.

The Italian column was made up of a mixed bag of light tanks, tankettes which were much like the British Bren gun carrier, armored cars, and tank destroyers. With the exception of the tank destroyers and the armored cars, none of the rest of the vehicles were on a par with allied armor, but they were well positioned to strike either the British or American landing force in the flank and armored vehicles of any type could be deadly against infantry.

There were approximately fifty vehicles in the column and no allied forces were in a position to block them or engage them in an effective manner. Allied air cover was tied up over the beaches, and the fleet firepower wasn't in a position to offer any assistance.

Reports from the plane Hal allocated to keep an eye on the Italian column made it apparent that the Italians were making for a tee intersection which would allow them to divide and sweep onto the beach from both ends or attack one or both flanks of the allied beach heads.

The paratroops had several bazooka teams, and Jack asked Schromber if his men could move fast enough to be in a position to hit the Italians at the intersection. If they could be stopped there, it would back up the column and maybe delay the Italians long enough for naval gun fire support to arrive. Schromber checked the map and told Jack there was no way he could move fast enough to get there in time. He might be able to catch the tail end of the column, but even that was pretty iffy.

Jack discussed the issue with Hal, then asked if Hal could fly Schromber's men to the intersection so they could set up an ambush. Hal said, "Sure, let me look at the map."

After a quick look, Hal just shook his head. "I can fly them there, but there's no place to land."

Jack looked at Schromber. "Do you have any of your parachutes left?"

Schromber gave him a *you've got to be kidding* look and told Jack, "Ah…sir, once we land, we haven't got any use for 'em. They aren't bulletproof, you know."

"Ah…Yes…I…Oh, never mind," Jack said, embarrassed that he'd asked such a stupid question.

When Schromber saw the look of disgust on Jack's face and watched him turn red, he thought he'd gone too far with his crack about the parachutes not being bullet proof and made the lieutenant commander mad. He immediately said, "Sir, we might be able to fire the bazookas from the airplanes."

Jack looked at Hal. Hal shook his head and said, "The back blast from the rocket would set the plane on fire."

"How about if a man leaned way out on the wing strut and fired the bazooka straight ahead? The pilot could aim the airplane at the target and the bazooka man could pull the trigger when the pilot was on target," Schromber suggested.

"H——l if you're going to do that, you might as well tie the bazooka to the wing strut and pull the trigger with a string!" Jack flared.

Schromber took a half-step backward, startled by the ferocity of Jack's response, but Hal said, "d——n, Jack, I think that will work!"

Jack barked, "Are you f——g kidding me? There's no way in h——l I'd ever ask a man to lay out on a wing strut and fire a bazooka!"

"No, no, no," Hal said. "Not what Abe said, what you said. We could clamp a bazooka onto the wing strut and fire it by using a piece of rope or a Bowden cable to pull the trigger"

Jack stood there thinking for a moment, then said, "Okay…If you guys think you can make something like that work…do it. Get whatever you need from Chief Grubowski and have him help you."

Thirty minutes later, Chief Grubowski and Master Sergeant Palmer came pounding up the ship's ladder to the bridge to tell Jack they had everything ready and were about to test fire the bazooka.

Jack slid down the ladder and ran to the bow where he could watch the test from the forward 40 mm. gun tub. Hal had an L-4 facing the cliff with its tail up on a crate sitting level to the ground. There was a big X painted on the cliff face one hundred yards in front of the plane. Jack signaled "okay" using his hands as flags. Hal reached into the cockpit and whoosh a rocket fired from the right wing hitting the X slightly to the right of dead center. Then another rocket fired from the left wing and hit the X square in the middle. Paratroopers ran to the bazookas attached to each wing and reloaded them. Hal turned and looked toward Jack on the bow of the LST. Jack signaled "Go," and Hal jumped into the cockpit. The paratroopers man handled the plane into the wind and a ground crewman gave the prop a swing. The engine roared to life, and Hal took off across the beach. He made a climbing turn and disappeared over the cliff.

Twenty minutes later, Hal dropped back over the lip of the cliff, taxied in, and motioned for the paratroops to reload the bazookas. He didn't even shut down the engine. As soon as the reloads were in place, Hal gunned the engine, turned into the wind, and was gone again. As Hal flew out of sight, a signal was sent from the cliff top that smoke and flames could be seen to the north. Hal was back in twenty minutes and landed again to rearm. This time, however, Jack noticed strips of fabric trailing from the fuselage and holes in the wings. While the bazookas were being reloaded Palmer pulled the fabric back in place, taped it down with duck tape, and slapped patches over the holes in the wings. As soon as the reloads and repairs were finished, Hal took off again. Smoke could now be seen from the beach rising above the height of the cliffs. Whatever Hal was doing, it was causing somebody a lot of grief.

Hal returned once more for reloads. Jack ran to the beach to try and find out what was going on, but Hal was just lifting off when Jack got there. Jack grabbed the first pilot he saw and told him to take him up so he could see what was happening.

Both men piled into a plane with the pilot in the back and Jack up front. Just as the pilot yelled "contact" and a ground crewman swung the propeller Jack saw a paratrooper with a Thompson sub-machine gun standing to one side watching. Jack yelled through the propeller blast, "Soldier, give me that Tommy gun and all the extra magazines you've got. I'll give it back when I'm through with it."

The paratrooper ran up holding his helmet on against the propeller blast, handed Jack the Thompson and half a dozen magazines, then threw a sack on Jack's lap, and yelled over the roar, "Here ya go, sir. You might want these too."

Jack looked into the bag and saw it was full of grenades. Jack smiled, slapped the paratrooper on the shoulder, and said, "Good thinking!" gave him a thumbs-up, and they took off across the sand.

The pilot kept the plane low as he flew north toward the smoke rising ahead of them. Trees and rocks flashed by to either side as the little L-4 made its way toward the towering pyres of smoke and flame which appeared to be belching out of the ground like the plume from Mt. Etna farther to the north. Jack searched the sky all around them, but there was no sign of Hal.

Suddenly, Hal's L-4 rocketed up in front of them like it had been spit out of the ground followed immediately by an explosion and streams of tracer fire. Hal did a wing over and went right back down in the opposite direction disappearing into the bowels of the earth only to pop up again followed by another explosion and more tracer fire. This time, Hal rolled toward Jack's plane and flew past heading toward the beach. Pieces of fabric were trailing from the tail, one aileron, and the wings. The body behind the cockpit looked like a sieve. Jack could see all the way through the plane in places as Hal passed them heading south.

Hal had caught the Italian armored column on a narrow one lane road carved out of the side of a hill. Where he was attacking them the hill fell away five hundred feet to the valley floor on the one side of the road and was up against a sheer cliff on the other.

When Jack's plane flew over the lip of the hill, it drew streams of tracer as soon as the Italians spotted it. The pilot hauled it around to duck back over the top of the cliff out of sight then the pilot leaned forward and yelled, "What do you want me to do, sir?"

"Fly along the edge of the cliff so I can see what's going on."

The pilot made a circle, and Jack threw up the top half of the side door, latched it in place, and dropped the lower half. He had a completely unobstructed view out the starboard side of the plane and could even lean out and look straight down. As they flew along the edge of the cliff, Jack could see Hal had caught the column of Italian armor and stopped it in its tracks. Vehicles were burning at both ends of the column. Hal destroyed the lead vehicle blocking the way forward and then destroyed the last vehicle in the column to plug the escape route. Then he began working his way back from each end destroying one vehicle after another. It was a mad house below. Men were trying to extinguish the flames on the burning vehicles and push them over the cliff to get out of the trap.

Jack's L-4 was pretty well shielded from the anti-aircraft fire from below, so Jack had the pilot swing around once more. This time, as they passed overhead, Jack cut loose with the Thompson and sprayed the men at both ends of the column trying to spring the column from the trap. This caused the soldiers to run for cover, but as soon as the plane passed, they were right back at it trying to extinguish the fires and push the destroyed vehicles out of the way.

Jack had the pilot make another pass and sprayed the men with hot lead again. On this pass, they started drawing fire. The starboard wing hung out over the edge of the cliff and the Italians were firing at the wing as the plane flew over. Jack told the pilot to duck back over the cliff and only pop out when he thought they were over one end of the column or the other. Jack pulled out a pair of grenades, pulled the pins with his teeth, and held the handles down. As soon as the pilot swung over the precipice, Jack dropped both grenades and the pilot swung back. The grenades landed among the working sweating men and blew up. They also set fire to a vehicle that was being used to push a destroyed tank over the edge.

Jack kept up the attacks alternately dropping grenades and spraying the Italian soldiers with machine gun fire. He didn't know how many passes they had made, but suddenly, an artillery shell burst on the top of the hill behind them and Jack told the pilot, "Let's get the h———l out of here."

The Navy had finally arrived and had begun shelling the coordinates Hal had given them. As Jack and his pilot made their way back to the beach he saw Lieutenant Schromber and his men scrambling across the broken ground toward the area being shelled. As they flew over, Abe's troops waved at the little L-4 and the pilot waggled his wings in reply.

When they landed, the first thing Jack saw was Hal's airplane sitting on the sand broken in half just behind the pilot's seat. When the pilot killed the engine, Jack jumped out and ran to the wreck of Hal's L-4 thinking the worst. Instead, he found Hal under the nose helping Sergeant Palmer unbolt the engine from the plane.

"D———n you're okay!" Jack yelled when he got to the plane. "I saw this wreck and thought you were dead."

"Yeah, well, I ain't, but I busted this bird trying to land. I guess she just had too many holes in her and not enough lift. She quit flyin' about four feet off the ground, dropped in like a rock and…well, you can see what happened. I'm tryin' to salvage as much as we can for spares."

Looking at Jack's plane, Hal said, "It don't look like you done my other bird much good either. What the h——l have you been doin'?"

Jack glanced over his shoulder and saw his pilot and several of Hal's maintenance people looking at the L-4 Jack had just returned in. The starboard wing was shredded, the starboard elevator was a shambles, and the fabric on the rudder was almost completely gone. Jack thought, d——n *I wonder what caused that?*

Before Jack could say anything more a soldier came running up to him and asked, "Sir, can I have my Tommy gun back now?"

CHAPTER 58

J ack had just returned to the ship when a message came in from allied command that the 422nd was to move inland. Hal took off with his remaining airplanes while his ground crew loaded everything back aboard the LST. Jack pulled away from the beach and towed his causeway with him to the American beach head where he unloaded the 422nd's supplies and equipment into waiting trucks. He'd also brought Hal's two crippled planes tied down on the causeway. Hal's men broke them down in a matter of a few minutes and loaded the airframes onto trucks as well. It only took Jack and Hal's men an hour and a half from the time the causeway was pushed up on the beach until the time the 422nd was gone.

Jack wrote his after-action reports on the way back to Tunis and filed them along with some other paperwork as soon as they beached. There was a load of equipment and supplies waiting for him and he immediately began to stow the cargo as fast as possible. As hectic as things were, Jack couldn't help but notice Boats had seen to it that two more airplanes and a pair of torpedo boats had been added to the kill list on both bridge wings. At the sight of the decorations, Jack broke into a smile that almost hurt it was so big. He'd never been more proud of anything in his life. That was when Lieutenant Young called the bridge and reported a Captain Cassidy was at the gangway requesting permission to come aboard.

Jack was checking the cargo manifest when Captain Cassidy was escorted to the bridge. Jack thought it odd that the Captain had a pair of SPs with him but didn't attach any significance to it. "Welcome aboard, Captain. What can I do for you?" Jack said as he stuck out his hand in greeting.

Rather than shaking Jack's hand, the captain turned to one of the SPs and said, "Arrest this man."

Before he could do or say anything the SP slapped a handcuff on Jack's wrist and cuffed his hands behind his back. "What the h——l is this about?" Jack demanded.

"You are under arrest for impersonating a naval officer, endangering the lives of the crew of *LST 121*, interfering with a superior officer in the execution of his duties, unauthorized use of Navy equipment, giving false testimony during induction, evading arrest, and incompetence. As of this moment, you are relieved of your command, your status as a member of the United States Armed forces and the United States Navy is severed. You will be taken to the nearest brig and held in custody until you are brought to trial to face these charges. Is that clear?"

Jack stood there for a moment and realized that the Navy had finally figured out they had inducted the wrong man. In a way, it was a great relief, but at the same time, he had come into the situation unwillingly, had repeatedly told the Navy they had made a mistake, and had documented his claim repeatedly in writing. He looked around at what he thought of as *his ship and his crew* and thought about all they had been through together; suddenly, he was angry. He was beyond angry he was mad as h——l, and he wasn't going to take it.

"Did I understand you correctly that I am no longer a member of the United States Armed Forces and the United States Navy?" Dealing with the law and legal issues was a major part of a superintendent's job, and Jack had become particularly knowledgeable of the ins and outs of the legal system. Oftentimes, a single word could change the entire course of litigation. Cassidy had made a mistake, and Jack wasn't going to let him get away with it.

"That's right," Cassidy said. "As of this moment, you are out on your ear."

"And you're sure about that, correct?" Jack replied.

Cassidy nodded his head and stood staring smugly at Jack.

"Okay." Then turning his back to the SP who had applied the handcuffs, he held his hands out as far as he could behind him and in his best command voice said, "Sailor, undue these handcuffs."

The SP looked dumbfounded. He looked from Jack to the captain and then began to unlock the handcuffs. Captain Cassidy bellowed, "Belay that order, sailor. You are under my command. You leave those cuffs exactly where they are."

Jack said, "Sailor, unlock these handcuffs. As you no doubt heard, I am a civilian. The Navy has no authority to arrest me or place me in irons. As a civilian, any charge brought against me must go through a civilian court. I have not been presented with a warrant for my arrest, therefore unless you want to be charged with aiding and abetting in a kidnapping, I suggest you immediately unlock these handcuffs."

Word had spread throughout the ship about what was happening and the bridge, both bridge wings, and the ship's ladders leading to the bridge were becoming crowded with crew members who were hanging on every word.

The SP looked around once more and, turning to Captain Cassidy, said, "I'm sorry, sir, but he's right." Then he unlocked the handcuffs and, looking at Jack, said, "I'm sorry, sir."

"That's okay. You were just following orders. Oh…and you don't have to call me sir. I'm a civilian now." The SP stood back and said, "As a matter of respect, I think it is called for…sir!" Then he saluted. The crew in earshot began to mumble their approval. Lieutenant Purvis pushed his way through the crowd on the bridge and said, "Boats, would you see that Captain Cassidy is escorted off the ship, please?"

"Aye, aye, sir!" Gardener bellowed. "Make a hole. Man coming through." Then he cleared the way for Cassidy to leave the bridge.

As Cassidy was about to step onto the bridge wing, he turned and said almost in a hiss, "This isn't over, Cole. Not by a long shot."

Jack looked Cassidy straight in the eye and said, "You are correct about that, Captain. This isn't over."

CHAPTER 59

It was bittersweet leaving the ship. On the one hand, it was humiliating. On the other, he should never have been there in the first place, but…the Navy made the mistake—Jack didn't. He did everything he could to explain that to them, but when it became evident that they were bound and determined to send him to sea or send him to prison, Jack had put everything he had into doing the job that needed to be done. Looking back, he could find nothing to be ashamed of and plenty to be proud of. After everything that had happened and everything, he and the crew had been through he felt he had earned the right to be there, but now he was being given the boot, tossed out on his ear like so much trash. It hurt.

Jack had no idea what was going to happen now that he had been declared a civilian, but he knew he had obligations that needed to be addressed. He notified Admiral Hunt that he had been relieved of his command; the admiral would now need to find someone else as his go to guy and the "most knowledgeable LST man in the Mediterranean." He wrote a fitness report for each of his officers recommending them for advancement and extolling their outstanding qualities. He also wrote the chief of staff of II Corps and presented him with a written report of Hal's actions against the Italian armored column as well as those of Gene Wilton the pilot who had flown the plane Jack was in. As a final thought, Jack wrote Admiral Springset and Admiral Beyard describing how well the causeways had worked and suggesting Pete Meriwether be recognized for the contribution he made to the success of the landings through his ideas on the use of pontoons to fabricate causeways and floating piers.

Once Jack had completed these reports, he dropped them into his out box, sorted the mail in his in box, arranged the correspondence into the usual piles, picked up his personal mail, looked around his cabin one last time, grabbed his seapack trunk, B-4 uniform garment bag, and headed for the main deck.

Jack was uncertain about how the crew would react now that they knew he was not the grizzled veteran they thought he was. He had never lied to his men, but by the same token, he hadn't gone out of his way to confide in anyone about his true background. Of course, he had been put in a position where if he had shared that information with anyone he would now be in Portsmouth Naval Prison. He'd been put in a lousy spot, but that wasn't his men's problem. They were there to do a job and depended on him to know what he was doing to keep them alive. Jack had done the best he knew how, and he'd done everything he could to keep his men safe. He knew that, but what would his men think now that they knew the score?

When Jack stepped on deck to leave the ship, all work stopped, and the crew crowded around the sally port, standing on every available hatch way, ventilator, and winch so they could see the "old man." He wondered what was going through their minds. He needn't have worried. A voice bellowed out, "We're with ya, skipper. Just tell us what you need us to do." That voice was immediately followed by every man shouting encouragement, cheering, and crowding in on him to show their support.

Jack stood there, looking into the faces of the men he'd come to think of as *his boys*, and it practically broke his heart to think of all they'd been through and having to have it end like this. He managed to collect himself and rubbing the back of his neck while looking up at his men said, "Gentlemen, by now, you all know that I've been relieved of command and why. I got into this kinda bass ackwards."

At that, smiles and laughs emanated from the crew. "I had no idea what I was doing or how to do it, but faced with the option of spending the rest of my life in Portsmouth Naval Prison or going to sea, well, the choice wasn't too hard to make."

This time, there was plenty of laughter. "This could have turned out to be a complete cluster f——k, but I got lucky because I got the best crew in the Navy."

A voice boomed out of the assembled men. "H——l, sir, you made us a great crew. We wasn't borned that way."

That brought a cheer from the crew and a chorus of "Yeah," "That's right," "You bet," and other affirmative statements from the crew.

Jack smiled and raised his hands for quiet. Once the men settled down, Jack went on. "You are the finest group of men I've ever known. I don't have the words to express how proud I am of each of you or how proud I am of this ship and all you've accomplished."

There were cheers and whistles among the smiles and laughs from the crew. At that moment, the piercing blast of attention on deck was heard from a bosun's pipe on the bridge. Jack looked up and there stood Barton, Boats, and Grubowski directly above the decorations on the bridge wing. Boats immediately piped salute the colors, and Barton stepped to the signal halyards where he hauled up a hoist and spanked it off the yard arm. When the hoist unfurled, it consisted of three braziers and a pair of pink panties. The ones the ship had collected as "war prizes." A roar went up from the crew that was so loud men on other ships in the harbor looked across the water to see what was going on.

CHAPTER 60

When Jack set foot on shore, he had no idea what he was going to do. He'd been cast adrift on foreign shores with nowhere to turn, no one to advise him, no place to live, and no idea how he was going to get back to the United States. The only thing he could think of was to go to the American Embassy in Tunis, tell the consul general what had happened, and see if the consul general could help him.

Jack hailed a cab. He was going to have the driver take him straight to the American Embassy, but it was coming up on noon, so instead, he had the driver take him to the Canadian nurse's compound hoping he might catch Shelley free and tell her everything that had happened over lunch. Instead, he was told Shelley would not be available until after her shift which wouldn't end until midnight. He left her a note and sent his gear to the embassy by taxi. He needed time to think before he spoke to the consul general so he decided to walk back.

As he walked along, Jack turned things over in his mind, trying to get a handle on the situation that faced him and figure out what to do. But by the time he reached the embassy, nothing had come to mind. When he approached the gate, the Marines on guard duty stopped him and one asked, "Excuse me, sir. Are you, Lieutenant Commander Cole?"

With a big smile, Jack said, "Not any more. They used to call me that, but I got promoted to civilian now, so it's just plain Jack Cole. Can I help you?"

The Marine looked embarrassed and said, "I'm sorry to have to tell you this, but we've got orders to arrest you on civil charges."

CHAPTER 61

After leaving the ship that morning, Cassidy had gone straight to the embassy and filed charges against Jack with the consul general. Once Jack showed up at the embassy, things began to move very quickly. Since the American Embassy was considered American soil, an American civil case could be tried on embassy grounds with the same legal effect as if it was held in the states. American law would apply, and the case would be tried as if it was in an American court room, the Consul General Hooker A. Doolittle, acting as the judge. A jury would be selected from Jack's peers, Captain Cassidy would act as the prosecuting attorney, and Jack could hire a lawyer, have one appointed by the consul general, or defend himself.

Cassidy was pushing for the trial to be held immediately. He would have been content to have the trial start the next day, but the consul general nixed that when he asked Jack if he was represented by counsel. Jack replied, "Represented? H——l I didn't even know I was being charged until I walked through the embassy gate."

Not having representation, the consul general declared the trial could not start until the defendant was provided with an attorney who could defend him. He assigned a junior legal attaché as Jack's council and gave him three days to come up with a defense. Cassidy objected to the delay, and after a heated argument with the consul general, he left the embassy fuming.

Even though things happened quickly, they didn't happen in a vacuum. As soon as the warrant for Jack's arrest was issued, the gunnery sergeant commanding the embassy guard contacted Boats and filled him in on what was taking place. Boats, in turn, reported to Lieutenant Purvis and then passed the word to the crew.

Lieutenant Purvis had been placed in command when Jack was relieved, but as far as he and everyone aboard were concerned, Jack was still the captain. The mood aboard ship was *the Skipper is in trouble and needs our help.*

Immediately, Lieutenant Purvis convened a council of war in the ward room with Boats, his chiefs, and all the department heads. Following Jack's standard procedure, Purvis suggested a plan of action, and they fell to making a list of things that needed to be done and then prioritizing them. Franklyn, Tyree Higby, and Lucius Tanner kept the coffee flowing and Bill Spence saw to it that there was plenty to eat while they worked out the details of their plan. Just past midnight, Shelley joined the meeting by the ship to shore telephone. She had gotten Jack's note and called him at the embassy. After Jack explained what had happened, she began to cry. But Jack told her everything would be okay. She just needed to be patient and have faith. He told her, "Don't worry, the crew is on this. I'll be fine. You'll see."

Even to his own ears, Jack didn't sound very confident, and Shelley began to cry again. Finally she got her emotions under control and found out she would be allowed to visit Jack while he was held under house arrest on the embassy grounds. This seemed to make both of them feel better.

Over the phone, Shelly told Lieutenant Purvis she would be able to see Jack so he gave her a list of things to tell him. Just before she hung up, Shelley told them her Uncle Lyon was a politician in Canada, and she could get his help if they needed it. Then she had to surrender the line. Dawn was just breaking when the plans were completed, and Operation Jail Break was born.

When Purvis closed the meeting, each man knew his assignment, and they immediately set to, to make the necessary contacts and set the plan in motion. The only possible fly in the ointment was the cargo run they had been assigned to make to Sicily. It would take three days if everything went according to schedule but could take much longer if they were held up unloading. They had finished loading their cargo the day before shortly after Jack left the ship. Their sailing orders were to be prepared to leave port and join a small convoy for the crossing to Sicily that day at noon. They had worked through the night on Operation Jail Break, and Lieutenant Purvis was ready to sail immediately. He wasn't about to wait six hours to get underway.

Leaving immediately would put Purvis well ahead of schedule. According to the sailing orders, they were to leave port at the harbormaster's command, rendezvous with the convoy escort outside the submarine nets, and form up for the run across the Mediterranean. The convoy would be slow; the best Purvis could expect from the transports, freighters, and tankers would be nine knots. Knowing this, Purvis had factored it into the plans for Operation Jail Break and immediately contacted the harbormaster after the meeting broke up. Following his discussion with Lieutenant Purvis, the harbormaster issued orders vague enough that they could easily be misconstrued to mean Purvis was to leave port immediately.

As soon as he cleared the submarine nets, Purvis sent a signal to the harbormaster informing him they were unable to locate the convoy. The harbormaster acknowledged receipt of the message while drinking a cup of very excellent Turkish coffee fresh brewed from his West Bend electric percolator and replied, "Take convoy course and make maximum speed. Join in route if possible." Then he settled back in his chair and enjoyed the rest of his coffee.

Grubowski kicked in the third blower on both engines and the ship was able to maintain a sustained speed of fifteen knots during the crossing. Dale was worried about Kriegsmarine and Regia Marina submarines operating out of Italian ports. They had proven quite effective during the early stages of the invasion of North Africa so Dale adopted a zigzag course and doubled his lookouts. They avoided any contact with submarines, but the zigzag course added additional time to the crossing.

When they sighted the Sicilian beach head, ships were spread from horizon to horizon. Attack transports, freighters, and LSTs were milling around waiting to unload under the watchful eyes of destroyers, destroyer escorts, and submarine chasers.

This is what Purvis had been concerned about. The military's standard operating procedure was hurry up and wait. This could create a huge problem for Operation Jail Break if it was not addressed. Anticipating something like this might happen, Purvis contacted beach master control, identified his ship, and asked for Commander Meriwether. "Jack, you old pirate. Long time no hear from. How you doing?" were Pete's first words over the radio.

"Pete, this isn't Jack. It's Dale Purvis. Jack isn't with us this trip. He's in serious trouble, and we need your help. Can you get us turned around as soon as possible?"

"I can't move you ahead in the unloading queue, but I've got a new section of beach I'm clearing to make landing sites for the LSTs. It's a long way from being finished. If you're willing to risk it, I think I can slip you in. Fill me in on the situation with Jack once you're beached."

"Yes, sir Commander, just guide us in."

Dale conned the ship up on the beach, and Mr. Jensen immediately opened the doors, dropped the ramp, and began to unload. Dale drove the ship's jeep down the ramp and looked for Pete on the beach. When he found him, Dale filled him in on what had happened, the charges that had been filed against Jack and the trial.

After Dale had brought him up to speed, Pete shoved his cap back up from his forehead and said, "You mean to tell me the Navy got the wrong man? Jack was never in the Navy and they told him it was either go to sea or go to prison? I'll be d———d. He's the best Navy officer I've ever worked with. That ain't right."

When Pete paused to think, Dale said, "Pete, you've really helped us by getting us in so quick, but I need another favor."

"Sure, what do you need?" Pete asked.

"I've got an idea. You remember those photo jockeys that came over with us on the invasion?"

"Yeah?"

"Do you know where they are?"

"I know where they're supposed to be," Pete replied.

"That's good enough," Dale said.

Dale told Pete what he needed, and Pete immediately sent one of his men in a Jeep to get the job done. Just as the last of the cargo was coming ashore, the Jeep came roaring back and slid to a stop.

One of the combat camera men that had been with the ship at the beach airfield jumped out and handed Pete a canvas satchel and a metal film canister.

"Sir, I think this is what you wanted. I hope it helps." Then the camera man saluted and jumped back in the Jeep. The Sea Bee driver popped the clutch and roared away to get the camera man back to his unit.

Pete tossed the satchel and film canister to Dale and said, "Here you go. If you think of anything else we can do to help, just name it."

"Will do," Dale replied. Then he saluted and headed back to his ship.

Dale had just hauled off the beach and was pulling away from shore when air raid sirens began to sound. A dozen or more Ju 87 Stuka dive bombers dropped out of the clouds into a hail of anti-air-craft fire and attacked the supply dumps, truck convoys moving inland, and the ships waiting to unload. A ration dump on the beach near the ship was hit by a five-hundred-kilogram bomb. The other four one-hundred-kilogram bombs of the five bomb stick landed long; two walked their way across the beach toward the water. Of the last two, one exploded in the water between the ship and shore and the other slammed into the after superstructure. The pilot roared over the ship, turned, and came back to make a strafing run. Just about every gun aboard got a piece of him. The plane exploded, and the flaming wreckage dropped into the sea about two hundred yards from the ship. There were no parachutes.

The bomb destroyed the ward room and the captain's cabin but did not penetrate beyond the main deck level. There were several men wounded, but none of their wounds was life-threatening. Purvis called for flank speed and exited the anchorage at better than fifteen knots. The damage control parties had the fires put out within minutes and the ward room cleaned up and closed to weather within an hour. The ward room would be ready for use by the time they reached Tunis, but the captain's cabin and everything in it was a total loss.

CHAPTER 62

The trip back to Tunis was a rough one. Dale had a timeline he was determined to meet and wasn't going to let anything prevent him from meeting it. A moderate wind kicked up from the west south west raising three- and four-foot waves on the ship's starboard quarter. Dale did not reduce speed, but the way they pitched and rolled and pounded into the waves it gave him some second thoughts about carrying that much speed for the entire crossing. There was also a hand full of men who spent their time hanging over the rail chumming the sharks that would have been in complete agreement.

In Tunis, the legal process was moving fast, primarily because Jack's assigned attorney didn't understand the game. He was letting things slide that he should have objected to and not taking advantage of the time allotted between the various steps in the judicial process. As a result, things were running almost three days ahead of schedule. However, even though they missed the arraignment and preliminary hearing, Dale made port in time for the beginning of the trial.

Once they were tied up, Dale left the ship. He stopped by the harbormaster's office to make sure both men had their stories straight and their reports matched. The harbormaster's secretary retyped a few pages where corrections were required, and Dale filed his report with the port commander where, after a cursory glance at the report, the commander congratulated Dale on shooting down the Stuka. Heading back to the ship, he stopped at the Canadian nurse's compound and left a note for Shelley asking if she could get a pass to come to the ship after her shift was over.

While Purvis was taking care of official business, the rest of the men followed up on the progress being made on their portions of

Operation Jail Break. Boats contacted the gunnery sergeant at the embassy for the latest news on the trial. The report wasn't good. The junior legal attaché assigned as Jack's defense attorney had specialized in international business law and had no experience in US civil law. He had no trial experience and had never been in a courtroom a day in his life. According to the gunny, the kid was doing the best he knew how, but that wasn't good enough. When they went before the consul general for the arraignment and preliminary hearing, the kid was so green Cassidy ate him alive. The gunny said if it hadn't been for the consul general asking for them the kid would never have presented a list of potential witnesses or evidentiary documents; he simply didn't know what to do. The consul even had to prod him into objecting to some of the things Cassidy tried to pull. The gunny said that without the consul's help, Jack would have been railroaded into a life term without the kid even knowing it.

When Shelley arrived at the ship, Dale met her at the dock. No one wanted any unwarranted aspersions cast on Shelley's reputation, so he outlined the plan for Operation Jail Break while they were standing on the pier. When he was finished, Shelley was hopeful, but she wasn't convinced it would work. She reiterated, "Don't forget I can cable my Uncle Lyon if we need his help."

Dale nodded his head politely and assured her that he hadn't forgotten about her Uncle Lyon. Then he immediately dismissed the idea. He didn't see any way a Canadian politician could have any impact on the outcome of a US civil trial being held at the American Embassy in Tunis, Tunisia.

When he returned to the ship, Purvis called his council of war together and asked, "Okay, where are we?"

All arrangements were completed and everything was in place, but the trial was progressing faster than anticipated, and there was a real danger things could get out of hand. Something had to be done, so Purvis decided to call in a favor Jack was owed.

CHAPTER 63

At dawn the following morning Major Herald Newman, formerly of Donovan, Leisure, Newton & Irvine in New York City, New York, currently JAG in command of the II Corps legal section, arrived at the airfield outside Tunis in the bombardier's seat of a Plexiglas nosed droop snoot P-38.

After a very interesting conversation with Chief Quincy Barton and Boatswain's Mate Art Gardener about Operation Jail Break, Newman was driven to the American Embassy in a US Navy Jeep serial number, 212020–122021 where he assumed lead attorney status for Jack Cole and immediately requested a stay until he was able to prepare a defense. Over the objections of Captain Cassidy, the consul general gave Newman two days to review the case and prepare the defense.

Unbeknownst to Jack, Major Newman was on loan as his defense attorney at the insistence of the chief of staff of II Corps. The chief of staff ordered Major Newman to handle Jack's defense after being notified by the ranking NCO in his records department that Jack had been arrested and was standing trial. The NCO passed this information to the II Corps chief of staff shortly after receiving a phone call from Boatswain's Mate Gardener. The chief of staff still remembered receiving the map tube marked Eyes Only II Corps Chief of Staff and felt it was the least he could do for an officer of Lieutenant Commander Cole's insight and understanding of the pressures of command.

Newman was originally scheduled to be driven to Tunis. However, when the pace of the trial picked up, rather than being sent by staff car, he left very early that morning from an air base outside

Casablanca with only a maintenance sergeant leaning on a motorized engine hoist to see him off.

Newman established an office on the terrace level of the Majestic Hotel and took a room on the fourth floor. He immediately began to interview potential witnesses who could vouch for Lieutenant Commander Cole's character, ability, bravery and dedication. He dug in and spent almost every waking hour over the next two days preparing for the trial.

Jack was kept under house arrest at the embassy which, except for the food, was quite comfortable. He had the run of the grounds and was given freedom of movement throughout the embassy buildings but was restricted to the embassy compound which was surrounded by high walls and guarded by Marine sentries. Major Newman came and went as he pleased and other than the inconvenience of the short walk from his office to the embassy had complete access to see Jack anytime he chose day or night.

Newman found no shortage of witnesses willing to come forward and vouch for Jack's character, his abilities as an officer, his bravery and his dedication to the war effort. However, as he interviewed each potential witness, Newman found there were a number of things not included in the charges against Jack that might have an adverse effect on the outcome of the trial if they surfaced during the proceedings. Lieutenant Commander Cole's dedication to the war effort and the lengths to which we would go to assist units in obtaining equipment they desperately needed was extraordinary, although in some cases irregular. As a result of the dedication, Jack was willing to show Army as well as Navy personnel, Newman developed a high degree of respect for Commander Cole's abilities, but became more and more apprehensive each time he interviewed a new witness. It was now very clear to Major Newman why he had been sent from II Corps to defend this low-ranking sailor.

The charges against Jack were impersonating a naval officer, interfering with a superior officer in the execution of his duties, endangering the lives of the crew of *LST 121*, unauthorized use of Navy equipment, giving false testimony during induction, evading arrest, and incompetence.

If Major Newman could keep his witnesses from expanding too much on the manner in which Jack was able to assist various units with their logistics needs Newman felt he had a solid defense and could win the case. But it all hinged on his ability to prove that Jack had repeatedly told the Navy he was the wrong Jack Cole. If he could do that, the other charges would be rendered moot as they were a result of following the orders he was given.

Major Newman contacted the Bureau of Navy Personnel and asked for copies of the letters Jack had sent informing them he had never been in the Navy and that they had the wrong Jack Cole. He soon found out that having made the request as a JAG in II Corps was a mistake. It became very clear to him that cross service requests of that sort were guaranteed to be tied up for months in endless snarls of red tape. Realizing he needed more horsepower, Newman requested the letters again only this time the request was sent through Navy channels over the signatures of Admiral Hunt and Admiral Beyard. So far, there had been no response.

Major Newman met with Jack and laid out the defense strategy he planned to use. After reviewing everything with him, Newman told Jack not to worry. He was not finished preparing the defense. He just needed the information he requested from the Navy. Once that arrived, the case would be assured.

CHAPTER 64

I t had been a torrid two days for Major Newman, but he was the type of lawyer who relished the challenge. He had worked constantly for almost forty-eight hours nonstop, but instead of being worn out, he seemed to gain strength and momentum as the start of the trial neared.

The trial opened the next day. By midmorning, the jury had been selected, and the consul general requested opening statements from the prosecution and the defense.

Cassidy opened with a recitation of the charges against Cole emphasizing the fact that Cole had no prior service in the Navy, maintaining he entered under false pretenses, and declared that he had falsely assumed command of *LST 121*, thus making each movement of the ship an unauthorized use of a Naval vessel which endangered the lives of the crew and the ship. Cassidy maintained that Cole was incompetent because he had no naval training and it was only through the skills of the properly trained officers and men of the ship that Cole's incompetence was prevented from turning into a complete disaster. From there, he continued, claiming that his efforts to apprehend Cole, as ordered by Admiral Bryton, had been thwarted as a direct result of actions taken by order of Commander Cole while trying to evade arrest. He closed by declaring that none of these things would have happened except for the fact Jack Cole lied about his identity when contacted for reinduction. Cassidy's assertion was that Cole did this for personal and monetary gain, which he would not otherwise have enjoyed as a civilian.

Major Newman's opening statement was short and succinct. He stated that the defense would show the Navy had made an error when updating its records to include the new government required social security numbers. As a result, Jack Cole was inducted because his name, and his social security number were the same as an officer who had served with distinction during the First World War, but whose social security number had been entered incorrectly. Jack had repeatedly tried to correct the mistake but was unable to convince the Navy of their error. This led to the Navy giving him the option of joining the service or going to prison. Therefore, all actions Mr. Cole took while in command of *LST 121* were a result of orders he received from the Navy. Newman then challenged the prosecution to show that Jack Cole knew he was subject to apprehension or that he was responsible for any action taken to evade or interfere with Captain Cassidy in executing his orders. He closed his opening statement by adding that the defense would show that even though Cole was forced to enter the service in error his performance had been far above what is expected of an officer of his rank and bestowed great credit on himself, the United States Navy, the United States and its allies.

The stage was now set, and the battle began.

CHAPTER 65

ollowing the opening statements, the consul general called a recess for lunch with the trial to reconvene beginning at 13:00 hours. Following the recess, Cassidy opened by presenting a log of the ship's movements from the time Cole took command to the present. He claimed that each movement was an unauthorized use of Navy equipment. Major Newman objected and claimed the prosecution was grand standing. He requested that the ships orders be subpoenaed and entered as evidence that Mr. Cole was sailing under orders on each ship's movement. It came as a surprise when Cassidy responded, "Yes, Your Honor, by all means, please subpoena the ship's sailing orders. I'm sure that will be most enlightening for everyone, especially the jury."

Doolittle looked at Lieutenant Purvis who was in the courtroom and said, "Lieutenant Purvis?"

Purvis stood and replied, "Yes, Your Honor?"

"Please see that the ship's sailing orders are brought to this courtroom as soon as possible."

Purvis silently looked at the consul general but did not respond.

"Lieutenant Purvis? Did you hear me? I'd like to see the ship's sailing orders as soon as possible. Please contact your ship and see that they are delivered here immediately," the consul general said.

Purvis cleared his throat and said, "Ahem...Your Honor, I'm afraid I can't do that, sir."

"And why is that?" the consul general asked rather testily.

"I'm afraid they no longer exist, sir. They were destroyed when the ship was hit while off the beach at Sicily, Your Honor," Purvis responded. "We were hit in the superstructure. The captain's cabin was completely destroyed along with everything in it including the captain's safe which held all the secret documents, orders and codes, sir."

"My, how convenient," Captain Cassidy said, sarcasm dripping from the statement. "Is it common practice that all orders, codes, and secret documents be kept in the captain's safe? Or is this just a convenient ruse to hide the fact that the orders never existed in the first place?"

Newman jumped to his feet. "Objection, Your Honor, that is slanderous, argumentative, and designed to place doubt about the creditability of Mr. Cole and his crew in the minds of the jurors. I move that statement be stricken from the records and the jury be instructed to ignore the prosecutions unwarranted accusation."

Doolittle banged his gavel. "Objection sustained. The jury will ignore that last statement by the prosecution. Captain Cassidy, you are out of line."

Major Newman immediately followed the consul general's admonition by stating. "Your Honor, the sailing orders can easily be duplicated and copies forwarded to prove the legitimacy of the orders Mr. Cole received."

Before Doolittle could respond, Cassidy said, "That may be true, Your Honor, but how will we know those orders will be legitimate? It is well-known that Cole has someone who is tipping him off about my movements. Who is to say that that same person or persons won't recreate bogus orders and send those instead? After all, they will be out of the chain of custody."

Newman exploded from his seat. "Your Honor, this is outrageous. Captain Cassidy is making assumptions which are totally without merit and calls into question not only the integrity of Mr. Cole, Lieutenant Purvis, and the ship's company of *LST 121*, but the integrity of the entire United States Navy."

The consul general banged his gavel repeatedly and declared, "Objection sustained. The jury will ignore the statements made by Captain Cassidy."

Then turning to Cassidy, the consul general leveled the gavel at him and said, "What you have done is unconscionable, sir. You will refrain from that type of accusation, or I will find you in contempt of court."

"Yes, Your Honor, my apologies," Cassidy replied, then turning away from the consul general and the jury he looked at Jack and Major Newman with the smile of a cat that had just eaten the canary. The damage was done; he had interjected doubt into the minds of the jury, which was exactly what he intended to do.

The remainder of the afternoon progressed in much the same manner. Cassidy made accusations based on flimsy evidence, Newman objected and the two spared over the validity of the accusations until the consul general sustained or over ruled the objection. Almost all Newman's objections were sustained, but Cassidy was attempting to place doubt in the minds of the jurors and was succeeding admirably. The only bright spot was Cassidy did not bring up the ice cream machine, the quad .50 caliber machine gun turrets, the Jeep, the deuce and a half truck, the modifications to the ship's engines, and the items Jack assisted shore units in obtaining to fill out their TO&E requirements.

When the consul general closed the proceedings for the day, Cassidy hadn't mentioned any of the items Newman was concerned about, however, Cassidy would continue presenting his evidence the following day. He had found out about the ship's records being destroyed before Newman knew anything about it, and Newman was very concerned about what else Cassidy might know that he didn't.

As they were leaving the conference room, Jack spotted Boats and Barton waiting in the foyer. When he pointed them out to Major Newman, the major said, "I'll see you in the morning. I need to talk to them about the BuNavPer documents and cover a couple of other things with them."

Newman immediately asked about Operation Jail Break. All they said was things were going as planned, but they had not yet heard from BuNavPer. Newman cautioned both men that a major part of the defense strategy centered on that information and asked if there was any way of checking on its whereabouts? Then he said, "If we don't get those documents here in time, we could lose this case."

Both men looked at each other, and then they left.

Major Newman had seen the look they had on their faces once before, but he couldn't remember where. Then it dawned on him it was the same look John Dillinger had on his face when he posed for a picture with his arm on the shoulder of Lake County Prosecuting Attorney, Robert Estill before he escaped from jail in Crown Point, Indiana.

CHAPTER 66

That evening, Shelley was able to come to the embassy to see Jack. They were sitting on the embassy terrace, watching the sunset, and talking quietly when Major Newman walked up and interrupted them. "Excuse me, Commander…Leftenant, may I have a word?"

Jack and Shelley stood to face Major Newman. "Certainly, Major. Have you met Leftenant Lindsey?"

"I don't believe I have." Removing his cover and tucking it under his left arm, the major extended his hand and, with a slight nod of his head, said, "I am very pleased to meet you. It's a great pleasure."

Shelley shook his hand and said, "Won't you join us, Major?"

"Thank you, Leftenent. This won't take long. I just need a quick word with Commander Cole if you don't mind."

Shelley started to leave, and Major Newman said, "Please stay. This won't take but a moment."

Shelley sat down and the major went on. "I am waiting on confirmation from the Bureau of Naval Personnel that you sent numerous letters notifying BuNavPer you were not the Jack Cole they were seeking. I have yet to hear from them. Is there anything you can think of that can be done to speed up the process?"

Jack thought for a second and said, "I made copies of everything I sent the Navy. There are copies of the letters in my personal files at Walnut Hill, and I also sent copies to the draft board. Will either of those work?"

Major Newman took a deep breath, thought a moment, and said, "I'm afraid not. Those copies would be outside the chain of evidence and not considered valid. We need the originals or confirmation that the originals exist. That is our only means of confirming that you indeed provided the Navy with this information."

"I see." Jack said.

"Is there any way you can think of that we can get someone in BuNavPer to find those letters and confirm them in time to use for the trial?" the major asked.

Jack thought for a moment, then his face lit up with a wry smile. "You met Boatswain's Mate Gardener and Chief Barton from my ship's company."

"Yes, I have. Two very extraordinary men, in my opinion."

"Yes, ahem…Yes, they are. As long as you don't ask how they do it, I'd suggest you contact them, tell them what you need, and let things take their course." Jack said.

The major looked askance at Jack and finally nodded his head once. "I see. Thank you, Commander. Have a nice evening." Then turning to Shelley, he said, "Leftenent," and with a flourish donned his cover, turned and left.

As soon as Newman returned to his office, he called the ship and spoke with Lieutenant Purvis, explaining he needed to speak with Boats and Barton. Dale said, "Just a moment, Major." and turned away from the receiver. Major Newman could hear Lieutenant Purvis tell someone to, "Get Boats and Barton up here like five minutes ago."

Purvis came back on the line and said, "Major, I'll have them for you in just a moment."

A few minutes later, Major Newman heard Boats' voice come over the line, "Boatswain Gardener, sir. I have Chief Barton with me. How can we help you, sir?"

"Mr. Cole informs me that as long as I don't ask how you do it he believes you two may be able to get both the BuNavPer sailing orders as well as the letters he sent to the Navy explaining he was the wrong Jack Cole. Do you think that is possible?" Newman asked.

As soon as he finished, Gardener said, "Way ahead of you, sir. We've been in contact with the senior yeoman in BuNavPer. He is looking for the letters as we speak. I expect to hear from him within the next half hour, sir."

Boats couldn't see Newman's eyebrows rise in surprise, but he could hear it in his voice. "Really, does he think they exist?"

"Oh, there is no question they exist, sir. He's seen them. Yeoman Burris is digging them out now."

"So they are not in Commander...er, Mr. Cole's file?" the major asked.

"No, sir, they are not, but they were stamped with the date of receipt when they arrived and were opened. So that ought to be good enough, shouldn't it?" Boats asked.

"Yes...Yes, it will," Major Newman replied. "But since they weren't in his file, we will only be able to be use them as evidence if we can present the originals during the trial to prove that the dates of receipt are valid and not added after the fact."

There was silence on the line as both men were thinking. Suddenly, in the background, Major Newman could hear another voice. "Say, didn't that babe the skipper's been seein' say she had somebody in the govment could hep if we needed it?"

"Who is that?" Newman asked. "It's me, Chief Barton, sir."

"No, Chief, I mean who is it that Leftenent Lindsey said could help?" the major asked.

Boats came back on the line. "I doubt there's anything to it major. Lieutenant Lindsey said, her uncle Lyon could help. But he's some politician in Canada so don't pay it no never mind." Boat's comment was dripping with derision.

"Hey...she said it." Barton complained defensively.

"Did I hear you correctly? Did you say Lyon? She wasn't talking about Lyon MacKenzie King, was she?" Newman asked.

"Hel...er, heck, I don't know," Boats replied. She just said her uncle Lyon was some politician in Canada, and he could help.

"Okay," Major Newman said. "You stay right where you are. I'll be right back as soon as I talk to Leftenent Lindsey. Don't go any-where—I mean anywhere! If this Uncle Lyon is who I think he is, I'll have another job for you to do. Say, speaking of that, how did you get a hold of this Yeoman Burris in DC? Nobody can get a phone call from here to the states without a special authorization."

There was a pause on the other end of the line, and then Boatswain's Mate Gardener asked, "Do you really want to know, sir?"

Newman thought for a second and then said, "Ah…No, I guess not."

CHAPTER 67

Newman slammed the receiver down, called the American Embassy, and asked to speak with Leftenent Lindsey if she was available. The operator said she would check and see if she was still in the compound and put him on hold. When the operator returned on the line, she told Major Newman Leftenent Lindsey was on her way out, but she would have the Marines stop her before she left the grounds.

Newman was on pins and needles waiting. He paced and fidgeted like a small boy waiting in line to go to the rest room. Finally, Shelley answered, "This is Leftenent Lindsey. Who am I speaking with, please?"

"Leftenent, this is Major Herald Newman. I just spoke with you a little while ago."

"Oh, yes, Major. What can I do for you?"

"I understand you have an Uncle Lyon. Is Lyon his first name or his last name?"

"His first name." She replied, somewhat surprised.

Cautiously, Newman asked, "He wouldn't by any chance happen to be Lyon MacKenzie King, would he?"

"Why yes…Yes he is. He's my mother's brother. We've always spoken of him as Uncle Lyon. He goes by MacKenzie in public."

"Leftenent, I've been told you think he might be able to help with the Cole case. Is that correct?"

"Oh yes, Uncle Lyon is rather gruff in public, but he is an absolute darling, and I just know he would do anything he could for me, if I asked him."

"Leftenent, can you wait for me at the embassy until I get there? I think you hold the key to resolving Jack Cole's case in his favor."

CHAPTER 68

Major Newman did something he hadn't done since he played left field for the Yale baseball team during his undergraduate days. He sprinted from his office to the American Embassy. He was passed through by the Marine Guard, found Shelley, and raced to the embassy communications center with her in tow. He then placed a call to the Prime Minister's residence in Ottawa, Canada, and handed Shelley the phone.

Since the call came from the American Embassy, it was assumed to be an official call and was patched straight through. It was 11:00 p.m. Tunisian time, which made it 5:00 a.m. Ottawa time. The call was answered by a gruff voice which demanded, "Who is this? Do you have any idea what time it is?"

Shelley's answer was, "Hello, Uncle Lyon. It's me, Shelley."

CHAPTER 69

When the trial resumed the following day, Cassidy picked up where he left off by continuing to list ship movements, which he claimed were each an illegal use of Naval equipment. Major Newman objected to each charge of illegal use of naval equipment and the two attorney's spared until the consul general ruled on the objection. This was frustrating, but knowing Newman would be unable to produce the sailing orders, Cassidy felt compelled to carry on if for no other reason than to build a preponderance of evidence showing Cole's willful disregard for military protocol.

The jury was made up of Navy desk officers of equal or higher rank than Lieutenant Commander Cole and civilian embassy officials who had no military experience but were on a civilian pay grade equal to or above that of a lieutenant commander. There wasn't a single sea officer in the group, and one thing Cassidy knew for certain, desk officers and civilian employees were notorious for their disdain of officers and other military personnel who chose to ignore the finer points of protocol and strict adherence to orders because during war time they felt the world walked in their shadow.

Cassidy closed the portion of his prosecution covering illegal use of naval equipment and immediately began to address impersonating a naval officer and giving false testimony during induction. He produced a ream of documents each of which contained Jack's signature. These documents covered every facet of the reinduction process, and Cassidy took great satisfaction in pointing out that nowhere on or among the documents was there an entry by Cole, any of the administrative officers, or the Naval clerical staff that Cole protested the actions. Cassidy's conclusion was that Cole had willingly signed each document in an effort to deceive the United States Navy and gain entrance to the service under false pretenses.

Major Newman objected, "Your Honor, what possible incentive could Mr. Cole derive from joining the Navy that he didn't already enjoy as county superintendent of schools for Wellborn County Nebraska?"

Cassidy quoted the pay and benefits Cole received from the Military pay chart. For a lieutenant, Commander Jack was to receive $3,150 per year in pay, plus housing, meals, medical and dental care, and an insurance policy of $10,000 in the event he was killed in action as well as mortuary services and burial at a military cemetery.

This had an impact on the jury and those in attendance. The average wage in the US was a little under $2,000, a Coke was a nickel, a month's rent was $35, and gas cost 15 cents a gallon if you could get any. The pay and benefits a lieutenant commander received looked pretty good to the everyday working man.

Major Newman replied, "Your Honor, that is indeed a handsome salary and benefits package. However, I have here a summary of pay and benefits Mr. Cole was earning before he was *forced* into the Navy."

Captain Cassidy jumped to his feet. "Your Honor, I object to the characterization of Mr. Cole as having been *forced* into joining the Navy. It is the prosecution's contention that Mr. Cole lied in order to enter the Navy under false pretenses. He was never *forced* into anything. On the contrary, he has gone out of his way to take advantage of the war time situation for personal gain which as I have shown is quite substantial."

"Your Honor," Newman replied, "the prosecution's *contention* does not make it a fact. That is precisely what we are here for today to prove that the prosecution's *contention* is false. Any term other than *forced* is a misnomer."

The consul general banged his gavel. "Major Newman, in the interest of time, I do not wish to prolong things by arguing over semantics. Please refrain from using the term *forced* to describe Mr. Cole's induction into the Navy and find another term."

"Would Shanghaied be acceptable, Your Honor?" Newman replied.

Before Cassidy could respond, Doolittle banged his gavel and pointed it at Newman. "Sir, you knew the answer to the question before you asked it."

Turning to Cassidy, he said, "Captain, your objection is sustained."

"But, Your Honor, I haven't made an objection," Cassidy replied.

"You were about to weren't you?" Doolittle asked.

"Yes, sir."

"There you go then. Your objection is sustained."

Turning to Newman, he said, "Get on with it, Major, and mind your impertinence."

"Yes, Your Honor, my apologies," Newman replied. Then speaking to the jury he continued. "As I was saying, gentlemen of the jury, I have here a summary of the pay and benefits Mr. Cole would be receiving if he had not been called to serve in the Navy."

At that point, Newman turned to the consul general with a *is that satisfactory* look on his face. The consul general nodded his approval, and Major Newman continued, "As county superintendent of schools in Wellborn County, Nebraska, Mr. Cole earned $4,000 in annual salary, a home was provided by the county, and his health and dental needs were provided at no cost to him by doctors in the community. If Mr. Cole joined the Navy for personal and monetary gain, I don't think he made a very wise choice, do you?"

"What about life insurance?" Cassidy asked. "I don't recall hearing about a provision for life insurance, mortuary fees, or burial? What about those expenses, sir?"

"Your Honor, gentlemen of the jury," Major Newman said, "I fail to see how Mr. Cole would realize any personal gain if the need arose to utilize any of those services."

This brought a huge laugh on the part of everyone in the courtroom. Only Captain Newman failed to see the humor in the response. He was serious.

"On that note, we will adjourn until tomorrow," Doolittle declared and banged his gavel to close the day's session.

It was now Newman's turn to give Cassidy a sarcastic smile.

CHAPTER 70

Major Newman immediately sent word to the ship asking Purvis, Boats, and Barton to join him at the embassy. When he had them altogether, he looked at Purvis and asked, "Well?"

Purvis shook his head and looked at Boats and Barton. Both men shook their heads as well. "Nothing from BuNavPer yet, sir."

With a frown on his face, Newman folded his arms across his chest and said, "s——t."

Barton glanced at the clock on the wall and then looked at his wrist watch, "Sir, I wouldn't get too excited yet. They's a Navy R4D bout to have engine prolems and land at the airfield. I 'magine it's gonna take a couple a days to get the parts and maybe another day to fix it. They's a couple admirals aboard prolly won't wanta spend the day at the airfield. I magine they'll grab a taxi and head to Naval Headquarters unless their driver gets lost an brings 'em to the embassy by mistake. I'm sure they'd be interested in this here trial, sir."

Newman just stared at Barton for a few seconds and said, "Engine trouble?"

Looking at his watch again, Barton said, "Yep, just about now I'd say, sir."

CHAPTER 71

Later that evening, as the consul general was beginning to think about dinner, he glanced out his office window on the second floor of the embassy and saw Admiral James B. (Jimbo) Hunt and Admiral William (Billy) Beyard walking across the embassy grounds accompanied by two Marines. He knew both men from the days when they rowed against each other in college. Hooker, rowed stroke oar for Cornell, while Jimbo and Billy rowed as members of the crew for the Naval Academy. They had struck up a friendship that lasted through college and continued to this day. Jimbo and Billy continued their careers in the Navy and Hooker started his career in foreign and domestic commerce, which eventually led him to a career as an international diplomat. Hooker left his office and met Jimbo and Billy as they entered the foyer.

Hooker welcomed them and invited them to dinner; both men accepted, and the consul general escorted them to his private dining room. After a few minutes spent catching up on family and friends the consul general said, "Jimbo, Billy, it's great to have you here. I assume you are here for Lieutenant Commander Cole's trial?"

Both admirals turned and looked at each other and Admiral Hunt asked, "What? What trial?"

"Lieutenant Commander Cole...Lieutenant Commander Jack Cole? He's being charged with impersonating a naval officer, interfering with a superior officer in the execution of his duties, endangering the lives of the crew of *LST 121*, unauthorized use of Navy equipment, giving false testimony during induction, evading arrest, and incompetence. I'm assuming that's why you're here, isn't it?

251

"We're here because our plane shot craps, and we couldn't get it through some French cab driver's thick head that we wanted to go to Naval Headquarters. What are you talking about a trial?"

Doolittle explained what was taking place. Neither man knew anything about the charges or the trial. It came as a very unpleasant surprise, and neither man was pleased to hear about it. They each had a special interest in Commander Cole and his abilities.

"Hook, Commander Cole and Captain Cassidy are both under my direct command and nothing has come across my desk about the Navy bringing charges of any kind against Jack Cole. As a matter of fact, I'm in a dog fight with Admiral Byers at BuNavPer over his being dismissed from the service. It's one of the most frustrating and infuriating things I've ever been involved in," said Admiral Hunt.

"Well, Jimbo, the charges weren't issued by the Navy that's probably why you haven't heard about them. They are civil charges and were brought by Captain Cassidy."

"On whose authority?" Admiral Beyard demanded.

"On his own, Billy." Then the consul general explained that Captain Cassidy had filed civil charges against Commander Cole and as consul general, he was obligated to adjudicate the trial.

Admiral Hunt asked, "Who instructed Captain Cassidy to file civil charges against Commander Cole?"

"As far as I know, he filed them on his own" was Doolittle's response.

"Hook, I'll want to see all of Cassidy's paper work when this is concluded," said Admiral Beyard.

"Certainly; would you like a copy as well Jimbo?" the consul general asked.

"Most definitely," Hunt replied. "Most definitely."

"Since we're grounded here until they fix our plane, I'd very much like to attend the trial," Hunt said.

"Me too," Beyard added. "When does it start?

"It's already started. Tomorrow will be day three. The prosecution is making its case now. Tomorrow or the next day the defense will begin their presentation," Doolittle replied.

"Well h——l, because we're marooned here, they'll be holding the conference we were supposed to attend at Naval Headquarters here in Tunis. People are flying and driving in as we speak. The conference will start tomorrow," Hunt said. "How long will the trial take?"

"I don't know, but I'd say two maybe three days more at the most," Doolittle replied.

"Well, Hook, I can't tell you what to do and I wouldn't even if I could, but I'd sure like to appear as a witness if that can be arranged," Hunt said.

"Add me to that too," Beyard said.

"Well, gentlemen, the list of witnesses for the prosecution and defense have been submitted, but if you can show that you have compelling new information that will have a bearing on this trial, I can add you at my own discretion. Just make sure you have something legitimate to add. I won't allow you to pull rank or intimidate the officers in the jury," Doolittle said, giving both men the evil eye.

"Who me?" Beyard asked. "Would I do anything like that Hook? Why you've known me since we were pups. You know better than that."

"Yeah, me too," Hunt parroted. "I'm offended you would even think such a thing, Hook. Why if I didn't know better I'd swear you were treating us like conniving children."

"That's the point," Doolittle said. "I know both of you, and I wouldn't say this to anyone outside this room, but you're both children at heart, and I wouldn't let either one of you date my sister."

All three men broke into laughter and then got down to some serious drinking and reminiscing.

CHAPTER 72

The next morning, a Navy Jeep pulled up in front of Naval Headquarters in Tunis Harbor escorted by a Navy six-by-six truck carrying six armed SPs. A boatswain's mate and a chief stepped out of the jeep and were followed into the building by the SPs carrying a film projector, portable movie screen, and a storage container. They marched through headquarters to the central conference room where the boatswain's mate knocked twice, in military fashion, on the conference room door. When the door was opened, the men marched into the room and began to set up the projector and screen. As the film was being fed into the projector, the SPs distributed packets of photos to each person in the room.

The brigadier general who was speaking at the time the Navy detail entered the room stopped and asked the boatswain's mate, "What's the meaning of this, Boatswain?"

"Just following orders, sir. This was sent over from Sicily. I was told the *old man* wanted it shown immediately," the boatswain replied.

"What old man?" the brigadier asked.

"Don't know, sir. Whoever is in charge over there, I imagine. That's above my pay grade. I'm just following orders, sir."

Whispers went through the conference room. "Patton?" "Montgomery?" "Ike?" "Bradley?" were all names that were bandied about.

When the projector was ready, an SP flipped the switch to start the film. The boatswain's mate saluted the brigadier general turned, and left, turning off the lights as he exited the room.

The majority of the officers in attendance were admirals or generals of various grades. No one attending the meeting was below the rank of full bird colonel or captain. The officers represented the Army, Navy, and Air Corps of the United States, Britain, and Australia. There was still some quiet discussion about which Old Man had sent the film and photos, but as soon as the first images flashed on the screen, the mumbling stopped, and the photos were set aside.

The film was black and white with no sound track. It opened with a handwritten title page reading: *Sea Bee Pontoons and Light Spotting Aircraft—Invasion of Sicily.*

The scenes depicted were rough footage that had not yet been edited and put into a cohesive sequential story line. As a result, much of what was seen happened at different times during the landing at different places along the beach head and did not depict the combat in chronological order. Some of the film was too shaky to be seen clearly; other parts were overexposed or underexposed as the cameramen ran from one piece of cover to the next trying to capture scenes of the action around them. Unedited film was to be expected this early after the invasion, and the officers were engrossed in what they were seeing.

Most of the film was from ground level or deck level and showed how the pontoons had been dropped from the sides of LSTs, bolted together, and run up on the beach. Interspersed were scenes of the actual combat. Bullets could be seen impacting trucks, tanks, and other equipment as it rolled across the pontoons and went straight into action. One closeup showed a Sea Bee commander standing in the open directing his men while under fire. Someone said, "That's Commander Meriwether. He's the man responsible for putting the pontoons into action." Nodding heads could be seen and affirmative statements could be heard throughout the room.

The next part of film was shot from the air. It showed an Italian armored column stretched out along a mountain road. Suddenly, a small Army liaison aircraft dropped into view from above and fired a rocket into the lead vehicle which exploded and blocked the road. There was a gap in the film and then the small airplane appeared again diving on the column. This time, the plane fired a rocket into the last vehicle in the column trapping the Italian armor rendering it incapable of movement. The little airplane was shown several times repeating the same tactics firing rockets into the line of vehicles causing mass confusion and whole sale destruction. Between scenes of the rocket firing airplane, another small liaison aircraft was caught on camera dropping grenades on the trapped Italians and strafing them with automatic fire from a Thompson machine gun.

This action caused a minor sensation among the officers viewing the film, and they began commenting on the action as it was taking place.

"There are some real fighting men."

"Look at the way they're putting it to those EyeTies."

"Who the h———l are those guys?"

"They ought to be recognized for this."

"Those are the type of fighting men we need."

"Etcetera, etcetera, etcetera."

The next shot was of several of the small airplanes gathered on a beach. A plane came in to land, and men ran out to rearm it. This scene was repeated several times.

"Those are bazookas tied onto the wings," one Air Corps officer said loud enough for all to hear.

"Every time he lands, that plane has more holes in it than it did the time before," a rear admiral said.

"Who is that man?" an Aussie colonel asked.

"Those men rearming that plane are paratroops," an Army major general said with pride.

The camera switched to another plane as it came floating in to land. It was so shot up that it dropped like a stone when the pilot tried to set in down. When it stopped rolling, a man jumped out with a Thompson submachine gun.

"Hey, that man is Navy. What's he doing in an Army airplane strafing an armored column?" a British armored officer asked.

The sailor began to sprint away from the airplane but suddenly stopped and turned to hand the Thompson to one of the paratroopers. In doing so, there was a brief instant where the man's face could be clearly seen. "d———n that's Commander Cole," Admiral Hunt blurted out.

The camera followed him as he ran toward the other airplane. He ducked under the wing, grabbed a man, and spun him around. Hal Dunwitty's face filled the screen.

The two men looked at each other, and both pounded each other on the back each obviously happy that the other was okay.

The film then cut away to pictures of attacking aircraft being fired upon from a ship's deck. Two airplanes were seen to go down in flames. The next scene showed tracers flying into the night followed by an explosion that was bright enough it clearly showed an Italian motor torpedo boat exploding. The next scene was of an Italian motor torpedo boat abandoned and adrift, sinking. Then the film ended.

When the lights came back up, Admiral Hunt shook his head slowly from side to side, a wry look on his face. Admiral Beyard burst out laughing. Hunt and Beyard recognized the boatswain's mate and chief when they entered the room. Both admirals had served with them long ago when they were ensigns and again several times as they rose through the ranks. Once a man had served with either of them, he would never forget them; it was Gardener and Barton.

Beyard jabbed Hunt in the ribs and said, "The entire allied command in North Africa has just been had."

Chuckling, Hunt said, "So has Captain Cassidy."

CHAPTER 73

C assidy droned on, adding document after document to support his claim that Jack had entered the service under false pretenses and had been impersonating a naval officer. When he completed the prosecution's case on the charge of entering the service under false pretenses, the consul general called a short recess. Newman had been watching the jury and judging by their body language and facial expressions they were convinced of Cole's guilt. It was obvious Cassidy had prepared his presentation with their bureaucratic thinking in mind. Documentation was their life. If the documents said up was down and down was up, then everyone should be walking on the ceiling. Common sense wasn't applicable in a properly managed and well-ordered bureaucracy.

Everyone rose for the recess and began to filter out into the embassy foyer where coffee and pastries had been provided by the embassy staff. As he stood and stretched his legs, Newman saw Lieutenant Purvis at the back of the room. Raising his eyebrows in a questioning manner, Purvis shook his head. The documentation Newman was relying on had not arrived.

Following the recess, Cassidy began to addressed Cole's interfering with a superior officer in the execution of his duties, and evading arrest. Cassidy laid out in great detail how he was thwarted at every turn by missed flights, canceled ground transportation, missing arrangements for rooms and meals, inaccurate information on Cole's movements, etc., etc. Cassidy went as far as to say that Cole mislead Admiral Hunt and Admiral Beyard into believing he was a legitimate lieutenant commander and abused their trust in him by participating in missions and planning sessions for which he had no training or experience and was totally unqualified. This in turn led Captain

Cassidy into reemphasizing Jack's lack of naval instruction and how because he lied to get into the Navy his utter lack of training had endangered not only the crew of *LST 121*, but the entire allied invasion of Sicily and everyone involved.

They were losing the case and Major Newman had to do something. He caught the eye of one of the Marine guards and motioned him over. He handed the young Marine a slip of paper and said, "Get this message to your gunnery sergeant immediately." The Marine private left the room and after a few moments returned to resume his post.

Approximately twenty minutes later, anti-aircraft fire could be heard coming from the direction of the harbor, and air raid sirens began to go off all over Tunis. The consul general gaveled the session closed, and everyone went to the air raid shelters. Major Newman made a point of making sure he and Jack were not in the same bunker as Captain Cassidy. Lieutenant Purvis joined them, and Major Newman steered them to a place where they could talk quietly until the all clear was sounded. When he was sure no one was within earshot, Newman turned to Purvis and asked, "Where are we?"

"Well, as fast as this trial has been moving, it put us behind the curve for a while, but we're all caught up now and are on top of everything," Purvis said. "Boats and Barton got their job done this morning and went back to the ship. Grubowski is waiting at the airport in the jeep, and he's got some of his snipes hanging around the Canadian Embassy keeping an eye on things there."

"Okay, what about Beyard and Hunt?" Newman asked.

"Spence has a buddy in the galley at Naval Headquarters and everything is taken care of. MPs from the 202nd MP Company are stopping traffic and directing every staff car that comes along to the parking lot at Naval Headquarters. The 407th Bomb Disposal unit is going through them with a fine toothed comb ostensibly searching for booby traps. They'll be able to hold them there until lunch easily. The last report I got, they had twelve staff cars and were getting more."

Newman looked at Jack and said, "You really shouldn't be listening to this, Jack."

Cole looked at him and said, "Listening to what?"

Newman and Purvis both got a chuckle out of Jack's answer.

CHAPTER 74

When the all clear was sounded, everyone moved back into the courtroom. The consul general gaveled the proceedings back into session, and Cassidy picked up where he had left off before the air raid sirens sounded.

They had entered the final phase of the prosecution's presentation—the part of the trial that Newman felt he had the best opportunity to disprove Cassidy's claims. The only thing left after this was the summation, and then it would be the defense's turn.

Newman sat there and let Cassidy describe how he was assigned trivial duties in order to keep him from going into the harbors and ports to find Cole, how his travel authorizations were regularly delayed, his ground transport and lodging were continually misplaced or never arranged, and how several times he was left motoring around in fleet anchorages unable to find *LST 121* when the harbormaster's records clearly showed that the ship was in port. The more anecdotal evidence he produced, the more worked up he became until he was finally standing in front of Cole and angrily accusing him of the charges instead of presenting to the judge and jury.

Red in the face and winded from his tirade, Cassidy finally paused to wipe perspiration from his brow and spittle from his lips. Newman chose that moment to pop from his seat and ask, "Point of clarification, Your Honor?"

Cassidy started to open his mouth, but Doolittle banged his gavel to cut him off and said, "Go ahead, Major. What is your question?"

Taking time to straighten his uniform jacket and collect his thoughts, he asked, "Your Honor, I am only a lowly Army foot slogger so I may not understand how things work in the Navy, and I am puzzled. Who is in charge of the naval detachment in Casablanca, Mr. Cole or Admiral Hunt?"

Cassidy practically shouted, "This is outrageous."

Doolittle, hammering his gavel, said, "Captain Cassidy, control yourself. This is a trial, not a back alley brawl. Your reason for asking this question is what, Major Newman?"

"Your Honor, if Admiral Hunt is in command of the naval detachment in Casablanca I fail to see how Mr. Cole could in any way be responsible for Captain Cassidy's duty assignments. The location of a ship in an anchorage is assigned by the civilian harbormaster. I suggest the problems Captain Cassidy has experienced in finding a specific ship may have been caused by the language barrier inherent between French and English. Regarding the problems the captain has experienced with travel and lodging arrangements it appears, from his testimony, that he should be more concerned about the efficiency of Admiral Hunt's staff in making his travel and lodging arrangements than in trying to concoct some wild story about Mr. Cole controlling all the clerical functions of Admiral Hunt's command."

Cassidy was stunned by the accusation and stared wide-eyed at Newman. The consul general looked at Captain Cassidy and asked, "Well, what about that, Captain? I believe the defense raises a good question. You have told us of your troubles, but you have failed to demonstrate how Mr. Cole is involved in any of these incidents."

Doolittle looked expectantly at Captain Cassidy and asked, "Well?"

Cassidy stood there for a moment clearly at a loss for words and the consul general banged his gavel. "Captain Cassidy, while you ponder your response, the court will recess for lunch. We will reconvene at one o'clock or as you military folks like to say 1300. Captain Cassidy, I will expect your reply and your summation when we return."

CHAPTER 75

T he courtroom emptied, and everyone in attendance moved
toward the embassy dining room chatting among themselves
as they went. When they arrived, they found the cafeteria
was full of high-ranking officers from the various allied commands.

Doolittle spotted Admirals Hunt and Beyard and joined them
at their table along with British Admiral Springset, an Australian
Brigadier, and an American Air Corps Major General.

After introductions, the Aussie Brigadier General said, "Thank
you for taking care of us. Didn't know what we were going to do after
the headquarters mess was shut down."

Doolittle looked surprised and said, "Well, we are always pleased
to help our gallant allies at any time, but I've been presiding over a
trial all morning and don't know what you are referring to."

"Oh, it must have been one of your people then. At any rate,
the headquarters mess was closed due to a broken steam pipe, and we
were all loaded into staff cars and brought here."

"Well, regardless of the circumstances, we are very glad to have
you," Doolittle replied.

"Mr. Doolittle, did you say you were presiding over a trial?
What trial would that be?" Admiral Springset inquired.

"We have a man who is accused of impersonating a naval officer, interfering with a superior officer in the execution of his duties,
endangering the lives of the crew of *LST 121*, unauthorized use of
Navy equipment, giving false testimony during induction, evading
arrest, and incompetence," Doolittle replied.

"That seems like an issue for the navy to deal with not the
American Embassy," the air corps major general said.

"Yes, I agree," the consul general replied. "However, in this case, the man was dismissed from the Navy and a civil charge has been brought against him. It's a very unusual case."

"Rather unheard of don't you think?" Admiral Springset said. "Who is the man in question?"

"His name is Cole, and that is him sitting over there next to that army major and navy lieutenant," Doolittle replied, nodding in Cole's direction.

"All five guests turned to look and the Aussie Brigadier barked, "That's the man we saw on the Sicily film earlier today."

The others looked closer, and both Admiral Springset and the air corps major general nodded their heads in agreement saying, "Indeed," and "Yes, it is."

"I say Beyard, you yanks have a d——n odd way of treating your heroes, what," Springset remarked.

At that moment, an air corps major entered the room looked around and made a beeline for the table Jack, Newman, and Purvis were sitting at. When he got there, Jack rose and shook his hand as did Newman and Purvis. Those dining nearby casually looked up to see what was going on.

At that point, someone said loud enough that it could be heard over the casual conversation in the dining room, "Those are the two men we saw in the film this morning."

Someone began to clap and in short order as they realized who was in the room, everyone rose to their feet applauding. Jack and Hal both looked around to see who was being applauded, and then an Aussie colonel reached out to shake Hal's hand. More hands were extended, and soon, everyone was stepping forward to congratulate Jack and Hal on their daring and bravery.

Both men looked bewildered but nodded their thanks and exchanged pleasantries with the officers as they shook hands and were slapped on the back.

The crowd finally broke up and returned to their seats. Shortly afterward, an embassy aid appeared at the dining room doorway and announced that it was time to return to the trial. The participants in the trial rose and headed toward the doorway. No one failed to notice that Jack and Hal were among those leaving. Out of curiosity, a group of the officers from the headquarters meeting trailed along to see what was going on. The group included Admiral Beyard, Admiral Hunt, and Admiral Springset.

CHAPTER 76

The consul general struck his gavel and called the court into session. After everyone was seated, he turned to Captain Cassidy and asked, "Do you have a response to the question Major Newman asked before we recessed for lunch Captain Cassidy?"

Newman rose and asked, "Your Honor, would you mind having the court recorder repeat the question so the jury might be reminded where we were before the recess?"

"Certainly, would you read back the question Major Newman asked before we adjourned?" Doolittle asked the court recorder.

The court recorder read aloud, "Your Honor, I am only a lowly Army foot slogger, so I may not understand how things work in the Navy, and I am puzzled. Who is in charge of the naval detachment in Casablanca, Mr. Cole or Admiral Hunt?"

In the back of the room, Admiral Hunt's eyebrows went up, and both Admiral Springset and Admiral Beyard looked at Hunt.

Doolittle turned to Cassidy and said, "Would you care to answer that, Captain Cassidy?"

"Certainly, Your Honor," Cassidy replied, glancing nervously toward Admiral Hunt before speaking. "Admiral Hunt commands not only the naval force in Casablanca, but the logistics and fleet train for North Africa, the North African coast, and the supply train to Sicily."

Newman asked, "May I ask for another clarification, Your Honor?"

"Certainly, go ahead," Doolittle replied.

"Again, please forgive my ignorance, but that seems to me to be quite a lot of responsibility. Is that not so, Captain Cassidy?"

"Yes, it is. It is one of the most demanding jobs in the European theatre."

"With all the responsibility Admiral Hunt has, would you say your travel arrangements were the most important item on Admiral Hunt's plate?"

Realizing where this line of questioning was going, Cassidy gritted his teeth and replied, "No, I don't believe that would be the case."

"So with all the thousands and thousands of tons of equipment and supplies men and materials needing to be routed from the United States to Algeria and distributed across North Africa would it be possible that your travel arrangements might on occasion be set to one side until more important items were taken care of like…I don't know say tanks, gasoline, bullets, and food?"

This brought a chuckle from everyone in the court room.

"Yes, it would."

"Then if I understand correctly, since Mr. Cole does not command the naval force in Casablanca or anywhere else for that matter, it would be reasonable to say that your grievances against Mr. Cole for directly interfering with your duty assignments, travel orders, housing arrangements, etc., are unfounded and have nothing to do with Mr. Cole?"

"You could say that," Cassidy mumbled quietly.

Newman said, "I'm sorry. I didn't quite hear that. What was it you said?"

"I said no, they do not," Cassidy responded angrily.

"So does that mean Admiral Hunt and his staff are at fault for the inconvenience you experienced?" Newman asked with a questioning raise of the eyebrows.

"Certainly not," Cassidy replied, cutting his eyes toward Admiral Hunt for a moment.

"Then, Your Honor, I ask you why is this an issue?"

"Well, Captain Cassidy?" Doolittle asked, staring at him with an expectant look on his face.

Without looking up, Cassidy reached down, picked up a sheaf of papers, and tapped them on end to align them before placing them back on his desk. Then looking up, he said, "Your Honor, the prosecution wishes to withdraw the charge of interfering with a superior officer in the execution of his duties."

"Your Honor, since the charge of interfering with a superior officer in the execution of his duties is no longer being brought against Mr. Cole, does that mean the prosecution still believes Mr. Cole is guilty of evading arrest?" Newman inquired. "The two seemed to be directly related one unto the other."

Looking at Cassidy, Doolittle asked, "Mr. Prosecutor?"

"The prosecution would also like to drop the charge of evading arrest lodged against Mr. Cole, Your Honor."

Newman had been looking at Captain Cassidy when he asked the question. He now turned and looked at the consul general.

"Very well," Doolittle said and banged his gavel. "Let the record show that the charges of interfering with a superior officer in the execution of his duties and resisting arrest have been withdrawn."

Newman said, "Thank you for the clarification, Your Honor."

Doolittle cleared his throat and said, "Ahem…Now that we have that behind us, are you prepared for your summation, Captain Cassidy?"

Adjusting his tie, straightening his uniform, and doing the best he could to recover his composure, Cassidy replied, "Yes, Your Honor, I am."

Cassidy launched into his summation reviewing the charges and providing a condensed review of the materials he presented as evidence on each charge. Following his summation, Captain Cassidy rested his case. The consul general declared a five-minute recess after which the defense would make its case. Cole's fate was now in the hands of Major Newman.

CHAPTER 77

Immediately after Doolittle declared the recess Major Newman looked to the rear of the room where he caught the eye of Lieutenant Purvis. In response to Newman's questioning look, Purvis slowly shook his head side to side. Major Newman nodded and said, "d——n" under his breath so no one could hear it but himself.

Newman had to play for time. Without the sailing orders and the letters, Jack had written to the navy explaining they had the wrong man Newman had nothing except Jack's word against the navy's and that simply would not be adequate. Scanning the foyer, he spotted the marine guard he had spoken with earlier and motioned him over. Newman handed him a note and told him to give it to his gunnery sergeant. The young marine disappeared returning a few minutes later. Shortly afterward, court was called back in session.

Taking his time and making a face as if he was puzzling over a major concern, Newman addressed Captain Cassidy, "Captain, as I've mentioned before, I'm a soldier, a foot slogger. I believe the Navy refers to us as doggies. I don't know anything about the navy and how you boys in blue do things. For my edification, could you please explain what the requirements are to become a lieutenant commander in the United States Navy?"

Cassidy responded, "I don't see why that is necessary. Everyone in the room of any consequence knows perfectly well what the requirements are."

The consul general banged his gavel, leaned forward, and looking down from his elevated dais, he said, "Excuse me, Captain Cassidy, this may be presumptuous on my part, but I consider myself to be a person of consequence. I am in this room, and I have no idea what the requirements are."

Somewhat sheepishly, Cassidy began, "Yes…Yes, Your Honor. I meant no offense, sir. To be considered for officer training, the candidate must be a United States citizen, have had some college education, pass a standard navy physical, and successfully complete the battery of tests prescribed for officer selection."

"I see, and is that the only way to become a current naval officer, Captain Cassidy?"

"No, if a man has been in the Navy, he is automatically considered as part of the inactive reserve and can be recalled in a time of national emergency."

"Are we currently in a time of national emergency Captain, Cassidy?"

"Of course we are. We are at war."

"Yes…Yes, indeed we certainly are."

"I am surprised that there are only two ways to become a naval officer especially in a time of national emergency. Or are there other ways to become a naval officer?"

"Yes," Cassidy said between clenched teeth. "As you well know, the specialist branches like the Medical Corps and Judge Advocate Corps recruit officers based on achievement of civilian credentials. These recruits are then put through abbreviated officer training classes."

"So are all these officers recruited and entered into the service as ensigns?"

"No," Cassidy answered testily. "These recruits are assigned their rank based on the level of their civilian accomplishments."

"So based on the skills and abilities a person possesses, could he be assigned a rank of…oh…say lieutenant commander?"

"Of course…In theory, a person could be assigned any rank the service feels is appropriate to meet the level of responsibility for the position they are assigned."

"I see," Major Newman replied.

"Your Honor, I would like to call my first witness." Turning to face the audience, Newman said, "I would like to call Admiral Donald Reynolds, Your Honor."

Admiral Reynolds approached the witness stand and was sworn in. "Admiral, could you please state your name, rank, and command position for the record, sir?" Newman asked.

"Certainly, Donald James Reynolds, Rear Admiral lower half. I command the harbor facility in Tunis, Tunisia."

"Thank you, Admiral. Admiral do you consider yourself a good judge of a man's ability to command a ship in the United States Navy?"

"Yes, I do."

"Do you consider yourself capable of determining if a man has completed his duty in a competent manner?"

"Yes."

"Thank you, sir. Do you consider yourself capable of assessing a man's capabilities for consideration of advancement or placement in the naval officer corps?"

"I do."

"Might I prevail on your expertise, sir, to suggest the rank a man might hold if he had the following credentials and accomplishments?"

"Certainly"

"A bachelor degree, a master degree, was CEO of an organization with a budget in excess of $100,000 per year, with two hundred employees, and a group of 1,200 young men and women as dependents of the organization?" Newman asked.

"Without knowing anything else, I would suggest administratively that person had the skills and abilities to handle a company-sized organization, perhaps a battalion."

"And what rank would you assign a man to hold a position such as you have just described?"

"A first lieutenant for a company-sized unit and a lieutenant commander for a battalion-sized organization."

"I see. Thank you, sir. In addition to the credentials and experience I have just described, what if this same man had commanded a squadron of six ships, a task group of eight ships, the ship he commanded earned a blue *E* for record amounts of tonnage shipped, his same ship shot down three enemy airplanes, assisted in the destruction of an enemy submarine, sank two enemy motor torpedo boats, he participated in the development of new beach landing techniques and directly participated in the destruction of an Italian armored column by strafing it and dropping grenades from a light observation plane?"

"With that record and accomplishments, I would recommend that man hold a rank no lower than full commander and be placed on the list of candidates to be considered for promotion to captain."

"Thank you, sir. I have no more questions, Your Honor."

Turning to Captain Cassidy, Doolittle asked, "Do you wish to crossexamine the witness, Mr. Prosecutor?"

"Yes, Your Honor," Cassidy replied.

"Sir, referring to the hypothetical man the defense just described what if this man had never been in the Navy, had never gone through officer's training, had never been to sea, and was suspected..." At this point, he turned to the consul general with a questioning look on his face.

The consul general nodded his head and said, "Good choice of words."

Cassidy went on, "Suspected of lying about his background and personal history during induction?"

"If he had accomplished—"

Cassidy interrupted the admiral, "A simple yes or no is all I'm seeking, sir. If the man the defense attorney described was suspected of being a, liar would you still make the same recommendation on his rank, sir?"

"As I was about to say—"

Cassidy cut him off again, "Your Honor, all I am seeking is a simple yes or no. Nothing additional is required."

Doolittle looked at Cassidy, a frown on his face, and then turned to Admiral Reynolds. "Please respond with a yes or a no, Admiral."

Reynolds cleared his throat, stared at Cassidy for a moment, then spat out the word, "No!"

"Thank you, Admiral. I have no further questions, Your Honor," Cassidy said.

"You may step down, Admiral Reynolds. Thank you for your testimony, sir."

Looking at Captain Cassidy, Admiral Reynolds stood, straightened his uniform, and with a loud, "Humph," stepped down.

Captain Cassidy had entered water's fraught with peril. Men like Admiral Reynolds, Jimbo Hunt, and Billy Beyard were old Navy and one thing Cassidy apparently had not learned in his fast rise through the ranks was you didn't f——k with old Navy.

Cassidy followed the same procedure with each of Newman's witnesses. Newman would pose a scenario using a hypothetical person to describe Cole's competence or ability and Cassidy would back the witness into a corner forcing him to nullify his testimony by asking if the testimony he had just given would still stand if the person in question was suspected of being a liar or of trying to steal money and services from the navy or used navy equipment without authorization. Cassidy was playing to the bureaucratic minds of the jury, and it was apparent he was winning. Newman glanced at the clock on the wall and called his next witness, Hal Dunwitty.

But before Hal could be sworn in, anti-aircraft fire could be heard coming from the airfield on the edge of town and air raid sirens began to howl. Doolittle struck his gavel and ordered everyone into the air raid shelters. Major Newman made sure he was in the same shelter as Admiral Hunt and the two had a brief conversation. When the all clear was sounded and everyone returned to the courtroom, a projector and screen were set up with an embassy staffer standing beside the projector.

Before mounting the dais, Doolittle quietly asked the staffer, "What is all this about?"

"Two sailors delivered this while everyone was in the shelter. They said Admiral Hunt may want to have the film entered as evidence." A slight smile crossed Doolittle's face as he walked to the dais and declared the court in session.

"Now where were?" Doolittle said to the courtroom at large and to no one in particular. "Oh yes, Major Newman we were about to swear in your next witness. Shall we proceed?"

"Your Honor, instead of calling Major Dunwitty, I would like to call Admiral James B. Hunt to the stand."

Cassidy immediately jumped to his feet. "Objection, Your Honor. Admiral Hunt's name does not appear on the list of witnesses provided prior to the start of the trial. Therefore, he cannot be called as a witness."

"The councillor is correct, Major. Why would you like to call Admiral Hunt to the stand?" Doolittle inquired.

"Your Honor, it is not so much Admiral Hunt I would like to call to the witness stand as it is new evidence which has been discovered that needs to be introduced," Newman replied.

"And what is this new evidence and how does it have any bearing on this case?"

"It has to do with the claim that Mr. Cole's lack of knowledge and prior naval service may have led to disaster on the invasion beaches of Sicily. On the contrary, this evidence will show that the outcome of the invasion was significantly enhanced due to the part he played in the development of new beach landing techniques and his personal participation in the fighting."

"I object, Your Honor," Cassidy declared. "I have not seen this evidence. What bearing could it have on this case if it was not available prior to the trial? How do we know this isn't another attempt by one of Cole's cronies to insert false information and corrupt the facts? He is suspected of doing so already, and this could just be another example of the extremes to which this man will go to take advantage of the United States Navy and reap underserved personal and financial gain."

Doolittle turned to Newman. "Well, it seems to me the prosecution raises some excellent points. What do you have to say about that, Major?"

Before Newman could respond, the junior legal attaché who was originally assigned to defend Cole reached up and tugged at the Major's sleeve. Newman turned and looked at him angrily.

"May I have a moment, Your Honor?" Newman asked.

"Yes, but just a moment," Doolittle replied.

Newman bent down, and the young man whispered in his ear, then pointed at something written on a piece of paper. Newman looked at the paper then stood up and looked to the back of the room. He smiled, slapped the young attaché on the shoulder, and turned to the consul general. "Your Honor, I withdraw my request to call Admiral Hunt as a witness and wish to call Admiral Anthony Springset instead. I believe you will find his name on the witness list originally submitted by the junior defense council."

Surprised though, he was Admiral Springset came forward and was sworn in. "Admiral, could you give us a brief overview, within the limits of secrecy, of your responsibilities during the invasion of Sicily?"

"Certainly, I was tasked with developing new invasion techniques to facilitate landing on the hard scrabble and boulder strewn beaches of Sicily."

"And on whose authority were you acting in this capacity?"

"Admiral Cunningham, commander in chief of the Mediterranean Fleet."

"I see. Within the limits of secrecy, how did you go about this, Admiral?"

"In brief, I gathered the most experienced men in the Mediterranean, posed the problems we faced, and ordered them to come up with a solution."

"Can you elaborate on the solution they developed?"

"I cannot."

"I see, and we certainly understand that Admiral. Could you tell us who was involved in the committee?"

"No."

"May I ask if Lieutenant Commander Jack Cole was involved, sir, and if he was what was his contribution?"

"I can only tell you that he was involved, and his contribution was significant. I would say critical to the success of the operation."

"From your statements, Admiral, would it be fair to conclude that, in your opinion, Mr. Cole is one of the most experienced men in the Mediterranean?" Newman asked.

"Regarding beach landings, the LST, and its capabilities, yes, absolutely."

"Thank you, Admiral. Is there anything else you would like to add, sir?"

"Springset sat for a moment staring up and to one side thinking, then said, "Yes, yes, there is. I received some film this morning sent straight from the invasion site. I have only seen it once, but I believe it will demonstrate the level of involvement Leftenent Commander Cole played in the landings at Sicily without divulging any sensitive information." Speaking to the room at large, Springset asked, "Do any of you gentlemen who have seen this film see any reason it should not be shown?"

There was no response to the question only the shaking of heads by those who had seen the film earlier in the day.

Captain Cassidy jumped to his feet. "I object, Your Honor. Entering evidence which has not been shared with the prosecution is most irregular."

Before Cassidy could say anything more, Admiral Springset said, "Young man, do sit down and quit making a nuisance of yourself. You've created quite enough bother as it is. Let's tread the flick, what?"

When nothing happened, Springset looked at the puzzled projectionist and said, "Turn the bloody thing on."

The lights were turned off, and the film began. Springset offered no narrative during the entirety of the film. At the conclusion, the lights were turned back on and he turned to Consul Doolittle and asked, "Do you have any questions?"

Doolittle replied, "Yes, Admiral. Did I see Mr. Cole's face in that film?"

"Yes, and you also saw Major Dunwitty's face in the film. Major Dunwitty please stand and be recognized for your gallantry."

Dunwitty stood and Admiral Springset said, "Near the end of that film, you saw both Major Dunwitty and Leftenent Commander

Cole in action against the enemy. The final scene was Leftenent Commander Cole's ship engaging Italian motor torpedo boats. He destroyed two."

Then turning to the jury, he said, "Make note of that. Your Honor, do you have any further questions?"

Doolittle replied, "I do not. What about you, Major Newman? Do you have any questions?"

"No, Your Honor."

Doolittle then turned to Captain Cassidy. "What about you, Captain? Do you have any questions for Admiral Springset?"

Cassidy looked at Springset and then checked his notes unsure what he should ask. It was obvious that Cole was involved in the fighting. It was also obvious that if Admiral Springset said Cole played a significant role in the development of new beach landing techniques his word could not be challenged.

After Cassidy checked his notes for a second time, Admiral Springset said, "Bother all, do get on with it, lad. There is a war on, and I don't have time to waste."

Then turning to Cole, he said, "After this nonsense is completed, I want you to report to naval headquarters in Casablanca and bring Meriwether with you, I have more work for the two of you to do."

Then looking to the back of the room, he added, "Is that all right with you, Admiral Hunt?"

"Certainly, Tony. I'll see that he gets there even if we have to break him out of jail and have him brought in chains." Then Admiral Hunt and Admiral Beyard both stood up and left the room. Admiral Springset stepped from the witness stand and left as well. The fact that he did not ask permission to do so was not lost on anyone in the room.

Newman glanced at the jury. He could tell by their body language that not all were impressed by what they saw on the film. Being brave under fire was one thing, but disobeying orders, lying, and fraud were entirely different issues. Cassidy had played to the jury like a maestro conducting an orchestra. He had spoon fed them just the type of information they needed to empathize with the prosecution and they ate up every word. Newman wondered if the film had helped or hindered his defense. If it hadn't helped, at least it bought him some more time.

But now, his time had run out. Major Newman had no more witnesses to call. He might be able to delay a few minutes on procedural issues, but that was all. Without the ship's sailing orders and the letters Jack had sent to the Navy, the trial would rest in the hands of the jury and Newman was convinced the jury would side with the prosecution.

As these thoughts were running through Newman's head, he noticed that the consul general had not asked him to continue. Newman snapped out of his reverie and looked around to see what had delayed Doolittle in calling for him to continue.

After the marine guard closed the door behind Admiral Springset, he marched to the dais and quietly spoke with Consul Doolittle. Doolittle listened carefully, then said, "Have him bring it in."

The marine returned to his post and opened the door for a man wearing a Canadian diplomatic brassard who delivered a diplomatic pouch and left the room. Doolittle broke the seal and opened the pouch where he found a United States Navy document folder. He broke the seal on that and examined the documents inside. He then handed the documents to the bailiff and, speaking to Major Newman, he said, "The documents you requested have arrived. Let's proceed shall we?"

CHAPTER 78

Addressing the unauthorized use of navy equipment first, Major Newman began dismantling the prosecution's case by producing the orders for each movement of the ship. After reviewing several of the orders, he turned to the jury and said, "I have before me the entire list of sailing orders issued for the movements of *LST 121* from the time she was commissioned until Jack Cole was relieved of command. I ask you how a man can be accused of the unauthorized use of Naval equipment when he is following the orders he is issued. Now you must forgive me as I am in the Army, but isn't it the Navy's practice to issue orders and expect them to be followed?"

This put smiles on everyone's faces and a few chuckles were heard.

As to the accusation that the incidents described were conducted with the intent to deceive or mislead the Navy; Newman asked the jury to consider how Cole had deceived or mislead the Navy by sailing the ship down the Mississippi and crossing the Atlantic as the commander of Task Group 4.7 under orders, which he produced in a very theatrical flourish and waved for all to see. This brought a chuckle from the consul general and some smiles and laughter from the jury.

In very short order, Newman was able to prove beyond any doubt than Cole was not acting on his own but had followed the orders he received. The only variation on those orders was the fact that Cole had completed his sailing dates ahead of schedule which under the emergency circumstances of the war effort was a benefit and hardly the act of an incompetent. He closed this part of the defense by saying, "Captain Cassidy has stated repeatedly that my client sought to enter the Navy by impersonating an officer in order to gain personal benefit that he would not otherwise enjoy as a civilian. I fail to see the advantage to be gained by taking a pay cut and rushing into a war zone ahead of schedule in order to be attacked from sea and air by a ruthless and aggressive enemy."

This brought laughter from those in attendance, which caused Cassidy to rise red faced and object, stating that this was a court of law not a comedy show. The consul general banged his gavel and reminded everyone to maintain their decorum, then added, "But I do believe the defense makes a perfectly valid point." He then cleared his throat and said, "Let's move on, shall we?"

"Yes, Your Honor," Newman said. "I'd like to introduce the correspondence between Mr. Cole and the United States Navy in reply to his summons to be recalled into service."

Doolittle handed Newman the stack of envelopes, and Newman began to read each summons followed by Jack's reply. He read them in chronological order which included letters from the local draft board stating that Jack Cole was known to them and had never served in the United States Navy. They also stated that for reasons unknown, the records assigned to Mr. Cole's social security number had been assigned incorrectly, the Wellborn County Draft Board having responded to the issue considered the matter closed, and had advised Mr. Cole that he need not respond to any further correspondence from the navy.

The summons sent by the Navy did not address or refute the claim that Jack Cole was the wrong man. Each summons clearly stated that Jack was to report to his local draft board and be prepared for reinduction when and if called to service.

Since Jack had reported to his draft board and followed the instructions they gave him, it was clear Jack had been caught in a bureaucratic snarl of red tape. Someone had dropped the ball somewhere, and it did not appear to have been Cole. Even to the most die-hard bureaucrat, it was plain that Jack had followed the navy's instructions to the letter.

Doolittle turned to Captain Cassidy, "Do you have any questions, Mr. Prosecutor?"

Looking very contrite, Cassidy replied, "No, Your Honor," and sat down.

Looking at Major Newman, Doolittle asked, "Do you have anything more for the defense?"

Newman replied, "No, Your Honor."

"In that case, I will accept closing arguments. Captain Cassidy, you have the floor."

Cassidy rose and made an impassioned plea to the jury to do the right thing and see through the subterfuge by Cole and his cohorts. He admitted there was the possibility of an error in record-keeping, but that did not excuse Mr. Cole's failure to note that in the paperwork he signed. Nor did any typographical error mitigate the danger Cole placed the men and *LST 121* in by going ahead and following orders he knew were not meant for him. He concluded by saying that good luck and the training the navy provided for the crew had saved the situation. He closed by saying good fortune, and a fine crew should not be ignored while incompetence and failure to adequately explain the possibility of an error were rewarded.

Taking a page out of Captain Cassidy's playbook, Major Newman appealed to the bureaucratic mind of the jury by asking them what other course Mr. Cole had than to follow the orders he was given. It was not the prerogative of the individual to follow only those orders he chose to obey. It was the duty of every man to take his assignment and do the best he could to complete it properly. He concluded that Mr. Cole is an outstanding example of the man who does not fail to do his duty to follow the orders he is given.

Mr. Doolittle advised the jury of their responsibility and sent them into deliberation. The courtroom cleared, and everyone moved into the foyer to await the verdict.

As the crowd milled around quietly discussing the possible outcome and the jury's verdict, Jack noticed a white gloved hand waving above the crowd, and after a moment, he realized it was Shelley standing against the far wall waving so she could be seen. The casualties from the fighting in Sicily had overwhelmed the hospitals, and Shelley had not been able to attend any of the trial sessions so far.

Jack wormed his way through the crowded foyer, and when he reached Shelley, he threw his arms around her and pulled her close. Shelley held her purse between them with both hands and pushed him away, saying, "Jack, you know I cannot be caught showing any public display of affection. That could get me dismissed." Then she smiled, and after a quick glance to make sure no one was watching, she pulled him into an alcove where they could not be seen, threw her arms around him, and kissed him.

They remained in the alcove until the bailiff announced the jury would be sequestered for the evening and a verdict would not be returned until the next day at the soonest. Reluctantly, Shelley stepped out of the alcove, straightening her uniform and patting her hair back in place. Jack followed a few moments later, and they strolled out onto the embassy grounds to discuss the trial with Major Newman, Major Dunwitty, Lieutenant Purvis, Boats, and Barton.

CHAPTER 79

Major Newman had been certain that the introduction of the sailing orders and the letters Cole had sent to the navy would assure they won the case. However, Cassidy had made a compelling summation, and the fact that the jury had been sequestered for the evening could only mean the jurors had not reached a unanimous decision and the question was in doubt. Whether this was good or bad, Newman did not know. They would have to wait until the next day for the verdict; it would be a long night.

Due to the heavy casualties, Shelley had not been able to secure a pass to attend the trial until that day. She was unaware of what had taken place, and Jack and the others brought her up to speed as best they could over drinks on the embassy terrace. Since Jack was still under house arrest, they retired to the embassy dining room for supper. As they were being seated, Jack was surprised when Admiral's Reynolds, Hunt, Beyard, and Springset had the maître d' pull two tables together so they could all sit as a group. Once they were seated and drinks were ordered, Admiral Springset said, "I say, Cole, what the devil have you gotten yourself into?"

Before Jack could answer, Admiral Reynolds said, "Commander, you may want to consider renouncing your citizenship and ask Admiral Springset if you can join his staff."

Everyone laughed except Shelley who looked around the table with doe eyes, then slipped her arm through Jack's and pulled him tight, smiling.

"Well, if it comes to that," Springset said, "you may want to consider Canadian citizenship. It looks like you may have an in there." Again everyone laughed.

Admiral Hunt looked toward Newman, Boats, and Barton and asked, "You gentlemen wouldn't mind explaining why those sailing orders and that correspondence arrived by way of the Canadian Embassy, would you?"

Newman turned and looked at Boats and Barton who in turn looked at Leftenent Lindsey. Shelley looked back innocently and said, "Oh, that was my Uncle Lyon's doing."

The four senior naval officers looked at each other puzzled, and Jack said, "Honey, maybe you ought to tell them who your uncle is."

"His name is Lyon King," Shelley said brightly.

The admirals looked at each other again, still puzzled. Major Newman said, "Perhaps you know him better as Mackenzie King, Lyon Mackenzie King, as in the Prime Minister of Canada."

All four men and Hal Dunwitty looked stunned. "Are you shi— kidding me?" Hal said.

"No," Shelley said. "He is the dearest, sweetest man. Mr. Gardener and Mr. Barton had the paperwork sent to the Canadian Embassy in Washington DC, and Uncle Lyon had it flown to Tunis. It would have been here sooner except Uncle Lyon had it sent to my attention, and it took a day for the embassy people to figure out who I was and how to find me."

Everyone turned to Boats and Barton with expectant looks on their faces. Barton didn't see the looks due to his fascination with a picture of Franklin Delano Roosevelt on the far wall at the end of the dining room, and Boats never noticed because he had a bit of lint on his left sleeve that resisted being removed no matter how much he picked at it.

Jack let them sweat for a few moments, then said, "Well, gentlemen? No one else in the Mediterranean Theatre seems to be able to get any communications in a timely manner, but somehow, you two managed to get original documents sent from the Main Navy and Munitions Building to the American Embassy in Tunisia in three days. Would either of you care to explain that?"

"Well, sir, it was actually two days. Like the Lieutenant said, it took the Canucks a day to find her," Barton replied.

Gardener gave him a withering look, and Barton said, "What? It did."

Shaking his head at Barton, Boats said, "Do you really want to know, sir?"

"Art normally I wouldn't, but in this case, I do. How'd you do it?"

"Well, Yeoman Andrew Burris is the ranking yeoman in Admiral Bryton's records department at the Navy and Munitions Building. Andy's a pretty good guy, but he's a lousy poker player. Anyway, he owed me $50 bucks from a game we was in at the Washington Navy Yard before I joined the ship in Evansville, and it wasn't too hard to convince him to drop off a records pouch at the Canadian Embassy. We oiled a few squeaky wheels from there on, and the lieutenant's uncle took care of everything else. Then bingo, it's here."

"I see, and how did you oil those squeaky wheels and make all these arrangements?" Jack asked.

Barton chimed in, "Well, sir, you remember the cash box we had welded to the mess room floor? We never did get it figured out what we was gonna do with it since..." At this point, Barton looked around the table rather sheepishly. "Well...you know. So the crew figured usin' it to hep out on this was the best thing to do with it and...well I think you get the idea," Barton said.

"Uh-huh, I get the idea," Jack said, shaking his head and smiling. "But you can't just pick up a telephone and make a call any time you want? How the heck did you two manage to pull that off?"

Before Barton could say anything, Boats jumped in and said, "Well, sir, in theory, that's correct, but there's pickin' up the phone, and then there's pickin' up the phone, if ya know what I mean."

"I don't suppose you'd like to share how you picking up the phone is different from say one of us picking up the phone would you?" Admiral Beyard said.

Gardener looked at the admiral and said, "Admiral, you an' me go back to the days when you was a wet behind the ears, Ensign, and I was crackin' heads to get the men to pay attention to yer orders. Is this Art to Billy, or is it boatswain to admiral?"

"We'd better make it boatswain to admiral."

"Then in that case, I don't think you want to know, Admiral... sir."

Beyard pursed his lips and looked at Boats for a few moments, thinking. Then he said, "Okay, fair enough."

Everyone laughed.

The salads were served shortly after that, and the conversation turned to other topics, among them Jack's chances of being acquitted. Purvis had been hitting the bourbon pretty hard along with Admiral Reynolds, Jimbo Hunt, and Tony Springset. Shelley was pensive but seemed to be enjoying herself for the moment. Dunwitty had just launched into a story about a cowboy who'd roped a pronghorn antelope, gotten pulled out of his saddle and was being dragged across the prairie when Lieutenant Purvis suddenly said, "Waita minute. I jus thoughta sompin' Maaayjer, we had some air raids at pretty coveen... cumveen...some pretty handy times. You don't know anythin' 'bout that, do ya? I mean they wasn't just a coinsa...coginca...They wasn't jus' an accident, were they?"

Admiral Springset said, "I say Purvis you're bloody right. Daft all if I wasn't wondering the same thing. Bit of d——n good luck that, what?"

Everyone looked at Major Newman who in turn looked at Boats. "Go ahead and tell 'em it was yer idea," Boats said.

"Well, ahem...I must say I learned a lot during this trial especially from the boatswain and the chief. When I needed a recess or time to think, I slipped the marine guard a note, he'd take it to his gunnery sergeant, who would contact the ship, the ship would pass the word to one of the ships in harbor or radio the airfield. It seems that to maintain your guns properly you need to test them every once in a while and when you're doing that if someone thinks it's because there is an air raid on, well, that just can't be helped."

When the laughter died down, Jack asked, "Is that correct, Boats?"

"Well, sir, you ain't got no idea how many friends you got in North Africa, and it's amazin' how far one frien'll go to hep another. That an' a few gallons of ice cream makes all the difference in the world."

"I say, you Yanks are a devious lot. I'm proud to say the Royal Navy and His Majesty's forces don't go in for that type of shenanigans," Admiral Springset said, looking down his nose at all present.

"Oh, I don't know admiral," Barton said. "The HMS *Ashanti* and HMS *Benbow* did the firing in the harbor and it was an Australian anti-aircraft battery that lit things up at the airfield."

Springset's eyebrows shot up in surprise. Then in the best English tradition of remaining resolute and unemotional in any situation he said, "Well, I'm glad to hear the lads are on their toes. I've yet to see a British man-o-war pass up the opportunity to exercise the guns. And it's bloody inspiring to hear the Aussies are so keen to keep their guns properly calibrated. D——n professional, don't you think?"

Everyone broke up. Purvis about fell out of his chair, and Dunwitty laughed so hard tears came to his eyes.

The meal went well after that, but the good humor gradually left the diners as their thoughts turned to the verdict that would be announced the next day. When things finally broke up, Jack found himself alone and after an extended stroll around the grounds retired to his room.

CHAPTER 80

J ack had no idea where he stood. Other than the pleasant banter during supper, Newman hadn't said anything to him after the consul general sent the jury into deliberation. He felt the trial had gone well, but it was just his opinion. The fact that the jury had been sequestered overnight did not encourage him. He assumed they were deadlocked which would mean at least part of the jury thought he was guilty.

Trying to shake off his worry, he sat down to write some letters, hoping it would take his mind off the trial. He was composing a letter in his mind when it suddenly dawned on him he hadn't read the letters he received on the day he left the ship. That brightened his outlook considerably. The one with the oldest post mark was from Angie Jenkins; he tore it open and began to read.

Angie was excited to tell Jack that she had enlisted and was going to Omaha the next week for induction and to begin her training to become a WAC at Fort Des Moines in Des Moines, Iowa. Jack checked the post mark and found Angie had by now been in the Women's Army Corps for over eight weeks. Angie went on and on about how important it was for everyone to do their duty and how eager she was to become an active part of the war effort. She said she didn't know what the future held, but she would try to write if she got the chance. Then she closed by saying, "I don't know if I'll ever be back in Walnut Hill after this thing is over. If I don't see you again, please know that I'll be thinking of you, and I wish you all the best in whatever you decide to do after the war."

There was another letter from Angie dated two weeks ago telling Jack all about her basic training and the other girls she was training with. She said she had passed a written exam and was being considered for the WAAF training program. She was scheduled to take an introductory flight with an instructor the next day to see how she handled herself in the air. She was as she put it *over the moon* about the possibility of learning how to fly. She closed by saying, "This is the most exciting thing that I've ever done. I never knew the world was so large or that so many opportunities existed. Please don't take this the wrong way, but this war has been the best thing that has ever happened to me. I'll write when I can and tell you all about what it's like to fly."

Jack thought about Angie the adventurous tomboy. He was glad she was getting the opportunity to experience life outside Walnut Hill. He knew from the tenor of her letter, he would never see her again, but he hoped she would continue to write.

There were two letters from Annette, which were full of the comings and goings in Pilottown and news from the home front about bond drives and all the construction that was going on across the state. Military camps were springing up everywhere. In New Orleans and Baton Rouge Higgins was building not only landing craft and PT boats, but Liberty ships as well. Consolidated/Vultee was building airplanes, and companies were being formed to build everything from mess kits to armor plate. There was a worker shortage and lots of the men and women who made their livings from the swamps and bayous were moving to the cities. She urged him to "Take care and don't let anything happen to you. You are cared for very deeply."

Jack knew Annette wasn't in love; she was infatuated with him, and he was flattered. Her brother understood, and Jack knew Rene had no expectations of Jack following the war. Jack assumed that once Annette had a chance to see a bigger world outside Pilottown her infatuation would fade, and she would either find a new life or go back to the swamps and continue her life as before. He liked Annette a great deal, but he didn't know her, and she didn't know him. That night, following the dance was a moment of intense desire, nothing more. As Rene had said, "Two sheeps they pass in the night."

The thought of Annette in his arms that night on the pier at Pilottown made Jack smile. The thought of Annette, Rene, and others he had met warmed him inside. It was good to have feelings and memories like that, but that's all they were—memories.

The letters from Angie and Annette cheered him no end. He felt much better about things and was in a positive frame of mind until he picked up his last letter and saw it was from Mr. and Mrs. Jenkins in Walnut Hill, Nebraska, postmarked shortly after Angie's last letter. He wondered why he would be hearing from Angie's parents; he had only met them a few times and had barely spoken to them. He didn't really know them at all.

Jack opened the letter, and after reading the first few lines, the letter slipped from his hands and a cry of, "Oh, no!" was wrenched from him which brought one of the embassy staffers to his door. "Are you all right, Mr. Cole?"

The staffer asked several times. Jack tried to answer but couldn't speak. Finally, the door was pushed open a crack, and the staffer stuck his head into the room. Jack looked at him and tried to say something, but again, he couldn't speak. Finally, he picked up the letter, handed it to the young man, and walked to the window where he stared out onto the embassy grounds.

The young man read the letter and didn't know what to say. He laid the letter on Jack's bed and left the room. He walked into the embassy lounge, found the consul general, and told him that Mr. Cole had just been informed a young woman from his hometown had been killed in a flying accident at Des Moines Airport outside Des Moines, Iowa.

Angie's death came as a terrible blow to Jack, try as he might, he could not keep his thoughts from focusing on her death. He kept thinking of the part in her letter where she had written, *This war has been the best thing that has ever happened to me.* He couldn't seem to get it out of his mind. His most disturbing thought was he had fought being inducted, and he was fine, but Angie had volunteered, and it had gotten her killed. He felt like somehow her death was his fault.

Jack did not sleep well that night, but it wasn't worrying about the outcome of the trial that kept him awake.

The next morning, the bailiff announced the jury was still in deliberation. All parties involved in the trial were requested to wait on the embassy grounds. They would be called when the jury returned with a verdict.

Pete Meriwether arrived early that morning in response to Admiral Springset's request. When he found he wasn't needed until Jack's trial had been concluded he caught a ride to the American Embassy to see how the trial was going. As soon as he walked into the foyer, he spotted Hal Dunwitty and Dale Purvis who were speaking with Admiral Reynolds. Hal spotted him and waved him over and introduced him to Admiral Reynolds. As the admiral was shaking his hand, he stared at Pete and said, "You look familiar. Have we met before?" Then he snapped his fingers and said, "I've got it. You were on the film we saw yesterday of the landings in Sicily. You were standing in the open directing your men while taking fire. I'm surprised you weren't wounded or killed. It's a pleasure to meet you, Commander. You set a very good example for your men and were an inspiration to those of us who saw you in action."

Pete had no idea what the admiral was talking about and said so. Reynolds looked askance at Meriwether and said, "Perhaps you are not aware of it, but one of the combat cameramen covering the landing captured you on film directing your men as they were assembling a causeway under fire."

"No, sir, I was not aware we were being filmed. I had good men with me, and they did an incredible job, but I don't recall being fired at. Perhaps you are thinking of someone else."

Hal looked at Pete and said, "It was you all right. The whole courtroom saw you. Admiral Springset showed the film as evidence."

"Evidence…Evidence for what?"

"To show that Jack wasn't an incompetent like the prosecutor accused him of being."

Meriwether still looked confused but let it go when the embassy staffer who spoke with Jack the night before approached the group. "Excuse me, Admiral, gentlemen, my name is Everett Wallace. I'm one of the junior staffers here at the embassy. I don't know if you are aware of it, but Lieutenant Commander Cole received word last night that a young lady friend of his from his hometown was killed in an aircraft training accident. He was quite upset. I thought you gentlemen should know.

"Ah s———t," Pete said. "How's Jack doing?"

"I don't know," Wallace said. "He was with the consul general earlier this morning, then met with Major Newman. I haven't seen him since."

After delivering the news, Wallace joined the conversation as the group talked quietly and speculated about the verdict the jury would return.

A few moments later, Major Newman and Captain Cassidy emerged from the consul general's office. Newman walked toward the group of officers while Cassidy began yelling for someone to take him to the embassy communication center.

"What in blazes is that all about?" Admiral Reynolds asked Newman when he joined the group.

"Doolittle informed Cassidy and I that a young female friend of Coles from his hometown was killed in a flying accident, and Cassidy went through the roof. He claimed it was a stunt pulled by Cole to gain sympathy and try to sway the jury in his favor. The consul general informed Cassidy the jury was in sequestration and knew nothing about the young woman's death. Cassidy refused to believe him so the consul general ordered him to leave his office. I took the opportunity and left too."

The three junior officers and Admiral Reynolds were shocked, but Wallace was furious. "I saw Cole last night right after he got the news. I've never seen a man so bereft as the lieutenant commander was after receiving that letter. Apparently, this young woman was more than a casual acquaintance. He was so upset, he couldn't speak. I stayed outside his door most of the night listening. I was afraid he might do something reckless."

"That's not like the skipper," Purvis said. "But thank you for keeping an eye on him. He won't say anything, but he could use a good friend about now."

CHAPTER 81

The bailiff announced the jury had returned and requested everyone to return to the court room. When everyone was seated, the consul general asked the foreman if the jury had reached a verdict. The foreman replied, "Yes, we have, Your Honor."

"Is it a unanimous decision?" Doolittle asked.

"Yes, Your Honor, it is."

Doolittle turned to Jack and said, "The defendant will rise."

Jack stood. But before reading the verdict, the foreman paused and said, "Your Honor, the jury would like to know if we could make a recommendation following the reading of the verdict?"

"Does it have anything to do with the verdict?"

"No, Your Honor, we reached a verdict shortly after beginning our deliberations. It has to do with the action to be taken following the reading of the verdict."

"The jury can certainly make a recommendation regarding sentencing. I will listen to your recommendation, but the final decision on sentencing will be mine based on the parameters of the law covering the charges."

A chill went down Jack's spine, Newman sat bolt upright in his seat, and Cassidy looked at the defense with an evil sneer of superiority. If the jury reached a quick conclusion, but their discussions dragged on long enough that they had to be sequestered. It could very well mean they wanted to make a recommendation on the punishment to be meted out.

"Yes, Your Honor, our recommendation—"

Doolittle cut him off. "Please read the verdict first, Mr. Foreman. I have already assured you I will entertain any comments you might have following your announcement of the jury's decision."

Cassidy leaned back in his seat with a broad smile on his face. Jack folded his hands in front of him. Newman scooted to the front edge of his seat and placed one elbow on the desk. Those in attendance held their breath.

The foreman cleared his throat and said, "Ahem… We the jury, in the case of Cassidy vs. Cole, find the defendant not guilty on all counts."

A collective sigh of relief came from those in attendance. Cassidy rocketed forward slamming both hands on his desk and gasped, "What?" Newman jumped to his feet blurting out, "Yes!" and looked at Jack with a huge smile on his face. Congratulations were shouted, and those near enough reached forward to slap Jack on the back. Jack sat down, folded his hands on the desk in front of him, and showed no emotion whatsoever. There was still the matter of the jury's recommendation, and Jack was not one to count his chickens before they hatched.

Doolittle banged his gavel to restore order in the court room. It took a few moments for everyone to settle down. When he finally had the courtroom under control, the consul general turned to the foreman. "Mr. Foreman you inquired whether the jury could make a recommendation. If you still wish to do so, now would be the time."

"Yes, Your Honor, we don't know if it is within our purview to do so, but the jury would like to have it entered into the trial record that we recommend Mr. Cole, the Sea Bee officer and the two pilots seen in the film of the invasion of Sicily be recommended for medals of valor for their gallantry and heroism while under enemy fire."

"Duly noted," Doolittle responded. Then turning to the court recorder, he said, "The recorder will see that the jury's recommendation is entered into the court record."

Speaking to the defense, Doolittle went on, "Mr. Cole, you have been found not guilty by a jury of your peers. You are free to go." Then he banged his gavel and declared, "This court is adjourned."

It was officially over. The trial was behind him, and Jack could relax while he figured out how he was going to get home. Everyone was shaking his hand and congratulating him. Jack, Major Newman, Hal, Dale, and Pete walked out of the courtroom together where

Everett Wallace and Admiral Reynolds joined them in the foyer. "Congratulations, Commander. Well done, Major. Now it's time to see about getting you back in uniform," Admiral Reynolds said. "We don't want to lose you again."

That brought a huge laugh from everyone. The tension broken, Jack could smile now, and everyone headed for the embassy bar. Wallace declared, "The drinks are on the embassy, gentlemen. Given the circumstances, it's the least we could do."

They had just turned and were headed toward the bar when Captain Cassidy emerged from the courtroom and confronted Jack accusing him of sabotaging the trial by fabricating a phony death and leaking it to the jurors. Cassidy then added he would not forget this, would appeal the ruling, and take him to court again. "I'll hound you until I get you. You are a miserable excuse for a human being, a liar, and a fraud."

Whereupon Wallace bunched him square in the mouth.

Admiral Reynolds looked down at Cassidy lying unconscious on the floor and said, "Mr. Wallace, I believe you mentioned something about drinks."

Carefully stepping around or over Cassidy, they left him lying on the floor and walked into the bar.

They were well into their second round when the consul general came into the bar followed by Captain Cassidy holding an ice bag to his jaw. The gunnery sergeant and two Marines were right behind them. "I understand there was a disturbance in the foyer," Doolittle said.

"I wouldn't really call it a disturbance, Mr. Consul General. I'd say it was more of an accident," Reynolds replied. "Captain Cassidy slipped on the floor, and Mr. Wallace made a valiant attempt to catch him. Unfortunately, Mr. Wallace was not quick enough, and Captain Cassidy fell, head first, onto the terrazzo."

"That's not true," Cassidy said, taking the ice bag from his mouth. "He hit me."

With an edge to his voice that would cut steel, Admiral Reynolds said, "I'll assume you are still woozy from your fall, Captain." Lightly tapping his Annapolis class ring on the edge of the table top, he continued, "I'm sure you didn't mean to contradict me, did you, Captain?"

Cassidy stared hard at Admiral Reynolds for a moment, then glanced at Reynolds's class ring as the admiral continued to tap it on the marble table. Cassidy got the message and said, "No, you are absolutely correct, Admiral."

Then turning to the consul general, he continued, "Mr. Doolittle, I am sure the admiral was in a better position to see what happened than I was. It is my error. Mr. Wallace must have been attempting to catch me, and I misinterpreted his actions."

Then turning to Wallace, Cassidy offered his hand and said, "I apologize, Mr. Wallace."

The two men shook hands, and Cassidy left the bar.

CHAPTER 82

Two weeks later, Jack found himself standing at attention while Admiral Cunningham pinned the Meritorious Service Medal, Bronze Star, and Air Medal to his chest, then moved to Pete Meriwether standing next to him and pinned the Legion of Merit and Bronze Star to his uniform. General Jimmy Doolittle then stepped forward and pinned the Distinguished Service Cross and Air Medal to Hal Dunwitty's chest followed by the Bronze Star and Air Medal, which he pinned to Gene Wilton's Tunic.

After salutes were exchanged and the band played, the admirals and generals off the parade ground the men who had received metals, awards, and decorations were dismissed. Jack searched for Shelley and finally saw her waiting at the edge of the parade ground by the reviewing stand with June.

A lovely young lady Jack had never seen before was there to meet Dale Purvis and an Army nurse strolled away with Pete Meriwether arm in arm. There were many WAVEs, WAACs, WRNS, WAAFs, ATSs, and local *jeunes beautés françaises* waiting for the officers and men who had just been decorated. But to Jack, none looked as beautiful as Shelley standing there in her nursing sisters uniform.

Jack swept Shelley into his arms and twirled around with her before setting her on her feet and kissing her as passionately as he could. Shelley, holding on to her nursing sister's bonnet, threw her head back and laughed. "I love you," she said, giggling. "I love you too, Shelley. We weigh anchor at 0800 tomorrow, and I don't want to miss a minute of being with you between now and then. I've got a jeep waiting, and there's a little bistro on the beach I'm dying to take you to. If we hurry, we can make it before they close the kitchen. We can eat, have a few drinks, and then I want to talk and swim and walk on the beach with you until the sun comes up. What do you say?"

"I say, mister, where is that jeep?"

Jack sailed the next morning with Shelley standing on the pier watching and waving with a brand new engagement ring on her finger as the ship exited through the submarine nets and made course for a place no one had ever heard of in Italy called Salerno. At Admiral Cunningham's request, Jack Cole had been reinstated into the United States Navy with the rank of full commander. Following the invasion of Italy, Jack was in action again at Anzio and later participated in the landings at Normandy. At the end of the war, he and Shelley were married in Ottawa, Canada. Lyon Mackenzie Smith gave the bride away, and Hal Dunwitty was best man. Jack took a job as superintendent of schools for the city of Ottawa and later, after gaining his Canadian citizenship, was elected to parliament where he served until his retirement. Shelley remained in nursing and eventually became head of the University of Ottawa School of Nursing. They had three children two boys and a girl—John Lyon, Herald Peter, and June Lindsey.

June left the nursing order shortly after Hal was promoted to lieutenant colonel. She returned to Canada after the invasion of Italy where she had her first child. At the end of the war, Hal took his discharge in San Antonio and immediately flew to Calgary where he and June were married. June's father gave away the bride and their son Herald Jack served as best man at the ripe old age of two. Hal did some wildcatting in the Texas panhandle where he brought in several wells and started the Stampede Oil Company. He and June spent their time between their homes in Calgary and Abilene until their retirement. They had four children.

Pete Meriwether stayed in the Navy and retired as a vice admiral. He married and divorced several times and finally retired to his home in the Florida Keys.

Dale Purvis took command of *LST 121* following the invasion of Italy and became Jack Cole's operations officer and righthand man in planning the amphibious landings at Anzio and Normandy. Dale had transited the Panama Canal and was well on his way to Hawaii when the war ended. After making several "Magic Carpet" runs, he oversaw *LST 121* being mothballed and placed in the reserve fleet. Dale left the navy went into management with IBM and retired as vice president of mergers and acquisitions. He and his wife bought a house at Lake Tahoe where Dale spent the remainder of his days teaching his children and grandchildren how to sail, fish, and swim.

The lovely Jennifer was waiting for Mr. Wesley when he was discharged in San Diego. With his savings and back pay, Bill bought a used 1936 Ford convertible. He and Jennifer drove straight to Las Vegas and were married at the first wedding chapel they came to. Bill was hired by Metro Goldwyn Meyer studios as a technical adviser for the movie *The Best Years of Our Lives*. Following the success of the picture, the studio offered him a job in public relations specializing in dealing with difficult clients. Jennifer was "discovered" while on the lot one day with Bill and made a career in the emerging television industry doing commercials and playing supporting roles in various soap operas.

Herald Newman returned to Donovan, Leisure, Newton & Irvine, where he was ultimately made a partner and cashed out with a very handsome retirement package when the company was sold.

Art Gardener finally retired from the navy and opened a surplus sales business with Quincy Barton. The two made a killing buying and selling military surplus. Boats moved to the Hamptons to run his end of the business, and Barton disappeared over the Sinai Desert when the C-46 he was using to smuggle arms to the Israelis was shot down by an Egyptian Supermarine Spitfire during the 1948 Arab–Israeli War. Two years after being declared dead, the ever-resourceful Barton was found to be alive and living on a private island he owned in the Aegean.

Following the war with the help of Herald Newman, Chief Grubowski patented several innovative ideas to enhance diesel engine performance and joined General Motors where he became project manager for diesel engine development. GM paid him a handsome royalty for use of his patents and bought the intellectual property rights on all developments he created thereafter. At the time of his retirement Grubowski owned four acres of the business district in downtown Detroit.

Everett Wallace stayed in the diplomatic corps and, after twelve years of continued service, was named Ambassador to Albania. He retired in the Finger Lakes region of upstate New York where he started a guide service for hunters and fishermen.

Bill Spence started a restaurant in Minneapolis, Minnesota. He hired Franklyn Ingolls as his maître d', and after a rocky start, it caught on and became one of the first integrated restaurants in the country. It was noted for having the best coffee in the Twin Cities.

Tyree Higby and Luscious Tanner went back to their hometowns married local girls and started businesses of their own. Tyree opened a barbershop and Luscious started an auto parts store.

Wilmer Burwell returned to Hamburg, Iowa took over the family farm and continued to ride bulls at local rodeos. He finally broke his collar bone at a rodeo in Sydney, Nebraska and said goodbye to bull riding for good. However, two of his sons took up the sport as did three of his grandson's. Wilmer named his farm Wang Leather Ranch.

Captain Cassidy eventually got it through his head that there was more to the Navy than rules and regulations, paper pushing, and sharpening pencils. He applied for sea duty, but no matter how hard he tried he could not get over his sea sickness. He resigned his commission and with help from Herald Newman became a prosecuting attorney for the city of New York.

In 1960, *LST 121* held a ship's reunion in Reno, Nevada. Every living member of the ship's company was invited as were Hal Dunwitty, Pete Meriwether, Herald Newman, Admiral Hunt, Admiral Reynolds, Admiral Springset, Hooker Doolittle, and Everett Wallace.

No one was left out and between Boats, Barton, and Grubowski all travel, meals, and lodging were covered at no cost to those who could attend. The opening ceremony of the ship's reunion was held surrounding the flag pole in the courtyard of the Mapes hotel. After a short speech welcoming everyone and thanking Boats, Barton, and Grubowski for "pulling this shindig together" Jack ran up a hoist and spanked it off the truck and finial. When the hoist unfurled, there flew a pair of pink ladies undies and three brassieres. The party lasted three days and went down in history as the largest single party ever held in Reno, Nevada up to that time.

The End

PICTURES

LST Bridge

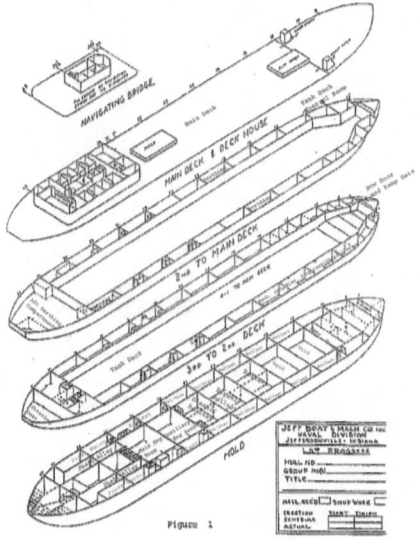

Cut Away Of LST Deck And Compartment Structure

LST Traveling Down River Toward New Orleans

LST With Deck Cargo

Submarine Chaser

LCVP Along Side LST

LST With LCVPs

LST Engine Room

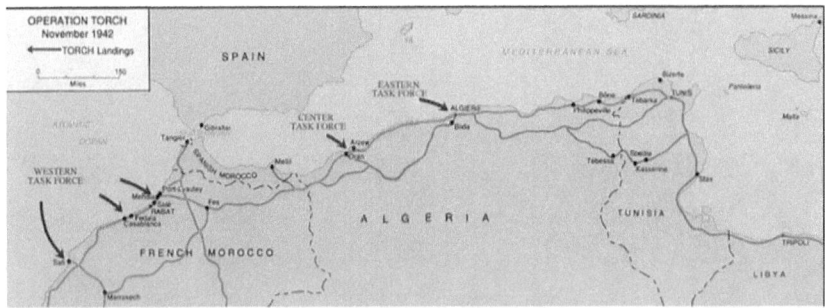

Operation Torch Landing Sites

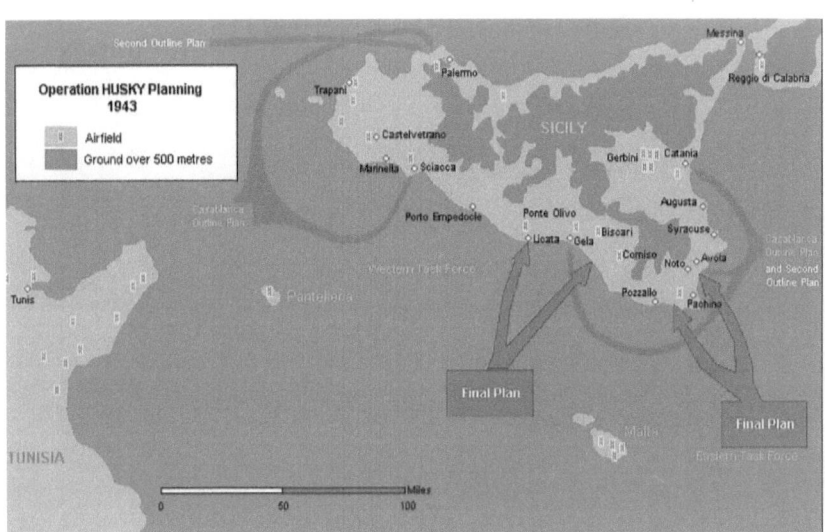

Operation Husky Landing Sites

Crane Loading Deck Cargo Aboard LST

LST With Pontoon Pushed Onto Beach

LST With Pontoon Lashed Along Side Ready To Be Deployed

LST's Beached For Unloading At Beach Head

Bazooka Armed L 4

LST With L 4 Raised Into Position To Be
Moved To Flight Deck For Take Off

LST Under Way With L 4 Poised On Flight Deck for Take Off

L 4 Flying Off LST Flight Deck

General Characteristics

Class and type:	tank landing ship
Displacement:	• 1,625 long tons (1,651 t) light
	• 4,080 long tons (4,145 t) full (sea-going draft with 1675 ton load)
Length:	327 ft. 9 in. (99.90 m.)
Beam:	.50 ft. (15 m.)
Draft:	• *Light*:
	• 2 ft. 4 in. (0.71 m.) forward
	• 7 ft. 6 in. (2.29 m.) aft
	• *Sea-going*:
	• 8 ft. 3 in. (2.51 m.) forward
	• 14 ft. 1 in. (4.29 m.) aft
	• *Landing* (with .500 ton load):
	• 3 ft. 11 in. (1.19 m.) forward
	• 9 ft. 10 in. (3.00 m.) aft
Propulsion:	2 General Motors 12-567 900 hp (671 kW) diesel engines, two shafts, twin rudders
Speed:	12 knots (22 km/h; 14 mph)
Range:	24,000 nmi (44,000 km.) at 9 k (17 km/h; 10 mph)
Boats and landing craft carried:	2 × LCVPs
Complement:	7 officers, 104 enlisted
Armament:	• 2 × twin 40 mm. gun mounts
	• 4 × single 40 mm. gun mounts
	• 12 × single 20 mm. gun mounts

ABOUT THE AUTHOR

 Jack Williams is the author of *The Curious Case of Commander Cole*. He retired from public education after twenty years where he was a teacher, administrator, and superintendent of schools. From public school education, he transitioned to industry education becoming an industry workforce development specialist, troubleshooting performance issues, and developing training programs to solve companies' productivity, efficiency, and quality control challenges for another twenty-plus years.

Jack has many interests not the least of which are flying, music, woodworking and metal working, hunting and fishing, and history. He and his wife, Sheri, have one daughter, one son, and three granddaughters. Jack and Sheri live in Missouri near Kansas City.

Jack has written several novels and many short stories. He was also a self-syndicated cartoonist for several years appearing in Midwestern newspapers as far west as Jackson Hole, Wyoming. *The Curious Case of Commander Cole* is Jack's first published work. Though he takes his writing seriously, he sees humor in the world around him and tries to reflect that in his writing.